The Complete Mystery of Matthew Alcott

HERITAGE OF SECRETS

MICHAEL OBORN

outskirtspress
DENVER, COLORADO

The Complete Mystery of Matthew Alcott
HERITAGE OF SECRETS

v3.0 r1.0

Outskirts Press, Inc.
http://www.outskirtspress.com

ISBN: 978-1-4327-8893-3

Library of Congress Control Number: 2012902576

PRINTED IN THE UNITED STATES OF AMERICA

Out of respect for two men, both scholars of courage and insight.
Rodger I. Anderson and D. Michael Quinn

Preface

In my experience it is in story that we are all connected. While this story looks to be about the circumstances and traditions of a single culture, it is not. It is about the human dilemma in all cultures in which behavior is based-on and shaped-by belief system values.

Thousands of cultures. Many languages. We assimilate ours in story elements relative to the hand that rocked the cradle. A fact without relevance doesn't exist. Our connectedness, one human to another, is inalienable. Our culture dictates the story environment. Relationships are the adhesive.

Where does the moon go when it is no longer dark? The wind blew hard the day father died. When it blows is father angry with us?

The moon and the wind were no longer experienced without reflection. They came to mean many different things. The value elements answering behavioral needs for a being no longer dictated by instincts species-specific choices are found in our stories.

Since the evolution of the cerebral cortex we became more autonomous in the quandaries we faced. Our behavioral options multiplied as we needed to fill in vast new dimensions stimulated by cognitive awareness.

As long as there are many different religions we have a chance. When the wall of separation between church and state is breached, history will have repeated itself and again there will be only one church. Since we cannot re-incarnate the founding fathers we will have "completely fucked up the end game." (Thank you Arron Sorkin for your brilliant and succinct way of making a point.)

With choice came the capacity for enhanced survival.

The plague of mankind is the fear and rejection of diversity, . . . The belief that there is only one right way is the root cause of the greatest threat to man."

Thomas Szasz

Acknowledgments

Robert Simmons for instilling confidence. Andrea Hurst for pushing. Sean Riley whose example continues to inspire. Dean Taylor for always being there. Brent Bingham whose support has never wavered. Gina Sue for too many things to enumerate, love, patience, and emotional support to name a few.

About the Author

The U.S. Army sent Mr. Oborn to Information Specialist School for training in media journalism. After graduation he was shipped to Camp Zama, Japan to manage a theater where he directed live stage plays. Mike is a Chemical Dependency Professional who, before retirement, worked with addicts and their families, and continues affiliation with, SAFE CALL NOW, a nonprofit organization that works with police, fire fighters, and other first responders experiencing the disease of addiction. He is a member of the Willamette Writers Association, Portland, Oregon and the Pacific Northwest Writers Association, Issaquah, Washington. He lives with his sweetheart of many years in Puget Sound.

A Prelude

There was a shuffling sensation. Matt moved to brush it away. He couldn't find his foot.

Dust filled his eyes when he tried to open them. It burned.

A current of awareness surged through him. *I'm hot. I'm not dreaming. I'm awake and I'm very hot.*

Something was wrong with his arms. They didn't move freely.

Searching. Reaching. No experience equated to what he was feeling. His efforts were feeble. Forcing his arms around, he found freedom down at his sides.

Nauseous, a slimy vomit welled up.

Inside? Was he wrapped inside something? A bag?

The sun was unbearable on his legs. Like a snake shedding its skin, he was able to force the bag over his head.

He found himself kneeling naked in the dirt, felt his head, brushed a gob of green slime out of his hair. Never could he remember being so hot.

He worked on a few deep breaths, struggled to his feet, and started hopping, one foot then the other. Everywhere he stepped was blowtorch hot. A lizard ran across his foot. He grabbed the burlap bag he had freed himself from and stood on it. *What's happening to me?*

Desert. In every direction desert.

The thought occurred that he was in serious trouble. In the pit of his stomach, helplessness was growing.

Shoulders burned like someone was holding hot coals to them. Off to his left next to a wash was a small rise.

He bent over, rotating the gunnysack back and forth, slowly making his way to the rise and praising God all the way that no one with a camera was standing behind taking pictures, and at the same time wishing there were.

Clawing up the other side of the wash left him exhausted. The dryness in his throat was becoming unbearable. He tried to swallow. Nothing but cotton.

Matt stood on the gunnysack to look about for some sign of civilization.

Great good God in heaven. Something. Couldn't tell what it was. A long way off.

The coarse fabric of the burlap bag was old and he was able to tear it. The two bottom corners made half-decent socks he could hold up by the middle part. Bent over with one hand between his legs, keeping the sack taut, progress was slow. A top portion he held over his head and shoulders with the other hand.

Shrubs with bony-like fingers tore at his hide. Milkweed, until it dried, was no immediate problem, but the devil in the desert is a fuzzy scrub cactus with needles that sting like bees.

Major fatigue now. His ankles and legs screamed pain. His knees were bloody from stumbling and faltering. Thirst increased. A leg cramp brought him to the ground. He attempted to shout. Pathetic foghorn of a sound.

It occurred to Matt that he might actually be dying. Twenty-seven years. Not a great life span. *Only played the hand I was dealt, Goddamn it*. He thought of his book, the book that now would not get written. Matt seemed to get a second wind.

Getting closer. It was a service station with a trailer in back. As he approached the buildings, a new silver 2005 Infinity pulled into the gas station. Matt's vision began to swim. The trailer was closer. He leaned on the wood railing, climbed the steps, and knocked on a door that took forever to open. Two human shapes were molasses images shimmering in and out of focus.

They were staring at him. Two wide-eyed young women, dumfounded, staring.

Where is the burlap cloth? Cover yourself.

Sweat-dried mud stains streaked his face and neck. His hair, clumped and spiked with dust, defied the telling of a natural color. Matt's mouth opened. No sound emitted from his lips.

The image the women were looking at was so bizarre it took a moment to make sense of it, but desert heat tells its own story.

The brunette, looking all of twenty, grabbed Matt by the right arm. The blonde by the left. Together they managed to lift him to his feet. Five feet ten, they put their heads under his arms and shuffled him sideways through the trailer door.

Matt blinked. There were five human shapes. They all had female voices.

As his vision cleared, the pain increased and he heard himself moan.

"Drink this." Another voice, female again.

He inhaled most of a bottle of water before the brunette took it away from him.

"Not too fast, mister," cautioned a girl with large, olive-shaped eyes.

His nakedness, he noticed, held no more significance to them than a loose hem on a skirt.

"Did I pass out?" Matt mumbled.

"Yeah, but only for a second," a girl in hip-hugger shorts said.

"Sorry to be a bother."

"Boring morning. Don't worry about it," the blonde said.

Matt wanted to close his eyes to hide from the embarrassment he was feeling. It seemed silly under the circumstances. Still, there it was. They were saving his life, but how often did a naked, single guy have five sexy ladies cleaning his wounds and otherwise fussing over him? In an odd way he was happy to be in so much pain—he didn't have to worry about embarrassing himself further with a woody. Or did he?

He flinched from the touch. A girl with red hair was gently smoothing lotion over his shoulders, back, and chest.

"Aloe vera and vitamin E," she said.

She stopped at his genitals.

"Here, you'll have to do that part. Otherwise, I'd have to charge you."

They laughed. Matt could tell they were happy with the fact that he was responding to their ministrations.

His vision was clearing. The laughing stopped. He looked up to find a plump, matronly-looking woman in a muumuu standing in front of him. All of five foot, her presence commanded the room.

"I've seen men do a lot of things to get laid. You beat all. What in hell are you doing in my store?"

Matt tried to think. Mouth open, he couldn't form a sensible answer for her or himself.

"Lincoln County sheriff is at the other end of the county. I called Clark County. A uniform from Vegas is on the way."

She introduced the girls. "Brandy, Pussy, Bunny, Bella, and Liberty. I'm Betty. What's your name? What happened to you?" she said.

"Matt, Matthew Alcott. Las Vegas. Where am I?" he asked.

"Vegas is ninety miles south. Tonopah is only twenty more miles on up the road."

In less than ten minutes a deputy sheriff came through the door.

"I was on my way to Death Valley. Dispatch rerouted me to you, Betty," the officer said.

The officer wrote down as much information as he felt he needed. When he ran out of obvious questions, he took a moment and read what he had written.

"From this I have to conclude you were drugged, transported from somewhere else, and left in the desert to die. Attempted homicide, only way I can think to call it," the deputy said.

Then, instead of Matt he looked at Betty, the proprietor in the muumuu.

"In my backyard," she acknowledged.

"Keep your eyes and ears open. Doors locked. Protection?"

"Sawed-off sixteen," Betty said.

"Be right back," the deputy said as he exited the trailer.

"Where's he going?" Matt mumbled.

"Service station. See if they saw anything last night," Bella, the brunette, said.

When the officer returned he asked Matt how he was feeling.

"There's a possibility I'll live. It's terrifying."

"We'll be leaving in a few minutes get you to the hospital gonna interview the girls first." One continuous flow of words as he disappeared into the back hallway of the trailer with Brandy and Liberty. Twenty minutes later the officer stood next to Matt.

"Okay. Think you can show me where it happened?" he said, adjusting his gun belt.

Matt, beet red, tried to get up. The girls gathered. Two pulled, two pushed. He grunted with pain where their hands touched him. Betty handed them a white sheet.

"Wrap him in this. Come back and see us now, y'all hear," Betty said.

They all waved. Hobbling his way in bare feet to the deputy sheriff's car, he saw the small red neon sign, Betty's.

Matt wasn't much help with directions. The officer wandered around in the desert looking for clues. Could find nothing.

Revolving red light winked as they sped ninety miles an hour toward Las Vegas. Deputy Sheriff Lyman didn't talk much the hour it took to drive south on I-95. Matt was going over yesterday in his mind.

LAS VEGAS
THE DAY BEFORE

When the Vegas temperature dropped to 100 degrees, Matt made a grocery run. Wasn't critical. Still had half a quart of Cutty Sark in the cupboard.

When he returned, the gate was open. Knew he'd closed it. Little Buddy, his dog, wasn't jumping all over him.

He almost stumbled as he closed the kitchen door behind him. An empty milk carton in the middle of a puddle of milk met his gaze. The floor of the kitchen was littered with broken glass, plates. Rice and coffee grounds were strewn everywhere. He slipped. Almost fell. A slice of bread was stuck to his shoe.

Was he hallucinating or was he seeing a rerun of his life? What wasn't broken was ripped apart, smashed, or cut up. Electrical cords to the refrigerator and the window air conditioners were cut.

"Bastards," Matt exclaimed.

This was exactly what happened to him a year ago in Salt Lake City. Matt went back outside, hollered for Little Buddy. Gate open, probably ran off. He didn't like the feeling that was creeping through him. He looked in the pump house to see if he still had running water. Little Buddy was lying on the floor, his neck at an odd angle.

"Goddamn coward bastards!"

His nearest neighbor lived diagonally across the street in a one-level with bleached-out wood siding. Like his own, the yard was little more than desert itself. The man who lived there, Pharmy, only showed up couple times a week. His real home was the Be Back Bar a block north of the Sahara Hotel and in the front of the old, derelict bowling alley. That's where they had first met. Knew Pharmy was home as he cut through the yard. The bumper of Pharmy's car was visible behind his house.

Matt knocked and waited. Felt he was being watched through a window. After half a minute Pharmy stood in the open doorway.

"What's happening?" Pharmy said, pushing the screen door open, cool air following.

"Have you seen anyone hanging around...stranger probably?" Matt asked.

"Why?"

"My place has been trashed. Killed Little Buddy too."

"You don't strike me as the kind to have enemies," Pharmy said, studying his neighbor more closely.

"You mean, other than half the state of Utah?"

"Any chance they might have gone to the wrong house?" Pharmy said, thinking it had been him they were looking for and not Matt.

"Happened to me before. An apartment in Salt Lake," Matt said. "Only I didn't have a dog then."

Pharmy seemed relieved. "You need to call 911. Get this on record. I don't mean to be short, but I gotta customer waiting. I'll make some calls. You know where to find me," he said.

It was getting dark as Matt ambled back toward his place. Nothing seemed different from this angle. He resolved to do exactly what Pharmy said, call the cops.

As Matt re-entered his house his breath caught in his throat. The walls were clean. The historical documents he had stolen from his former employer were missing.

In Salt Lake he'd worked for three years as a historian for the church. It had entailed entering the bombproof archives in Salt Lake City's Cottonwood Canyon, making copies, and taking them back to his office to analyze and catalogue. There was a sinking feeling in his chest. Years! It had taken years to find and compile the information in those records, not to mention the most important document of all, the lost revelation itself, which painted the genesis of the church in a whole new light. Without those documents how could he expose the truth, let the lie out of the closet?

Pinned up to study. It's how he liked to work. He used walls like law enforcement people used a crime investigations whiteboard. Instead of shuffling through a stack of papers, he could stand or sit and peruse several at the same time. Now, along with the lost revelation, they were gone.

He hadn't noticed this before he talked to Pharmy. Were the documents gone before he walked across the street? He went into the living room to see if those walls had also been stripped clean. That's where memory failed.

LAS VEGAS
HOSPITAL ENTRANCE

Officer Lyman's voice startled Matt.

"Killed your dog too?" Deputy Sheriff Lyman asked as they pulled into the emergency entrance of Sunrise Hospital.

"Little Buddy. Yeah. Friendliest little brown-and-white mutt you ever saw," Matt grunted.

"You can't think of anything they might have been after...anything of value someone might have wanted?"

"No sir."

"Have you pissed anyone off recently?"

"Not that I can think of, no."

Chapter 1

LAS VEGAS, NEVADA
SUMMER 2005

The young ER doctor insisted; one overnight to monitor electrolytes.

"It's not the worst sunburn I've seen, but you can't be too careful," he added.

The next morning Matt returned home just in time to receive the call from his boss, editor on the City Desk at the *Las Vegas Sun*.

Matt was an embarrassment to the newspaper. Jack, his editor, was through making excuses for his drinking.

"Given you more slack than I have anyone, Matthew. Best of luck to you," Jack said.

Jack liked Matt. Only made the firing harder, but the word had come down from above.

"You get off the sauce, call me. If you do a freelance piece I'll definitely look at it," Jack added.

Getting laid off at the paper hurt, but it was nothing like that morning a year ago when his wife moved out and had him served with divorce papers. It was the last blow in a chain of heavy hits that ended in his being fired from his job as historian for the church. Hired times two. Fired times two.

At least I'm consistent.

Never forget that day. He was at the bottom of his life. His gut ached like everything inside had turned to stone. Felt he'd have to improve to be depressed. Suicide displaced rational thinking. Nothing made sense anymore.

"Is there not somewhere in this bleak existence a life worth living?"

He repeated it over and over as he drove. It wasn't worth it. Found himself driving to his folks' home to get his shotgun. His mind, floating in a vortex of malaise and hopelessness, wondered what gauge of shell would be appropriate for a task of that nature. He remembered using all of his shells during bird season last year. *Wouldn't you know it. I can't even do this right.*

He'd been working in the archives in Cottonwood Canyon, studying the personal papers of Brigham Young. For the past few months it was the only place he felt any peace of mind. Matt wheeled his old beater toward the 6200 South Canyons exit from I-215 and continued east to the canyon where the signs read to Snowbird, Alta, and Cottonwood Canyon.

It was on that day, on the lowest day of his life, he stumbled onto the most exciting discovery of his life. The memory was vivid, as bright and moving as the day it happened.

Matt was surprised access had not been denied. He had been expecting it.

He read his notes, returned to his last point of reference. He was sitting down, pinching his nose as per usual for a minute due to the dryness of the air. The inside of his nostrils felt like they had turned into paper.

He carefully lifted the cover leaf of one of Young's journals. Noticed a portion of the inner face had come unglued. With his fingers he checked to what extent the aging might have occurred elsewhere. *Wait. Hold up. What is this? A slight wrinkle. A lump?*

Carefully. A pair of tweezers. Gently, slowly, he worked the thin lump out.

Matt found himself looking at one of Joseph Smith's revelations. But wait a minute. That was impossible. Matt knew them all, every revelation Smith had received. Or did he? Was this one he had never seen before?

"Holy…!" jumped out of his mouth.

Matt reared back in his chair. Glanced about to see if he had been overheard.

"Holy shit! What is this? Have I…?"

For three years he had researched and compiled information about Joseph Smith's life, some of which no one had seen since the early eighteen hundreds. The prize was the lost revelation and by all indications the last revelation.

Matt stood in his kitchen, the mess he had to clean up all around him. A twinge. What? The word again. Suicide. It came slicing back, penetrating sanity. From the day of that discovery the *S* word had not been big in his consciousness. Until now. The documents were gone.

Now without those records how could he write his book? It had given him a reason to go on. And it was the only reason he hadn't driven to his folks' home that day when he knew they would be in church to collect his shotgun.

It seemed like he was starting over, only he had nothing to start with. *Someone doesn't want me to have that research. They know where I live. Fool! Why didn't I see this coming? Wait…*

Matt charged out to the van and flung the rear doors open.

"Yes!" he shouted.

In plain sight. There they were. Several weeks back while covering the night desk he'd made a copy of the whole set.

Still, it was close. Too close.

LAS VEGAS
THE BE BACK BAR

Pharmy, Matt's neighbor, was exactly where Matt figured he'd be, bar stool included. His office was the Be Back Bar in the front of the old bowling alley, one block north of the Sahara Hotel. As Matt approached, Pharmy patted the stool next to his.

"I put out some feelers. There's been a white...Jesus, what happened to you?" Pharmy said when he saw Matt's face.

"Someone drugged me. Left me for dead in the desert."

Matt summarized his night and morning in the desert.

"You gotta problem, man. That's attempted freakin' murder," Pharmy said before continuing. "There's been a big guy in a white pickup truck hanging around driving the back roads. Wears a brown fedora, if you can believe that."

"Doesn't ring a bell," Matt said, searching his memory.

Pharmy finished his drink. Pushed the empty glass away.

The man looked like he was allergic to food and lost his razor the week before. Matt didn't have a clue as to his real name. Was a pharmacist who had lost his license, but continued to sell drugs, only now he did it out of the trunk of his car.

Pharmy had managed immunity to being arrested by supplying the devil's dick to many of the city's most respected and politically powerful hierarchy. As long as he was not a problem, he was left alone, even watched over for the special service he performed.

As a newspaper journalist Matt discovered Pharmy had an elaborate working knowledge of the city's political sewers. When writing copy, Matt had learned to lean on him for intel and confirmation.

"Did I see a *sold* sticker on the Realtor's sign in front of your place?" Pharmy asked.

"Yeah, done deal."

"Time for you to disappear."

"Looks like my only alternative. How's one go about that kind of thing?"

"God. You are from Utah, aren't you? Go to this address." Pharmy scribbled on a napkin. "Guy in a wheelchair. Give him

$500 cash money and your driver's license. Don't worry; he'll give it back to you. He's gonna take your picture. Sit out in your car for fifteen minutes. When he opens the door, go back. What he gives you bring to me." Pharmy pulled out a cell phone. "What year were you born?"

"1976."

When Matt returned, Pharmy shuffled through the papers.

"Memorize your new social security number, and the high school you graduated from. When you're ready to be someone else, hide everything with your old name on it. Don't show this new driver's license for two days. Takes that long to process through some computer or something. Okay?"

"Too easy," Matt said.

"Stroke of luck on the new last name, Matheson. Matt works for that too. You still living in the house?" Pharmy asked.

"No. I have till the end of the month, but I feel safer in one of those by-the-week motels in Henderson...at least until the check clears."

"Timing has to be good."

"The property doubled since January. After the mortgage company and the escrow company and all the other pirates took their percentages, it is still the largest chunk of change I've ever seen."

"You gonna cash out, get rid of the credit cards?" Pharmy asked as he lit a Marlboro.

"Yeah."

"Don't use a bank."

Matt waited for an explanation. Short on patience.

"You gonna tell me why or do I have to beat it out of you?"

You could count the times Matt saw Pharmy laugh on one hand and have fingers left over. This one ended in a coughing fit.

"Thanks. I needed that," Pharmy whispered as he caught his

breath. "Casinos, dummy. Start an account at one of the casinos. You pull thirty or forty grand out of a bank in cash...gets everyone's attention. Withdraw the same from a casino, hardly noticeable."

LAS VEGAS
A WEEK LATER

The last day before the new owners moved in, Matt went back to pick up a couple of things. Almost dark. Phone was supposed to have been turned off, but there was still a dial tone. Matt knew where she'd be. Punched in her office number.

The crisp, clear alto voice he loved to hear purred in his ear.

"This is Professor Eve."

His stomach tied a great, giant knot in itself.

"Hello. This is Eve," she repeated. "Matthew?"

Silence.

"Is that you, Matthew?"

Her voice turned warm, like an electric blanket feels on a cold night.

"You are a bad boy, Matthew."

An anguished pause.

"Call me when you quit drinking." Her voice caught.

After the way he'd treated her, he couldn't force a word out of his freakin' beak.

Click. The line went dead.

"I'm sorry," he said.

Packed and ready, a lump of anxiety in his throat, Matt pointed the van toward the Be Back Bar. A letter of introduction from Jack Holiday, his old boss at the *Las Vegas Sun,* to one of the editors at the *Los Angeles Times* was neatly tucked away in his briefcase.

Change. That's what he needed. New name, Spencer Thomas Matheson, nickname Matt, address at a post office box in Henderson, Nevada.

Anyone inquiring as to his whereabouts at the *Las Vegas Sun* would look to California.

He sat on the stool next to Pharmy, answered the bartender's glance with two fingers extended, after pointing to the drink in front of Pharmy.

"I'm out of here," Matt said.

"Where? Wait. This is where you lie to me. If you find the perfect bar, call me," Pharmy said, as if he were offering an opinion on the bleak decor of his present circumstances.

"Worthy project. What's it look like?" Matt said.

"The perfect bar? Where nobody knows your name; where the clientele are witty, short on hypocrisy, and there's an agreeable lady in every booth," Pharmy said as he slid off his stool. "Come on. I got something for you."

Matt followed him outside, where he opened the trunk of his office. A carpenter had owed Pharmy money. The obvious reason. Drugs. He had the carpenter design, build, and install layers of cabinets in the trunk. They were stocked with controlled substances, primo street product, and prescription drugs.

"Here. This is a prescription for no pain and this for no worries." He handed Matt a small container of Percs and another of Valium. "Covers just about any emergency. Work faster if you chew 'em."

"How much I owe ya?" Matt said.

"Fuck it. Gonna miss reading your stuff. Put me in one of your goddamn books."

"I want the story. Your story. License being pulled, everything."

Pharmy looked at the ground. Shook his head.

"Just standing here talking to me is dangerous. Stupid too."

"I'm an investigative reporter. Color me stupid."

"Worry about yourself right now. Maybe I'll see you again. You know where I live."

Matt watched him walk back into the Be Back Bar. Knew something had happened in the past and someone important had used him as a scapegoat. Now he was daring them. Matt had a gnawing feeling this would be the last time he'd see Pharmy alive. He hated those impressions. They were often right.

Chapter 2

DROPPING OUT OF SIGHT

As Matt drove east, it seemed his life was filled with stories of greed, injustice, hypocrisy. More than just being a journalist on the City Desk. He glanced back at the cardboard box next to his clothes and books. Research. Three years' worth.

How can they stop me now? How can anyone stop me from writing my book when I don't exist? The self-righteous, religious, true blue, love your neighbor, do-gooder, bastard radicals that are dogging me are being out flanked.

The rearview mirrors reassured. No one following. It had been a close call.

From now on, everything with cash. Gas, motels, restaurants, etc. No credit cards. No phone calls. No communication with anyone until the damn book was written and the deception exposed.

Matt's stomach stopped aching beyond the typical discontent that had been with him since before the divorce from Carol in Salt Lake.

Long and frugal, the highway stretched out like a finger pointing. But where? No destination. Freedom? Yes. God yes. *Freedom from the self-righteous testacies in Salt Lake that want me shut down.*

For the second time in his life Matt had no place to go, no one waiting, no one to share it with and if, by some quirk of fate, he died, no one who would give a damn.

It will be as though I never lived.

He took a pull from the pint of Cutty next to him on the seat.

Fine. . . suits me fine.

Cutty, medicine for the lump of self-pity in his throat.

Full scope of the plan; get used to the new name, drive until something says, this is the place. Night work. Perhaps a custodial thing, school or building maintenance. Nothing to distract. The book comes first.

Matt could tell you about a cowboy tavern in Kansas City, Kansas, or the inside of a bar full of university students in Ames, Iowa, but little else about the country he was driving through—except the discontent.

Waiting for him in whatever town he stopped was the malaise, throbbing. The days seemed to blend into each other without contrast. Today, a blurred repetition of yesterday.

A day in Haverford, Pennsylvania, a week in Waukesha, Wisconsin, the towns came and went.

Money getting low.

Cooler, autumn nights.

Headed, east. Southeast? God no. Lean northeast.

Stay drunk.

Avoid crowds.

Chapter 3

RESURRECTION CORNER, NEW YORK
LATE FALL

The near empty gas gauge caused Matt to wheel right at the off-ramp, but it was the name that hooked him. When he read Resurrection Corner his foot relaxed. A religious community? Curiosity and a dry throat driving.

A one-tavern town, not the kind travelers stop in. He idled into a diminished hamlet that had obviously seen better days.

Night had already eclipsed day. Main Street. The businesses—what there was of them—were closed. A few streetlights winked out a direction. A half-dead neon sign blinked....try...cant...as he approached. Tried everything. Can't do shit. It mocked him. Closer, it read Country Mercantile.

Resurrection Corner slept in upstate New York as though drugged under a quilt of leafy maples. The streets were covered in autumn's costume. Rusts, yellows, and reddish browns swirled up, around, and behind his taillights. Wouldn't have given it a second glance if he hadn't been exhausted and in serious need of a bracer.

"Where am I?" he said as though there were someone to answer.

The words ONE HUMP were all he could see until he came to the middle of town where the street ended. Right or left; the timeless dilemma. If he had turned right that night he would, one mile down, have reconnected with the highway and who knows what might have been?

The half-lit sign on the left loomed lonely below a crescent moon, the lower end pointing to the words THE ONE HUMP BAR.

Reminded him of a couple of thirsty wise guys a long time ago looking for The King's Tavern, only it was under a star not a moon. Might have had the same thought Matt did—a drinking establishment with a great name cries out for a pit stop. Needed to piss something fierce. Only a few customers in the place.

Matt, tired to the bone, spoke softly, a lament, as though narrating his own journey.

"Any man who had the inspired irreverence to name his drinking establishment the One Hump Bar in a town named Resurrection Corner has my respect. Within the rigid confines of the status quo, he too may have ranted against the sham and pretense of civility. Out of sheer respect, I will spend coin, imbibe in strong drink."

Following a visit to the men's room, Matt found a stool at the end of a twelve-foot bar with a ninety-degree turn that ran another twelve feet to the wall.

"Started to snow yet?" the man with the limp behind the bar asked as he placed a coaster in front of Matt.

"Close," Matt answered.

"We don't get many strangers here. What brings you to The Corner?" the bartender inquired.

Two thousand years before, an identical dialogue passed between a saloonkeeper and three wise dudes after finding a parking place for their camels.

"Am looking for an inn, a motel for the night. Preferably cheap, fresh straw if possible. Any recommendations?"

A yellow jeep pulled up in front of the bar. Easy to see out through the large picture windows.

Two women entered, hung their coats on wooden wall pegs next to others. Without answering Matt, the barkeeper placed two wineglasses on the bar where it started to make a ninety and head toward him.

Matt checked them out. The taller had an angular face with raw-boned features. Not a model, but wouldn't kick her out of bed. The shorter he couldn't get a good look at. All he could tell was that she was the color of toast, maybe Hawaiian. She flitted around the room like a butterfly, said something to each person in the place before she went behind the bar and gave the bartender a quick hug.

Matt knew he looked like hell, but didn't give it much thought until the butterfly whispered into the bartender's ear, "Who's the smelly drunk?"

The bartender shrugged.

His hearing was keen enough.

"Matt. Name's Matt."

The butterfly shot one grimaced glance in his direction as she floated back around the bar and stood behind her friend. It looked like someone peering out from behind a tree, only half her face exposed. She whispered something Matt couldn't hear. He looked into what he could see of her face, realized he was staring, and moving to pick up his drink, knocked it over. The bartender cleaned up, put another drink in front of him.

"Didn't plan that," Matt said, forcing himself not to look where the giggling was coming from.

"No sweat. On the house."

When he looked up she was still staring at him from behind her friend. His inclination was to give her the finger. Matt concentrated on his drink instead.

"We don't get many strangers here. You just passing through...I hope," the butterfly, still standing behind her friend, said.

Feeling out of place, a familiar emotion, Matt didn't answer.

Savvy to her moods, the bartender reached for the remote control to the television.

"Where you from?" she pressed.

He sipped his drink. Having no desire to incite an incident, Matt ignored the question.

"Let's see how the game's going," the bartender said, turning on the television.

Thank God, a legitimate use for TV, Matt thought. When he glanced at her again, disgust was written all over her face.

"Name's Matt. I'm not looking for any trouble," Matt said quietly to the bartender.

"James J Flannery. Call me James J," the bartender said, offering his hand.

James J added some house wine to the girlfriend's glass. As he did he looked at the butterfly.

"Cool it, Little Sister," he said.

She acted hurt.

"Your money's good in this bar," he offered, glancing at Matt.

Matt had no way of knowing that James J had been where he was, nor that he had seldom seen a drunk get sober, but there wasn't a decent chap inside waiting to happen.

The bartender looked at the schoolteacher whose name was Raven, and who was already looking at him, and said, "The resemblance is uncanny, wouldn't you say?"

"I'm getting that too," Raven said.

Matt wondered what they were talking about. Like a stiff drink on an empty stomach, when he first looked into the butterfly's eyes, Matt sensed something, long dormant, shift. Pretty, but no raving beauty, this butterfly. Matt tried to shake it off. Like moth to flame, he was drunk with her, his eyes helpless to their own rule. Loathed himself, he couldn't stop looking.

Matt attempted to monitor the animated conversation at the elbow of the bar. He listened for names, clues. The taller lady with long jet-black hair was a schoolteacher who obviously had parents who were Edgar Allan Poe fans. Named their daughter Raven. Her delicious and hostile friend with large black eyes and brown hair remained nameless.

A better view, Matt figured she was Italian or maybe Spanish. The two chirped away without a break in the conversation for the hour they were there. If his life depended on knowing the content of their conversation, it would be forfeit.

The one named Raven had two red wines. The nameless other, the butterfly, had one and drank only half of that. Amazing the things he paid attention to. Matt couldn't trust anyone who didn't finish their drink.

Chapter 4

JAMES J FLANNERY & THE NEW RELIGION

James J Flannery's bar was at least three things: It was the place he displayed Knuckles, his Harley, a name spoken in reverence, and it was a drinking establishment, but it was also an ongoing, eight p.m. Friday evening and nine a.m. Sunday morning collecting place for AA types.

Any drunk on the wagon could drop in anytime, occupy a bar stool, order what in this bar was called an RC, otherwise known as strong recovery coffee, and strike up a conversation with whoever. Half of James J's pigeons would do exactly that when having a rough day. Everyone, drinking or not, had an opinion, and often the drinkers were known to give excellent advice about staying sober.

All over America, taverns and restaurants opened their doors early on Sunday mornings for recovery meetings, but this was the only one that was held in a bar during drinking hours that anyone in the town knew of.

People talking. Sounded like they were on the other side of a wall. Matt felt as if he had hair growing on his eyeballs when he opened them. When he tried to raise his head, he found himself lying in a large booth next to another booth with nine ex-drunks, sitting in an Alcoholics Anonymous meeting, sharing their experience, strength, and hope.

Working on it, Matt determined that he was in a drinking tavern, on a Sunday morning in a town he'd never heard of, and he had a hangover that would turn a rhinoceros into a whimpering puppy. As images came into focus, he realized he was staring at the most immaculate hunk of shined chrome and black paint he'd ever laid eyes on. He recognized the Harley-Davidson logo, which was confusing and caused him to recheck his surroundings.

"What's your name?"

Loud and shrill, it was a female voice and it was closer than the Harley. Matt worked both eyes into focus. Standing in front of him with her hands on her hips was an apparition.

"Do you know where you are?" the apparition with the voice asked.

It was the butterfly, the one called Little Sister. She was close, too close, hovering. Her presence, clean, fresh, and all too comely, was intrusive. Matt, shamefaced, hadn't showered in days and wasn't sure if he had pissed his pants or not.

She walked away, thank God; then, seconds later reappeared with a coffee and shoved it under his nose.

He felt cornered. Wished she would go away. He banged his head on the table. It made an awful noise and hurt like hell. Matt tried to take the coffee, but spilled it. His hands trembled so violently the butterfly backed away, horrified. He made a passing gesture to wipe away the spilled coffee with a sleeve.

She retreated to the AA meeting and sat in a chair where she could watch him, as though he might turn into something even more horrible.

Matt became aware that someone was talking. It was the bartender from last evening and he was talking in an alien lingo. By the end of the meeting Matt had managed to right himself.

As each member of the meeting filed past, they welcomed and thanked him for reminding them how they used to be. He later learned, that's the way you treat everyone new in AA. The reason simple. The likelihood of Matt ending up in an AA meeting and being in the wrong place was so remote it could be compared to jumping off a Trump Hotel and not hitting the ground.

Skin crawling, eyes growing hair, he took a fix on the last stool at the end of the bar, sat, and tucked his hands between his legs to hide the trembling.

"How about a beer?" he said to someone behind the counter.

James J spoke. "Acute withdrawal. This will help a little."

He tossed a small packet of aspirins in front of Matt.

"I'll never again criticize another man's demons," Matt said.

"Yeah, I get that," James J said.

Matt frowned when he saw the butterfly staring at him two bar stools away. He closed one eye in order to see her better. "What's your problem, lady?"

"What you are doing to yourself will kill you," she said, her words as crisp as potato chips.

Matt thought of something Dorothy Parker was once credited with saying and mumbled, "Promises. Promises."

"Ugh," she said, leaning away from him.

James J made some concoction, part of which was blackberry brandy, and gave it to Little Sister.

"What's this?"

"Help him hold it while he sips," James J instructed.

"Me?" she said, holding the glass like it might bite her.

"I know how he feels, and it would be nice of you."

Her mouth fell open, an expression of horror and disbelief.

"That shit-faced drunk? You can't be serious," she uttered, shoving it away from her and toward the drunk.

Matt attempted to drink the concoction by himself. Spilled more than he swallowed.

Watching, her eyes widened. She looked at James J and pointed. "You were like that?"

"More times than I can count," he answered, while drawing a draft for a customer.

The bar had a small kitchenette in the back. The butterfly emerged with a cheese sandwich slathered with mustard. She seemed satisfied with herself as Matt inhaled it. Didn't take her eyes off him until the last bite was gone. With a change of attitude and a grimace of disgust, she kept offering the glass with the blackberry brandy in it.

It was evident to the town citizens occupying bar stools that Sunday noon that Little Sister, whose name was Cate, could not tolerate Matt and at the same time could not stay away from him. He offended her like an itch that needed scratching.

Matt was slowly becoming human. When she was otherwise occupied, he looked to James J, nodded in her direction, and said, "Open to suggestions, here. How do I get away from that?"

James J laughed. "Call it penance," he said, and went to help another customer.

WINNING THE LOTTERY

Matt wouldn't bet against anything anymore. *If life is about change, God help me, I may have won the lottery.*

Over time Matt managed enough of the bits and pieces to put together a picture of James J's life. His wake-up call came on a dark night on a black, wet street, riding his beloved Harley. The accident was horrendous. The driver of the car not a scratch.

After the doctors sewed him back together, one leg was shorter than the other. The surgeons were still complimenting themselves at having reconstructed James J, and James J was proud at having rebuilt Knuckles, his Harley, using as many of the old parts as he could find and salvage.

He was in the hospital for two and a half months. As soon as he could sit in a wheelchair, he found himself being wheeled downstairs to an Alcoholics Anonymous meeting without so much as a "We recommend."

"Thanks anyway. I'm good where I am," James J said to the head nurse.

"You have a choice?" she said, morphing into the form of a Nurse Ratchet.

Seems the head nurse on swing shift had recently buried a yellow husband who died from cirrhosis of the liver. Looking down on him in the wheelchair, she said one thing to James J as she instructed the orderly to wheel him to that first meeting.

"Until you find a doctor to tell me otherwise, I'm God on this ward. I will only tell you this, AA doesn't work…unless you want it to."

Matt learned that when James J Flannery returned to the One Hump, he was well on his way to guru-ism as a recovering drunk. Some said he felt worse about what he had done to his Harley than to himself.

He'd sobered up, sure, but sobriety didn't dissolve his ownership in the bar. Nor could he conceive of parting with his beloved Harley. Another hog lover would understand this without added explanation, for a 1949 knuckle header was a premier collectable.

At a non-biker's curiosity as to the nature of the Harley-Davidson mystery, he would put it in ecclesiastical terms: "There are two great religions native to American soil—the Mormon Church and the Harley-Davidson motorcycle."

Knuckles, a modern shrine, stood upright, low slung and proud, as honest a machine as ever graced the roads of America.

"Had God done as well with Adam as man did with the Harley-Davidson motorcycle, mankind would not be so ready to declare good or evil that which could not be defined in a roomful of dying children," he told Matt one afternoon.

Town was so frugal the town council met after the evening AA meeting, seats already warm, same tight asses already in place. The AA meeting would last until either everyone who wanted to share had a chance or one point five hours had lapsed. The town council meeting might last ten minutes depending. The two meetings often got mixed up.

Drunk On Life was the name of the Friday evening meeting. The Sunday a.m. meeting, Sweet Surrender. Both were growing and often filled the bar down to the last chair with people from as far away as Danville and Palmyra.

The first few days without a drink, Matt's stomach felt like a bucket of angry piranhas. James J would talk him through it. His voice had a soothing, knowing quality that helped the minutes inch by.

"When I stopped using and boozing, I found a stranger wearing my boots."

He was wiping down the bar. An early morning before customers were expected.

"For the first time in years I was without my painkiller, Johnnie Walker. Everything I felt was like harsh, exaggerated. Got so I couldn't read the newspaper. Story about this guy in the next county beats up his girlfriend and her kid. Thought I knew the bastard. Found myself sitting in my truck. No shit. I had a baseball bat on the seat next to me and was going to beat the son of a bitch unrecognizable. He was half my size."

"I'll never make it," Matt said, head in his hands.

"The intensity. You've been numb for years. Feeling again. Scary as hell." James J watched Matt holding his head. "Without my anesthetic my nervous system was in shock. For you and me, natural is drunk. The rational thing, put you in an emergency room with a scotch IV. Every cell in your body is pissed. Stuff that used to matter don't, and the things that you couldn't give a shit less about before now do. Total freakin' chaos."

"Torture."

"The desperate angst that goes with needing a drink and wanting not to is known only to us. Normal types haven't a clue what we're all about," James J said.

That knowing piece of information kept Matt sober for five full minutes. A moment of needed respite to catch his breath. Wondered if writing would take his mind off a drink. He thought about the box of documents.

Digging through the van he found a couple of yellow writing pads. The box of copied documents took longer. It was stacked in sections by date. Carefully he worked a few pages loose, marking the position with a stray, dirty sock.

As a newspaper journalist he had learned to focus. The thought offered some hope.

A SAFE PLACE

A handful of documents, a couple of yellow pads, Matt moved into a back booth. Grace be to the God of hangovers, it took, became the daily routine. It was a great place to write. Quiet during the early hours. Coffee. People to talk to if and when he wanted.

From the vantage point of a quiet booth in the rear of a bar with a weird name, Matt watched the little village of Resurrection Corner unfold and came to realize Cate, the butterfly, was more than the town greeter. She was mascot to its hopes and dreams. She was its heart.

It worked like this: Gladys, Carl's wife, was looking for a block pattern with bears on it for a quilt she wanted to start. Mrs. Stein, principal of the elementary school in Danville, was giving a speech at the New York State Teachers Convention in a month and was looking for humor about teachers to "spice up my delivery," as she put it. Raven's daughter, Robin, wanted to be a computer animator and one day work for Pixar Industries. Elbert and Doris Hanley had a son anxious to be a computer analyst or programmer, maybe work for Microsoft.

The school needed computers desperately. The three old relics they had came over on the Mayflower and were divided up between twenty-nine seniors, twenty-three juniors, and forty sophomores. All were things-to-be-done that the butterfly jotted down in some invisible notebook. Until she had dealt with each, in some useful fashion, it remained in the active file, her head.

James J had opened one of the supply rooms above the bar for Matt to sleep in. Any Utah boy worth half his salt has a sleeping bag in his rig.

From the beginning, Matt was one of those, a project. Getting sober and being broke, while not entirely inseparable events, did put him within the reach of Cate's things-to-be-fixed radar.

One cheerful afternoon the butterfly came through the door of the One Hump, having solved the problem of one Matthew Alcott, homeless, Utah, ex-drunk, bad boy.

"Hey, James J," she said, sliding her curvy little derriere onto a bar stool near Matt. With her came a hint of vanilla. "Guess what?"

The two men glanced at each other as James J set a mug in front of her and refilled Matt's.

"Matthew doesn't have to sleep on the floor anymore, like a bum," she said, looking at James J.

Everyone in the bar stopped what they were doing, except Matt, who started to laugh, "Well don't hold back, little sister. Speak your mind," he said.

As they had yet to speak a civil word to each other, everyone thought he was egging her on. What they didn't know was how nice it was to be included, instead of excluded, in conversations.

It was the contrast between the way he had been treated by his friends in his hometown and the way he was treated now in The Corner.

In Salt Lake, Matt had gone from being the recipient of benevolent smiles and firm handshakes to averted glances and offered backsides.

But not in The Corner. Didn't matter how odd he was or what he believed, these people still included him in their camaraderie...with one exception.

"I'm not your little sister," she corrected Matt, the hint of vanilla stronger.

"How can this local bum be of service?" he cheerfully responded about himself.

She addressed big brother, not Matt. "Matthew can rent the room above the hardware store." She was referring to the Country Mercantile store owned by Doris Hanley and her husband, Elbert.

Matt didn't have a job or the prospects of a job. With only a few hundred bucks left and not wanting to add to his status as a bum, he waited for James J to say something. It was, after all, him she was speaking to.

She glanced at Matt, but continued to talk to James J. "It has a bed and a kitchenette and it's cheap," she said.

She waited. All were listening. A wrinkle formed between her eyebrows. Like the oaf Matt sometimes felt of late, he sat transfixed, looking into eyes he could fall into. They were his soul's distraction, clear, dark, forever.

Cate began to fidget on her stool. "It's...it is really very cheap rent."

She was, again, looking at James J.

Matt felt he should say something, but thinking vanilla, nothing came to mind.

"If he wants?" she said, starting to flush.

James J was looking at Matt, who didn't know that for Little Sister, waiting was a form of agony. While he was still trying to put all this together, she jumped in again.

"And the first month is free."

By this time James J had grown very nervous. Knowing she would sell the farm if need be, he leaned toward Matt. "Say something."

"He's obviously too dumb to take advantage of a good deal," she said.

Matt was watching, not thinking. His mouth opened. Nothing came out. Knowing Little Sister, James J addressed Matt. "For God sake, say yes."

Collecting himself, Matt said, "By...by all means. Sure. And who do I thank for this? Doris? Elbert?"

"Talking to you is like talking to a vacant lot," she said as she spun off her stool and headed for the door.

James J took a deep breath. "Cate. You thank Cate."

"I've offended her. What did I do?"

The people in this town had learned to expect this kind of outgoing concern, which, until you got to know Little Sister, bordered intrusive and eerie.

Distracted by hormones that were no longer being made toxic with saloon spirits, Matt tried not to gawp at her every gesture, her every change of expression. Not easy—his eyes were governed by a different law; they would not leave her alone.

Matt had felt lust's predatory nature many times. He had also felt protective and respectful toward some women, but never before had he felt the urgency of both at the same time. It was confusing. Compelling and confusing.

There was something vulnerable and unattainable about this siren. The closer her proximity, the more he felt like an awkward teenager with a rock in his Levi's. What made it worse; she hovered like a nurse in a critical care unit.

When she sat at the One Hump touching a mug of coffee to her lips, he wished he were the mug. Corny. Brain dead. Had never felt this way about anyone. Eve, with her wit and sophistication, came closest, but this was different. There was something about this butterfly. He wanted her like he never wanted anyone before. The minute she entered a room, composure went south. Fool sat on a bar stool brain dead.

"The name?" Matt said. His finger pointed down at the polished wood surface of the bar. "I take it the camel wasn't from Mongolia."

"You're fast," James J said.

"The story behind the name, must be a good one."

"My ol' man's bar. Wish I could give you something earth-shattering, but no. In his day, it was said, he was the only man in New York State to own a camel. He thought it would be good advertising, but owning a camel can get old real fast. At ten years of age, guess who got to shovel the shit?"

Matt nodded.

"You had to know my dad. Another drunk with grandiose dreams. Thought it would be a kind of poor man's Barnum and Bailey publicity. Anyway when he discovered it cost more to keep the camel than it had advertising value, he tried to sell it. No one else was that dumb. Finally it died of old age or the winters, one or the other. Losing was what my dad did best."

Matt was fingering a napkin, posturing nonchalant, the real name he wanted to talk about on the tip of his tongue.

"Speaking of names . . . "

Matt could not see himself calling her Little Sister, not with the random thoughts that kept jumping unannounced into his head.

". . . you call her Little Sister. What's her full name?"

James J avoided the question, or so Matt thought. He pulled a beer for Carl, mixed a vodka tonic for old Mr. Wylie, put some peanuts and a Coke in front of Kirk the delivery driver, stopped in front of Crazy Helen, who nodded at Alice, who was talking to Al Fritz and Arnold the florist when the bar went silent. The hair moved on the back of Matt's neck. To this day he knew or thought he knew when people were talking about him.

Matt was impressed with this bartender's cultivated gift for participating in various ongoing conversations, while at the same time never losing track of who needed what drink and what had been said.

"I've met some real fools in my day," James J said.

Crazy Helen went, "Fools. Real fools," and blinked at Matt.

Matt glanced around the bar. Everyone was staring at him.

"Matter of fact, I think I've known every kind of stupid there is," James J said.

Never missed a beat making drinks. His hands had poured for so many years, they performed independent of whatever else was going on. And, of course, a secret in this town was merely something new to talk about.

"I've watched fools lose their life savings," James J went on.

As he said it, he refilled Crazy Helen's wine. She smiled at Matt, whose hands went cold. James J turned back in Matt's direction.

"I've seen opportunity knock and no one answer."

Matt could tell James J had given more than a little thought to what he was saying and braced himself. "Look," he said, "I don' t mean to appear dense, but should I be standing when you finally get to the goddamn punch line or whatever the hell it is you're getting at?"

James J propped one black motorcycle boot up on the well-worn edge of the stainless-steel sink directly across the bar from Matt. "If you successfully push this girl away from you, I know I'll have met one of the all-time, world-class, prize fools."

By lowering his voice and drawing the word out, *fools* was delivered with considerable emphasis. He put another beer in front of Wally, the town sheriff.

Matt did a quarter turn on his stool. Nothing but eyes.

"You still lynch people in this town?" Matt half seriously inquired.

Wally, looking straight ahead at Matt's reflection in the mirror, said, "I've never seen her like this about anyone."

"Demented. The bunch of you. She hates my guts."

"She would be good for you," Crazy Helen challenged.

"That's the way it works with her," Wally added.

"Contrary to your flawed opinion of yourself, pal, you're not such a bad chap," James J added.

The whole room, all regulars, went, "Hear, hear."

Matt was scared of her, although consciously he wasn't aware of it. He had her in some ivory tower of pure perfection, and he was a bottomed-out, worthless drunk. Where he felt dirty, used up, and useless, she was healthy and happy. And if she would be good for him, it was definitely time to run. Nerves still fried from booze, he was scared of everything, especially his own feelings. Thinking out loud, "God, I need a Cutty."

James J rapped his knuckles on the hardwood surface as might a hanging judge handing down a sentence a hundred years before. "Your nervous system's a joke. Give yourself the benefit of the doubt. Meanwhile, stop treating her nice. It only confuses her."

Four weeks dry at the time. This was a first, an ultimatum to approach the most bewitching, contrary creature he had ever laid eyes on or . . .

Everyone went back to what they were doing. For a moment he wondered if what happened actually had.

"Cate with a C," James J said. "Her name is Cate Lynn Sudani."

Matt moved in. Threw his sleeping bag on the mattress in the big room above Hanley's hardware store and started making trips up the outside staircase with his chattel.

The first transfer was a box of research. He set it with satisfaction on the rickety kitchen table and scanned the walls. He then made the mistake of looking in the box. Documents began arranging themselves into stacks and piles around him.

Until the light began to fade, he realized he hadn't eaten all day.

Matt turned to see Cate standing in the open doorway. *Look cool, be witty.*

"Hey," he fumbled. "Just…moving in. Aaah, one more load."

He walked past her and down the stairs. She stayed in the doorway and attempted to make sense of what she was seeing. The walls were covered with documents that he had been either pinned or taped in place. Hardly a square foot that wasn't clustered with papers at eye level.

Matt brought the last load up from the van. She stepped out of the way as he inched past her, dropped a suitcase on the bed, and turned back toward the doorway. It was empty.

The One Hump Bar door opened. All eyes shifted to Cate as she came through.

"That man ignored me. Talk about arrogance. And can you believe it; he's wallpapering the place with old letters or something. We're talking dumb. No, change that. We're talking weird and dumb."

"It's research," Matt said, letting the door swing shut behind him. "I am, was, that is, a newspaper journalist. Just a little project I busy myself with."

She hadn't realized he was right behind her. It was obvious she was chagrined at having been caught with attitude showing. Matt figured snob and took the stool at the opposite end of the bar.

"Pour yourself a coffee," James J said to Matt.

Two straight pinch lines grew between Cate's eyebrows. James J, her big brother, had never said that to anyone but her.

"Matt's going to handle the bar for me when I need a day off," James J announced.

Cate slipped off her stool, left the bar.

"It's working," Crazy Helen said.

"Doesn't know what's in store for him, does he?" the sheriff said, looking at Matt in the bar mirror.

Matt opened a bag of peanuts. His mind was doing a hundred miles an hour. Decided to act like he hadn't heard what they were talking about. Drank his coffee, said nothing. Chin on hand, he feigned indifference.

One early morning, Cate came in to have a coffee with James J and found Matt spread out in one of the back booths, head down, writing on a yellow pad. She stood looking at him like something risen from the dead. Turning to James J, she spread her hands out in front of her, palms out, and waited. James J lifted his shoulders and dropped them.

This was her territory, her time with her big brother. Not to wake her mother and just short of a hop, skip, and jump, she would brush her teeth as she cut through a yard, wiggle through a hole in a fence, yet in her pajamas. She loved to ramble on about whatever she was thinking when her eyes opened. Big brother always listened without interruption. No new neighbors in years. Resurrection Corner was the town time ignored. For Cate Lynn Sudani, this had been a sacred time.

Her face worked itself into a squinty-eyed frown. Everyone knew everyone and everyone knew everything about everyone. But not this Matthew. He was an enigma.

Indignant, she crabbed over and stood in front of him and in a voice much too loud for this time of day said, "What are you doing?"

He looked up. "Aaaah, good morning, organizing notes…mostly."

"You're one of those smart guys, aren't you," Cate said, trying to be sarcastic.

"I don't know what you mean," he said, putting the pen down.

"You're writing about us, the Corner, aren't you?" she said as if she had discovered the most horrendous secret upon which weighed the future of Resurrection Corner and everyone in it.

Matt could see what she was getting at. He wondered how he might explain it to her.

"I'm in the process of writing a book. It would be called an exposé, but it has nothing to do with Resurrection Corner. It's about a large corporation in another state, Utah to be exact. That's it. What I'm doing."

Cate's head tilted to one side. She was looking at him sideways, while trying to read ink on yellow page. After a moment she sat on the edge of a cushion at the other end of the booth.

"Corporation?"

"Yeah."

"Our town is incorporated."

"Most are."

"Where you from?"

"Utah."

She had him. Caught him in a lie.

"Wouldn't it be smarter to write it in Utah?"

"There are people who don't want me to write it. It's safer here. No one knows where I am. Besides, I like it here."

"You like it here. Huh! I thought so. You're in trouble. Admit it. You're hiding from something...the law. Aren't you?" she said, delighted with herself at having caught him lying.

"Well, something, but not the law."

"So," she said, coming to her feet. "I was right about you; a smart guy, a charlatan. I'll bet you think we're just a bunch of hicks."

James J, watching, was clearly amused.

She turned to James J. "What time does the sheriff get here?"

"I think he had an arrest this morning, something about an overdue library book."

"When he gets here, tell him I need to talk to him and it's important. I'll be right back," she said, completely missing the sarcasm.

Matt, empty mug in hand, strolled over to the bar.

"I think she's gone to change into something a little more appropriate for arresting criminals," James J said.

"Got time for a short story?"

"Lay it on me," James J said, refilling his own coffee as well at Matt's.

"You already know a lot about me. Couple things..."

Matt brought him up to date about his old job, the documents, and having his apartment and his home trashed. Related the incident in the desert when he almost died.

"There are others floundering like I was. They need to know they are not alone. It's crucial that no one who used to know me knows where I am. Using an alias at the moment. Thing is, I've not felt unsafe here. Resurrection Corner is like a town the mapmakers forgot. Makes it the perfect place to disappear, write my book."

"Who are you hiding from, if I may ask?"

"One of the richest institutions in the world."

James J reached for his mug of coffee, leaned against the back wall where the various bottles of liquor were lined up. When a man does a fourth and fifth step with you in AA, you know him like few other people do. James J sipped his coffee before he spoke.

"One drunk to another, is this a revenge thing?" James J asked.

Matt mulled it over. "Yeah, partly perhaps, but more important, I feel compelled to make sense of the past so today can make sense—if that makes sense? And there are others like me. We've been betrayed. I'm hoping I can make it easier for them as well."

James J whistled.

Matt sat up.

"Yeah. A bit heavy."

A lighthearted laugh erupted from both men. James J continued.

"To end up in the desert like that, what you have...it must be pretty damaging."

"You could say that. When published, my research will disclose information heretofore unknown regarding the early days of the church. The documents show a staggering parallel between Joseph Smith and Hugh Hefner."

The new resident and the first night above the hardware store,

Matt tried to sleep. Futile! Something bothered him. It was the butterfly. Next afternoon he was talking to Doris Hanley when he saw Cate coming from the school where she was a teacher's aide.

"You got a minute?" he said.

"For you?" Cate said.

"Yeah, I'd like to show you something."

She almost said no. Curiosity, however, along with the near proximity of Doris softened her attitude toward the annoying new resident to Resurrection Corner.

"Okay."

He started toward the outside stairs that led up to his apartment. She saw Doris wave through the window, waved back, and followed him to the open doorway. Matt walked to the middle of the room. He turned slowly while pointing at the walls.

"I don't know who I am."

"Hey, good come-on line," she said, not trying to hide her distrust of him.

"It's complicated. I mean, in one sense, sure, I know who I am. In another I'm sorting things out. A year ago I was a...I don't know how to say it...I was a different person. I used to work for a church. It was the one I had been born and raised in."

Warily, she entered the room. Sat in the only chair.

"One day, without so much as ten minutes' notice, they locked me out of my office," he said. The circumstances flashed through his mind.

SALT LAKE CITY
A YEAR BEFORE

Matt stopped by his dad's office at the church. Brother Clayborne, First Counselor in the bishopric, was coming out of the building as he was entering.

"Dad with anyone?" Matt said as they passed.

Brother Clayborne hadn't offered his hand. Ordinarily it would shoot out, grab his, and pump his arm off. Not today.

"What keeps you in Salt Lake?" Brother Clayborne said, scurrying by.

Matt was stymied by the sudden, off-the-wall question.

"What?"

"Do you know what you're doing to the bishop?" Brother Clayborne said.

Matt recovered, understood. Clayborne was trying to protect Matt's father from Matt.

"Don't I have the right to think for myself?" Matt said.

"Over intellectualizing the church, you justify denying your testimony of the gospel."

"I...I don't...but isn't that the same..."

Brother Clayborne threw a hand up, dismissing both the conversation and Matt. He drove away, an elevated chin leading.

It had been that way for months. Friends, acquaintances. The treatment was the same from everyone.

"You'd have thought I masturbated at high noon in the middle of Temple Square," he'd said to a non-Mormon professor at the University of Utah, one of the few friends he had left in the valley.

It was the last straw. Matt looked in the glove compartment of his car. The wedding ring. The engagement ring. They were both there. He turned the car toward downtown Salt Lake.

Matt walked out of the side street where the pawnshop was and on to State Street. He enviously watched normal people doing normal things. Their lives looked full. A purpose behind their step. Each had someone waiting for them, someone who would be happy when they arrived.

The divorce—the civil part—would be final in a few months. He had just hocked the rings his ex surprised him with a few weeks back. She didn't want him or his cheap jewelry. She placed them in his hand like they were dirty. Her revenge. How could he blame her?

It wasn't enough money to pay the rent, but it was enough to get out of town.

Robot numb, Matt then drove to his office. Objective? Clean out his desk. Some vital papers he wanted to keep.

He parked, reached for his briefcase, and squinted against a bright Salt Lake sun. Odd. His hand trembled as he extended the plastic access card. Nothing happened. It did not evoke the usual guttural noise that accompanied the opening of the latch mechanism. Maybe he put it in crooked.

A cardboard box next to the door caught his attention. His name, Matthew Alcott, was hastily scribbled on top. He pushed the flap back, skimmed the contents: small desk clock, squeeze ball, fingernail clippers, half-eaten Baby Ruth bar, his frayed Dostoyevsky. Everything with two exceptions, none of his hand-scribbled notes nor the picture of his soon to be ex-wife. Reasoned he didn't need a picture of a beautiful shrew, but damn it, those notes were vital.

It was stupid to leave them in the office last night. If he hadn't been so tired, he never would have. Five yellow legal pads congested with notations. They had been generated over the four years he'd worked in the archives of the church.

He had made copies of every document he felt was vital and spirited them out of the office. Some, if they got out, would be a considerable inconvenience to the church. Others would be downright embarrassing. And others yet would be devastating. The information in them, like the lost revelation, was priceless.

Those were safe, but his notes in the yellow pads held the cross-references to people, times, events, and places, linking them together in historical context. If he lost them, it would take months to regenerate them.

"Welcome to the worst day of your life," he said to himself as he walked toward his car.

He'd been saying that a lot lately. It was as though someone had placed a spell on him. Feeling undressed and juggling his briefcase on top of the cardboard box, he walked as casually as he knew how back to his car. The only parking space available had been in the middle of the front parking lot. It seemed to take forever to load the box in the backseat, get in, and start the car. Only ninety people worked in that building. He felt undressed and like half of Salt Lake City had come to see his precious ass get the boot.

As he pointed his old beater toward the exit, he glanced up. There he was, Burgess, on the second floor. Old money bags, ex father-in-law, was standing in a window, a half smirk smeared across his face.

BACK TO THE PRESENT
RESURRECTION CORNER

Cate was looking at Matt, waiting. He realized he had been lost in memory.

"Today I'm my father's greatest disappointment. My mother won't speak to me unless she's had her Prozac. My wife, who was the daughter of a very important man in Salt Lake, divorced me. That's it…what I've been doing…attempting to make sense of things. It's what this is all about," he said, his hand in an upward sweeping motion, indicating the walls.

Cate rose, started reading some of the papers pinned to the wall.

Matt watched.

"It looks super boring," she said, moving to read another.

"Historical documents of and by themselves can be pretty dry."

After a minute she turned and looked at Matt.

"You are obsessed with this. Am I wrong?"

Matt was surprised. She didn't know him. How could she know?

"Probably not. But right now all I can think about is a drink."

He sat down on the bed directly across from where she was reading.

"If I tried to explain it further, we'd be up here for a week. Would you mind walking to the One Hump? I could use a coffee and a little James J."

She did. It was the way he said it. She almost pushed him. At the One Hump, Cate went behind the bar and, smiling at James J, pushed him out of the way to claim the coffeepot. She poured Matt a coffee and stood, pot in hand, watching until he began to sip it. Smiling, she then absently shoved the hot container at James J, who deftly caught it without seriously burning himself. He watched her walk around the end of the bar and place herself on the stool next to Matt, still smiling. James J blinked, reached for another mug, put it in front of her, and filled it.

After a minute people sitting around the bar started talking again.

Cate was walking fast, wanted to talk to her friend Raven, and was hoping her light would still be on. She opened the back door and went into the kitchen.

"Good. I need a break," Raven said.

Raven had been correcting exam papers. She stretched and rose to her feet.

"Let's have tea."

"What do Mor…Mormons believe?" Cate stammered.

"Where did that come from?"

"When I get that far I'll let you know. What are they…Mormons?" Cate said, sitting down.

"Well, let's see. It's been a while since I've talked to that side of the family. Aaah…they believe in polygamy, used to practice it. Aaaah… they baptize people after they die. Aaah…oh, you'll love this one. They believe God cursed Cain with a dark skin for killing Abel. As a result, everyone on earth with a dark skin descended from Cain and are damned or something," Raven said, chuckling at the absurdity. Placing two cups on the table, she looked over her glasses at her friend, expecting a nonchalant response.

Cate's expression was anything but. Her eyes blacker, narrower.

"Honey, you've been putting up with this white elitist crap all your life. Don't let this throw you," Raven said, ever taking her defense.

"Matthew comes from a church that teaches that my daddy was damned, my daddy and me?"

"It's a belief system, a perceived bias." The teacher in Raven was rising. "Not factual. In any sense of the word." Raven poured hot water into the two cups and sat. "Come on, what happened today?"

"Matthew is from Utah. He's hiding."

"Honey, can he help it if he was born in Utah? Can you help it you were born in The Corner?"

"He's a Mormon," Cate insisted.

"Mormons don't drink alcohol or coffee. I don't think Matt qualifies as much of a Mormon."

"He told me the church locked him out."

"Have you talked to him? Do you know what he thinks?" Raven said before changing the subject. "It's late. Robin's with Grandma Nighteagle. Why don't you stay over?"

Cate was silent, didn't touch her tea.

"Ask the man. Surely you're not afraid of him?" Raven said. She knew her friend. When Cate Lynn got wound up, she was her own worst enemy.

"I know this. The Corner would be better off without him," she said, wishing she hadn't; wishing she could save him from alcohol, wishing she wasn't so mixed up about him.

Cate rose, moved toward the door.

"Where are you going?" Raven asked.

"I'm not sure."

Matt lay in the dark, the moon reflecting through the windows, and wondered what he was doing sober in a town called Resurrection Corner. The building had a schedule of adjusting squawks as the temperature dropped. He was listening to them for the second time. Knew he wasn't going to sleep tonight. Again.

The single overhead light was a depressing yellow, hard to read by. No lamps. He could open the refrigerator, read by that light. That would work. Head would get cold though. He couldn't help thinking a few shots of Jack would get him through the night. A switch in his head flipped. He remembered a half-full bottle of Cutty neatly tucked away in a duffle bag in his van. First time he thought about that bottle in a month. Perfect. *There is a God after all*. One or two nips. That's all. Get him though the second empty, cold night in this bleak, hollow cave in this dreary nowhere town, in this lonely, fucking universe.

Matt sat up. Devil's brew. A sure cure for what ails and it was only a stairway away. Fumbled for his sneakers.

Chilly outside.

No reason to bother with pants if I move fast.

The steps complained as he descended. No matter. There was no one to hear it. The Hanleys had closed up and gone home hours ago. The lights at the One Hump were out. His hand searched the duffle, found the bottle, its shape so familiar and with it the feeling of guilt and relief. Felt like he was robbing a nursery of its last quart of milk.

He looked up. A silhouette, empirically feminine and one he knew by heart, was standing in the street. It looked like Cate had magically stepped out of one of the glass windows in the front of Hanley's store. *Shit. Caught*. The bottle hanging from his hand. At that moment Matt would have had to chin himself to see through the laces of his sneakers. He was about to chippy on his sobriety.

What must she think of me now?

Cate moved closer.

"My father was black," she blurted.

Matt realized it was too late to hide the bottle.

"Aaah...yeah, I heard that."

"He was from Asmara, Eritrea."

"North Africa, yeah."

The long pause that followed was forever. Matt shifted his weight.

Cate looked away, then back.

"What's your problem? Do you have something against talking to me?"

"I did...talk to you...I thought."

"That's all you can say?" she said.

"Is there something I'm supposed to say?"

She looked away again, the silence awkward. "Never mind. I, I thought...never mind." She turned to leave.

Matt reached, grabbed her wrist. She tried to pull away. He could see she was crying and wouldn't let go.

"What do you want me to say, Cate? God, I'll say anything you want."

If lip response were not a natural reflex, Cate may have chipped a tooth. Tears flooded. It was like kissing in the rain.

A bottle of whiskey made a thud in the dirt.

She felt him quicken. "Oh," a muffled sigh, "and I thought you were short on wit."

They held each other as though letting go would mean waking up. Cate moved in the moonlight to the stairs, her hand holding his.

As he undressed her, she seemed fragile and shivered against the cold. In the sleeping bag she was unbreakable. An urgency moved in him. At the same time he was in no hurry. The faintest hint of vanilla enveloped them, caressed his senses.

He'd never known anyone give herself so completely. She savored every caress, urging and surrendering at the same time. It was a mutual kidnapping, trapped in a pulsating current of suspended time. There were rambling rapids and deep, drifting pools of moment. Both hung on for dear life.

Chapter 5

SALT LAKE CITY
ELDER FARLEY HARPER

The television screen blinked its harsh, blank stare at the large sleeping man. Farley Harper had an irregular snore that rattled the thin walls of the mobile home. He woke with a jerk, looked around. The wind. He closed his eyes, let his head fall back into his memories. Within two exhales he was snoring again.

In the movies that Farley favored, the heroes, the private dicks, were loners who protected the innocent. Phillip Marlow, Mike Hammer, Sam Spade, Popeye Doyle. He never missed their movies, even went on Sundays. They were a special breed, those detectives. They always worked outside the law. But Farley didn't dream about them. His dream this windy night was filled with the things he couldn't have.

He was at the Sugarhouse Mall. As he walked toward the Cineplex box office to buy his ticket, he stared at the two pretty girls behind the glass. Closer, he knew they were talking about him.

"I told you so. Here he comes," she said.

It was the nineteen-year-old teller with the short, blond hair and the narrow-set eyes. Farley had seen her many times. Looked like the new girl was in training.

"Only detective movies, really?" the trainee asked, looking at the way he was dressed, brown suit and tie and the brown Fedora.

"Last time it was *The Maltese Falcon*."

"He's so big. How do people behind him see?"

"He always sits in the back row on the left side," she said. "When he's here, I never go on that side."

Farley walked slow. They were talking about him. As Farley approached the window, the new girl put her hand over her mouth. It was to hide her smile. *She likes me*, Farley thought.

"*French Connection*," he said.

He paid for the ticket with five dollars in change. The teller pushed the ticket under the window and into the small chrome tray, trying not to return his gaze, but too curious not to.

"Thank you," she said.

Farley thought to touch the brim of his hat with a finger, as he had seen Sam Spade do.

"Oh...my...God. I've got goose bumps," the trainee said as he turned to enter the theater.

Farley knew she liked him.

"Told you. Just don't be in the lobby when it's over. He likes to hang around and look at you. Pretends to be reading about the coming movies."

Maybe she will talk to me after, Farley thought.

"Creepy doesn't cover it," the new girl said.

Chapter 6

RESURRECTION CORNER
MORNING

The sheriff's car came around the corner and moved up the street toward the One Hump. The early morning sun caught a reflected glint of light. The sheriff's brow wrinkled. He parked in front of the bar, got out, and walked back across the street onto the vacant lot next to Hanley's Hardware store.

He stood quietly, brow losing its wrinkle. His hands moved to his hips. A half bottle of Cutty Sark sat in the middle of the vacant lot. It was pointing up. Wide open, the rear doors of Matt's van both added to and answered the puzzle that was unwinding under the sheriff's hat. Trained eyes couldn't miss the shoe prints in the dark soil. Two sets, one larger, trailing off in the direction of the stairs attached to the outside of Hanley's building.

There was a crunching noise in the dirt. James J stood next to the sheriff, a mug of coffee in each hand. Together the two men stood sipping the dark brew. After a moment, the sheriff pointed to the indentations made by shoes in the dirt. James J's eyes followed the trail to the steps. His imagination completed the ascent up to the apartment door at the landing.

James J leaned, picked up the bottle of scotch. The sheriff closed the van's rear doors. The two men walked back across the street to the bar.

Cate woke to find Matt writing. A half circle of yellow pads formed around him at the kitchen table. A folded piece of cardboard answered the problem with the table's short leg. That day Cate commandeered another chair, two lamps, and a small wood table. Another day dishes, towels, and the ugliest phone Matt had ever seen. Another, a used computer was waiting for Matt as he entered the loft. That was the name they gave their place, the loft.

Being in a relationship again…what to expect? Curious how there were so few hard and fast rules. Each relationship new and different, like haploid chromosomes coming together to form a new variation on life. None before exactly like this, none after. Carol, Matt's first wife, could chisel stone with her tongue, her words. Cate didn't fight, she pouted.

SALT LAKE CITY
WIFE NUMBER ONE
TWO YEARS BEFORE

His memory of Carol, wife number one, was mostly in the bathroom in front of the mirror. She couldn't pass up a mirror.

Matt was leaving for work.

"I'm gone," he hollered over his shoulder.

She stormed into the kitchen, makeup half on, monster curlers crowning her head.

"We're supposed to multiply and replenish the earth, and you can't get it up. What kind of man are you? Where's your priesthood?"

He never could after that.

"You remind me of that asshole who used to be president. No balls Clinton."

Horny as hell the minute he left the apartment. That's when he realized their love was selfish, one objective…the release of hormonal tension. Their marriage certificate had been license to use each other. She gave to get, not to give. He guessed they both did. They were taught to have sex for one reason, babies. Their spiritual leaders were clear on the subject. Said, oral is immoral, no extended pleasure, no embellishments, get on with, and only with, the business of babies. Mechanical, deliberate. Void of spontaneity, it seemed to him.

RESURRECTION CORNER
THE PRESENT

In the early mornings, Cate watched and dozed under a quilt of her mother's making as Matt wrote. They were happy in one large room above Hanley's Hardware store. It was impossible to heat in winter, and the toilet gurgled like a haunted trombone. The floor slanted to port if you were headed to the john and starboard if you were looking for the Cocoa Puffs.

Meanwhile Matt was invisible. He didn't renew the license tabs on the van. He didn't sell it. He didn't drive it. He didn't communicate with anyone from Salt Lake or Vegas. Phone in Cate's name. Everything with cash. He put his name to nothing. No one knew how to find him or if he still existed. There was safety in being invisible.

Cate didn't read his pages, she counted them. Two or more pages per day was met with a smile, a kiss, and sometimes an even greater bonus. A one-sentence day earned him a pat on the chest and a "Don't fret. You'll do better tomorrow. I know it."

Her candor gnawed at him, cutting away the deposits of cynicism and self-pity. The lady splintered his carefully crafted wall of sarcasm. When she slept, watching her breathe was the most contented he had ever felt. Awake, she sucked the excitement out of every minute. No question, he was in way over his head. No question, he loved every minute of it—even to the toleration of that damn Minnie Mouse telephone she brought with her when they moved into the loft.

He was learning from Cate to play, to enter into each day as an adventure. They lived, walking three degrees off vertical, happy as birds on a fence. Matt was scared. How in God's name did he deserve this?

"Do you feel it?" he said.

Most people didn't know what Matt was talking about until he'd said three sentences. Cate knew almost before he opened his mouth.

"I saw color in the maples today," she said.

"We won't need the fan tonight."

She followed him to the window and, pushing in front of him, put her hands flat against the glass. Trumped by gentle autumn, summers long, hot reckoning was over. She trembled and leaned into him. When her nipples grew hard, Matt lost the power of rational thought.

After. They fell exhausted into an autumn-like serenity. He took instruction in the language of soft whispered things, drifting in that moment of perfect contentment between heightened excitement and delicious slumber. Matt was convinced nature designed this after-place for man alone, because woman, insecure at its approach, invariably began conversations that could not wait until morning. Even when love was good and honest, Cate sensed something. Her fear spoke to him.

"Do you love me?" she said.

"Uh huh."

"Are you sure?"

"Uh huh."

"Will you say the words for me?"

"Uh, uh huh."

"Now would be good."

A deep breath, his voice thick with sleep.

"I love my Cate. I love her before and I love her after."

His shoulder where her cheek rested told him she was smiling. He continued his sleepy ode.

"I love her in the morning. I love her in the night. I love her tomorrow and I love her forever."

Trembling fingers covered his mouth.

"Don't say that!"

There was hurt in her voice.

"Don't say you love me forever. You can't. Forever is from nowhere, and you're not hard, so you don't have to lie to me."

Cate turned over, curled up in a little ball, and went to sleep, her back against him. By now he was refreshed. Would get up and write, but his arm was under her head. It would be hours before sleep returned.

Matt had no defense against the undesirable memories at times like this. He could side-step them by day, but at night they would loop and re-loop without pity. In revisiting those times he was struck by their strangeness. Two years, yet his old self was so different. Was like another dimension with some of the same actors, only aliens wrote the dialogue. The images still pulled at him, aroused emotion, but it was another person in another time.

SALT LAKE CITY
A MOTHER'S LOVE
TWO YEARS BEFORE

"Contrary child," his mother mumbled.

He'd heard it before. Knew what she said. The words spoken next were loud and heartfelt.

"You are an embarrassment to this family."

Matt drove to his apartment in Salt Lake on automatic pilot, his reluctant old beater with bald tires navigating. He remembered the smooth feel of the steering wheel, but not the ride. Knew, because his hand hurt where he pounded and wrenched at the wheel.

"I don't need this," he said, the windshield throwing it back at him. "I'm out of here. Pack tonight."

But where? he wondered. Parts unknown. Too much to deal with now. Figure it out in the morning.

He slammed the car door, the only way it would stay shut, and walked with his briefcase to the apartment. The deadbolt turned without resistance. *That's odd*, he thought. The hair on his neck moved. Matt inched the door open and stood dazed. What had not been turned upside down or inside out was broken, slashed, or ripped apart. Everything he owned had been trashed.

A sudden weakness, he leaned against the doorframe, his heart hammering in his chest. *Who,* he thought, scanning the hall.

THE WRITER'S LIFE

Matt would wander into the One Hump for a coffee almost without realizing he had done so. James J would pour the mug full. He would nod to those who said hello. Distracted, the mug would hang at his chin, pause midair. A moment later he would be gone, the coffee untouched.

Subjecting deeper and deeper into the character of Joseph Smith opened up elements of his own personality Matt had not considered before. Everything hinged on that. The Church, the doctrines, the beliefs, the behavior of its leaders, the multiple marriages...all pivoted on what made Smith tick.

What does it take to get a woman to spread her legs for a man? Not just the academics of it, Matt had to understand the psyche of a man who thrived on the adulation of women.

Once a month there was a matter James J needed to attend to. Matt would take over as bar keep. The Mormon boy tending bar. Believe that. He began putting in a couple half shifts at the One Hump when James J needed to take some time for personal business.

James J was gaining a reputation as an AA, CA, and NA speaker all over New York State. Sometimes he would get board, room, and travel expenses to speak at conventions in other states. He and Knuckles were famous. He sported a before-and-after blow-up of the bike that would go with him.

Dunn's Hollow was different, not exactly AA as Matt could figure it. A business of some kind. Last Wednesday of the month. It was some time before Matt put together what Dunn's Hollow was all about. All he knew at first was that it had something to do with battered women.

James J and the bike had become a legend. The Harley was a 1947 beauty with ape hangers. What came out of the accident was a sober bartender with one leg shorter than the other, served up good RC, recovery coffee, or a mean martini in a bar with the vintage Harley-Davidson bike on permanent display. Both he and Harley offered up a moment of pride as strangers walked through the door, stood, and looked at the upward swing of the high Y-shaped handle bars and the strangely shaped headers looked like knuckles on a fist. Muffled exclamations of credulity were not uncommon in the ambience of drinker and ex-drinker. They came through the door, all kinds.

"Damn beauty. She fire up?"

"Ninety all day."

"You really don't drink?"

"Affirmative."

"Yeah? Do a line now and then, man?"

"Drug of choice was more before I got smart and quit."

Followed by a roar of laughter from unbelieving bikers from Phoenix or Houston or, on this occasion, Salt Lake City.

"A meeting's as good as a drink any day," he declared to the bikers who came to see the before-and-after pictures of Knuckles and/or absorb some of James J's fellowship.

"Only problem is you have to sit through ninety meetings in ninety days in order to reverse the inflow of self-centered horse shit you've been feeding yourself, God knows how many years."

The black-leathered Harley owner from Salt Lake City sneered through one side of his face, "Ninety in ninety? The hell you say."

James J apologized to no man. A member of the AA Angels, he knew that self-honesty was the truer ride.

One sluggish afternoon after writing all morning, Matt made the coffee extra strong at the One Hump. Was waiting for James J to leave for Dunn's Hollow when the glass in the front windows began to vibrate. Matt pivoted on his stool and looked outside. The air was split with the sensuous vibrations of two Harley engines he'd never seen in the Corner.

Two half-drunk, black leather jackets parked their bikes and entered. Easy to see these two bearded bikers had a chip on their shoulders. Obviously they had been offended by the story of a sober Harley. They looked around until they saw Knuckles, paid no attention to James J.

"Jack Daniel's, water," the shorter of the two said, ordering.

"Black or green, don't matter. Whatever this cheap joint stocks," the other said.

They stood ogling Knuckles while James J poured. That done and acting like they owned the place, the two bragged and drank until finally James J disappeared out back.

He returned in his riding leathers. Looking a foot taller, he put an empty water glass in front of each of the two egos. He reached for the Black Label Jack Daniel's and began to pour. The dark amber fluid inched up the glass slowly. Questions began forming in the faces of the two bikers. One finger, two fingers, three fingers, four. The taller of the two strangers licked his lips. Tension mounted. First one glass then the other. The silence grew louder.

Expectation hung in the air like smoke. James J screwed the lid on the bottle super slow. He set the bottle down between the glasses with a solid thud. When he finally spoke it was deliberate, measured.

"You haven't got a hair on your ass if you can't walk away from this drink and keep up with me for the next three hours."

James J didn't wait for an answer. He turned and left by the back door.

The two loudmouths at the bar sat scratching themselves and looking at the booze when the distinct throaty vibrations of another Harley started down the alley in back and pulled up in front of the bar.

Every eye turned to see one of the factory-designed modern Classic Harleys sitting in the middle of the street. On the side of the gas tank, when James J dropped his boot to the street, you could see it, the chrome-plated plaque. If you rode a Harley, you knew the inscription read "Designed by Willie G. Davidson for James J" and under that, "Good Riding."

James J began pulling on a pair of jet-black leather gloves.

From one of the bikers Matt heard, "It's a Factory Fat Boy."

"Goddamn," the other said.

One rev of throttle rattled the glass in the windows. Gauntlet flung! The two half-drunken, discombobulated bikers stumbled all over each other attempting to grind through the door at the same time. James J gave his bike some serious throttle and pulled away. Three hogs left in a wake of thunder headed for the highway.

It was late when James J returned and fixed himself a fresh coffee.

"I shouldn't do that. Not as young as I used to be."

It was all he said.

Friday night AA meeting at the One Hump. An accountant with a Harley from Danville named Fonzie was scheduled to receive his four-year birthday coin. He joined Matt in the bar before the meeting.

"I been trying to put two and two together, and James J won't say a damn word. What happened last week?" Matt asked.

"It was classic, man. We hooked 'em up. James J didn't tell you? Ain't that just like that SOB? The timing was a God shot. He pulled into our meeting with the two strays just as it started," Fonzie said.

Matt had been to that meeting with James J. Biker meeting. Almost needed an interpreter to understand the lingo. Fonzie walked Matt through it.

"The two loudmouths shut up, listened only. Both skeptical as hell. As the meeting ended, James J announced that the two new guys had volunteered to make the delivery. Everyone knew what was going on. Salt Lake bikers thought they did too. Coke deal. Mules for cocaine delivery. Bikers reckoned that just because this bunch didn't drink anymore, that didn't stop them from moving product. Everyone needs coin, even dry sombitches.

"The taller one, whose name was Bart, spoke to his partner. 'Gang initiation. Hell yeah.'

"They jumped at the challenge. Our group secretary brought out the pouch. Gave it to the short guy, who thought to take a quick peek inside until James J stopped him."

"'Wrong move, man.'

"We head out. I take the lead. James J and two others brought up the rear, the new guys sandwiched in tight between the other bikes. I took us past the sheriff's office. Had to have shit their pants when I honked and we all waved. Give my left one to have seen their faces."

Matt listened as Fonzie laid out the whole story for him. "The two bikers were led to a house at the end of the lane in Dunn's Hollow, far side of Dansville. White picket fence, looked like a cottage in a calendar. Door opened as they drove up. A girl about eighteen years old with the last stages of a black eye came out and held the gate as they walked in.

"'What took you so long? We've been waiting ten minutes.'

"James J and I went in with the Salt Lake bikers. We were in the playroom with the children and the young mothers. There was a baby, couple toddlers, and a six- and seven-year-old. A lady, about five foot two, looking not all that much older herself, came from the next room, wiping her hands on her apron. She greeted James J. and me with a smile that seemed to gather light and illuminate the room where she stood. She then turned to meet the two strangers, who were having trouble taking their eyes off the nun's habit she was wearing.

"'Wanted to do this in person this week, Sister Angela. Got two new recruits. These gentlemen are from Salt Lake City, here to see how it works, possibly start their own shelter,' James J said.

"The two Salt Lake bikers, still smelling of road and whiskey, gulped. Was pure pleasure to see their bewildered expressions.

"James said, 'Don't pay any attention to the smell, Sister, it's a... just a...part of the initiation.'

"Sister Angela Maria, plain, clean, and polished to a high gloss, stepped forward, took the black pouch, and held it to her breast.

"'Four thousand dollars?' she asked, looking at us.

"We nodded. She nodded, turned to the two road warriors. 'You are so tall. Would you bend down for me please?' They looked at each other, not knowing what to do. James J pointed to the floor. 'On your knees.'

"They looked like anything but gentlemen. Scared rabbits with bushy beards. Sister Angela performed a blessing, crossed herself, and said, 'God bless and keep you. May the Lord love and protect you.'

"Poor hungover bastards. It was all they could do not to blubber like fools.

"Sister Angela turned to the mothers.

"'Girls, a little gratitude is not out of order here. If they say they are not, feed them anyway. They are men after all.'

"Two of the young mothers led the two Salt Lake bikers to chairs, and the toddlers, too young to have developed a sophisticated set of fears, climbed on and jabbered away at the now moist-eyed men in black leather. Children can be so trusting, and alcoholic bikers can be such maudlin fools."

Fonzie clarified the whole situation for Matt. "Residence Eight is a safe house for battered women with children. James J had suggested it to some of the bikers in his home group couple years back. Couldn't be part of AA because of its bylaws, but individuals from those groups could form a charity thing of their own and be responsible in its support. The idea took. Twenty bikers. Three qualifications. All had to be hog lovers, actively involved in AA, clean and sober at least one year.

"'Molly has a wet diaper. I'll change her,' a mother said to one of the Salt Lake bikers.

"When her mother reached to take the baby away from the black-leathered giant, the baby began to cry and the biker said, 'Don't matter. She can piss all over me she wants...I mean, it don't matter, little sister... I mean ma'am. She's good right where she is.'"

The two Salt Lake City bikers couldn't wait to get outside where they could fart and hide their feelings behind a couple of thousand rpms. These were the kind of men who laugh in the face of a judge passing down a sentence, because in their hearts they know short of death that's probably where they belong. The shame of what he is, where he's been, and what he's done against the purity of child and young mother is more than he can balance in a brain that is at home doing ninety on a freeway. The chance to offset the waste and carnage of the past against the preservation and care of these innocents was a dream with muscle.

In the bleak, desolate region of the soul, these road warriors knew there was something they could dare to care about.

It was time for the Friday evening meeting to start.

"We better get over there," Fonzie said.

"Don't leave me hanging. What happened?"

Fonzie continued talking while they made their way to the large booth used for the AA meeting.

"There were two more bits of business went with James J's dare. The men in black stood in the road outside of Residence Eight. James J handed them a nine-by-fourteen manila envelope they used for just such occasions. It contained generic copies of incorporation papers and bylaws for a non-profit corporation.

"'You ain't worth a cold turd on a flat rock if you don't go back to Salt Lake and start a Residence Eight. Get a bunch of sober drunks on bikes to support it. Be good for some freaking thing in your hungover, useless lives,'" Fonzie told Matt what James J said.

Fonzie continued.

"'Thing like this never occurred to me, man,' Bart, the taller of the two bikers, said. 'I thought a coke deal was goin' down, man, and we were the test mules. Then you hooked us up with a bunch of little babies slobberin' all over my ugly ass and mothers no older than my daughter, and a nun for God's sake blesses me, thinkin' I was helpin' them. Holy snot, man. I did nine years—hard time. Watched my daughter grow up in snapshots. Ten years old when I got out, my wife still won't let me see her, my own daughter. She was right too, nothin' but a worthless dirt bag piece of shit.'

"Feeling sorry for himself, this blubbering road warrior stepped to one side, put a finger against the side of his nose, and blew. Reversed his hands and shot another goober seven feet out from the other nostril.

"'Never been worth a damn to anyone, but I got more hair on my ass than any man alive,' he said.

"'It's true. Bastard's crazier than I am, and this is so crazy it makes sense,' Gabe, his partner, testified."

Fonzie kept talking as they took their places in the booth.

"Can it. A good meeting starts on time and ends on time," James J said, interrupting Fonzie's story.

It was Matt's turn to chair the meeting. He grabbed How It Works and the Preamble, which were read at the beginning of every meeting, and galloped through them super fast.

"My meeting. My format. I'm calling on Fonzie to finish the story. What happened to the two Salt Lake bikers?" Matt said.

"Not relevant," James J countered.

Everyone at the table objected. "Keep talkin'," they all agreed.

Fonzie started over. Brought everyone up to speed.

"We told the Salt Lake bikers there was one more order of business before they were done. Told them about a delivery of bad milk to the house, the second time it had happened. They needed to discuss a better business arrangement with the local dairy. Any suggestions?"

James J was annoyed, but knew he was outvoted. Fonzie continued.

"These Salt Lake bikers were like four hours from a drink. You could see the circles of self-pity under their eyes—up until they heard about the milk. The one called Bart turned white. You could see the cold fury working through him. 'Fuckin' A. Where is this fuckin' dairy?' Gabe, speaking reverently, as if we were in a church said, 'Can we hurt 'em?'

"James J told them, 'Sister Angela says no violence.'"

Fonzie is living the story, loving the reaction he's getting from the other ex-drunks at the meeting. He leans into the table and almost whispers, "For a moment no one speaks. Then a face full of teeth shows up in the middle of this Bart guy's beard and he says, 'But the owner can drink his own piss, right?'"

Everyone at the AA meeting hoorayed and high-fived each other for the benefit of James J.

Fonzie turned the meeting back over to Matt, who called on a few others to share, and the meeting ended.

It was after and Cate was, as usual, fully awake. Matt almost had to hold his eyes open with his fingers. She continued to babble until phase two kicked in where Matt got his second wind. Something said she needed this time, the two of them. It didn't matter what they talked about so much. She just needed this kind of one-on-one time with her Matthew.

He'd long since learned to surrender to her better wishes. While she seemed to be intellectually challenged about many things, Matt had learned that in matters of the heart she had exceptional insight. Be an hour before sleep returned anyway. He'd been thinking about the safe houses James J was affiliated with.

"Tell me if I understand this." He rolled over and propped his head up on an elbow. "Twenty adrift bikers found a neglected chunk of real estate, ordinarily wasn't worth saving. Rather than rebuild, they descended on this tear-down with hammer, saw, and dream. Twenty bikers. Yellow paint stains on black leather," he said, taking a deep breath. "Whose idea was it?" he mumbled, rolling to his back again.

"His," she said.

"White picket fence, flowers. It's a picture-perfect cottage with a dormitory added in the back." Cate could hear the respect in Matt's voice. "What started in relative obscurity in a small town in upstate New York is taking on the trappings of something epic. Do you know there is an affiliate now?"

"Yeah." Cate drew closer, threw her leg over his, the position in which they usually fell asleep.

"Only in America. A union of differences where even PTSD types could find an idea worth believing in and the freedom to grab hold and hang on. No matter how you look at it, for them it was a chance for redemption. The regular guy, the nine to fiver, is thought of as the backbone of the Democratic experiment, but to these road warriors, it's a way to believe they, too, are a piece of the American pie. The Mongolian Horsemen of America, these guys. Mavericks to the marrow, they know they are not cut out for domestic tricks. Loading a dishwasher or punching a time clock is work beyond the cognitive capacity."

Cate was rubbing his chest, gently, encouragingly.

"Once in Saigon, and for reasons most will never know, the pleasant dream is for other men. Resigned to wind and roar of adrenaline high, they roam the land looking for honor lost. A bottle of Jack in a saddlebag carries the moment they know will never come. Feeling left out, they stay out, telling themselves not for me. Then epiphany! Something they can believe in shows itself. A maverick heart, yellow paint stains on black leather, the color of hope, a sense of belonging. A bunch of dropouts contribute to the American dream."

"I don't get to see the newspaper guy very often," she said.

"Scribbling. Just scribbling."

"You should write it down," she said, drifting off.

"Those guys ride at the poetic heart of America. Couldn't forget it if I wanted to."

She slept, tucked in next to him, a snore as light as a butterfly's wing. He drifted, languishing in its rhythm. His last thought before drifting off, *I don't deserve to be this happy*.

It was a candor that took getting used to. Grounded in the nest Cate built, Matt's discontent vanished. He was pumped. Enthusiasm high. The perfect bar had become the perfect town.

The computer, one of Cate's little miracles, used up most of Matt's day. An accumulation of thumb tacks, translucent tape, and sticky notes lay on windowsills and tabletops.

Walls lost their character, became an extenuation of history. Copies of newspaper clippings, journal entries, land deeds, letters, meeting minutes, and other documents hung at every accommodation the walls could offer except one. To the wall at the rear of the room next to the bathroom door hung a single page. Handwritten, it read...

On this, the 27th day of June of our Lord, 1844, be it known unto Brother Young, I, Joseph Smith, speak unto you of the new and everlasting covenant. Whereupon more was promised more is given.

It has been made known unto me the reason the Lord commands celestial marriage. Verily, I say unto you our precious sisters do not carry the seed of truth. Eve by her nature deceived man. Verily, woman is not apportioned to understand the precepts of heaven. Her special calling is of the profane.

Therefore, she must administer unto man in order to provide the earthly bodies that man might progress and enter into exaltation according to the commandment God gave unto Abraham.

And again, verily I say unto you, men alone hold the keys of the kingdom. Touching on these matters, the Lord thy God commands every man with the duty of the priesthood. We must carry the burden of wives and concubines into the millennium where righteous men will rule during Christ's reign. It is to us to sow the seed of righteousness throughout every nation, people and tongue.

Verily I say unto you these are the fullness of times. To deny celestial marriage is to invite damnation. Behold, the laws of men are as nothing to the Law of God. The seed of your loins is the promise of the future. Nations of the righteous await. Because the Lord commands it there is no sin in it.

Now Brother Brigham, the saints have seen enough persecution. Take the Church west into the great territories where a nation of cities and towns can grow under the eternal covenant of holy marriage. Our discourses about the great Salt Lake Basin are in your faithful hands. The Lord will direct you.

Now the Lord commands Brother Richards. Henceforth, he is to remove himself from the presence of his prophet and to place himself at the most remote area of the jail and so remain, keeping himself beyond the reach of danger. No matter what comes to pass he is to remain separated from his prophet. He is to carry this letter in his boot until it is safe to convey to the next President of the Church.

Thus sayeth the Lord God. Amen.

Fear chokes at your prophet. Tomorrow is a curtain he cannot see beyond.

I fear I am now from Eden come.

Matt wrote in the mornings. When sleep eluded, he wrote. A newspaper journalist emerged from behind a wall of inebriation. In the loft, a mug of coffee in hand, Matt could be found staring transfixed at a piece of paper pinned to a wall at eye level.

A finger tapped the document hanging in front of him. The tapping might continue until a remembered connection sent him aimed at another wall. The urgency of message both clear and elusive, something said and something left unsaid. A last revelation as well as a lost revelation. It was the completion of a question, a discussion. It was answer. It was the Lord speaking through his prophet, bringing clarity to the befuddled, fear-ridden minds of men. Questions kept him awake.

"To deny celestial marriage is to invite damnation."

In the middle of the night Cate would be awakened as he read aloud, struggled with the meaning of the words. She lay awake watching, listening.

Disney Studio dreamt up a telephone that looked like Minnie Mouse. It made a noise like a dentist's drill feels, but louder. When writing Matt unplugged it, if he remembered. He'd never told Cate how much he hated that ugly varmint, nor would he, but when Minnie rang, Cate would reach in anticipation. Matt would grind his teeth.

He had thought of chucking it in Lake Ontario until he found out it was the gift of a loving father to his teenage daughter the year he had the heart attack and died. That off-key rodent would be with them forever. Begged the question, how much will a man suffer for love? So he surrendered to the fact that they were three: Cate, he, and an off-key mouse named Minnie.

If you are a writer, a telephone is a threat to sanity anyway. He was further challenged when Cate came home with one of those long extension cords so she could move about while talking.

For some reason only Carl, who once worked for the telephone company, could explain why cell phones didn't work well in and about Resurrection Corner. Some kind of signal problem along with the cost of a new transmitter station. The cost was prohibitive.

When Cate cut up a salad, head cocked to one side, the black cord skipped about behind her like a kangaroo's tail. It stretched into the john, drawing a horizontal line from the phone's cradle to the doorjamb a quarter way up from the floor, where it then did a U-turn and disappeared into the small room where she and General Commode were temporary comrades. The door stayed open and it was not because of the black cord, a thing he would come to know at a later time.

When Matt was finally able to put it together, he thought to query Raven first, to be sure.

"There is a reason, but it should be Cate that tells you," Raven said.

Matt was working on a way to bring up the subject of Cate's ex, John. Raven must have said something to Cate, because Matt had been asleep for an hour when he realized Cate was sitting up in bed, talking to him. He looked around just to be sure. She did jabber in her sleep once in a while.

"Are you telling me you were not a virgin when we met?" Matt said.

Cate threw a pillow over his head.

"I look like him? That's why the reaction when I drove into town."

Matt, of course, knew about her ex, John, but any excuse to tease, get a reaction, was golden, and he would have all he could get.

"Hush now or I won't tell you any of it," she said, putting a finger to his lips. "Why I hadn't noticed before or listened to my friends I don't know. I'm not so much stubborn as naive, I think."

Matt tried not to look like he agreed. She ran her hand over his face, as if to wipe away the expression.

"John's friends didn't laugh unless he thought it was funny. I didn't fit, but I didn't know it. You know me. I talk to everyone. That was hard for John. It was like he was always closing doors instead of opening them, shutting out what he couldn't control.

"Today I understand. The poor man was scared to death. He was afraid he would lose me if I were not dependent on him. It started innocently enough. 'I just want you safe while I'm not here,' he told me. When we love a man, our desire to believe him is natural, I think. At least we want to believe him," she said, searching Matt's face for his reaction.

Matt stretched his legs. He was amazed. Her degree of sympathy for this asshole blew him away. He wanted to cut the guy's balls off, and she was justifying his treatment of her.

"In that way I was dependent on him, but you know who the real prisoner was?"

"We all are, honey. Every man alive is your prisoner."

Cate reached for his T-shirt. Chest hair with it.

"Ouch," he said, attempting to protect himself.

"Then listen. He was the prisoner of his own smallness."

"Smallness, yes ma'am."

She rolled her eyes, went on with her story.

"And I forgave John. That's why, for you and me, divorce is out of the question."

Having lived with the female of the species before, Matt had developed some verbal skills, the ad lib being one of them.

"Uh-huh," he said.

"Uh-huh. Is that all you can say?"

"Okay. I don't get it," Matt confessed.

"We can't get a divorce if we are not married," Cate said.

A triumphant smile followed, and he knew somewhere behind that smile it made sense. Suddenly Matt wanted her so bad he started to breathe in rapid, short breaths.

"James J and Mom found me locked in a closet. It was one of those small, odd-shaped closets under the stairs. There was a space under the small door where I lay and watched the light fade. I felt so alone. I sure didn't want anyone to know. The poor man was jealous of everyone I talked to."

Matt didn't say anything. He was contemplating the guy's balls in a meat grinder.

"I get all weird inside when I'm alone in a dark room," she said.

"You're okay outside?"

Cate nodded.

Matt needed a moment to wrap his mind around what he just heard. He slipped out of bed and looked at the hinges on the bathroom door. There was no rust. He wiggled the door a little while he lifted the pins out of the hinges with the help of a butter knife as a wedge. He leaned the door against the wall and jumped back in bed. Cate clapped with glee. Triumphant.

The coffee was hot, dark, and bold. Of itself the rich smell had a waking effect. It was an hour before the sun would break through the layer of fog that blanketed the little village of Resurrection Corner. As he brought his computer up to speed, reading his notes from yesterday, he sensed a nagging impression. He was seeing Joseph in a new light, in the same way he looked at Paul, his brother. A kind of a kinship was taking place.

One of Smith's first scribes was a young, wide-eyed Oliver Cowdery, who had, in the early days of Smith's ministry, become his right arm.

OLIVER COWDERY

The two men had been together all day. Joseph had arranged to have Oliver Cowdery boarded with the widow, Sister Lewis.

Evening, Oliver had just come through the door. He was excited from the experiences of the day.

"I've been with Brother Joseph now for almost a month. I can t help thinking he is the one chosen of God. I believe him to be. I know of no other way this could be," Oliver said.

Sister Lewis was, herself, new to his teachings. She stopped what she was doing, wiped her hands on her apron, and sat in the straight back chair next to Oliver at the table.

"What a wonderful thing that must be," she said.

"Today Joseph had a revelation from the Lord. As usual he had asked me to scribe for him."

"As you have been," she said.

"Yes, yes, as I have been, but suddenly I was writing my own name and it was the Lord telling me that I have the divine gift of revelation. After Joseph embraced me with such joy I know he too was excited by the revelation. It was as though we are brothers in a cause common to the glory of God. I cannot tell you how I feel. For years I have floundered without direction. Today I have a path and it is straight and true."

Sister Lewis saw tears in Oliver's eyes. She was moved as well.

"I am a blessed man," he said.

It was through Oliver's eyes Matt connected with Joseph that first time. Without worrying about point of view, he had learned to let the pen run. When he did, things happened that were often insightful. It had taken him back to time and place and given him an added sense of the character of Joseph. How he believed in what he was doing.

A glimpse inside Smith, but it was enough. Joseph was flying blind, allowing the Lord to direct his course. There was a freshness Matt hung on to. He sensed the revelation as Smith's surprise as much as Oliver's. How it had been exciting for both of them. Oliver was twenty-four years old at the time. Insights like this were priceless.

This was a Smith he was comfortable with. He could not respect the cardboard cutout, one-dimensional hero he had been raised to believe in. He could respect a hero with a hole in the sole of his boot. The whole picture was changing. He saw the bravery and risk-taking in a different light. Smith could not accept much of a world that was so contrary, and he refused to become cynical for a long time.

Mainstream protestant Christianity said, man was saved by grace alone and not by deeds. No. No. No. Not so. Joseph felt the hand of God in teaching his followers; a man's good deeds were valued in heaven. Because he said it, he believed he was directed to say it. What he perceived as revelation was God guiding his thoughts. Why else would he think those things if they were not the Almighty using him for His own purposes? Joseph felt the connection to the prophets of old.

More and more he was seeing an ordinary man whose natural instincts had begun turning into liabilities in the presence of the drug of his growing power. A few months before his assassination in 1844, Joseph had himself anointed King over Israel.

Nauvoo, Illinois had a higher population than Chicago at the time. Smith looked beyond a governorship. He spoke in private circles of the presidency of the United States. Matt assimilated his hopes, dreams, and felt his outrage against the nonbelievers who would bring him down. He felt Joseph's fury against the fearmongers who would keep mankind chained in ignorance.

The time demands of a growing church were astronomical. Joseph had to be everywhere—meetings, speeches, land purchases, overseeing construction, declaring revelations, conducting municipal meetings, and he made it a point to welcome immigrants and settlers until it became an overwhelming task.

The larger the church grew, the more lawsuits there were to deal with. He was being accused of doing any number of horrific things, like locking women in a room for days if they refused his advances.

A reference in a journal entry would hint of Smith's wife's unhappiness. Emma felt neglected as any wife would. On top of that there were rumors of Old Testament marriage. Emma's jealousy escalated until home, a place where we nurture and refresh, became a thicket of thorns for Joseph.

Like old Money Bags, Matt's ex-father-in-law, Smith's wife's father disapproved of Emma's choice of husbands. Matt felt a vicarious sense of revenge at Joseph's womanizing. He couldn't help wondering if Joseph Smith had felt the way he did. Matt began to defend him, judged against the backdrop of his humanity, and not the otherworldliness taught by his priesthood teachers. Yet Cate was not Carol, Matt's ex, and the feeling was uncomfortable. All he had to do was think of how cheating on Cate would make her feel, and he felt like his head was in a vise. Cheating on Cate didn't compute. But there it was for Joseph, cheating on Emma felt vindicating.

What did Smith do when his wife Emma said, "I have a headache"? The more she said no, the more he needed her.

"It's the wrong time of the month. I'm all bloated," Cate would say to Matt.

Matt had been playful. Cate said she didn't feel like it. Wounded and indignant, Matt began to dwell on a stiff urgency.

Matt wondered if women knew how dutiful the male mind was about sex. Men were cursed with two and one-half times more brain cells devoted to sex than women. He told her this. She ignored him.

Men didn't ask for this. Came with the damn territory.

Matt was writing when Cate climbed the stairs to the loft. As she opened the door, he hit save and got in the first word, an accomplishment not all that easy. Cate would have itemized between two and four things she needed to inform Matt of and without which his survival and hers, no matter how trivial, would be seriously affected. Playful, he started talking as the door opened.

"Darwin was a fraud," Matt said.

She set a sack of groceries on the table.

"And all this time I thought Darwin was your buddy," she said. She walked over and felt his forehead. "No temperature."

"The whole thing's a fraud. Survival of the fittest is one of God's jokes," he said.

"When will I know what you're talking about?" she asked.

"Sex, of course."

"Of course," she mocked.

Cate turned her back on him and began putting groceries away.

"Yeah. I did a survey...a sex survey," Matt insisted.

As he said it, Cate shifted her weight, looked back at him, and rolled her eyes as if to say, okay, say it, get it over with.

"Survival of the fittest does not answer the primary question. How does a man bed a woman, for instance, with an acid claw for a tongue? Implication? God has to exist, otherwise how do you explain the temporary blindness men have to suffer at certain critical moments in order to procreate?"

Her hand made a fist. Matt grabbed a chair, held it between them.

"D. I., that's what. D. I. alone solves the problem," Matt said.

"D. I.," she said, her tone threatening.

"Divine Intervention. Adam wasn't getting the job done. God intervened, introduced a testosterone myopia, rendering Adam hormone blind. It's a temporary thing. Delirium. A temporary delirium. You know, apples and all that."

"I'll give you some divine intervention," Cate said, a clenched fist in front of her.

When a man makes a fist, you see it in his shoulders, his whole frame. When Cate made a fist, it hung in front of her, an independent thing unrelated to either her arm or her body. Trying not to laugh, Matt backed away, the chair between them.

"An Arabian sheik knows these things. Why else the harem?"

Backing gingerly away, he threw another barb in her direction.

"And my polygamous ancestors...they know. They understood the role testosterone plays and why God punished Adam with so much of it for eating that goddamn apple."

He let her catch him. The fun of it.

"This is reserved for a smart-ass Mormon boy," she said.

Matt didn't think she could punch that hard. Letting her catch him…it was always worth it. Playful. Human and playful. He was starting to get the hang of it. He could laugh at himself now. Seemed to be something healthy in feeling safe enough to act silly with Cate. Being playful with the most intimate person in his life felt right. There was a refreshing warmth to their love. He celebrated her. Himself. Them. But it added dimension to Matt's understanding.

Relationships demanded a playfulness from time to time. With Smith so many were offended by his actions, he couldn't let down his guard. His relationships with the women of the church were always new. They were serious conquests. There was no playfulness, no one to act silly with. The essential human quality, the missing element, being able to act silly, let the old cortex reboot.

Matt felt sad for Joseph.

He'd learned from the historical documents in his possession that Joseph Smith experienced a great deal of ridicule from Emma's family. Her father, Isaac Hale, strongly disapproved of the young man. One of Emma's brothers had said something on a fishing trip that caused Joseph to throw off his coat and call him out.

"Let's settle this now," Joseph raged.

He examined the documents. Feeling Joseph's frustration, Matt pounded on the table, paced the room, until downstairs Doris told Elbert to go upstairs and tell Matt to keep the noise down.

Matt was familiar with this kind of mental anguish. It had been the same with Carol's father, President Burgess. Until the perfect revenge presented itself, it was a crust of angst running through Smith. In Joseph, Matt felt a vicarious rancor.

Revenge came, eventually, in the form of Fanny Alger, an exciting seventeen-year-old come to live in the Smith home to work as a hired girl. The clandestine moments that followed were Joseph's first affair according to the records Matt had discovered in the archives of the church.

A romantic liaison would be adultery. But hormones, like hunger, came with their own urgency. The brain being a creative organ, it reached, demanded, and searched for answers.

Smith knew of a religion practicing polyandry in the next county. He knew his Bible. The Lord had spoken and Sarah, being barren, had given Hagar to Abraham to wife. Joseph did the math; he married the women he secretly courted. Called it a heavenly marriage, one that would come into its own after the resurrection. So the marriage took on the authority of a celestial license, but the bed—the conjugal bliss—what could be said of that?

The real problem, mostly unsubstantiated and unpublished until Matt's exposé, was that some of those women were already married. Would you believe it, their husbands didn't take kindly to the ecclesiastical rhetoric Smith was so good at.

Smith had solved his problem. He was game to the flush of procreation, yet had little regard for women. His was a unique and convoluted ideology, justifying one behavior, condemning the other side of it. He was slave to his instinctive need to procreate and masterful at shielding his actions in theological grandiosity.

Emma's father, Isaac Hale, had wished his daughter dead rather than marry Smith and had made his feelings known. It was something Matt could identify with in his first marriage. It was the evening the D word was spoken for the first time.

SALT LAKE CITY
THE "D" WORD
TWO YEARS BEFORE

Every evening Carol had something planned. Following the honeymoon she simply put herself in charge of their social life, just as she had with her father when her mother passed away the year before they started going together. At first he welcomed it, something else he didn't have to deal with. Now, he was burned out on her snooty, entitled friends. The idle chatter, the gossip, so boring it terrified.

Carol had them scheduled for some church thing her father, Ezra D. Burgess, was also slated.

Evening traffic moved around him. One idiot honked. Married a year now, he felt helpless at those events and captive to the boring babble of gossip that never changed. Not once had she asked him what he wanted to do. He dreaded the evening's tedium. No doubt Jack the Ripper had the same kind of day.

They had fought that morning, as usual, and he shuddered at the thought of the scene he was facing. His palm was sweaty as it turned the doorknob. He laid his briefcase on the kitchen table.

"We're going to be late. You'll have to shower later," her voice carried from the shower.

There was an edge to her words.

"I have to work. You go without me," Matt said.

He heard the shower door click and wanted to run. Carol bolted from the bathroom.

"How dare you. I've made plans, damn you."

It surprised Matt as much as it did her. Weary of the daily combat, he heard himself say it.

"Okay, I fully agree, I'll give you a divorce, any terms you want."

It amazed him, when, in saying what he was thinking, he blurted out the D word. Would never have guessed the beautiful girl in white, kneeling across from him during the marriage ceremony in the temple, could hate with such malice. The dull ache in his stomach sharpened.

Six months after they were married for time and eternity, Matt started wishing eternity was already here. Small heavenly harem would at least afford a few alternatives, and hormones being what they are, maybe if he were dead, he could get laid once in a while and by someone who didn't despise him and the size of his paychecks.

She froze, mouth open, dripping over the bedroom rug. How many times had he seen her without a stitch on? The bathroom light behind, her wet, glistening body betrayed any sanity he had left. Anger mounted. He was repelled by her. He wanted her so bad he was shaking.

"Who said anything about a divorce?" she said.

"You did. I'll sign anything you want. Just leave me one gonad."

She just stood there, a past runner-up to the Miss Utah contest. Ugly innuendo and cruel insult, her specialty. A tongue that lashed with the precision of a surgeon's scalpel. Indignant, she shoved her face in his. The closeness, the smell of her, a perverse urgency, he reacted before he thought and pulled her wet across the bed. They gave new meaning to the reproductive dance. On their wedding night they were both virgins, awkward, unsure. With her appetite grew, Matt would be spent. She would just be getting warmed up.

Brother Clayborne, Matt's priesthood quorum leader, like an elephant in the room, not infrequently came to mind when they were making love. Bald and shaped like an egg with a marble on top, he was also the first counselor in the bishopric. Matt would squeeze his eyes tight, hoping to shut out the image, only to see it brighter.

"It's our conjugal duty," Brother Clayborne would say, "righteous admonition to multiply and replenish the earth. Producing offspring is the woman's responsibility to the Lord and to her husband."

Matt couldn't help reflecting on the fervency with which he tutored his boys, as he called them, in their covenant with the Lord. *Methinks he doth protest too much*, words that would loop and re-loop, leading him to deduce that for Brother Clayborne, who had no children, getting laid was probably a quarterly event. The serious expression was the giveaway. How often had he heard him say those exact words?

"Our responsibility is to provide physical bodies for spirit children anxiously waiting in the pre-existence to be born into this world. And brethren, remember, no hanky panky, the oral stuff is strictly forbidden. Against God's mandate," he would insist.

Making the beast with two backs, by church canon, would involuntarily pierce consciousness. Shakespeare's prose—an image so ludicrous—would obsessively repeat, until he wondered if he was afflicted with an obsessive-compulsive disorder. On a few occasions, the distraction had rendered him unable to maintain a firm conviction in his work. But not today. Today it was like he and Carol went blind, both helpless participants in the great plan of salvation, the bio-logic of the life urge. In ancient pre-man the pelvis tilted forward and big brain took on a vertical posture. God then put the hormone in charge and homo erectus, erect, became the higher law.

"He's so hard. I don't think Conrad could scratch him," she said, referring to her cat.

"Why do we always call that part of me 'him'?" Matt said.

"He's so independent. We should have him incorporated," Carol said.

We should have him knighted, Matt thought.

He knew one thing; there was no church in bed that evening, only the sacrament of life.

Carol kept pushing him back on the bed and shoving her knees in his ears. He was jealous. Six times, he calculated. Lucifer would blush. Matt felt like a sperm donor.

After. She lay contented, spent, on the bed her father bought them. Her father? He never thought of that before. Old Money Bags was in bed with them. Matt wondered if there would ever be an end to his humiliation.

President Burgess had presided over the Cottonwood Stake as long as Matt could remember. They seldom spoke, which suited Matt fine. On rare occasions, like at Stake Conferences, where it would be too awkward not to shake hands, they did.

Carol didn't notice that her two men didn't speak to each other. With very few exceptions, her father, a widower, was always where they were, or was it the other way around? Matt wasn't quite sure. At least he would be rid of Daddy Money Bags.

Matt never cheated on Carol, and while she was a world-class flirt, he didn't think she did either. They were taught in Sunday school a healthy relationship required honesty, which seemed perfectly straightforward, until Matt came up against what he thought honesty was and found he was the only one who thought that way.

He rolled off the bed, walked around to her side where the phone was, dialed her father's number. She watched his manhood, at half threat, keep time with his stride until, that is, he dropped the phone in her hand.

"Divorce it is. I'll let you explain it to Money Bags."

By God he still had some class left. For a long while he'd known something was missing between them. They never spoke casually of little things. She never confided in him. She did with her father. He knew that.

"Daddy, we're not going to make it tonight."

Matt couldn't help thinking the love had been heat, and what he'd taken for romance had been hormones.

"I have a splitting headache, Daddy."

There was a pause while her father talked.

"Thank you, Daddy. I love you, Daddy," she said.

When was the last time she said she loved me? he wondered. As she put the phone in its cradle on the nightstand, her eyes turned to slits.

"Prick."

While President Burgess and Isaac Hale were not a precise match, the parallel was compelling. Not acknowledging Matt in church gatherings was a putdown. It was as if he had berated him in public.

He sensed the revenge in Joseph and knew the conquering soliloquy never stopped against his wife's father, Isaac Hale.

In Joseph the drive to right all wrongs was the Lord's voice made tangible. Through Joseph, the Lord spoke of one and used another. Matt wrote with interpretive license, at the same time pushing himself to guard against too broad a license, that which he gleaned from historical record:

THE PERFECT REVENGE

The servant girl, Fanny, peered out of the spaces between the boards in the barn wall and watched Joseph quietly closing the rear door. Quickly she loosened the strings of her bodice.

As he entered the barn she ran into his arms.

"I will never love another," she whispered, her breath as sweet as honeysuckle.

She stood motionless, allowing his gentle caresses as he kissed her hands and her eyes.

"You are the heaven and the earth to me," he said.

Their whispered coupling alarmed the white stallion in the next stall. It pawed at the side boards. Both to silence and to measure the sweet innocence of her, Joseph held her lips to his. She was as if catatonic in his arms. The white stood quiet and time stood the test of its own threat. Straw and night gave over to celestial vibrations. He spoke an unutterable chant, the only ear his own.

To blaspheme against me is to blaspheme against the Lord. I have saved the daughter of ridicule. My love wells up from the spring of truth. It is done. It is ever done. I complete the Lord's covenant. I am no more a conquered people. I am but a little east of Eden.

Pregnant, Fanny had to be sent away from the Smith home.

The writing could be frustrating. Thoughts scrolled out with electric speed. The keyboard had trouble keeping up. He obsessed over Smith's struggle, identified with his frustrations.

Smith could not accept the society of his time and place. There was a pettiness to the everyday inconveniences other men were content to suffer. The mundane held no adventure, no dream of greatness. For Smith ideas burned and pulsed. Capturing the great man's struggle was paramount.

Mother Smith taught Joseph to read, and it was the odd home that did not have a Bible in the new frontier of upstate New York. So how did the man of ideas grow and learn and adapt, or, Matt wondered, did the ideas grow him? The nail spawned the hammer, thought the idea, idea the word, word the language, language the story, story a bible of stories. Mankind's problem; he can't go from point A to point B without a frame of reference, and Smith challenged the frame of reference.

Groundwork ready-laid. Hell, heaven, fire, and brimstone firmly planted in every breast. His was to but tweak the existing model to reflect a new salvation.

That and a natural charisma. Smith saw his eloquence with the word as the divine substrate of his ministry. Between imagination and a charismatic presence, he expanded the parameters of social custom and reshaped the threads of Christian tradition, until Matt wondered how the man could have done otherwise. It was drug of story and it was the kingdom of God story anew, reawakened, urgent, a restoration.

RESURRECTION CORNER
LATER THAT DAY

"You'll never guess," Matt said, leaning against the countertop of their little kitchenette.

"What?"

He was drying the dishes, Cate washing the mismatched and chipped bowls.

"James J asked the question today, the big no-no."

She turned, looked directly into his eyes. "About your book?"

"Yeah."

"You have to give him credit. He resisted for a long time."

"Almost three years."

"Did you fudge?" she said.

"Didn't dare. Did my fifth step with him. You know. In AA. Knows when I'm lying before I do."

"What did he say?"

"Nothin'."

"He didn't?"

"Well, not right off. You know James J. He waits for his advantage. Then, just as I reached for my coat he said it."

Matt did a bad mimic of him for effect—James J standing behind the bar, looking off in the distance—almost as though talking to someone else.

"You know what resentment is?" Matt, mimicking James J, said.

"Yeah, but I know you're gonna tell me anyway," Matt said.

"Resentment is wearing a pair of black pants and having to piss so bad you can't hold it. No one else knows or gives a damn. The only one uncomfortable is you."

"I don't suppose you gave him one of your lopsided grins?" Cate said, giggling at her own cleverness.

"James J said resentments destroy more alcoholics than anything else."

She could see he'd stopped being playful. Two and one-half years sober, Matt was asking a serious question.

"What do you think? Is it revenge, my book?" he said.

They had watched addiction destroy people along with their families, resentments being one of the main causes. She had cheered for them when they held an insignificant brass coin and expressed a throat-choked gratitude for a mere thirty days of sobriety.

Matt had asked Cate casually. She watched his complexion change, a shade of gray spreading. She knew he was serious. His sobriety had been hard won.

"You're sorting out your life," she asserted.

Matt knew there were some things about which Cate was terminally naive. He also knew if it was about matters of the heart, he'd better pay attention.

"But I'm not writing about me. I'm writing about the life of another man," Matt said.

"If you understand him, you'll be able to forgive him. Then you can forgive yourself."

"There's that word again...forgiveness. What's to forgive? Things are the way they are. Resentments I get. I'll work on those. Forgiveness...I don't get it."

In the night, half awake, Matt dreamed. Joseph had followed a hard road. Being God is one thing; being human is so much harder.

Chapter 7

SALT LAKE CITY
PRESIDENT EZRA BURGESS

President Burgess moved his hand away from the calculator and jotted a note in a thin, leather notations notebook. He spoke aloud to the empty room as he wrote.

"Thirty thousand per hour consulting fee times two hundred average hours over the next few months equals six million dollars."

Carol, his daughter, bounced into the long room that was her father's study. An odd room, long and narrow with a twelve-foot ceiling. After the added set of bookshelves were built across from the large gun case, the room narrowed in atmosphere and felt like a wide hallway.

Carol had shown Matt her father's guns one day when they were courting and he was not at home. She touched a release switch and the glass doors opened. Most of the guns were antiques. A Browning twelve gauge with inlayed engraving for bird hunting. One handgun; a nickel-plated, thirty-eight, police special revolver. Carol had fired all of them.

"My very own Colt for personal protection," she had said.

The desk was positioned in front of a floor-to-ceiling window at the end of the room. The smell of leather and oak carried throughout the house.

"Talking to yourself again, Daddy," she said, planting a kiss on her father's cheek and wiping it off with a thumb in one fluid gesture. "We're gone. See you there."

As suddenly as she exploded into the room, she was gone, the room quiet.

Burgess smiled. He knew of no one who could move the full length of his den with the speed his daughter could, but then, she had been doing it since she was a toddler. What a joy it was to have her back in the house.

He glanced back at his notation. The best part of the deal, the money would be under his control. Essentially, he would be writing the checks and paying himself.

Burgess drew a half a circle, wrote a small "5" behind it, and for a moment contemplated its simplicity. After a moment he completed the circle and added a zero behind the five.

He'd done his homework, had made himself aware of the etiology of the circled number fifty. The secret name for this band of elderly brethren: the Council of Fifty. More shadow government than rumor, it was none other than Joseph Smith's Council of Fifty established before his assassination in 1844.

Following the trek to Utah, the Fifty became a thorn in Brigham Young's style of strong, personal leadership. Crafty, he maneuvered to disband the Fifty. However, a select few held the thread of its priesthood viable, believing in Smith's original premise, which was to consider, discuss, and act on political and/or financial matters that affected the church.

After Young died, the Fifty inched back into existence as the least observable office of the priesthood. One requirement for membership, however, had changed. The Fifty were no longer recruited from the general membership, but solely from those with a considerable monetary balance sheet.

Burgess rose and for the edification of no one but himself said, "Ever the Lord provides."

He looked at his watch, reached for his suit coat, tucked the small, thin, leather notations notebook in his left, inside suit coat pocket, and left for his appointment.

Chapter 8

ROCHESTER, NEW YORK
THE AGENT

"It's a book burning," Matt said.

Cate and Matt drove to a bookstore in Rochester where an author was reading from his recently published novel. An hour's drive through Palmyra and Manchester, arriving late, Cate sat at the back and Matt stood. They listened until Matt could take no more of it. He bent down and whispered in her ear.

"A good flow of words is conceptual music, and this guy's writing isn't bad until he puts voice to it. He's butchering his own book."

Matt was confirming an earlier assumption; no author should be allowed to read his own prose.

"Should be a bloody law. Good writing draws the mind into an ecstasy of images, and this guy's elocution is abysmal. They should shut him down before someone hears him and burns his book."

"Hush. Let me listen," Cate said.

Matt had told Cate his brother Paul might be there.

"He's going to introduce us to Hamilton Gloss, a New York agent who represents the reading author. Some Canadian chap, name of Gifford or Clifford or something. Paul does legal work for the agent in Utah."

Matt had called Paul to see how the folks were. It had been three years, and as the book was almost finished, he felt somewhat safe about catching up on things.

The agent, Hamilton, did not strike Matt as city folk. Wide, bushy, salt-and-pepper mustache, eyebrows the same. He was lean, well tanned, and was wearing a sport coat with a turtleneck sweater. More the country gentleman. Paul was in a suit and tie. He and Hamilton had some further business in New York. Matt and Cate were wearing Levi's.

Paul told Cate and Matt he was happy to introduce them to Hamilton.

Matt interrupted.

"Don't you believe it, honey. Not for a minute. Paul flew out here for the tax write-offs and the fresh air. Never admit it, but he'll make any excuse to get out of the Land of Oz. How are Mom and Dad anyway?"

At the end of the evening, as they were about to go their separate ways, Cate put her hand out.

"It's wonderful to finally meet you, Paul. Thank you for introducing us to Mr. Hamilton."

Matt was watching his brother while they talked.

"It's Mr. Gloss, Cate," Paul said.

"He is so distinguished and handsome, to me he looks like a Hamilton," she said, eyes dancing, teasing.

Hamilton was amused.

Paul was disarmed and said to Matt, "I think you've met your match." He then addressed Cate. "Please don't thank me. It's good to see this bum sober. I'm giving you full credit."

"No secrets in our family." Matt's words dripped with sarcasm.

Hamilton huffed in his mustache.

"Some of my best friends drink too much. They are all authors."

That's when he asked the forbidden question, the one Matt was dreading and hoping wouldn't get asked.

"Tell me what you're working on?"

It was the first question little brother had on his mind and the last he knew better than to ask. Paul looked at Matt, waiting, a half smile running across his face like he had just got the better of an old argument. Paul could only guess as to the nature of the book, and that's the way Matt wanted it for now. *Think fast*, he said to himself, deciding it was best to ignore the question.

"You really think I can do this?" He looked up at little brother, who was an inch taller than he.

Paul gave him a knowing look, but no dummy, still had the last word.

"I'd hate to say which you do best—write or drink."

OUT OF HIDING

Two weeks after meeting the book agent Hamilton Gloss, Matt had carefully proofread, printed, wrapped, and addressed the latest version of his blood, sweat, and tears. Until the one-room post office in Darwin's Place opened, it sat, an ominous presence, on the wobbly half table where Cate and he prepared and ate their meager meals. Every time she passed it, she kissed the tips of her fingers and patted it. It had taken over the loft and made of itself a thing of worship.

Using his real name happened by attrition. Paul knew nothing of an alias. Simply introduced Matt as his brother, an Alcott.

The package, pristine and foreign-looking, sat on the kitchen table next to a half-empty cup of coffee. Brown butcher paper had been used to wrap the box it was in. Cate had tied it with a narrow white ribbon for luck.

Matt was pacing, checking his watch.

"We should drive it into New York. I don't trust the postal service."

Cate usually rode to school with Raven and was getting ready to meet her.

"Don't be silly. Mail it. Go talk to James J. I'm late," Cate said as she kissed him and bounced out the door.

It was clear and sunny, and Matt parked the yellow jeep in front of the small post office and carried the wrapped manuscript under his jacket to protect it from the elements. Everything went into slow motion as he approached the little stand-alone post office, looking for all the world like something left over from a century before. Monumental day. Expectation running amuck. Commitment wavering. The door opened as it should, which in an odd way surprised him. There was nothing barring his mission or admission.

Licking his fingers, the pudgy postal clerk put down his pastry, completely missing the large gob of cream filling clinging to the underside of his thumb. While Matt waited he watched the clerk smudge the yellow goo over his manuscript. Chubby hands, still sticky, pitched Matt's life work into a hopper ten feet away.

A one-man post office, but his lob was good for three points. Matt tucked the receipt in his wallet, turned to leave, and encouraged the image of the man being sucked down in a whirlpool of bile and baby bottom.

Chapter 9

SALT LAKE CITY
THE CLUB

Brother Angus led the way to the chamber used for services and general meetings. Burgess was at his side. As the door opened, an aphorism hanging on the opposite wall met his gaze. The heavy, maple wood frame and Castellar lettering articulated one of the club's provocative mottos.

A MAN
IN PARTNERSHIP WITH THE LORD
KNOWS SUCCESS IN BUSINESS
IS NO ACCIDENT

Seeing it, Burgess smiled. In Utah fiscal prudence and monetary success were hallmarks of a man's spiritual acumen. No one knew this better than he did. There was another reason Burgess felt motivated to become a member. Something his old friend Brother Angus had said to him.

At discussing Burgess's invitation to membership, Angus had been forthright with his old friend.

"Don't think for a damn minute, Burgess, that this is a retirement club. You're joining one of the most powerful bodies of men in the world. Not something beyond ourselves we want known, mind you. Depending on what is going on around the world, we may meet two or three times a week on urgent matters touching the church."

Angus removed his hands from his trouser pockets. He wasn't through talking yet.

"Which reminds me, there are rooms if you wish to stay over. Swimming pool. Some of the members live here. Heart monitors are available if necessary. We have male nurses around the clock. Damn good ones, too. It's a hell of a deal."

"I can see you haven't changed," Burgess said.

"Yeah, they still get on me now and then for cussing, at least they try. I repent too damn fast."

Burgess had been waiting to see if he was on the short list for being considered for an apostleship. After talking to Brother Angus, it no longer seemed all that important.

The room seated fifty, exactly. As they approached, he heard a subdued rumble of male voices. Except for a few wheelchairs, each man relaxed in an overstuffed lounge chair accented for comfort. Brother Angus pointed to the six-inch rise at a far wall with three large, blank plasma screens displayed to one side. One straight back chair stood by itself.

"That's you," Angus said, motioning toward the chair.

Burgess was shaking hands, working his way through the brethren to that small dais at the corner of the room. He knew or had met all but four faces in the audience and was still talking with two old acquaintances when Brother Angus spoke again.

"Any damn time, Burgess."

Burgess smiled and stepped up on the small dais.

"Brethren," he said, and was immediately interrupted.

"You don't have to stand in this room, brother. Some of us have lost that art," a Brother Lohen said.

Laughter spilled across the room. The wheelchairs testified to the fact that sitting during a meeting was as proper as not.

The room was made up exclusively of Mormon businessmen, all in good standing in the church and all independently wealthy.

President Burgess addressed himself to the fifty. He could speak freely, that is, with considered care, for today he wanted to make a positive impression.

"I cannot accept the honor at this time. You know I preside over the Cottonwood Stake, but I assure you, I will take the weekend and ask for the Lord's guidance in this matter. You will have my answer on Monday."

President Burgess's businesses needed little of his direct attention anymore. He had picked his subordinate managers wisely and trained them well. In addition to his real estate holdings, he owned a specialty insurance company and a credit management firm. There had been a partner, but Burgess bought him out years before. In the recent past he had devoted more time to presiding over the several wards in his Stake than as the chairman of the board of his own companies.

"What's to pray about, Burgess? Six million dollars and it's damn near free!" said one of the brothers in a wheelchair.

Laughter.

"Don't pay any attention to Brother Garfield, he prays more than any of us," Brother Small said.

Again laughter.

Burgess would be representing the interests of business throughout northern Utah. His own firms would benefit, new contracts, new business relationships, and he would have sixty-two million dollars at his disposal to keep things tidy.

The Church, of course, could not be involved. However, it was understood that all of the church's considerable security resources would be at his disposal, and they were as state of the art as any in existence.

Anything that would have a negative effect or a suspected negative influence on the good name of Utah business would come under his scrutiny. Anyone who might jeopardize business enterprise in the state would be swiftly dealt with.

This was where the conservative arm of the Church exercised its quiet authority. Their arrival at this sidebar niche in the hierarchy of the Church had something to do with the fact that the richer the member, the larger the tithe.

"Give 'em hell, kid," Brother Post said. He was ninety years, still walking, and as some pointed out, still straight as a post. He extended a hand to Burgess and added, "You're not squeamish, are you?"

"I've never been accused of that, Brother Post."

"We need young blood in this place. You're gonna fit in nicely around here," Post said.

"Thank you, sir." Burgess tried not to look amused.

"He's good for the place. Makes some of us feel young," Angus offered.

Someone held the job of sergeant at arms in defense of the good name of the Church at all times. Burgess had $62 million at his disposal. His predecessor, listed as terminal, had moved Burgess into this position. If he did well, he would be ordained to this office in the Melchizedek priesthood.

The membership fee, a mere $6 million, became a shrewd bit of business manipulation. To become a member, nothing would have to come out of his pocket. His apprenticeship: deal with problems. Buy them off, deflect them, stop or minimize depending on what is necessary. The only stipulation, do so quietly. At the end of the year, Burgess would realize a one-time bonus of ten percent of the $62 million.

It was, and was to remain, a secret alliance, and as it would generate no income, the only tax liability would be Burgess' $6,000,000 consultant compensation. At the other end, when he paid the membership initiation fee, it amounted to a wash. Shrewd business heads in this group. The rich making it easier for the rich.

It was an opportunity for Burgess to further prove his leadership skills and become one of this elite band of influence in protection of the Church throughout the world. While it was a notch below apostle, it was the dream of any good Mormon businessman.

The evening light coming from the windows beyond testified

in silhouette to the presence of a man kneeling in front of a couch. President Burgess was in prayer.

As God is,
man may become.
As man is,
God once was.

Penned in his own hand inside his copy of the Doctrines and Covenants was this Mormon maxim. At an important moment calling for wisdom and guidance, you could find President Burgess on his knees in reflection and prayer.

His father, deceased, had been an Idaho potato farmer and as per custom had given his son this copy of the Doctrines and Covenants when he left for his mission at age nineteen. It lay now inches from his bowed head. If he did well, if he was a good shepherd of men, the celestial kingdom, along with many wives and children, would follow.

Burgess thought of himself as a member of a very elite group of wealthy, intelligent men. All were the anointed of God's Melchizedek Priesthood and one of the most powerful forces for good on earth.

Chapter 10

RESURRECTION CORNER

Weeks had gone by since Matt signed a contract with the agent Hamilton Gloss. He hadn't written a word since. Felt as uncentered and off-balance as an engine that needed tuning. Late one afternoon while toying with a *Foreword* for the book, the phone rang. He had forgotten the unwritten law to unplug the damn thing while he worked.

If it's peace of mind you want
pull the mouse's tail.

Well damned if he hadn't, and wouldn't you know it, that's when the call came.

The computer screen and he were conferring with each other when the obnoxious vibrations commenced. Space rape. Matt set himself to ignore Minnie's off-key noise, which only made it worse. Unless he was expecting a call, it was rare he would yield. The trick, as the man said, was not to mind, feign indifference, but never let the repulsive rodent know it betters you. He clenched his jaw.

If he relented he might have to talk with someone and about subjects dull and otherwise terrifying. Minnie Mouse screamed her annoying distractions before he remembered Carl was going to call about scheduling one of the small remodels the two of them were working on. He hit save, angled across the room, and snapped the black rodent from its cradle.

"Yeah, Carl."

"Matthew, is that you?" a voice said.

"Yeah."

Mind search. A familiar voice. Who?...Surprise! Matt had forgotten about this man, agent man, phantom of the literary world. Didn't think he'd hear from him for some time.

Awkward. His tongue stumbled over itself.

"Matt, yes. Me. I mean, is this the elusive agent, Hamilton Gloss from New York?"

"Matthew. I have news," Hamilton said.

"You hate my book."

"I've sold your book."

"You don't understand my book."

"You are published, my good friend—will be, that is—published," Hamilton reassured him.

Matt felt the floor drop from under him.

"That's good, isn't it?"

He was hit with a sinking feeling and a jolt of anxiety at the same time. His throat threatened to close. Hamilton's voice was breathy, like he was calling from a treadmill at his gym.

"You sound winded," Matt said, wondering why.

"You'll never believe the advance, Matthew. Lord knows I don't believe it myself."

When Matt heard the amount of up-front money Hamilton had sold his book for, his legs began to buckle. Compared to what Cate and he had been living on, it was a sum vulgar to the ear. A thought swam though...someone was playing a joke on him.

You think you can plan for a thing like this, anticipate the day, and imagine what it will be like, but when it happens it's never what you expect. A peculiar kind of power, money. Like booze, it alters the way you think, feel, act.

Matt and fiscal prudence were casual acquaintances at best, and what does any man want, after all, but total autonomy, absolute authority, and an eternal erection? No warning. Its sudden onslaught jarred him like an earthquake.

"My God, Hamilton. How many zeros is that?" Matt whispered.

Losing the battle with gravity, he went around the corner, dropped the lid on the john, and sat.

"This is all in the negotiation stage, right?" he asked.

"Three hundred thousand dollars. A third of it now. You gave me authority to accept the offer?"

Shock...Matt's mind reached for something familiar to hang on to while he reoriented, or tried to anyway.

"It's not like you are the new kid on the block. You worked for a newspaper. I know they called the *Las Vegas Sun*. Your reputation stood solid," Hamilton said.

"Say it over. No. Don't say it over, it won t do any good. After the third zero my brain is in uncharted territory," Matt said.

Hamilton guffawed. "Listen, it's late. I'm exhausted. I've been with the publisher all day. They pretty much like the book as it stands. Figure out when you can come into the city."

"What's wrong with when the check's ready?"

"I'll relay that message to them and get back to you." Hamilton hung up.

Matt tried to absorb what had just happened. He kept looking for something to compare it to. Sudden prosperity is not easy. Nothing fit. Nothing he could get a handle on. He felt like a man tumbling through space, unable to find an upright posture.

The old double-hung wood windows with half the putty missing provided evidence of the day's retreat. He started to laugh. Not the kind of laughter you can hear. The kind where the diaphragm cramps and the stomach muscles make little jerks and someone standing behind you might think you're sobbing quietly. The two are not far apart, after all. Matt sat, the cold working its way up through him, in shock.

There would not have been a trace of reality to Hamilton's phone call if he had not been sitting on the john, looking at the cracked yellowing tiles below him and holding a Minnie Mouse telephone in one hand.

Matt chalked a message on the small notepad Cate used for her grocery lists and pinned it to the outside of the door where she could see it without going in.

At The Hump.

Only half a block away he needed people, not to talk to, just to be around to distract him from the barrage of crap gathering between his ears. As the door closed behind him, a dark sky was making its intentions clear. A lazy snow beginning.

Jennifer, a top debater at her high school, was jogging toward him.

"Hey, Matt," she said as she flew by.

"Give 'em hell on Friday, Jennifer," he called out, turning to watch her run.

"Count on it," she said, waving.

He watched her ponytail bounce to the rhythm of her gait. Matt felt overwhelmed. Needed a drink. Out of the question. How to find a footing? Where are you, Cate? How do you celebrate without booze is the same as saying, how do you celebrate without celebrating?

He grinned at snow that wasn't in a hurry. A dreary emptiness prowled the night and he laughed at all things dreary. Matt could trust a dark sky, a cold night.

He chose the end of the bar with the fewest people. Nodded at those who said hello. James J reached for the cardboard coaster and poured him a mug of hot black Colombian medicine.

"You look like you just saw a ghost. You okay?" James J said.

"You still remember how to make a bourbon highball?" Matt said.

James J did a double take. Dog-faced, Matt put one finger on the bar, a point in front of him and to his right about six inches.

"Bring me a bourbon highball," Matt said, his voice matter-of-fact.

James J had something of wit to say about everything that happened in his bar, with but one exception. And this was that exception. How many AA meetings had they sat through together? About ex-drunks who go back to the bottle, James J was humorless.

He turned his back on Matt, gimped to the other end of the bar, and resumed his conversation with the sheriff and old man Collins. Little waves of noiseless laughter continued to jerk at Matt's belt. In a few minutes his mug needed a refill. He hoisted it to shoulder height in front of him. James J moved back slowly and stood in front of him.

"Cup's empty."

James J poured while scrutinizing Matt's expression.

"Prove it. Bourbon highball," Matt said, tapping the point in front of him he had previously indicated.

James J reluctantly made the highball and placed it in front of Matt, who moved it deliberately to the spot he had previously pointed.

"I'll have another," Matt said.

With that the word went out. Matthew was at The Hump getting drunk.

In no less time than it takes a lie to become immortal, people started pouring through the door. He watched people watching him in the big mirror behind the bar.

Cate rushed into the bar, Raven behind her. Arnold, owner of the florist shop where Cate sometimes helped out, was behind Raven, followed by Crazy Helen in bathrobe and curlers. Cate looked at Matt and six highballs neatly lined up in fence formation in front of him. The four stood as though their shoes were nailed to the floor. Cate's eyes were as big as bar room coasters.

Matt knew if he looked at her he'd lose it.

"Ya know, you're the slowest bartender I ever met. I'm going to buy this bloody bar and fire your lazy ass," Matt said.

Nothing moved. No one spoke. Five stretched-out seconds, the longest anyone in Resurrection Corner could remember. Matt pivoted on the stool toward Cate, who hadn't moved. Their eyes locked.

"They bought my book."

Matt did everything in his power to keep his voice steady.

Cate's eyes were question marks.

Raven made a strange, high-pitched noise and grabbed Cate. Matt raised his hand and spread his fingers.

"Five zeros, honey."

His voice broke.

Raven made another high-pitched squeal only louder. James J leaned over the bar, not sure what he heard.

"You have a publisher!" Raven shouted.

"It's a done deal."

Matt forced himself to say it, to say it out loud.

Cate, with her lower lip protruding, hadn't heard anything anyone said. She was staring at the drinks in front of Matt. The bar went silent again, like that split second before a bomb's impact. If someone had dropped a pin at that moment, it would have sounded like the crack of a rifle shot. James J Flannery exploded into a great belly laugh, came around the bar, and pulled Matt into an enormous bear hug. Only another drunk would have understood.

"He ain't gonna drink 'em, little sister. Your ol' man needed to order them like he could."

The place went nuts. Raven was jumping up and down, hugging Cate. People started slapping Matt on the back. Before he knew it, he had seven coffees lined up in front of him on the bar. Everyone was buying. Even the sheriff.

While new snow spread a four-inch white blanket over Resurrection Corner, Cate, Matt, and James J talked the night away. Matt had to repeat the telephone conversation he'd had with Hamilton half a dozen times.

"How many zeros was that?"

To celebrate the occasion, James J removed the knife he carried in a leather holster at his belt. With his thumb he rotated the blade into the open position and locked it in place. Thumping his knuckles on the hard, wooden surface of the bar, he placed the knife in front of Matt. Matt handed it back.

"Your bar. You first."

James J carved a $ with a vertical slash through it into the glossy surface. Matt followed with a three, two zeros, a comma, and three more zeros, and put the knife in front of Cate.

"Needs a date."

She wrinkled her nose and pushed the knife away

"My bar will be famous, little sister," James J said.

Cate giggled like a teenage girl. The pink tip of her tongue pushed out through her lips and she carved away.

Two men laughed like they had lost their wits.

Exhausted, Cate Lynn and Matthew climbed the steps to the loft.

"Attempting to realize you're in a new tax bracket is hard work," Matt mumbled.

He unplugged Minnie and threw his Levi's on a chair. In bed a timid voice next to his ear whispered.

"You scared me," Cate said.

"It was callous of me. Wasn't thinking. Won't do it again. Promise."

Matt realized he had just lied to the one person who meant the most to him.

"Honey?" he said.

"Uh huh?"

"All future lies?" Matt said.

"Uh huh?"

"They won't be about booze."

"Promise?"

"I promise."

Chapter 11

ONE WEEK LATER

Cate was working at the school. Matt had just bought a bus ticket to the city. Little desire to be alone, he headed for the One Hump, where he found the sheriff, old man Collins, and James J reliving Sunday's pathetic display of batting by the Red Sox.

"Even Matt hits a home run once in a while," old man Collins said.

The three men looked at Matt and laughed. He lifted his coffee to them in a ha-ha-very-funny salute.

"I write one book and now I'm the brunt of the town's jokes. The Red Sox yet. Cold. You guys are cold," he said.

Memories and idle thoughts jumped about like bats in a barrel while he sipped his coffee. The anemia of his former paychecks as a church historian carried a hero's halo. Yesterday's near poverty testified to a fallen state of grace. He wondered if money would change him or Cate. Peace of mind seemed impossible today. He could hear his mother s voice in his head as if she were standing next to him.

"Matthew has sold his soul to the Devil. He is a wicked child employed in the service of the evil one."

Instantly he needed a drink. He began reflecting on the first man to discover the fermented grape. What followed was freely shared with the sheriff, old man Collins, and James J.

"Everyone thinks it was euphoria, ya know..." Matt said, interrupting.

The three stopped talking and looked at him. Matt didn't look into the blank expressions. Distracted by thoughts of woe, he continued...

"...couldn't be more wrong. People think it was euphoria that made alcoholics out of men. Well, I got news. The first man to drink discovered it was the antidote to truth. Thereafter, they couldn't make the stuff fast enough."

Matt took a deep breath, let out a long, woeful sigh, and pivoted off the stool. As he opened the door to leave he heard the sheriff say, "That's the saddest thing I ever saw."

He figured they were still talking about the Red Sox.

As he walked away, he idly wondered what it was they were laughing at.

Cate was putting together an overnight bag. He was steeling himself for a long bus ride into the city to see Hamilton and meet the people who would publish his book.

"I feel like the guy who said he didn't trust happiness. I don't trust tomorrow anymore."

"Matthew?" Cate said. He looked up. "We've never been apart."

They held hands all the way to the Greyhound bus stop except when Cate ran into the florist shop to tell Arnold she'd be a few minutes late. Arnold waved shoo at her and blew Matt a kiss.

He liked the guy, waved back. Homo or no, Arnold was alive, a condition not many people could put on their resume.

Chapter 12

SALT LAKE CITY
FARLEY HARPER

"Elder Walker should have let me whip on them," Farley said, between bites.

The half sandwich looked small in his hand.

"Wouldn't do any good. We never run out of infidels. Same in England where I was," Jedediah, his older brother, said.

"Did they hurt you?" Farley asked.

"Nah. We always saw it comin'."

The small lunchroom provided sandwiches and soup every day for the workers at Deseret Industries, a welfare subsidiary of the Mormon Church. Jedediah, the manager, was afraid Farley would eat too much and there wouldn't be enough for the employees. He put his sandwich on his brother's plate.

"Have you finished loading that flatbed, yet?" Jedediah asked.

Farley had worked all morning loading the flatbed with the forklift for his brother.

"I should have whipped on them. What they did to us in Flint, Michigan wasn't right."

Farley had seen it on KSL television. All of Salt Lake was grieving for two missionaries turned up missing in Russia.

"I got a surprise for ya. Come on, I'll show it to ya," Jedediah said, heading for his office.

Farley followed.

Jedediah patted a video player sitting on top of a television set. He picked up a video and handed it to Farley.

"The story of Brigham Young after the prophet was shot and killed. It's about bringing the saints to Zion. Tape plugs in like this."

"I know how it works," Farley said.

They both stood back and watched the screen come to life. Tyrone Power featured.

Without taking his eyes off the screen, Farley sat on one of the office chairs.

"I can't sell it, so the box and the video are yours. Plugs into your TV the same way."

Farley went to a bookstore that sold anti-Mormon literature, justifying the visit as necessary to his special calling, and bought the book about the biblical Samson of Mormonism, Porter Rockwell. Every night he read out loud the Danite pledge Joseph Smith had written that was included in the book.

DANITE PLEDGE

In the name of Jesus Christ, the son of God, I now promise and swear, truly, faithfully, and without reserve, that I will serve the Lord with a perfect heart and a willing mind, dedicating myself, wholly, and unreservedly, in my person and effects, to the up building of His kingdom on earth, according to His revealed will. I furthermore promise and swear that I will regard the First President of the Church of Jesus Christ of Latter Day Saints, as the supreme head of the Church on earth, and obey him the same as the supreme God...and that I will always uphold the Presidency...I furthermore promise and swear that no Gentile shall ever be admitted to the secrets of this holy institution or participate in its blessings. I furthermore promise and swear that I will assist the sons of Dan in the utter destruction of apostates, and that I will assist in setting up the kingdom of Daniel in these last days, by the power of the Highest and the sword of His might. I furthermore promise and swear that I will never communicate the secrets of this degree to any person in the known world, except it be to a true and lawful brother, binding myself under no less a penalty than that of having my blood shed. So help me God and keep me faithful.

Joseph Smith's own words forged the covenant men made with God to protect the prophet and the Church from the Church's enemies. Where his finger smudges had obscured the words, he made up new ones or skipped over them.

Farley knew he would prove himself one day, and that his time would come. He knew it because his father had told him so. He pored over the short, sparse scenes in the movie that showed the man people spoke of as the prophet's bodyguard. As the scene began he would speak the words.

"Orrin Porter Rockwell, protector of the prophet."

The way Rockwell rode his horse, sat in the saddle, all were indelibly memorized. Farley played the video until it broke. He refused to let his hair be cut like Rockwell. When it started to look comic, his brothers talked it over and decided on a course of action. Bribery. The tradeoff was an all-you-can-eat at McDonald's after the haircut. Farley smiled. Reckoned he'd just grow it back.

He'd spent last Thanksgiving with Jedediah's family. He remembered how pretty Mindy, his brother's wife, was and how her breasts pressed against him when she hugged him. The loneliness stabbed deep when he thought of her.

One day when Jedediah stopped by with a pizza, Farley said something that puzzled him.

"When I am taken through the veil, they will all honor me and they will be sorry."

To others, Farley said nothing, but Jedediah was his closest brother. He trusted him.

"Sorry about what?" Jedediah asked.

"One day a great cry will go up. People will rejoice in the servant of God. Then they will all be sorry," Farley insisted.

"When you were on your mission, Elder Walker taught you a lot, didn't he," Jedediah said.

Farley knew by the expression on Jedediah's face that Jedediah was worried about him.

FLINT, MICHIGAN
TWO YEARS BEFORE

Elder Walker had been assaulted on the streets. Had ducked tomatoes and eggs by the locals and gang bangers in Flint, Michigan's neighborhoods many times.

"Mutt and Jeff. Get the hell off our streets."

They heard it almost every day both from kids and adults. The taunts were familiar fare to Mormon elders in many parts of the world.

Elder Walker, five foot eight, was from Mountain Home, Idaho. He wore his hair in a crew cut and loved spaghetti.

"Pay no attention to them," he said to his new companion.

They were an odd couple, going from door to door to preach the gospel. In his weekly reports Elder Walker had recounted those violent street confrontations to his mission president, Brother Melrose. His last letter had said, "Praise the Lord for the likes of one Elder Harper. At seven feet two he intimidates the local rowdies. We are seldom harassed anymore."

Elder Walker had received a call, approved by his mission president, from Bishop Harper, who explained to Elder Walker that Farley might need a little more special help than the ordinary new missionary in the field would.

They labored together for more than a year.

Farley learned by repetition until it became ritual. There were mechanical things he could do, but about words in books he found little that pricked his attention. Walker was studying to become a teacher and used his large companion to expand his teaching skills. He realized that Farley's interest did not wane when he was listening to stories.

The early days of the church were fraught with tribulations that supplied story after story of heroism. An ominously appearing task became an anticipated hour of entertainment and education for both men.

After a day of knocking on doors, attempting to find people receptive to the truth, Farley would say, "Tell me the story about the man that helped the prophet."

"What was that name again?" Elder Walker, always the teacher, requested.

Almost everything he did was to evoke and stimulate Farley's mind. This had never been done before. It helped. Some Saturdays, with a little praise and coaching, Farley even managed to make spaghetti.

He would scratch his head, look around, until, "...O...Porter Rockwell."

"Excellent, Elder Harper, excellent," Elder Walker praised. "Okay, but only for you. I won t do it for anyone else."

By now Farley recognized teasing. He would smile, lift Elder Walker's hat, and pat him on top of his head.

After the evening meal when the dishes were done, Walker would tell the story of Orrin Porter Rockwell, Son of Thunder, Man of God, Protector of the Prophet; the man the prophet foretold would not die by bullet or blade should he not cut his hair.

"Ended up he had many names," Walker might begin. "We know that Joseph and Rockwell knew each other from 1831 when Rockwell was baptized after he heard the prophet speak. Joseph was twenty-six and Rockwell seventeen, so he looked up to Joseph."

"Rockwell loved the prophet," Farley interjected.

"A few years later Rockwell was living with his wife in Jackson County, Missouri, when the lieutenant governor of that state, a man named Boggs, persuaded the governor to issue an extermination order on the Mormons," Walker said.

"Ex-term-in..."

"—ation," Walker would coach.

"—ation," Farley repeated. "Ex-termin-ation, extermin-ation."

"Remember, like ants. Call the Orkin man. Exterminate the ants," Walker said.

"Exterminate the ants," Farley said.

"Which means?" Walker said.

"Exterminate the Mormons," he said proudly.

"You got it. What happened after that...hundreds of Missouri men on horseback raided the Mormon towns and villages, burning homes and beating people. They wanted them out of Missouri."

"Boggs worked for the devil," Farley said.

Walker nodded. "Day after day they raided and plundered. Nameless marauders savaged and burned many Mormon settlements. It continued for years."

"They whipped on Mormons," Farley said, looking to his companion for praise.

"Many were killed and suffered severe injuries. One night when Rockwell was away, his brother-in-law was flogged and clubbed. His wife and mother and father ended up standing in their fields watching their homes burn. The prophet was becoming increasingly vexed over the way the saints were being treated."

"Rockwell could not read," Farley interrupted.

"That is true. He was a man of action. The prophet knew that what the saints needed was protection. He started a secret society. What was it called?" Walker asked.

Farley thought hard, but nothing came to him. Walker put his index finger in the air and wiggled it. A large hand went to the table and drew a large "D" with his finger. After he drew it, Farley said, "Danites."

"You will be telling me the story before long."

Farley beamed.

"Do you have your bible open?"

With pride and confidence Farley reached for his bible. He pulled the long black ribbon that opened at Genesis 49:17. He leaned forward and looked at the words carefully.

"Dan shall be a serpent by the way, an adder in the path, that biteth the horse heels, so that his rider shall fall backward."

Farley faltered as he read, but got through it. Smiling and still confident, he sat back to listen to Elder Walker continue.

"The sons of Dan were kept a secret for a long time. Orrin Porter Rockwell came to be known as...?"

At this point Walker would pause and look at his companion, waiting.

Farley pounded the air, looking like he was directing music. "... Danite...Chief."

"Right again. Over the years the Danite Band became feared and reviled by the people of Missouri. To become a member you had to take a blood oath to protect the leaders of the church, the Kingdom of God, and other Danites. By 1838 this Boggs guy was the governor. Well, by that time the prophet had a revelation stating that God would send The Destroying Angel to exterminate the bad guys...and we both know who that was..."

"The Destroying Angel would whip on Boggs." Farley's voice was strong when he said it.

"Four years later Rockwell moved his family in with his wife's mother. He didn't say why. He just unhitched the wagon, got on the horse, and rode off."

Farley looked puzzled.

"He wanted to keep it a secret, but some members rumored that he had gone to fulfill the prophecy. As it happened Governor Boggs was shot through a window in his study, two bullets in the skull, two in the neck, but it didn't kill him. No one saw who did it, but Rockwell had such a reputation that eight days later he was arrested and jailed for the deed, and he spent nine terrible months in jail on half rations and no change of clothing and was released without conviction. They couldn't prove he did it. Barefoot, he walked all the way to Nauvoo, Illinois, a journey that took weeks. He came into town unshaven, unwashed, half starved, and in rags and found the prophet at a party."

Farley's eyes didn't blink as Walker related the tale.

"People took him for a beggar and told him to leave. Did he go away?"

"He would not leave. I want to see the prophet, he said, over and over." Farley pounded the table as he said it.

"Finally someone informed Joseph Smith that a beggar was at the door and wouldn't go away. He was so filthy that the prophet didn't recognize him until he came closer and looked into Rockwell's eyes. He recognized his old friend. After hearing what happened, the prophet blessed Rockwell and here's what he said..." Walker looked at Farley. "It's your turn..."

Farley found the paper with the writing on it and read, "I prophesy, in the name of the Lord, that you, Orrin Porter Rockwell, so long as ye shall remain loyal and true to the faith, need fear no enemy. Cut not thy hair and no bullet or blade can harm thee."

"Since there were many plots to murder the prophet, Smith asked Rockwell to be his bodyguard. It was a great honor. After a long pause, Rockwell answered him," Walker said.

Again, Walker looked at Farley, indicating that it was his turn.

"What was his answer?"

Farley did not have to search long before pointing to himself. He said, "Your enemies are my enemies."

"The prophet commissioned Rockwell as the avenger-in-chief for the Lord. It was said that many died under the bloody hand of atonement for which the prophet had commissioned him, and he faced many a bullet and blade. So how did he die, Farley?"

"A heart attack," he said, placing his hand on his own chest.

"Yes, he died of a heart attack in 1878 in Salt Lake City."

"I'm your bodyguard!" Farley said.

"In a very real sense, you are, Elder Harper."

Chapter 13

RESURRECTION CORNER
THE PRESENT

They were standing next to the Greyhound bus that would take Matt into New York City to meet his new publisher.

"I haven't had a good chat with Mom in a week. That's where I'll be tonight," Cate said.

He knew Cate would not stay alone in the loft. When he first met her mother, a disapproving wall of granite he would walk an extra mile to avoid, he was amazed. Cate had her mother's features, but the personality contrast was striking. Cate was happy, gregarious, and always thinking of others. So his first impression earned him a punch to the midsection.

"You are adopted then?"

Fist in stomach. She knew her Matthew was teasing. Cate walked in front of him, backwards, finger-in-face lecture. When she did that, his insides turned to jelly. The giant urge to duplicate her delicious image was overwhelming.

"My mother is a wonderful lady. I'm all she has since Daddy died. She'll grow to trust you after you've earned it."

"Getting on your mother's good side will take ten years," Matt argued.

"Two."

"Three already."

"You have to help."

The bus driver entered the bus. A wave of anxiety shook Matt and he reminded himself he'd only be gone one or two days. He fantasized going to the bank together and having her make the deposit into their account. No one earned that money more than she did.

Last on. The bus driver sat waiting. The people behind the bus windows watched like mannequins with fixed expressions. The bus driver cleared his throat.

"We can have pizza instead of soup. I can get fat and have fat babies," she said.

"Come with me to New York."

She thought about it. "Only two days. Go and hurry back."

He moved to the rear window of the bus and looked out. She was smiling and waving like he was coming home, not leaving. The diesel engine growled, cleared its throat, throbbed. Cate held his gaze until the bus turned a corner, waving all the while.

Chapter 14

SALT LAKE CITY

"Elder Walker was my teacher," Farley said to his brother, Jedediah. "He told me I am a loyal servant of God and I would have a wife some day. It's the Lord's commandment to have a wife. Elder Walker has a wife now. He wrote me a letter. I'll show it to you."

Jedediah read the letter. It was innocent enough and thoughtful of Walker to continue to include his one-time companion in his thoughts. He was beginning to understand. Said so to his younger brother.

"Elder Walker told me what you did when you and he labored together. Because of you many people were able to hear the word of the Lord. Who is questioning your loyalty to the church?" Jedediah asked.

Farley looked down at the ground, scuffed at the dirt with his foot.

"You understand that, don't you?" Jedediah queried, trying to make a point.

"You have a wife," Farley, sick with wanting, said.

Jeremiah shoved the box with the last piece of pizza closer to Farley, who ate it in silence.

"I know you're lonely, little brother. Damn it, I'm lonely for you."

Farley had heard it in Sacrament meeting. A member, when bearing her testimony, related the story of her son's near brush with death in Chile on his mission. He remembered the skirmishes with street gangs in Flint and became upset.

"If I had been there I would have whipped on them," he said to Jedediah.

Farley remembered what his father had said to him.

SALT LAKE CITY
BEFORE FARLEY'S MISSION

"You are a little different, son, but in God's Kingdom there are many mansions," his father said.

"I know it, sir," Farley had said.

"It has been hard for you. I know that. But the obedient of God are his chosen. God knows you and loves you. In His time you will come to know your own special place."

"Yes sir," Farley said.

"Keep the faith. Honor your priesthood. Always be loyal to our general authorities, and you will come to know your own special calling in God's kingdom."

To Farley it was rejection. His father never told him he loved him, only that God loved him.

Chapter 15

NEW YORK CITY

The drone of the big bus tires provided a hypnotic accompaniment to his half-awake dreams. Because of Cate, Matt experienced the peace of mind to withdraw into that expanded place within where bits and pieces fit together into meaningful wholes. Collected impressions had lain waiting to be tapped and shared. Matt found Smith's creative core where heady dreams were born. All he had to do was add his muddy boots and mended socks to the aspiration of kingships, presidencies, and Godheads.

The air brakes woke him. Matt stepped down out of the bus and looked into Hamilton's face. Mr. Congeniality on the phone. Not the person he was shaking hands with now. Hamilton was cold and distant.

"Something has come up. They want us at their office, now, this evening," Hamilton shared as they walked.

Matt stopped. "What's going on?"

"Not fully up on it myself. Tell you what I know on the way."

Matt felt his chest tighten. He had done it again—one more time, the fatal error—let himself count on something. James J's last words when he left the One Hump were aimed directly into that place where the addict was most vulnerable.

"Expectations can drive an alcoholic to drink," James J had said.

Hamilton sensed the mood change. "Deal's not off."

Matt hadn't slept well on the bus. Little sleep last night. In the cab to the publisher's office, the muscles in his neck felt like tight straps of leather.

Chapter 16

SALT LAKE CITY

Farley first met President Ezra Burgess when the office of the presiding bishopric asked Burgess to intercede with a member of one of his congregations.

A rally of sit-ins took place when Farley happened to be in the neighborhood. Physically he stopped the group of people from demonstrating against his church.

Rather than subordinate the job to the proper bishop, Burgess was curious about this defender of the church. He thought he knew who it was and wanted to be sure.

"Injury lawsuits could amount to a serious liability, not to mention the negative publicity. The media pays more attention to you than to what the demonstration was about," Burgess explained, pausing.

Farley was holding his hat in front of him with both hands. He didn't fully understand what his Stake president said, but did know that the pause meant it was his turn to say something.

"Yes, sir."

President Burgess treated him with such kindness that day, Farley knew he was a great man and needed protection. It was only great men who treated him with kindness.

Farley thought of Elder Walker, his favorite companion, who he protected in the mission field. Now there was someone else, an important man who needed his protection too.

Chapter 17

NEW YORK CITY

A man in a uniform met them at the entrance.

"It's on the third floor. Right side," the gaunt-looking security guard said as he relocked the door.

From the elevator Matt and Hamilton entered a small, no-frills conference room on the third floor. Chairs, table, people. No phone. Not even an artificial plant in a corner.

Hamilton introduced Matt to his editor, Samantha Perness.

"Please, call me Sam. I'm so happy to finally meet you. What a marvelous book you've written," she said.

She was tall and thin with short brown hair. Matt had to look up to meet her eyes. She in turn introduced him to her secretary, who was even taller and had rounded shoulders from stooping to compensate for her height. Glenda something. The door clicked behind them. He turned to see another woman in a neatly tailored olive suit enter. This one, the house legal, he did not have to strain his neck to connect with. What Mickey Spillane would call a classy broad.

Five in all. Two men on one side of the table and two women on the other. The legal, Susan Vincent, took the chair at the end away from the door. Matt's head was buzzing; he had enough anxiety for at least two people. Best thing, shut up, wait. It was his editor who did the talking and, God bless her, she didn't mince words.

"We received a second-party offer to purchase your manuscript, Mr. Alcott. It's a kill fee and it's for a considerable amount of money."

"It's a direct buy-out, Sam," the attorney Vincent interjected.

"Yes," she said, turning to her secretary, Glenda something. "Do you have it?"

Glenda handed her boss an off-white envelope. Sam pushed it into the middle of the table in Matt's direction. It rested there, on the glass surface. Five pair of eyes focused on it like the last piece of chocolate. Matt knew if he picked it up, his hand would shake. He slid it in front of Hamilton, who took his cue, opened the envelope, and laid it in the middle of the table where Matt could read it. The damn thing was for two million dollars.

Matt had not had a drink for over three years, but at that moment that was what he wanted. It was all he wanted. Felt like he already had the hangover. Glad he wasn't in a bar and wished he were. The old philosophy; got the hangover, all I need is the cure. A shot of Crown Royal would fix everything. A bottle would put the world back on its axis.

The first name on the check was his publisher, Bloomsburg & Walbridge, the second, Matthew Alcott. To cash it required both signatures.

"Someone wants to own your manuscript outright, Mr. Alcott… we can only assume to stop publication."

He felt like his brain had quit on him. He sat looking at more circles than a pearl necklace. Matt always got angry when he was confused.

"You call me mister, I start looking for my dad. Call me Matt or Matthew."

Screw good manners. He was pissed. The fear of his own vulnerability made him even angrier. He shoved the check back in the direction of the legal and looked away.

Hamilton sensed his frustration and shifted into agent mode. He picked up the check and, waving it, addressed the other side of the table.

"What's going on here, Sam?"

Sam looked to the attorney.

"We know this is sudden. Us as well, but it is no hoax. I called the bank of origin. They know of this check and they will honor it. It's a legitimate offer," attorney Susan Vincent said.

"Tell me this didn't originate in Salt Lake City?" Matt said.

"The attorneys for the principal are a well-respected Salt Lake law firm, yes."

"And...?"

'"That's the hitch. The express qualification is that the presenter remains anonymous."

"Who's representing the principal?" Matt wanted to know.

"The law firm of Tanner and Welsely," the attorney answered.

The room was quiet, everyone looking to him. Matt attempted to make sense of his thoughts, but something was out of plumb.

He rose from the chair. "Where's the restroom?"

Secretary Glenda started speaking to her boss, who was talking to counsel. Matt turned his back on the whole thing. The water was too deep at this juncture. He needed to breathe. Matt threw cold water on his face. When he returned, attorney Vincent turned toward Matt.

"I was told any further information was not relevant. You have to agree, Mr. Alcott, excuse me, Matthew; the offer is more than generous. It might even break some kind of record."

Something didn't sit right. The book flashed through his mind like a rifle shot, all of it, every tortured word. Three women and an agent were staring at him. The image that came to mind was not tactful, but not inappropriate either. Frustration won out.

"What would you say if you had just given birth to your first child—you're holding it on your stomach and someone walks in and says they will pay you to smother it?"

You could've cut the tension in the room with your hand. Secretary Glenda's glasses dropped to the end of her nose. Counsel stiffened.

"What do you recommend, Sam?" Hamilton asked.

"If we publish we will make out all right, but to split two million without all the publishing expenses makes good fiscal sense. I believe you should ask yourself how much you would make if we published. Few authors ever see this kind of money," Sam said.

"Why tonight? Why couldn't this wait until morning?" Matt pushed.

"Did I imply that? I didn't mean to, not entirely," Sam said.

Matt got a whiff of cigarette as she spoke. His editor smoked.

"The offer dies tomorrow, midnight. We thought you would appreciate as much time as possible," Vincent added.

"Either way we would ask you, come back in the morning and sign another book deal with us. Your style works well with a couple of ideas we have in line to develop. No one can stop you from writing, after all," Sam added.

Hamilton did a U-turn in his chair. Looked at Matt.

"Say mid-morning," Hamilton added.

Matt was still rattled, rose to leave.

"There is one more thing," Sam said. "Time is of the essence. I'm to tell you that day after tomorrow the offer will be null and void and a new offer worth one million five will replace it."

The confusion drained out of him. Matt took a deep breath. Everything became clear.

"And the day following? One million, right?" Matt said.

They were all staring at him. Matt knew the mind set. He remembered Burgess, a shrewd businessman he had been related by marriage to his first wife.

"Yes, actually," the legal said. "How did you know?"

Chapter 18

SALT LAKE
FOUR YEARS PRIOR

The phone hadn't rung in days, since Carol moved out. It startled him. Matt grabbed it, as much to stop it from ringing as to see who it was.

"Hello."

"Brother Alcott, this is President Burgess. Would you mind stopping by my office in the morning?"

It was the second time his soon-to-be ex-father-in-law had approached him for anything. Matt couldn't remember exchanging three sentences with the man. The divorce papers had already been filed. What could he want?

That his wife's father was well off was an understatement. His several companies paid him a million annually to stay away from the office, what chairman of the board really meant.

President Burgess was head of the largest Stake in the Church, which put him high on the list for advancement. When an opening in the Quorum of the Twelve occurred, he was as close to being put on the short list to be an apostle as anyone in the church.

What had given Matt the willies was the thought of eternity with him, patriarch to her side of the family. The man was a refrigerator.

As he thought about that—a man who always gets what he wants—he knew he had to be careful. Burgess would be looking for something he could use as leverage against him for some reason. There was a reason. For a man like that, there was always a reason.

Carol and he were married civilly, by the authority of the state for life, but they were also married in the temple by the authority of God for eternity. This meant two divorces. Matt had to agree to a civil divorce and a temple divorce. The light went on. Nothing had been done about the dissolution of the temple sealing. That had to be what he was calling about.

What Burgess didn't know was that Matt had no desire to be bound to Carol in this life or the next. Not anymore. She was right out of a fashion magazine beautiful. She knew her mission in life was to turn men's heads and make women jealous. She was unhappy if she didn't get her way and worse if she did, blaming the outcome on Matt.

Easy to forgive a woman who can't cook if she's good in bed, but you can't pump iron twenty-four hours a day. They'd only been split for a couple of months, and he heard she already had a lawyer on the hook. Only time Matt ever felt sorry for an attorney.

"What for?" Matt said.

He didn't want to look too dumb, which was dumb.

"Let me put it this way. I think you would be unhappy if you didn't," Burgess said.

He had Matt. Huge curiosity. The man was born with something up his sleeve.

"At the Stake House?"

"My office downtown."

It was his building. Matt knew that much. His holding company managed his properties in Ogden, Provo, Salt Lake, and God knows where else. He owned among other things motels, office buildings, a hotel, and several industrial properties. More, much more. Matt didn't know the extent of it.

"What time?"

His turf. Who cares?

The next morning Matt parked and entered the building. Burgess' office and personal staff were on the top floor, level sixteen. As the elevator door whispered open, three people looked up from their desks. Matt no longer felt small. He felt minuscule.

First time in this building. Elegant and austere. The windows were floor to ceiling and tinted. His personal secretary was a middle-aged woman with silver hair and a face that looked like it hadn't changed expression in decades. She was the perfect fit. Secretary Perfect. Exactly what Matt would have expected for Burgess.

The only thing standing between him and Daddy Money Bags's office, where he assumed Burgess was waiting. A security guard was standing a few feet from her desk, attempting to look important.

It didn't take an excessive amount of intelligence to figure nothing got past her unless it was her express desire.

He walked fifty feet on the most beautiful multi-grained marble he'd ever seen. Her desk was flanked by two others, worker bees under her direct supervision. They were sitting, but Matt had the impression their inner posture was more like standing at attention. Eyes peering over computer screens. He didn't know how Secretary Perfect managed it, sitting down while he was standing, but she briefly glanced down her nose, expectorated ice, and said, "Go on in."

A slight motion of her head indicated the door behind her. Matt had the feeling he was big-time fodder for gossip in this building. The guilt he promised himself would not bother him swelled to infinity.

Daddy Money Bags was standing in the middle of the room. Out of habit Matt reached out to shake hands. Burgess turned, avoiding the gesture, left him pointing four fingers and a thumb at the view through a window.

"I have a letter for you from the First Presidency," he said as he walked behind his desk.

"You have a letter for me? Gosh, I had the impression the postal service handled the mail."

"I asked the First Presidency to expedite the matter, and then there was the problem of an address. Where do you reside nowadays?"

There was nothing on the large mahogany surface of Burgess' desk but a phone, a leather appointment book, a gold pen with black trim, and an envelope. It was the envelope he extended to Matt.

While he read the first paragraph, Burgess punched a button on the console. "See that I'm not disturbed." He then addressed Matt. "I want to make this easy, Matthew."

What happened to Brother Alcott, Matt wondered. The sudden need for fresh air left him light-headed. It was the most well-appointed, yet uncomfortable office he could remember being in. It reminded him of its owner, Old Money Bags, who had just motioned him to sit. More of a command than a gesture of goodwill.

He couldn't see himself sitting in front of this man whose voice dripped with authority. The mahogany desk between them and the chairs were designed to place him at an inferior level so Matt would be looking up. He clearly did not like the way this was going. Matt remained standing.

"When my wife passed it was a difficult time. I know how hard it is to be objective under emotional circumstances."

Burgess put one finger on his desk, pointing down. It seemed to anchor him as he continued. "You and I know the First Presidency will only grant a celestial divorce under certain conditions."

Matt didn't know, but he knew he was about to find out. He was having a rough time with the divorce, anyway. It was tearing him apart, but he wasn't so far gone he couldn't see that Money Bags was fishing, attempting to find a better angle from which to manipulate him. This man never did anything without thinking it through, stacking the odds in his favor.

Matt's impulse was to walk. Why did he have to endure this crap?

Burgess was not getting his way.

"You have been working hard for the church, doing important work. I understand hard work. I've worked hard all my life," Burgess said, carefully measuring each word as he spoke. "Can you tell me a little about the research you do for the church?"

Matt figured, *Here it comes.*

"Nothing complicated," Matt said dryly.

It was an answer not to his liking, forcing Burgess more into the open.

"Has it had anything to do with the way you feel about the church?"

Matt could be cagey too.

"I don't understand your question."

Burgess scoffed, but attempted to mask it. He made one more effort to elicit damaging information. He leaned back in his chair.

"I called Bishop Alcott, father to father. We would both like to know, do you still have a testimony of the gospel?"

"That's between me and God."

Burgess looked out the window. It was obvious he was shifting gears, coming at Matt from a different angle.

"Another man can respect your dedication, your industriousness. Unfortunately," President Burgess touched his chin thoughtfully, "it's the kind of work that doesn't pay well."

"Is that why you asked me here, to point out the nature of my poverty?"

His goddamn silk tie, a conservative teal, cost more than Matt paid for rent.

"Matthew, I have no desire to part enemies," Burgess said.

Matt almost looked at his feet to see how deep the bullshit was getting.

"As a matter of fact, I want to help you. I would like to give you a small gift of money to add some little compensation for the work you have been doing."

Surely he can't think I'm this stupid.

Carol's mother died before Carol and Matt started going together. Since then all Burgess ever thought about was his daughter. He'd walk through hell for Carol.

"Let me explain myself. I'd like this entire divorce thing to happen as quickly and quietly as possible. The proper perspective is very important here. And, of course, this is no one's business. An agreement between gentlemen. I imagine you could use," his eyes, like calipers, were measuring Matt, "five thousand dollars to compensate you for the work you have been doing."

The idea of that much money in one lump put Matt off balance.

"Can we...? I need to back up a little. I'm confused. You want to give me five thousand dollars? Just give it to me."

"For the work you have been doing for the church."

He had started out in awe of President Burgess, all that money and the president of a Stake. Not now. Not anymore. This rich bum was a snake and he'd done it again. Old Money Bags had stepped in to rescue his daughter.

Matt stood holding the letter that would sever Carol and him forever. He opened it again, ignored Burgess, and re-read another paragraph, savoring it like a man who loves pain. The official language, authoritative and legalistic, smacked of a curse dooming him to an eternity of emptiness.

The letter spelled out certain essential requirements. Matt, being a man with the priesthood, must first consent to the divorce, and second, he must also rule on her worthiness to get a temple recommend in the future so that she could remarry for eternity if she desired. It was a surreal moment. He turned his back on his ex-father-in-law, skimmed the letter again. Matt had to convince himself that it did, indeed, say what he thought it did. He could feel Burgess' eyes on the back of his head.

The way it played out, Matt, the rejected and scorned, was now judge and jury over her life. This was one of those church doctrines not advertised. You find out when you get there, not before. Until he approved of a church divorce between them, and until he sat in moral judgment of Carol, remarriage in the church for her would be next to impossible. The irony was thick as molasses.

Women could not hold the priesthood. Men only. If a woman wanted to go to heaven, she had to marry a man who had been ordained with God's priesthood.

The civil divorce would be easy, but in the eyes of God, good only until death. Beyond, in the place called hereafter, the poor girl reverted back to being Matt's ol' lady and for nothing less than eternity. He couldn't resist savoring that little piece of sweet revenge...at least for the moment. That's when he thought of the $5,000 again. That's when everything fell into place.

Without looking at old Money Bags, Matt could tell he was fuming, holding himself in. Matt didn't have to grant her a temple divorce. She could secure a civil divorce and with her looks remarry another man no sweat. The revenge? She could not marry again for eternity because she would still be Matt's wife in the hereafter. That would kill President Burgess, a man on his way up in the hierarchy.

Matt? As a man, he could make a small tithe offering for a couple of months, sit through a few meetings, and marry again immediately, if he was so inclined...for eternity too. For him, a male member of the church, Joseph Smith made it as easy as collecting butterflies.

Old Money Bags must have noticed something in his demeanor. Matt couldn't help but reflect on the irony of Smith's fertile mind. He almost said out loud what he was thinking, Revelation from God. Old Testament marriage. Testosterone fantasy. Woman, it's my way or the highway. Smith, you genius, you outrageous genius.

It was the man who had to grant the eternal divorce. Five thousand dollars to write a letter to the First Presidency of the church. Meanwhile Carol was powerless and at the whim of his injured male ego. Matt looked up from the letter. Burgess was staring directly at him, eyes like a cobra.

"You want a letter from me now...right now!" Matt said.

It occurred to Matt what a naive fool he must look like.

Burgess squeezed the words out like they were distasteful.

"The First Presidency will accept a handwritten letter, yes," he said, opening a drawer. A yellow legal pad appeared in front of Matt.

"And then you write me a check?"

"Exactly. And when the eternal sealing has been..." he searched for a word that would not offend,"...reversed, I will see that you get this."

As he said it, he reached in the drawer and extracted a banded stack of crisp one-hundred-dollar bills. Matt realized that if Burgess had said anything different, it would have been out of character. The man was used to getting what he wanted. In this building everyone was on the payroll, his payroll, and Matt was standing in his building.

Matt folded the letter and put it in his jacket pocket. As he turned to walk away, Burgess picked up the stack of one hundreds, threw it in the drawer, and slammed the drawer shut.

"A week from today this is reduced by half."

Chapter 19

SALT LAKE CITY

Somewhere a phone was ringing. Burgess' eyes opened. Another ring.

"On," he said.

The room illuminated with soft light. He glanced at a wall-mounted flat screen, which came on giving him the hour, the date, day, and temperature outside. It was nine minutes before his usual wake-up time.

An unfamiliar voice came over the phone.

"Good morning, President Burgess. My name is Joseph Woodruff. I am the assistant to Brother Tanner of Welsely and Tanner, attorneys at law. Brother Tanner asked me to call you to see if you could meet with him at six-thirty this morning. Do you know where our offices are?"

"Of course. What is this regarding?"

"I'm warned not to discuss it over the phone, President Burgess."

"Are you in your office now?"

"Yes. If you park on the first level, a security guard will meet you there and bring you up," he said and hung up.

Burgess pressed the intercom on the phone.

"Bring the Mercedes up. I'm driving myself."

President Burgess exited his car as a man in a blue windbreaker, tan slacks, white shirt, and black tie walked toward him.

"President Burgess. It is good to see you again. Brother Lundgren, if you will remember."

"Brother Lundgren. Yes. Are you still with the SMC?"

"Ever since you hired me sir, yes."

They shook hands. Brother Lundgren led him to a freight elevator that whisked them to the tenth floor.

Sleeves rolled up, Brother Woodruff had what looked like a two-day beard. He was standing at the elevator when it opened.

Lundgren stayed on the elevator. Woodruff escorted President Burgess to a conference room that had no knob on the door. It was key latched only. On the table lay an unbound manuscript, the pages of which were spread out over the large, polished table surface. Woodruff indicated a chair. Both men sat.

"Brother Tanner is parking as we speak. He told me to go ahead and begin briefing you. It seems an inactive member, a Brother Matthew Alcott, is about to be published in New York."

Burgess stiffened. The name hung in the air like a grenade with the pin removed.

"That is not a big deal ordinarily, except that four years ago this man, this Alcott, worked as an archivist or a historian for the church. His book," Woodruff's head tilted to indicate the spread-out pages of manuscript on the large conference table, "if published, will disclose information heretofore unknown regarding the early days of the church."

At that moment Brother Tanner entered the room and offered his hand to President Burgess. He was wearing a royal blue suit and a blue silk tie a couple of shades lighter than the suit.

"Thank you for coming, President Burgess. Sorry about the early hour," Brother Tanner said.

"On the contrary. You did the right thing," Burgess said.

Tanner sat down facing him.

"I will make this short. This manuscript can be broken down into basically two parts. The main body of the writing is about the prophet. It deals with him personally and his relationship with women. References with discussion make up the latter half. I might be more accurate to call them expanded references. It's all damaging. It discredits the character of the prophet. Obviously it's based on incomplete information. It's laced with historical innuendo and inaccurate assumptions and it mentions something about a lost revelation. There are a host of implications of sexual impropriety and promiscuity on the character of the prophet. It reads like smut, just short of pornography."

Questions were forming. Burgess took a deep breath. He did not want to miss anything Tanner was saying. This was not easy considering his feelings for his ex-son-in-law.

"And we're not looking at a small, independent publisher. The book is owned by one of the big six publishers. What we are just learning is, it prints only mass runs. It's what you see at Costco and in grocery stores."

Tanner paused at this juncture and looked at Woodruff.

"This came from the twenty-sixth floor."

Woodruff handed the memo to Burgess. One sentence it read.

This manuscript is potentially damaging to the interests of the membership.

"When?" Burgess said.

"Three o'clock this morning. A full quorum. They're still in conference," Tanner said.

"Is there any way I can get a copy of this manuscript?" Burgess asked.

"Explicit instructions state that no copies are to be made. Anyone needing to review the manuscript is to do so behind locked doors, and only in the presence of Welsely, myself, or Woodruff," Tanner said.

He then turned to his unshaven assistant, Woodruff.

"Would you read the section I highlighted to President Burgess? I need to make a call."

Woodruff gulped. "Aloud?" His hand paused, a visible trembling. "I prefer not to, sir."

"I can certainly understand. Show President Burgess the section." He turned to Burgess. "I want you to see for yourself the level of degradation to which this Alcott has subjected the prophet. This is only a sample, one of many."

Woodruff shuffled through several pages and handed them to Burgess.

"About 1840," he said.

Burgess began scanning the pages.

Emma was angry with Joseph. As with no other person, his frustration increased.

"I can take no more of this plural marriage gossip the women speak of behind my back. I want the truth, Joseph. I will have the truth or I will take the children and leave," Emma said.

She dabbed at her eyes with a lace hanky.

Joseph felt weak and helpless when she did this. Anger welled up until he did something he had never done before. He dropped to one knee and holding Emma to him, he looked up into her eyes.

"Mine enemies would defame me. It has been so with all the prophets."

"Sounds like a fiction. I mean the way it's written," Burgess said.

"It is meant to sound that way. That's why it's so dangerous. Fiction being promoted as fact. This Alcott takes the position of defending the prophet rather than impugning him. States he is applying common sense to the prophet's life. He claims it's based on research. Here's another."

*The writings of John C. Bennett, Mayor of Nauvoo and Assistant President of the Church (*) have been called by many of today's critics as vindictive. Some of what he said in the Sangamo Journal had to be credible or it never would have seen ink. (* History of the Church, by Joseph Smith, Vol. 4, page 431)*

John Bennett states in his articles for the Sangamo Journal, Springfield, Illinois, between 1836 and 1842 that Joseph had women locked in a room for two days if they would not consent to be his wife. This is preposterous. This is one of the newspapers Abraham Lincoln both announced his candidacy for President in and campaigned in. It could not be labeled as a gossip rag.

Unpublished portions discarded at revision give new perspective to Bennett's personal relationship with the prophet.( ) These were lost until now. The question remains how did Smith present himself to a woman in a way that would favor his desires? The answer is simple. He would drug them. His drug was the word. It was the rhetoric of the day. His language was of the gospel of forbidden desires.

*The following account is slightly embellished from the previously lost text. It is informed and based on common sense and Joseph's character.(** Portions discarded at revision points, Mormonism EXPOSED, by John C. Bennett, 1842)*

The clouds loitered on the horizon. It had rained all night, but it was already warm. Joseph leaned the reins right and the gelding stepped over the wagon rut and started along the path to the Ridgemont farm. The door to the cabin opened. Morning sun splashed over the lower half of Olive's dress, accenting the small waist and spreading breasts. His breath quickened as the door closed. Joseph tied the sorrel at the water trough by the barn. He paid no attention to the mud from last night's rain as he walked past the vegetable garden and back to the front of the house. He raised his hand to knock. The door swung open.

"Good morning, President Smith," Sister Olive Ridgemont said.

Her voice was soft and soprano and, Joseph thought, as sweet as an angel.

"Please Sister, Brother Smith, call me Brother Smith," he said.

As he spoke he smelled cinnamon from the open door. His pulse raced at the sight of her. He was carrying a leather bound Book of Mormon. The smile that spread across her face seemed to issue from her whole being. For a moment he felt speechless as though someone had stopped time. Joseph forced himself to look away lest he sweep her up in his arms.

"Your home is lovely. I see your touch at every wall," he said.

He turned, as though looking at her home. Joseph wanted to make sure she saw him from the back, a view he was told was as handsome as his long face and straight nose. He had worn his dark coat with the high collar, accenting his dark brown hair.

"Here it is," he said, "the book I promised."

He presented the book with both hands as he would a precious jewel.

"Your knowledge of the Bible is a tribute to God. Let this be the companion witness to the coming of Jesus Christ," Joseph said.

"You honor me, President... Brother Smith. I will cherish it as I am skeptical of it, giving it equal weight in my mind and prayers."

"You have been sent among us for a reason, Olive. May I call you Olive?"

"Yes, please do."

She and her parents were recent migrants to the new city. Her parents had returned to New York State to complete the sale of their properties and bring the balance of their belongings to Nauvoo. Olive had stayed behind to feed and water the animals. At twenty-seven she was yet unmarried, a condition her mother blamed on expectations too lofty for any man.

"We spoke of celestial marriage you and I, a week now, was it not," Joseph said. "Have you prayed about this?"

"I do not oppose such a thing, I confess, but my prayers are yet unanswered, Brother Smith," she said, unmindful that she was holding the Book of Mormon snug to her breast.

"President Smith, I am engaged to be married. My fiancé only waits to complete an apprenticeship before joining me here," she informed him.

"He must be a wonderful man to have your heart, but I speak not of the finite flesh, but of the soul and an eternal partnership in the presence of the Lord. Let me remind you, sweet sister, that your fiancé has not been anointed with the holy order of Melchizedek. He cannot take you into the inner circle where your soul will be entwined with the Lord of Hosts for all eternity."

Olive's breath drew in, emitting the slightest whisper of a sigh.

"If you would have me in the celestial kingdom I am the more blessed. You must pray for guidance. I beseech you. Ask the Lord if you are not of his elite?" Joseph went on.

She stepped closer to him, "Yes, it is a promise I will keep."

Joseph's hands rested gently on her shoulders.

"The Lord has revealed to me, sweet sister, that we are to form a holy union in his name. Let us pray together."

They knelt at a chair facing each other.

"Oh Lord, our God, we, your servants, come before you. In answer to your call we humble ourselves, knowing that you are here with us. We know we are called upon, Kings and Queens to your commandments."

As Joseph whispered his prayer, his breath touched her ear. She took his hand in both of hers with a firmness that ran shuddering through his being.

"God's commandments are not always written in words, but in the heart," he said in a baritone whisper.

The transaction that followed was written in the holy book of secrets. One sigh lay on the breath of another. Her face on fire, flames of desire held order to the chaos of creation. How strong she was surprised him.

In the hushed shuffling that followed, he spoke softly in her ear as from the holy book itself.

"I am a great storm coming, King of the twelve tribes. In my loins the truth coils waiting to come forth. Oh Lord, joining me now in holy covenant is the daughter of Eve. Multitudes will flow from us."

As breathing worked its way back to normal and they lay in each other's arms, Joseph folded inward. He went to that place where none were allowed, repeated his private communication with Almighty God. A whispered thought, a true transmission, but for one ear only, that of his Lord.

"I conquered the daughter of ridicule, completing your revenge, O Lord. Mine are no more a conquered people. I am yet East of Eden a little."

The sun had moved across the floor, announcing to Joseph he would be late for the meeting with the Council. He thought, "Brigham is there. That bunch can start without me."

"This is a predestined moment ordained by the living God," Joseph intoned as he buttoned the flap of his britches.

"There's more," Tanner said, moving to another place in the history.

Other than pursed lips and set jaw, Burgess had not moved, his face a grimace of loathing and hate.

Olive became a part of the inner circle of polygamy. These were ladies who thought of themselves as an elite enclave of high-church leaders. They identified as either well educated or spiritually exceptional. Olive thought of herself as both. She had waited. She had known to wait for God's finger. There was no equivocation. She knew her part in the great plan of salvation and the considerable mission assigned to women by the Lord. The glorious nature of God's plan thrilled her. She felt and conducted herself a queen at Joseph's side, though she seldom stood there.

Tanner stopped, laid the paper down. He addressed Burgess, the tone conversational.

"The Church is comprised of over fifty-five percent women. Can you imagine their impression of the prophet after reading this?"

Burgess said nothing. An inner resolve spread though him. Tanner continued.

"We are charged to act with haste and prejudice. In the past we have bought out small, independent publishers, guaranteeing to defray legal damages, if any develop. Anonymously, of course. If this were an independent publisher we might offer between fifty and three hundred thousand, but this is a major publisher. They can print virtually anything they want. Buying them out, something called a kill fee, would have to do two things; it would need to be a substantial sum, and it would have to include the author; otherwise, what's to stop him from selling it to another house."

Burgess knew the stubborn nature of the author. Remembered

the $5,000 Alcott chose not to take at the time of the divorce. He thought about his daughter and how she had been deceived. The thought infuriated him. His shoulders tensed. Matthew had escaped from the jaws of death once. A reckoning would come. Burgess reminded himself,

The Lord works
in mysterious ways

"If knowledge of a lost revelation got out, there would be no end to it. I'll put it this way, if this book is published, the integrity of the restoration with be challenged and the good name of the church will be linked to *Playboy* magazine forever,"Tanner said.

Burgess agreed, the news media would have a feeding frenzy.

"This antichrist needs to be dealt with decisively."

Nor did Burgess want to end up in a bargaining hassle with the publisher.

"Have you a suggestion, a figure the publisher might take seriously?"

Tanner looked at the table, the manuscript. "I'm thinking a million plus."

"A two-party check. Force agreement between them," Burgess added.

Driving home Burgess felt a surge of glacial ice spread through his gut. He could see the headline:

Church Buys Controversial Book.
The Lost Revelation, a cover up.

From the point of view ofThe Council of Fifty it would be his failure. He inched the throttle forward.

When he took the position as CEO of the Alliance, one name

given him for confidential work was the law firm he had been quickly summoned by this morning: Tanner and Welsely.

The hasty meeting with Brother Tanner confirmed what had to be done. What President Burgess did not disclose was that one Matthew Alcott was once married to Burgess' only daughter. As he drove away from the meeting he couldn't help thinking,

Vengeance is mine,
sayeth The Lord,
His wonders to perform.

Burgess needed to think. His den was where he wrestled with the problems of the day. If he had only known sooner. He thought of Brother Lundgren, reached for his telephone book.

One phone call to the SMC, the Strengthening the Membership Committee, one of the church's security teams, did the trick.

The telephones at the offices of Paul Alcott, attorney at law, would be bugged the following night. He would be alerted if the name Matthew Alcott were mentioned. Being on the board of directors of the SMC had its advantages.

"Daddy?"

It was Carol, his daughter.

"Daddy? Can I disturb you please?"

Strict orders. No one was allowed to intrude when he was at prayer. Carol had gotten away with it when she was a child.

President Burgess did not respond.

He felt there was something unknown about this whole issue of the book, and there was no room for failure. Matthew Alcott must be stopped. With that he thought of Brother Farley Harper and recalled the Stake Conference when Farley had saved the day.

STAKE CONFERENCE
A YEAR BEFORE

An unhappy member who had been out of work for some months began shouting at President Burgess for the return of his tithe money so he could feed his family. It was in the foyer of the church. Hundreds of people were milling about. Two of the brethren attempted to step in between Burgess and the angry member, but were ineffective. He was a strong man and highly motivated. Farley walked him out of the building by the collar of his jacket and left him on the grass.

Guaranteeing that he would be no further problem, Farley stood by the front doors and quietly watched as the man considered whether or not to try again.

Burgess couldn't put his finger on it. Most people found Farley Harper strange. Possibly it was because he was a quiet man, almost withdrawn. A large person who doesn't talk much can come off a little frightening, different anyway. But Burgess liked Farley, felt sympathy toward the big man.

What impressed Burgess was that Farley seemed to know his place. People said he was a little slow, but Burgess had never found that to hinder his loyalty to the church or his ability to carry out a specific task.

Chapter 20

NEW YORK CITY

It was late. Matt waited at the elevator for Hamilton.

"We are to turn all manuscript copies, computer discs, and research materials over to the attorney in the morning," Hamilton said on the ride to his room in the hotel.

"I sent it. Should be in your office."

"We'll take it with us in the morning. You'll have to sign a document certifying that no other copies exist."

"No sweat," Matt said.

Agent Hamilton would get one hundred and fifty thousand. Matt would receive a tidy eight hundred fifty thousand dollars, U.S., but money was not what Matt was thinking about.

If there was any man on earth he detested more than Ezra D. Burgess he couldn't name him. How many times had James J warned him—if you hold a resentment, that person owns you. At that moment his ex-father-in-law owned every cell in his body.

With other people getting on and off the elevator, they couldn't talk freely, but Matt was so rankled he couldn't stop himself.

"Ever feel like you been bushwhacked?" Matt said to Hamilton, the group in the elevator listening.

"Every time I get divorced," a lady said.

She was in her fifties with heavy makeup and gray roots beginning to show. Hamilton nodded, acknowledging her. The elevator door opened. No one got on. No one got off.

"You can do an awful lot with that kind of money," Hamilton said.

"Are you married?" the lady asked.

"Happily," Hamilton said.

"Not you," she said.

The elevator door opened.

"I needed to understand Smith," Matt said as they left the elevator.

Hamilton sat in one of the hotel chairs.

"Help me understand the people behind this," he said.

Hamilton figured it was part of his job to counsel his authors. In matters like this, asking the right questions was vital. His author needed clarity, and he definitely wanted to keep him around. It was no mystery that Hamilton Gloss was old school.

"I'd kill for a scotch and water," Matt said without thinking. This was accepted, even encouraged behavior in AA. Hamilton had never been to AA.

Hamilton opened the chrome door on the small cabinet. Four bottles of airport beverage stood at attention. Matt watched, said nothing, as Hamilton tucked them into his jacket pocket. Matt knew if he let himself think he needed a drink, nothing short of a small cohort of sumo wrestlers could keep him from it.

"I have a friend," Matt said. "Roger Andrayson. Man wrote a book, *The Faith That Failed: A Biblical Examination of Mormonism*. The publisher did a twenty-five thousand first printing. The books were ready to be distributed to the bookstores when all communications ceased. The publisher stopped answering his calls. Written communications were not acknowledged. Eventually Roger sued. When the litigation came to an end, the judge agreed there had been a breach of contract. The judgment added damages to what would have been his royalties. Roger said he made out better than if every copy had sold."

"Catholic church doesn't bother with this sort of thing," Hamilton said, attempting to understand it.

"Mormon Church does the same most of the time. When something comes along that strikes at the core of their authority to ensure obedience and loyalty from the membership like Roger's book, it acts.

Unfathomable power and influence. Rich, quiet, and jealous of its image. About this kind of threat, there is no hesitation," he said.

He took a deep breath and started over, slower, easier.

"The inner circle has three classifications; faith promoting, no threat, and non-faith promoting. If it's labeled non-faith promoting, no further discussion occurs. Some prearranged action is set in motion without so much as a nod. The problem is neutralized with an efficiency and an expediency as indifferent as a computer virus."

"Talk about image conscious," Hamilton said.

"The most appearance-conscious institution on the face of the earth, more so even than the pharmaceuticals and the oil companies."

"Is there someone you want to call?" a thoughtful Hamilton asked.

"I will, shortly. Is this your first experience with Mormons?"

"Completely off the wall," Hamilton said.

"What would you do?"

"Your decision. All I can do is advise. I really think you need to sleep on it," Hamilton said, getting up to leave.

"Copout."

The words slipped out before he could stop them.

"You want me to make the decision for you?" Hamilton said.

Matt rose, leaned his head against the wall with a thud.

"Honestly?" Hamilton posed.

"Need all the help I can get."

"If you don't agree to the two million...?"

"You think I'll regret it for the rest of my life," Matt answered. It was, of course, the obvious answer.

Hamilton opened the door. "I'll see you in the morning."

As the door closed behind him, Matt reached for the phone. No answer at her mother's. James J did not answer. He let it ring for a long time at Raven's house. Tried the loft, hoping Minnie Mouse would wake the whole damn town. Wait. Hold it. A flag went up.

Matt put the phone in its cradle. Wondered how dangerous this could be for Cate. The publisher did not have his answer yet; still, would she be in any danger?

With thoughts of Cate, sleep eluded.

Almost 4 a.m. *Might as well find some coffee*. He stood in the shower and let the hot water pound until easy breathing followed shallow. He would buy out the Hanleys, turn the hardware store into a comfortable home for Cate, convert the loft into a writing studio the envy of any author alive and...and...and...in time he would write the book he wanted. He would fashion it differently, but it would be written and, oh yes, he would make sure James J was treated by the best oncologist on the planet.

Chapter 22

SALT LAKE CITY

Quarterly Conference. President Burgess extended his hand. "Brother Harper. Good morning."

"Good morning, President Burgess, sir."

You grow a strong grip in Zion if you are a man. The handshake, man-to-man, is more than a custom, it sets a tone, confirms a brotherhood.

"Brother Harper, could I see you tomorrow?" President Burgess asked.

The appointment was for a set time and at a different address from either his business office or the stake house. President Burgess had been more casual than usual. That evening Farley shined his shoes and wondered what the meeting was about. Shined his shoes again. There was no man alive he respected more.

A few minutes early, he parked down the street and walked into the parking garage of the office building. He passed a storage room with the door ajar. A light illuminated the interior. He looked in.

"Brother Harper, come in, come in. Close the door behind you."

One folding table, two folding chairs. Fluorescent lighting. President Burgess extended his hand.

"Your father and I knew each other. I don't believe you knew that. Goes way back to our missionary days."

"No sir," Farley said.

"A good man, Bishop Harper. We labored together in the... Let s see, it was called the..."

"The Southeastern Mission, sir," Farley said.

"That's right. I believe it is two missions today. My regret, your father and I were never companions, but we knew each other. Both from Northern Utah, we chatted at reunions."

Farley smiled or expressed what for him was a smile. When President Burgess asked him to, "Please sit down," he felt less uncomfortable with the stake president than he ever had. Instructions had always taken place standing before.

The only chairs in the room were metal, folding, temporary. When Farley put his weight down, the chair felt shaky, as though it might twist and collapse. He leaned forward, put more weight on his legs. An awkward position, he said nothing. Farley's size had often been a source of embarrassment.

President Burgess spoke slowly. As always what he had to say was meticulously thought out.

"As you know, Brother Harper, the Church has many enemies. Of late they seem to multiply. There comes a time when we can no longer turn the other cheek, but must strike a blow for the truth."

He paused to allow a comment if Brother Harper felt so inclined. Farley was listening intently. This had always impressed President Burgess. He became more direct.

"I had to ask you once to refrain from acting when you had come to the aid of the Church. Do you remember?"

Farley thought about it. Said, "Yes, sir."

"This time it is different. The Church needs you. Will you come to the aid of the Church?" There was a pause. Farley had an answer. He looked for it.

"Your enemies are my enemies," Farley said.

At this point his legs were beginning to cramp. He moved to adjust his weight.

I think I know this man, President Burgess thought. *Always quiet, shy, no doubt due to his size. Can he follow directions?* He had, so far, and he had completed an honorable mission for the Lord. He reminded himself, *The Lord provides.*

"I need a man who can work discreetly, who can follow a person without being seen."

Farley nodded.

"Business is business," President Burgess said. "Apparently the job you did three years ago in Las Vegas did not have a lasting effect. Again I don't need to know the details."

Because of the awkward posture, the strain Farley was feeling was becoming unbearable. His leg began to quiver.

"If you will remember, we had to discipline a man who had stolen a box of important papers from the Church," Burgess reminded.

"Yes sir. I remember. In Las Vegas."

"It looks like he didn't take our threat seriously. Do you think we can do that again?"

"Scare him," Farley said.

"Yes, scare him. Would you know what to do?"

The awkward posture was becoming intense.

"He is one of Lucifer's own and would do injury to the Church," Burgess continued. "Brother Harper, we are at war with evil. Of course, the true church is always at war with the dark forces, and I know that you're a peaceful man. If you choose to say, 'No, but thank you,' I will understand."

Farley could take no more. He came to his feet, a great cramp knotting in his left leg. When he spoke he sounded raspy, like Robert Mitchum with a cold. The words were those he learned in the mission field.

"You can count on me, President Burgess."

Farley stood as he always had, with his hat in front of him, both hands at the brim. It was the Mission Field posture, polite, ready. President Burgess was positive. This was his man. He bent down and picked up a briefcase. Placing it on the table between them, he took out two large manila envelopes.

Chapter 22

SALT LAKE CITY

It had been a long day for Farley. As he drove home he was hungry and tired, stopped and bought a large root beer shake, three monster burgers, and a double French fry at the Burger Factory.

He ate in front of the television set, as always. A few hours later he woke remembering. President Burgess had mentioned a more practical mode of transportation. He went out to his pickup. Two large envelopes lay in the front seat.

He thought it was play money for a minute. Counted out fifty one-hundred-dollar bills. Farley had never seen this much money in his life. There were addresses and pictures of Matthew with Cate sitting with Paul Alcott, his brother, in a bookstore in Rochester, New York.

The storage facility did not have a gate. Advertised, twenty-four-hours-a-day access. The key opened B-22. Farley stood looking into the dark at the shine he could see under a layer of dust on a four-door gray sedan. He transferred his tools for working with locks into the trunk of his new ride. It didn't take five minutes to make the trade. As he drove away, the 1965 white pickup remained behind the overhead door.

The next day Farley drove to Provo and back. Get the feel of her. *The big question, do I need a gun?* He remembered what President Burgess had last said to him: Do your work quietly. There is no profit in ostentation. A display of power would defeat the Lord's purpose. Ostentation. His brother Jedediah had a dictionary in his office and helped him find the word and understand it.

"A guy that's strong like you doesn't need to show off that he is strong," Jedediah said.

"A secret?"

"Yeah, like that," Jedediah agreed.

That evening he walked into the Sugarhouse Mall and didn't have to stand looking at the long folding knife with the shiny eight-inch blade. The man behind the counter showed him how to open and close it.

A special man for a special work. He practiced manipulating the big knife.

The Lord made me different for a reason, a reason not many are inclined. He could see it. Everywhere he looked, the Church had enemies.

"The Church's enemies are my enemies," he said to the windshield.

The day following he drove his new car north to the Malad Pass at the Idaho-Utah border. The day following south to Nephi City and back. *This is the Lord's test of me*, and Farley's foot would push the throttle forward. *My loyalty will be known*. He walked slowly like Robert Mitchum. He ate at truck stop diners where the food was good. Chicken-fried steak and gravy, one of his favorites. He saw the waitresses in their sins and thought he should marry them so that they would no longer be sinners. He left extravagant tips, two dollars.

Farley knew that he was now part of the great eye of God that is in the Salt Lake temple and that one day he would have many wives and they would all vie for his affections.

"I will be fair. I will show no favorites," the windshield glass would return his voice, sounding as it did when he said his prayers at night.

He was busy that first week. A new television set, video player, and those kinds of videos that he must view in order to understand the workings of the Devil's mind.

Farley knew that when a man fears the Lord, he will be good and no longer do things that hurt the Church. He remembered the finger of President Burgess pointing at the eight-by-ten picture of the man who had written a book. It was the same man he had left in the desert without clothes.

"We must see that this man is made to fear the Lord." He could still hear Burgess' words.

In the movies he liked, when a detective was on a job he studied the pictures of his subject. Farley looked at the pictures of Matthew Alcott. He stared at the pictures of the pretty Hawaiian girl with him.

Chapter 23

NEW YORK CITY

Hamilton was at the front desk of the hotel when Matt stepped off the elevator. They shouldered their way the two blocks to his office, where they were to gather up all the reference materials and backup files to deliver to the legal in the tight skirt.

Hamilton introduced Matt to Louise, his secretary.

"It's very nice to finally meet you," Matt said.

Gray hair in a tight bun, she looked as proper as a paper clip. Louise offered the hint of a smile over her computer screen, seemed busy with something urgent.

Matt followed Hamilton into the back office, where he found him frantically moving and throwing things about. In contrast to the front office, where everything was neat and tidy, the rear two offices looked like it would take two days to find something.

Hamilton came out of the back office, used mostly for storage, into his own office. Almost in a panic, he dialed Sam Perness.

"It's not here. The book. His files. Nothing is in this office."

A strange look like a shadow moved across Hamilton's face. Putting the phone down and missing the cradle, he addressed Louise in the front office.

"When you found the door unlocked this morning, did you look around, see if anything was missing?"

"The front office. Nothing was missing or out of place. Back there, I would have no idea."

Matt almost smiled out loud. A divided office; her territory, his territory. Hamilton retreated into the back office.

"They already have it, don't they?" she declared dryly.

Matt put Hamilton's phone back in its cradle.

The intuitive flash gave little warning. Hamilton was squirming, some ongoing debate. Matt knew immediately who the backbone of this small business was.

"Okay. I'll have the locks changed and bars put over the windows this week."

He spoke reluctantly, like he had been coerced into it.

"Upgrade the locks, Mr. Gloss. We don't need bars," Louise said.

"All they have to do is break the glass," Hamilton pointed out.

"Bars would offend our clients, and I refuse to work in a prison."

Hamilton started to sit down, but came right back out of his chair as if he had been spring-loaded.

"We'll be late if we don't get a move on."

Last-minute instructions to Louise. Check for two million waiting for them. Reminded Matt of his newspaper days. Didn't matter how good the piece was he'd written, if the powers that be did not print it, wasn't a damn thing he could do. Didn't work for a newspaper anymore...still everyone seemed to have agreed, don't be a fool. Take the money.

While Hamilton and he were waiting for the elevator, Matt had one of those afterthoughts that nag like a toothache that's just beginning. He felt boxed in, cornered, realized it was Hamilton's secretary that was troubling him. Monitoring their conversation that morning was interesting. Something in that office didn't square up.

"Need a minute," Matt said.

He left Hamilton standing with his finger on the down button, his mouth open.

Matt knew sometimes he offended and his opinions were not infrequently met with curious expressions, but there was a respect in him. It was not for the high and mighty, the celebrity, or the CEO. It was for the man, the guy, the one who does the work. It was for the carpenter who swings the hammer and the machinist who swages the tool. Same in the office. While some talk, others do. In an office, it's the secretary.

Intuition at high rpms, Matt stepped back into Hamilton's office and dropped his overnight bag in front of Louise's desk. She stopped typing and swiveled her chair toward him, one eyebrow arched. Matt found myself standing in front of a pair of steady, discerning gray eyes. There was no equivocation in them. This lady knew who she was.

He asked a question. Thought he already knew the answer, but had to confirm it.

"You've read my book?"

"Yes."

It was as though she were ordering office supplies, confirming the kind of toner used. "You could do me a great service?" Matt said.

Matt noticed a respect in his voice. Nothing planned, but real nonetheless. He had come to this town for a reason. The need that drove him, riveted his posterior to a chair for untold hours writing and revising—years of work. His book would hit like napalm, expose acres of fraud.

Nor was it courage that drove him. Courage had little to do with it. There was a hunger in Matt. He wrote and as he did, he changed. First, it was bitterness, loss, and betrayal that composed words. Boring and self-serving, it got old. New file. Start over. The wonder of Joseph Smith, of what he had created. His was a war against stupidity, arrogance.

New words scrolling out. This time he was discovering what made Smith tick. He wrote to express these newfound insights. Compassion followed. Matt found himself writing a book about a man creating his own life. One in the other, he found the human in Joseph Smith and, sensing the connectedness, began to gain new insights into himself.

"No one has said one word to me, but I have a problem. I have written a book. I like to think a good book. Beyond killing it, no one seems otherwise interested," Matt said, frustrated.

Her eyes, gray and cobra steady, softened.

"Before I agree to its abortion, I need to know...was...was it a good book or just a commodity for barter?"

She sat silent looking steadily into Matt's eyes. Then, a hint, a knowing look. Honest and wily. As she spoke, her eyes began to shine.

"Matthew Alcott, it is a brilliant book. The last revelation certainly gave us a new perspective into the genesis of the Mormon Church, but it was your sympathy for Joseph Smith and what drove him that gripped me. It has empathy and insight. I can actually sense your respect for a driven man at a peculiar moment in America's history. I could tell you empathized deeply with him. You were sensitive to the needs that sustained him and to an intellect that could not be contained. It gave me goose bumps to read what you wrote about him. He, like Hefner, fought against titanic odds. You made Joseph Smith something he never has been, a real person. When that mob shot him, maverick rascal that he was, I wept."

A shudder moved through Matt. Hamilton had returned, was standing in the doorway. Matt didn't know what to say. She seemed to understand and continued.

"That personal connection to his intimate feelings and motivations is precisely what makes your research live. The documents you are exposing to the world are reinforced by your treatment of an exceptional man at a pivotal time in our country's history."

He bent, picked up his bag. He had written desiring to find something. What? Peace of mind? In the whole island of Manhattan, at least one person beyond him thought it was a good book. This dear woman understood his passion, connected with it. In doing so, God bless her, she set him free.

Back to the real world. Commodities and profit margins. The power of promotion. How many people can say they worked for three years and made a cool $1,000,000 for their efforts? His publisher was a heavyweight, a threat. Trade on it. Matt felt like a newspaperman again after the Sunday edition is read, forgotten, and in the Monday morning trash. Who cares? Take the money.

"We're late," Hamilton said.

He looked at the picture on the wall behind her. It was of a man running at dawn through a park or forest. It was entitled Dedication.

"Hamilton, if you don't make a partner of this lady, you're a fool."

As usual when he felt something deeply, he spoke before he thought. As he followed Hamilton back to the elevator, her words hung in the air behind him.

"Not interested in any partnerships. But I will say this to you, Matthew Alcott. If you take the money, something meaningful will be lost, and it won't matter if you ever write another word."

Chapter 24

SALT LAKE CITY
THE CLUB

"As you know, many books have been published that discredit the Church. The presence of another seems almost tiresome, but this new book has special circumstances that justify a different course of action. It is an exposé that includes a new and damning revelation by our first prophet never seen before." Burgess paused, let the body of men listening absorb what he'd said. "The twenty-sixth floor has labeled the book non-faith promoting."

President Burgess was addressing some of the richest men alive. Some of these men were wealthy beyond even his dreams. Few men he looked up to, but for those fifty in this club his admiration was difficult to suppress. He felt he was finally where he belonged.

The club was well appointed with oak trim and paneling. Men-only employees, all members of the Church in good standing. Forty-eight-hour shifts. Half alternated at a time, leaving a complement familiar with the last twenty-four hours.

There had never been a gentile in the place. Nor a female. Priesthood only. He was shown a room and introduced to a man dressed in a gray suit as the head of house security. There was another man also in a gray suit watching a bank of security monitors. The gray suits were well tailored, but ordinary. In here, they were clearly security personnel. Outside on the street they would look like any regular husband on his way home from work. Gaining access required both voice and visual verification.

The Council of Fifty carried a lot of weight in the Church. It was invisible weight, but real. Burgess knew his selection to head up the Alliance was two-fold; it kept an arm's length buffer between the Council and any dirty work needed to be done, and it offered the initiate an opportunity to prove himself worthy of full membership.

Burgess understood his words and actions were being measured. He felt a little smug, but was careful not to let his confidence show. The proper attitude was vital.

Seclusion, privacy, and camaraderie for fifty older, rich men. The primary function was to consider, discuss, and act on church-political issues. They had made themselves comfortable in their work. Outside of Utah only a few people had heard of Joseph Smith's Council of Fifty.

A swimming pool, Jacuzzi, steam room, and other exercise equipment had been added over the years. A full time masseur, male nursing staff, and a small cooking staff. Vitamin and hormone therapy was conducted under the best medical care available. Employees were hired for their loyalty to the restoration of the gospel of Jesus Christ and the ability to be discreet.

While comfortable, it was a fortress equipped to monitor almost any media or Internet event desired by the membership.

Burgess, sitting, made his report to the committee.

The rumble of voices was audible.

"This book speaks directly to the authenticity of the restored gospel." President Burgess again paused to let that sink in.

"How valid is this last revelation?" Brother Smyth asked.

"The author claims to substantiate its credibility, but then the book reads like smut. Until we can evaluate its source, refuting it is his word against ours."

There was a hush in the room.

"What steps have you taken?" It was Brother Angus who spoke this time.

"I've made an offer to buy the manuscript. Considering what's at stake, and with the advice of church counsel, I put up two million dollars.

I didn't stop there. I had a team collect every trace of the manuscript at the agent's offices and at the author's home. These, along with his hard drive, are in Salt Lake in safekeeping. At this time the only manuscript not in safekeeping with us is with the publisher, as far as I can tell."

"Why two million?" Brother Angus asked.

A Brother Stevens in the audience made known his voice. "One of my subsidiaries publishes nonfiction. From what I know that's a goodly sum. I'll back it up with a phone call."

Burgess addressed Brother Stevens.

"Thank you. Let me be sure you have my phone number. The attorney for the publisher made the offer clear last evening, and as I offered half the money to the publisher, I believe I have made them our advocate for the sale."

"Bravo. Bravo. Amen," were heard randomly throughout the audience.

"I also made it a self-limiting, descending offer. Its total value is only worth one point five million today. Tomorrow one million. I should know by the end of the day."

"Wicked! Brilliantly wicked! Remind me not to do business with you, Burgess," a brother waving his cane said.

The meeting was over. Brother Angus approached Burgess. "Would you stay and dine with us?"

"Can I take it to mean shades of things to come?" Burgess inquired.

For a moment Angus had a strange expression. He was looking for another member. Spoke to him briefly before turning back to Burgess.

"You know, as a matter of fact it would. You have already been accepted by the full membership, and we are to treat you as one of us. Your ordination, of course, is pending Brother Volcker's passing." Angus looked at his watch. "I think we have time...are you up for something enlightening?"

They walked down a hallway that ended at an elevator. There was only one button: down. Angus pushed the button indicating descent.

The elevator stopped. The door opened to total blackness. Angus stepped out, pushed, and held a button for a brief moment. A generator kicked in and began to hum. Angus flipped a toggle switch and lights came on, illuminating a tunnel with a conveyor belt obviously built for human transport. The visual narrowing of the tunnel indicated it went on for some distance.

"Easier if you get on before I start it," Angus said, having a little fun at Burgess' expense.

He was obviously enjoying his role as tutor to the soon-to-be new member. President Burgess sat in the chair next to him. At one point the conveyor stopped and they boarded another.

"Only the most righteous of God's servants see any of this," Angus announced.

President Burgess thought he knew everything there was to know about the Church. He began running through an index of possibilities in memory.

As the conveyer expressway slowed to a stop, another tunnel opened up at their right.

"That way leads to the Church Administration building. We are now..."

Burgess smiled. "Directly under the temple if my sense of direction holds."

"Very good. Very good."

A stainless-steel door opened automatically as they approached. Beyond was an anteroom that had two benches built at the walls.

"We leave our shoes here," Angus explained.

Up a small flight of stairs they opened another door, beyond which was a long, narrow room. Two rows of chairs. One behind the other elevated. Both faced another room beyond a glass wall.

Brother Angus touched Burgess' shoulder.

"Speak freely. No one can hear us. We can see them. They cannot see us."

Burgess blinked. It was a part of the temple he had never seen. Two male technicians, dressed in surgical scrubs, were working at a medical station. A bulky white chair with wheels was being pushed into the room by a woman in a white dress.

The chair carried a motionless lady with a white half hood that covered her eyes and nose. The lady pushing the chair turned and exited the room, leaving the wheelchair and its passenger. As the wheels of the chair were locked into place by one of the technicians, the chair converted itself into a table with extended stirrups. The white sheet covering the unconscious young woman was folded back, exposing her genitalia.

Angus pointed to a large appliance built into the wall. One of the technicians was reaching for the handle. As the door swung into the open position, exposing pre-prepared vials of an aqueous solution, he spoke.

"Seed of the righteous. Yours will be in there soon."

"Seed…as in…" Burgess left his question hanging.

"Sperm. That's right," Angus said.

The men in olive-colored surgical scrubs began working over the girl. Within sixty seconds the entire procedure was completed and the table was converted back into a wheelchair. The woman who had transported the lady into the room re-entered and wheeled her out.

Burgess nodded toward the door the wheelchair exited through.

"To the anointing room?"

"Yes. It started with Brigham Young in the St. George Temple, which as you know, was completed and in service before this temple. He never explained why, but you'll agree, I think, the reason is obvious."

Burgess searched his mind.

"I've heard of something…a…a truth gene."

"Our scientists have decoded it. Something to do with an allele on the Y chromosome that enhances cognitive perception," Angus said.

Burgess was silent.

"It's a lot to digest. Let me explain it to you this way. My granddaughter married a young man she met in college. His family is from Cuba. He converted and they were married two weeks ago. Will my grandchildren have a testimony of the gospel?"

Angus left the question in the air for a moment.

"Keep in mind, women don't carry that specific gene. It's the Y gene. Men only. How can my progeny have the fullest advantage? You and I want our families intact in the next estate," Angus said.

He paused again. Burgess seemed to have withdrawn.

"Two weeks ago I entered this room. I was blessed to be able to watch my granddaughter being inseminated. For obvious reasons semen from the Council of Fifty were excluded that day...to insure mine were not in that batch—appropriate quality controls. There is a great comfort in knowing my progeny will have a testimony of the true gospel." Angus paused to let that soak in before pointing to the other end of the room. "Did you notice the door at that end of this room?"

Burgess turned and squinted down the dark barrel of a room. The door was painted the same color as the wall. It was hard to determine the real color in the subdued light, maybe pewter, maybe steel gray.

"The changing room is beyond. I put on my temple clothes. A flight of stairs and I met them in the sealing room, where I performed the ceremony uniting them forever," Angus said.

"Artificial insemination. That brings up a question..." Burgess said.

"The hymen?" Angus submitted.

They watched another young woman being wheeled into the room.

"There is a technique. I don't know what it is, but the sad fact is there are not that many intact hymens anymore. You probably noticed that the pubic area was partly shaved on the last girl."

Burgess nodded.

"A constant reminder, the war with evil is never over," he said as he looked at his watch. "Aw! Here we go. Time to start back. You are about to taste the most amazing trout you've ever eaten. We seed a lake, annually, Wyoming, in the high Uintahs. Caught this morning. Couldn't get any fresher."

It had been a strange experience at the very least. Stranger still, Burgess found himself thinking about his businesses. Over the years he had made thousands of decisions that affected his employees, their families, other people. Their lives took directions that were the direct result of his needs and goals. With what he had just seen, Burgess began to perceive the magnitude of leadership at a more divine level. He couldn't help reflecting on the oft-repeated Church maxim,

As man is,
God once was.
As God is,
man may become.

He realized his spiritual journey had just entered a new level of responsible leadership.

After what he had seen in the viewing room below the temple, Burgess was silent. The conveyer belt moved them along, returning them to the elevator. As it did he became aware that Brother Angus was watching him.

"It's humbling," Burgess reflected.

"That was my reaction," Brother Angus said, adding, "One gets the impression President Young knew things he couldn't tell us."

The Executive Lounge had ten tables for dining. Fresh Rocky Mountain trout, with thinly sliced almonds and fresh lemon. Angus made it clear, they did not talk business at dinner. It was because of the waiters and other staff.

"I believe this is the best trout I have ever eaten," President Burgess said.

"Caught this morning by our own people. They time it to land at first light. Fish right off the pontoons. Sometimes one or two of us go along. Pilot calls when they have sixty or so cleaned and on ice. One of our vehicles meets them at the airport," Brother Angus said.

Chapter 25

NEW YORK CITY
PUBLISHER'S OFFICE

The legal, Susan Vincent, was wearing a beige suit this morning. It lent a softer look to her features. Sam and the secretary entered together. The minute Matt sat down he wanted to get up and run. His stomach felt like he had eaten lead for breakfast. *How come?* he wondered. The deal was done. Everyone was in agreement.

Take the money, but wait a minute. I didn't write the book for money. All those hours. You couldn't pay me to do that again. My book was a labor of love. I wrote to complete my life, to know finally who and what I was and to share that process with others who were floundering and felt empty, alone, betrayed.

Life was a process, an ongoing experiment, not an end game. He realized that there comes into some lives a moment that renders all others insignificant. It stands by itself, a force beyond consequence, and like a bullet in flight, when it strikes, it changes things.

For Matt freedom was about being able to say yes to a drink. He couldn't quit until he realized he had the power of choice. The most valuable thing in the world was not money. It was about the way he felt about himself. While everyone was talking, Matt started scribbling on a piece of paper. When he finished everyone was looking at him.

"This money didn't come from the Church, did it," he said, looking directly at the beige suit.

It was a demand not a question. The attorney knew he had figured it out. At least some of it.

"If I have one regret in all of this, it's that I didn't get to read your book," she said.

Matt sensed she meant what she said.

"Can you...will you tell me who the private party is?" he asked.

"Honestly, I don't know."

He believed her. A crosscurrent of doubts and questions had been running through his head all morning. The loudest voice was from a new friend, a lady who didn't pull punches. "If you take the money something meaningful will be lost, and it won't matter if you ever write another book."The pain in his stomach eased back. He folded his scribbling once and pushed it in front of Sam.

"Is this legal?" Matt said.

The room went silent. Sam read carefully, laboring somewhat over his cursive.

"Is this word substantive?" she asked without looking up.

"Yeah."

Sam handed it to the legal, who after reading it answered, "Date it. Have Hamilton and one other witness it. There's no mistaking its intent," the legal said.

"This is the way you want it, then?" Sam asked.

Matt rose from the chair. Hamilton turned white. Glasses slid down the bridge of the secretary's nose.

"This is for you." He pulled a computer disc out of his pocket and placed it in front of Sam.

A nudge of intuitive feedback from dark experience, Matt suspected, said play it this way. Get the ball rolling and vanish. Keep your head down. After the dust settles come up for air, see where the flak has done its damage. Typical drunken ostrich, head in sand, he thought.

The note in Sam's hand read:

Samantha Perness

I accept your offer to publish my book.You are herein authorized to act as my editor. Make any changes you deem necessary, keeping my agent's office informed and in the loop. Any substantive changes to the storyline and writing are to go through Louise Nellis and Hamilton Gloss, who are also authorized herein to sign the contract for me. In the event of my death, Cate Lynn Sudani, of Resurrection Corner, NY is to be named owner/beneficiary.

The accompanying disc is the latest revision and has all the backup references authenticating its factual basis.

Please have your business office deposit two equal checks to two bank accounts; one into the New York State Bank, in Resurrection Corner in the name of Cate Lynn Sudani, and the other in my Salt Lake City bank, deposit slips enclosed.

Signed: Matthew J. Alcott, Date:

Witness: Hamilton Gloss, Date:

Witness Sam Perness, Date:

Sam jumped in, "We will need to confer. How do we contact you?"

"Go through Hamilton and Louise."

"A phone number?"

"Hamilton and Louise."

It was a lie, but what the hell.

"I have to catch a plane. May I use the phone in your office?" Matt said.

Sam nodded and pointed across the hall.

Chapter 26

NEW YORK CITY

Good old Hamilton surprised him again. Last thing Matt expected. He got in the cab and rode with him to the airport. There was a standby available on the next flight to Salt Lake City, luck or destiny, one of those guys. Matt offered the cabby an extra twenty to make haste. What the hell? What's a twenty to a rich guy?

"Check in, in less than an hour. Can you make it?" Matt inquired.

"Get in," the cabby said, rotating his flag into the upright position indicating a fair. He alerted those behind that his cab was about to enter traffic.

"So how did the people in Utah find out about your manuscript?" Hamilton asked.

Traffic slow. Driver didn't seem to have his heart in his work.

"Is there a faster route?" Matt asked.

"This is best way, pal. Believe me. Sy's my name. Driving's my game."

Matt realized he was feeling an emotional reprieve from the anxiety of the past few days.

"Couple different ways. I'll bet there are at least six people work at Bloomsburg & Walbridge Publishing who are good Mormons. If you did not take information like this, that a book about us, the Mormons, was being published to your bishop, you would be censured by him when it did. It is your sense of duty to the Lord and Church that motivates. The other way? If you have unlimited resources, what's to stop you? I mean, if you can afford the computer talent, you know, specialists that can make a computer do handstands, you can back your way into any PC on the net. And listening devices, high-tech toys, micro stuff? Privacy is something from history. Today? Only a matter of money. With five different security teams, the Church always needs people, so who does the Church employ?"

Hamilton was listening, but not nearly as intently as was the driver. Cabby's eyes were burning holes in the rearview mirror.

"So who's on the cutting edge of investigative technology?" Matt asked.

"FBI, CIA," Sy, the cabby, said.

Both looked at the man in the front seat.

"There's your answer," Matt said.

"You know this?" Hamilton asked, ignoring the cabby.

"Church hires 'em, FBI retirees. No secret. Several authors have covered the subject of church security and Mormon shadow governments."

"You're saying FBI retreads take jobs in Utah for the Mormon Church," Hamilton said.

"Yeah. Why not? For retired security specialists the pay is probably excellent. They don't necessarily need to be Mormons. They're used for surveilling anyone for any reason. Screw the ethics."

"You'll be blackballed by your own people," Hamilton added.

"Already happened. The minute I began thinking for myself," Matt said.

The voice is sharp with little resonance, like he had been talking over the noise of engine and traffic for years. "If they're shootin' at ya, ya must be doing something right," the cabby said, smiling into the rearview mirror.

Matt noticed cars in the other lanes were moving at a faster pace than their cab was.

"Excuse me, but are we in the slow lane?"

"Don't worry about it. Those are to off ramps. I'll get you there. Name's Sy, 'n I don't lie."

Hamilton surprised Matt. "It's a hell of a book, Matthew."

This was the first direct compliment he'd received from his agent.

"My book's not just a commodity?"

"I confess, Louise threatened to quit if I didn't take it on. She's only threatened to do that one other time. You see, I didn't have a choice. I'm the boss, but she outranks me."

"Let me guess. I would take you for Catholic?" Matt ventured.

"Didn't know it still showed."

"Me too," came from the front seat.

They ignored him.

"So what do you believe down deep in that Catholic heart, Hamilton? Are Islam, Rome, or Salt Lake City all that different? One and only one true religion?"

"I haven't found any legitimacy to that question since I was seventeen, but there is something I'm curious about. If the apple falls close to the tree, are you the exception?" Hamilton said.

Matt knew he was thinking of Paul, his brother. "Downhill side I guess."

"Your brother is a good attorney. Certainly has done well by me. Where does he stand?" Hamilton said.

"We try to avoid the subject. Ninety percent of his clients are members. You do the math."

"Is he aware of the content of your book?" Hamilton asked.

"Little brother will have a coronary. Can't wait to get that phone call."

Traffic was against them. Cabby's eyes moved back and forth. "My brother-in-law's a Mormon. He's the bishop of his ward."

Hamilton shifted his weight in the seat. He was clearly offended by the man.

"We've enlisted your services for the business of transportation. I'd appreciate it if you would confine yourself to driving."

"Nice guy, my brother-in-law," the cabby said.

"This is a private conversation," Hamilton added.

The cabby moved his head to make eye contact with Hamilton. Indifferent smile. "My cab, pal."

Ignoring him, with effort, Hamilton directed his attention back to Matt. "There is a question I ask all my authors."

"Yes?"

"I've found a good book affects its author. Did anything like that happen to you?"

"Oh. A before and after. One day I'm writing. It's early, still dark out. My fingers stop mid sentence and I walk over to the window and look out. Why did I turn east when I sold my place in Nevada? Always thought I'd end up in LA. So only then did I understand. My book's a New York story. What Smith did became a western way of life, but its origins are pure New York. It was a new country, just defining itself. Smith's mother saw something unique in her boy, and a mother's influence is nothing if not far reaching. Easy to overlook. The only entertainment was the tent preacher. Not much of a social life unless Smith went to church, attended bible classes. Beat the hell out of sitting at home if you're fifteen. Methodist was the closest. I think of Joseph as the Hugh Hefner of the 1800s. Did you know Hugh Hefner was raised a Methodist? Much of that was of a puritan ethic they both took offense to and both were obsessed with self-documenting their lives, as if writing it down made it real. Both with the written word launched their own destiny. Do you remember the Playboy philosophy? Like Smith, Hefner challenged the existing order; Joseph with celestial marriage decreed by God, Hugh with the glory and grandeur of rational love as God designed us biologically and spiritually in his magazine. Both men challenged and changed cultural attitudes, and both provided housing for some of the favored concubine. Realized as I consulted my research, I'd been raised in a philosophy that grew out of an area so saturated with evangelizing preachers it was called the burned-over district. Theatrical fire and brimstone notwithstanding, a good tent preacher could no longer make a living. Too damn many of them. It's all Smith knew. How could I leave things like that out?

"That was Smith's school room. Mine was in Sunday school and in the back room of a grocery store listening to stories about the war. His was listening to the Bible thumpers; Methodists, Congregationalists, New Baptists, plus a bunch of new, weird religious movements. Next county had a religion with plural marriages, another with a woman prophet. It was a new country and new religious novelties were popping up right and left.

"Without a sense of direction or of belonging, people need a charismatic leader. It's what the founding fathers couldn't do, give people a sense of self-worth. A constitution that did not dictate behavior easily turns to magic. And with no king to tell them what was what, they were without direction. All they had was what the founding fathers were running from. They fell back on the only thing they knew, religion. It was easy to believe Joseph because he believed it. He later claimed and wrote that until age fourteen he was confused, couldn't accept everything he was hearing. His mind shuffled ideas. People felt better when around him. Bill Clinton charisma. Something happened. Ya know...we get caught up in our lives. In those days most families, if they had no other book, always had a Bible. To learn to read, it's what your mother hands you, teases you along. 'How many *A* letters can you pick out in the first line? For a cookie?' And you show her with fingers. This many. Later, long winter evenings, nothing else to do, you read for a minute, close the Bible, look at your mother, and recite verbatim the Sermon on the Mount. Is your mother impressed? It was she who brought you along, her pride, her joy. It's her praises you trade on. A drug, that praise. Smith read and reread the Bible. Even today's soaps can't compete with the Bible. Love, sex, revenge, murder, rape, torture, abandonment, betrayal, repentance, sacrifice, including the slavery of many wives and concubines. Add testosterone. What else is polygamy if not a form of survival of the fittest? Billions of pushy, bullheaded little spermatozoa with but a single directive, the prime directive, penetrate that one little ol' defenseless egg. Between 1841 and 1844 the guy manages to marry on average one a month. Can you imagine? We're talkin' busy. Some of those ladies had living husbands and children," Matt said, taking a deep breath.

Hamilton interrupted, "Proof?"

"There, in the archives."

Cabby was looking in the rearview mirror more than the road. "I gotta read it. What's the name of your book?"

"The book will not be in print for some time yet," Hamilton said. Turning to Matt, "Why did the Church stop doing it...polygamy?"

"Didn't happen easy. Federal cease and desist order came down in1887 called the Edmunds-Tucker Act. The LDS authorities in 1890 did a dancing act, said they ceased the practice when in fact they went underground. Practiced in secret for another sixteen years."

"Did they?" Hamilton said, leaning toward him.

Matt's hand came up, thumb pointing to his chest. "So where do you think I came from? One historian, Yale guy named Quillan, estimates fifty thousand descendants alive today from the polygamous marriages performed underground between 1890 and1906."

"You can back this up? You have records? Verify all this?" Hamilton said.

"The disc I gave to Perness," Matt said.

"I can't help wondering what your life expectancy is," Hamilton said.

Matt laughed. "Why do you think I put you and Louise in charge and Cate as beneficiary? After I met you I stopped hiding, even started a bank account in Danville for Cate. A safe deposit box holds my will, everything to Cate."

Hamilton frowned. "What in God's name possessed you to apply common sense to Joseph Smith's life?"

"Until I fumbled my way into his flaws and weaknesses, I couldn't connect. After that, there were times I could not keep up." Matt glanced at his watch. "I'm in a bar when it happens. This cocktail waitress with a low blouse comes over, leans forward, and asks what I want to drink. We're talking bridgework. Not monster boobs, but not average either. I wasn't sure what I ordered until she brought it. I forced myself to look at her eyes, but I couldn't, for a minute, tell you what color they were, but I know damn well I could do three thousand words on her cleavage. When your ol' lady has a headache you want her even more, right? Smith never physically forced a woman in his life. I feel good about leaving the record clear on that."

"It's our humanity compels," Hamilton said.

"The book is factual, by and large, but common sense influenced conclusions."

"Did he begat with all of them?"

Sy looked like he was watching a tennis match. Between the traffic and the rearview mirror, his neck was working overtime.

"No way to verify the extent of the sex. There were children though. We justify our actions. The lies we tell ourselves have costs, but we all do it. He was the president of the Church, leader of his people, healthy, strong, and handsome to a fault. The power of words flowed. Testosterone fire pumped through his veins. God said and he made it happen. Hell, if they looked anything like the cleavage in front of me in that bar, I would have given them all my special nine-month pregnancy test and started a whole new religion to boot," Matt said.

"Viva la cleavage," Hamilton said with a wave of his hand.

"In Salt Lake it's called a faith-promoting image," Matt sighed. "Joseph Smith, a one-dimensional hero. A man who never spits or breaks wind. Women Smith married were romanced to be coy about the relationship. It was, after all, God's holy order. Hormonal opiate. The itch to procreate. Mix evolution's drug with sacred symbol. Add to the stolen moment a velvet tongue and what do you have?"

"Celestial sex. Heavenly intrigue. Sensual intensity," Hamilton exclaimed, shaking his head.

Matt had been watching a small sports car top down coming up on his side. Driver, a tasty blonde with furtive eyes, did not miss his gaze. Her short hair danced in the wind.

"A heavenly toss in the hay. Natural bestseller," Hamilton added.

Her eyes danced the way her hair did. The lady knew how to drive a clutch. Obviously having a good day, she shared a little of it. Flashed a quick smile at Matt.

Close to the airport now. Matt could smell burnt airplane fuel. He watched a 747 climbing skyward. There was an urgency in Hamilton's voice. "Where did the Book of Mormon come from?"

"Did you ever read it?"

"No one ever sent it to me looking for an agent."

"Get a copy…skim the book. Reading it, far too tedious. Ask yourself this, how many men took the social order by the throat and shook it? Smith had the brass to write the third testament. Wrote his own Bible. Steel huevos. Started The Eternal Life Truth Company, aka the Mormon Church. I sometimes wonder what Smith would say if he could see his church today," Matt said.

"Meaning?" Hamilton cocked his head toward him again.

"Net worth, for instance."

"How much?"

"Undisclosed. Tax exempt. Ten percent income from maybe half the thirteen million membership every payday."

"What's the going estimate?" Hamilton asked.

The cute blonde in the sports car was back. Matt smiled at her.

"Super conservative estimate, fifty billion, I'm told. No debt to speak of."

"Good Lord. No debt! What do they do with all that money?"

"Investments. All kinds. One that teases my imagination? Check this out… They own a lot of developed real estate, but it's the undeveloped real estate that spikes my curiosity. Large chunks of it in every state in the union." Matt shook his head.

Hamilton broke his gaze. Stared out a window. "Two million to buy your book isn't even petty cash," he said.

"Think we should have countered for more?" Matt said, attempting to be humorous.

"This Joseph Smith. If the favorite fantasy is many wives, what's really going on? Is it phallic worship? At the prime of life testosterone affects everything a man does. What is the most popular fantasy—harem filled with agreeable ladies that cannot get enough of my…?" Hamilton was thinking out loud.

"Priesthood." Matt completed his question for him.

Sy's smile was permanent now. "Like having your own personal whorehouse."

"God's brothel," Matt agreed.

"Good title for a book," Hamilton offered.

"There is one. I heard the author speak once. One of those hyphened last names. Andrea E. Merit something."

Sy was giving the finger to a truck driver.

"What did your wife think of all this, your first wife?" Hamilton asked.

"Outside of men-only meetings, it's seldom mentioned. You wanna get lucky tonight, not really a subject you want to bring up at dinner."

Hamilton shifted in his seat like he was trying to adjust his thinking. "Good Lord. The psychological implications…?"

The cute blonde in the sports car shot ahead.

"People really know so little about Mormonism. Think they do, but mostly they haven't a clue. Did you know that next to Catholicism the Mormon Church is the largest sect in ten states?"

"I can't believe that," Hamilton said, shaking his head. "How about your mother?"

"Now there's a woman. In the morning before she takes her

Prozac, I'm her womb's betrayal. Wait an hour after it hits and I'm her wonderful Matthew."

"My sister married a Mormon. Takes a turquoise and white capsule every day," Sy said.

"Ever curious about it?" Matt asked.

"Should I be?"

"Back when—college days—I ask a friend who is now a professor at BYU."

"The church school?" Hamilton interrupted.

"Brigham Young University, Provo, Utah," Sy said.

Hamilton's chin elevated itself a full inch. "Well of course it would be, wouldn't it? Do you mind?"

"You need to get a life, man," Sy said, shaking his head.

"Question!" Matt threw out. "Which state leads the nation in prescription antidepressants?"

It took Hamilton a moment to follow Matt's drift. "I'm sorry?"

"Almost two to one. Mostly women being treated for depression. Stat is from a study by the pharmacy department, University of Utah."

No one spoke for a moment. A scowl was working its way across Sy's face.

"Do you think they will still try and stop publication?" Hamilton said.

"They've gone to a lot of trouble already."

"I have heard of a Mormon mafia," Hamilton said.

Matt shifted uneasily. "I don't think so. I don't know."

"The Jesuits of LDS business. My office was robbed last night. Would Cate be in danger?"

Matt swallowed. "Wanted an answer to that question all day. Was going to stay at her mother's last night. I'm sure I've kissed my hard drive good-bye."

"How could they know about me?"

"If you could wrap your head around the mind set, you wouldn't need to ask. First loyalty; not family, not employer, not even self. First loyalty? The Church. An employee working for the publisher. Pockets of us everywhere, Hamilton. You think it's an obscure little church, think again. More Mormons in the U.S. than either Presbyterians or Episcopalians."

Sy was bringing the cab to a stop at the ramp in front of check-in. As Matt extended a hundred, Sy put the flat of his hand up.

"You're free, pal. He pays. Gonna read your book too. Gonna send a copy to everyone I know. Hey. What's your name?" Sy said, extending his hand.

"Matt Alcott."

Sy and Matt shook hands, and Matt turned back to Hamilton.

"I don't mean to frighten you, Hamilton, but if you got a little this morning it's in a memo to Salt Lake by now. An office door key is nothing to my people. This is the third time they've done it to me."

"Get another agent," Hamilton said in jest.

"Convert Mormon. You get your wish."

There was a pause.

"How many wives can I have?"

Chapter 27

NEW YORK TO SALT LAKE

The weather outside United flight 2167 was a clear 59 degrees. Inside it was the equivalent of a dense, high-pressure weather front. Felt like they loaded the plane using a garbage compactor. Sardines have more room.

Matt detested shoulder-to-shoulder travel. Only person he wanted that close was Cate. He didn't fly well anyway. Every breath he took, someone else had run it through their lungs first. Sober, Matt was no passenger. Nothing to do but try to relax. There, he said it, "try," the rocking-horse word that guaranteed a state of anxiety.

Pushed himself to review what had happened in the past twelve hours. Contract was signed. Money was being transferred. Cate would be taken care of. It was hard not to think about her. He had no desire to have a bunch of perfect strangers watch him wipe tears from his eyes. Couldn't help himself. Knew if she was to be safe, he had to break the connection, maybe for a long time. For her sake. After…when the book was on the shelves. Maybe then. Cate's safety…above all else.

The lady sitting next to Matt was starting to act funny. A small packet of tissues presented themselves in front of him. He followed the arm to a pleasant smile on a stewardess.

"This may help, sir. Can I get you something to drink?"

Hell's revenge if he got off the plane drunk.

"Coffee."

Louise, the lady with impeccable taste, was firmly established to make decisions for him, if it became necessary. Matt would call, work through her. He trusted her and he knew Hamilton listened to her.

Beating himself up with expectations. If things got dicey in Salt Lake there was Park City. Since 1881, the naughty, prodigal, almost-suburb of Salt Lake City would be where he would migrate. Drunk in Park City more than once. When you can no longer tolerate the intolerant, you move thirty minutes east into an old mining town in one of the upper valleys of the Wasatch Range, next door to Paul Newman's buddy, Butch Cassidy.

The engine noise droned. Flight was like a ship on a sea, endless, eternal, going backward in time toward a yesterday of shame and betrayal.

Had called little brother from his editor's office. Left a message. Coming into town. Sober. See ya when I get there. Until his book hit the shelves, Paul would be civil. After, who knows, and besides, what better place to hide than in the lion's den?

Following a visit with little brother he would call his old high school buddy Rodney Overton. Rod had picked up a PhD in psychology at Berkeley and was now clinical director of the largest drug and alcohol rehab facility in Salt Lake. Try that on for coincidence. Matt had Rod's business card in his wallet. Three years plus without a drink. Eager to surprise him.

It was Cate's voice he wanted to hear. Impossible, considering. Maybe one quick phone call at his brother's office. Wished he were there to see her face when the bank called to apprise her of the deposit in their account. Thinking of her kicked his heart up a notch, fear with it. *What will happen now that he turned down the offer? Where is the danger? Nuts. I'm being paranoid.*

Matt was desperate to hold her. *Give my left gonad to feel her in my arms.* Almost said it aloud. Closed his eyes, the khaki-green baggy army pants she sometimes wore, the frayed army hat she positioned a dozen different ways. He'd pay a king's ransom to smell her hair, listen to the music of her voice. Somehow he'd known this day was coming. Loneliness moved through him like refrigerated blood.

What right do I have to anyone, let alone her? Ultimately I destroy, and I destroy best those I love most. Amazing how my mind poisons itself the closer I get to the city of saints.

"Sir, sir. Please fasten your seat belt. We are beginning our descent into Salt Lake City Airport."

Matt walked out of the plane feeling like he'd run all the way. He counted three bookstores in the airport alone. As he worked his way through the tarmac he wondered what it would be like to see his book on display. What layout and color? Would there be a small picture of him on the inside rear flap? Would anyone recognize him? Would crowds descend on him, chanting, "Go home, apostate-traitor"? Not a thought he cared for at the moment.

He couldn't help thinking that he liked the feeling of anonymity. A freedom to it, like being invisible.

As he walked toward a cab he noted the smog. Had forgotten this part of Salt Lake. The mountains acted like a dam. Smog could layer up like floating pancakes over the city until your eyes watered.

Chapter 28

SALT LAKE CITY

Paul's building smelled of paint drying. Tenth floor, he walked into the reception area. Paul's door was closed. A young typist in a dark green skirt with a moss green and white blouse was guarding the gate. She might have been his niece, except she didn't recognize him. He'd never realized that before. The young girls in Utah all looked alike.

"Where's dummy?" Matt asked.

He was pointing to his brother's office and hoping that Paul would hear. It took her five whole seconds to figure out who dummy was.

"Brother Alcott is…" her voice went up. "Do you have an appointment?"

Obviously, she existed in a bright, tight little bubble of decency, dignity, and proper etiquette. Obviously, she was offended that anyone would call her wonderful boss anything but handsome, thoughtful, kind, and intelligent. Matt asked her for a piece of scratch paper. She let him know that he, of all people, was not her boss.

He hadn't had coffee in over three hours. He was in a city he didn't like. Without thinking twice, he took a right, opened Paul's office door, walked over, and sat in the chair behind his desk. Typist followed, flushed with outrage. The yellow pad in front of Matt was full of Paul's doodling. He tore it off, picked up a pencil, and printed in large strokes a quick note for little brother.

At Weller s Book Store. In need of bed. Couple nights. Much to tell. Back one hour.

"Leave this right here. He'll want to see it the minute he arrives. Needs to be warned."

She snatched up the yellow pad. Her victory.

"Who shall I say wrote it?" the secretary said.

So it was thrust and parry and Matt still hadn't had his coffee. He picked up the pencil again, extended his hand for the legal pad, and waited. Reluctantly she handed it over. He wrote, for her benefit.

Black sheep, Alcott Clan.

Underlined it with a broad stroke, and looked directly at her.

"Be sure dimwit sees it."

He left her standing in Paul's office trying to figure out who dimwit was.

Matt had thought to call Cate, but thought better of it until Paul was in the office.

Matt counted multiple coffee shops as he walked.

"I must have landed at the wrong airport," he mumbled to himself.

Coffee brewskis in Salt Lake City storefronts? *What's this world coming to?* He stopped in one, picked up a latte.

Many an hour he'd spent rummaging through Weller's stacks of books.

There was a new trolley system, as quaint and green as it was utilitarian, thanks to Brigham Young, who had insisted on wide streets. All had taken place for the winter Olympics a few years before.

Smell was familiar. Nothing had changed in Weller's Book Store. Knew right where to go to find it. Copy of James Coates' *In Mormon Circles*. Coates had been a journalist in the region of the Rocky Mountains for years. Made him the perfect author for Mormon subjects. Insightful, in-depth, well researched, no ax to grind, and did not belabor the work with over-big, important-sounding words to show how intellectual he was.

Matt approached a middle-aged lady with perfect hair who had been working there for years. She thought she knew him and was about to speak until she saw the title of the book. The temperature in the store dropped ten degrees. *In Mormon Circles* was not a book she would stock if it were her store. In her opinion it told too many lies about her church. Matt refused the bag she was about to put it in and left.

He turned into an alley. It was a shortcut back to little brother's office. He opened the book as he walked. Had already read it, but had misplaced his copy and he wanted to review one chapter. A third of the way into the alley a gray sedan was parked at a skewed angle, making it difficult to pass. There was a large man standing next to it.

"Excuse me," he said.

The big guy didn't budge. Still leafing through pages, Matt moved to go around. There was a tug at his shoulder. A shadow moved over him.

Paul Alcott, attorney at law, returned from sitting in on an affidavit being conducted in another attorney's office. A man he was defending.

"Did my brother show up?" he asked, heading in the direction of his office.

"A very rude man came in. There is a message on your desk," his secretary said, following and still defending herself from the uncouth man's visit. "He said we are uncivilized."

Paul looked at her, waiting…

She caught herself. "Oh. Because we don't have coffee."

"That's him."

"He said he would be right back," the young secretary added.

"Don't count on it."

"What?"

"If you're looking for him, you won't find him. If you want him to go away, don't turn around."

The look on her face...?

"My brother is a drunk," he added.

"Oh!" she said, horror blushing through her.

Chapter 29

SALT LAKE CITY

Not sure, but it was cold and dark. Took Matt hours, days, to figure out that he might be inside, not out. Hard to hold his thoughts. Sometimes coherent. Teeth chattering cold, bones of ice, he begged for the sting he had come to know was the needle of oblivion.

"Come back, please," he heard his own words echo.

Hard to know what is going on when you have nothing to hang your thoughts on. Vague images floated on an ocean of random, amorphous wreckage. Flotsam dreams.

Fuzzy wuzzy was a bear, there's the rub, fuzzy wuzzy, cheap aftershave, turn on the lights, thank you. No arm by God. No arms by God. Goddamn cold. Why is it dark?

Hours, a day later, did I just say that?

Clothes, what's with the clothes, feet somewhere, cold proves it, freezing, arms? How can I scratch my nose? Get away, aftershave, after what cheap aftershave, boar's breath, lousy digestion. Tickles. Scratch my ear, goddamn it. Fetid breath, sour, quit tickling my ear. Paper is it? The needle, asshole. Where's the fucking needle, thank you?

Some shadowed place.

Matt awoke to the screeching complaint of old hinges and a beam of searing bright light.

"I serve at the behest of God and you are a thorn in His side," a voice, deep in a dream, said.

"Who, thorns, vomit dreams, make sense for God's sake. Warm water? Piss alert! At least it's warm, thank you. Straight shots vodka, thank you. Toast the train, vomit the silence, quit it out, burns, puking proves it. I know you're there. Hey, hey, who fuck is it? Remember. Wrong people do the dying."

The click. Sounded like?

"Hey. Stop that shit. You cutting? Is that a knife? I said stop it."

"Vengeance is mine, sayeth the Lord," the voice said, echo following.

"Hurry. Pain says hurry. The needle, thank you, whale piss, boar's breath," Matt said, days running into weeks.

"I am God's avenging angel and you are a thorn in His side," again the voice.

"Run, Matt. Run," Matt called out in the darkness.

A flashlight rolled across the floor, stopped at a wall. A zipper announced its purpose.

"Recluse can smell, recluse knows. Hey, cut it out. Who's pissing? Jesus is pissing on me. Wrong people do the pissing."

In and out. Five minutes later or was it a week? Matt swam up toward the light.

"Hey, shit breath, where are you? I could use a little help here. Perverse prick, murderer, traitor, murderer of churches. Someone will hang for this, thank you, heartaches, son. Jesus pack a toothbrush," he said a minute ago, a lost minute.

"I am the son of thunder and you are a thorn in His side," the deep voice said.

The echo. The tunnel. Light fading. The world moved. Matt's head flopped.

"What are these? Arms. One. Two. One, two. Ouch. Am I moving?"

"Make up your mind...why is the street pushing my face, stand up, thank you, dummy, clothes, ouch. Streets go somewhere, don't they!" Matt heard his voice without an echo. "Cold. Why am I naked?"

Cobblestones made of ice. Walk, fool. You're free. Whoa. Easy. Steady there, fella. Where did you get them legs? My God, I have legs!

Hold the street out of your face with your arms. Crawl. That works. But where? Where to go? Don't I have to be from somewhere? Oh, God that hurts. Light hurts. Focusing fun in an alley. Smells dark like mushroom.

"Mushrooms grow on pizzas."

An alley in what valley? I can smell it. Pizza in an alley.

"Jesus, I'd kill for a pizza."

Alleys go somewhere. What's a pizza joint doing in my alley?

Matt stood, but not without great effort. He blinked. It was getting colder.

"What city is this?"

Amazing no matter in what city you find yourself, there are pizza joints and yellow cabs. "Steady legs. Push with the thumb, pull the shiny chrome thing. Handle works. Pull."

To his amazement a cab opened its mouth.

"Big dog."

Matt's self-talk, pushing through the fog of mind.

"Here doggy, doggy. Out you go."

He fell into the cab.

"Good doggy," Matt slurred.

Matt saw a woman looking at him, mouth open.

"Yellow cab. Nice yellow cab, take me to Twelve Step House," Matt said, patting the seat.

A guy appeared in the front seat.

"You need some clothes on, fella. I can't fare you without clothes."

Matt scrambled through the pants he was carrying.

"Hey, that's our cab. Where's my dog?" someone said.

"Twelve Step House," Matt repeated, "Here's money."

Matt threw a handful of money into the front seat, a fifty, some twenties. The light was torture on his eyes.

"My God, he doesn't have any clothes on," someone said.

Matt looked around. Someone was laughing.

The cabby took one look at the money.

"I'll be right back," he said to the waiting people. "Five minutes tops."

"Find my old buddy, Rod," Matt said.

Bump, bump through the night. "Jitter joint. Take me to the jitter joint."

Random thoughts came and went.

"Streets are for sleeping. Drunks are for laughs. Something hard to sleep on. God, I'm getting tired of hard things."

Chapter 30

TWELVE STEP HOUSE
SALT LAKE CITY

The day over, several patients at Twelve Step House were hanging out in the recreation room. Some were playing cribbage, others spinning grandiose yarns about the primo drugs they had used before treatment. The screeching of rubber on pavement caused everyone to stop what they were doing.

"What the hell?" Yoyo said, twisting in his chair to look.

Pearl had been sitting between Connie's legs getting her hair brushed. She ran to a window and cupped her hands around her eyes to cut down the glare.

"Taxi. Dumped somethin' in the street," she said.

"People throw kittens in plastic bags in the street," Connie said.

Yoyo, gaunt and stringy, pushed in between Connie and Pearl.

"S'not a cat," Yoyo said.

"I think it's a man," Pearl said, pushing back.

Yoyo quit the window, went to the front door, and opened it. Several patients scrambled after him to watch a taxi squeal out, speed away.

"Oh my God. He's bare assed as a baby," Yoyo exclaimed.

A car swerved to avoid hitting a naked man lying in the middle of the street. Above the trees in the distance, you could see the brightly lit statue of the Angel Moroni atop the Salt Lake City Temple.

The windows and front entry facing the street filled up with patients crowding to see the strange picture in front of Twelve Step House. Tiny Tim, a six-foot-two male attendant with the athletic frame of a weightlifter, pushed his way through the crowd and bounded into the street. He circled, carefully scrutinizing the body. What he was looking at, a nude man dumped by a taxi in the middle of two lanes of asphalt, did not make a lot of sense. He waved a car to go around.

"Yoyo,"Tiny shouted.

Yoyo was standing with other patients in the entry.

"Yeah? What?"

"There's a stretcher in the back room. Get it."

A biker on a Harley came to a stop.

"Tiny, is that you?" the biker said, flipping his visor up.

"Did you just pass a taxi?"

"Yeah, stompin' on it," Gabe, the biker said.

"You didn't get a cab number by any chance?"

"Sure. I memorize cab numbers for a hobby. This the way you kick people out of treatment?" Gabe said, leaning on the handlebars of his Harley.

"Can you believe a taxi dumped him like this?"

"You want some help, get him inside before his balls freeze?" Gabe offered.

"I got it covered. I'll catch you later."

"Can't wait to tell Bart how you run this place."

He rotated the throttle forward.

Yoyo returned with an aluminum and canvas litter and placed it at his feet in the doorway.

"I got it."

Tiny gestured to bring it.

Yoyo didn't move.

"I don't need it over there."

"You told me not never to go past the goddamn door,"Yoyo said.

Yoyo folded his arms. It was a triumphant gesture he was delighted with himself to be able to make, as though he had just won an argument.

Tiny Tim's shoulders dropped. He spoke deliberately. "You wanna see me break something?"

Yoyo scurried into the street with the litter.

"What happened to no exceptions? Probably not an exhibitionist, huh."

Yoyo squatted, squinted, and repelled away from the body. "Jesus! He's black and blue all over."

"Tell the nurse to call Dr. Overton," Tiny said.

Yoyo's eyes were as big as walnuts.

"My God. He smells like an outhouse in a brewery. Is he dead?"

"Go, I said!"

Yoyo dashed off, flailing his arms in the air.

"Someone beat the shit out of that poor fucker. Get the nurse. Get the goddamn nurse."

"No ID, but I found one of your cards in his pants. Clothes were scattered all over the street," Tiny Tim said.

Matt could hear, tried to open his eyes. The light was killing. He loved the peace the voices kept cutting into. A man was bending over him with a stethoscope. Rod's face, but more mature and with a white beard. Doctor Rodney Overton was talking to the nurse, urgent, demanding. Matt sensed he was in trouble.

"CBC, electrolytes, chem seven," Doc Overton said.

The nurse placed a blood drawing kit on a stainless-steel tray.

"Pneumonia," Rod announced. "I can smell the alcohol, but what are these lacerations on his buttocks? Needle marks everywhere. I want to start him on a broad spectrum antibiotic immediately." He turned to Tiny.

"Run his blood work over to St. Joseph's lab, stat. Be sure they fax the results the minute they have them."

"Librium for now?" the nurse asked.

"Can't. Toxic liability at this stage. We have to find out how much alcohol is in his system first. I want a blood pressure q/15 until I say otherwise."

Matt's eyes had closed again and he couldn't get them to open, but he could hear the voice of his old high school buddy. They had been inseparable during their junior and senior years. Finally forced his eyes open, Seeing Rod's face delivered a jolt of adrenaline. For a moment he was alert.

"Rod you gotta teach me to drink, man."

People were crowded in the doorway; some laughed. Matt thought to laugh with them, but nothing came out. He did manage to get an arm in the air, a half wave in it.

Yoyo was standing in the doorway.

"He smells worse than day-old shit."

SALT LAKE CITY
FOUR YEARS BEFORE

Matt blinked, looked at his watch. He'd been numb, staring at the debris about him for some time. After the shock eased he thought, *My life is comedy for the hopelessly depressed.* There was a sense of emptiness, a cold ambience bone deep and disconnected. He hadn't felt warmth from anyone for a long time. He thought it was emotional exhaustion or maybe that was the same thing, but if taking the next breath had required anything beyond an automatic response, it never would have happened.

Twenty-seven years old. Rent due. He didn't have a pot to do anything with let alone piss in. Everything he owned except his suitcases had been butchered. In a desperate moment he had thought of donating his Mark Twain collection to the University of Utah library. He reminded himself, that's what people do who are getting ready to off themselves. He didn't have a friend to talk to, not in this city. There was an old high school buddy, Rod Overton, but Rod was at Berkeley working on his doctorate in psych. Should leave him a note. Here, shove this up your PhD. There is a sense to it, a redeeming value to suicide. You don't shrug it off lightly. Where and how? Poison? Drug overdose? Shotgun?

Shotgun. Where? Not inside. No. A free get-out-of-jail card on some deserted road. The fact that it should have been a frightening thought did rattle him some. Searching for an alternative, Matt came up blank. He'd never felt so worthless. There were no words that he knew to take comfort in.

Traitor! Add coward to traitor. It was then, with his head in his hands, that he thought of it. Strange thought. One he had never had before. Alcohol.

SALT LAKE CITY
TWELVE STEP HOUSE

Matt came to again, reached, managed to grab Rod's shirt. Pulled hard.

"There are no innocent smells," he said, looking into the repulsive grimace Rod's face had formed.

The rest was gibberish.

Yoyo laughed so hard he wet himself. Hurried off to change clothes.

Chapter 31

FOUR YEARS BEFORE

Twenty-seven years on planet earth and Matt had never been to a party where alcoholic beverages were served. He knew what people did in the movies when they were desperate. They went to a bar and ordered...what? He'd never been in a bar. He'd never ordered a drink. Utah had state-owned liquor stores that were the sole and only source of alcoholic beverages. He had never been in one. He didn't care about the movies, but if alcohol changed things, well, what else was there to say. He knew where there was a liquor store.

For the first time in his life he was contemplating an alcoholic beverage. He didn't have a clue as to kind, type, taste. This would require some research.

He addressed the problem as he drove. It was a redbrick building with a glass storefront. Matt parked around the corner, just in case. Moved quickly. Didn't want to be seen.

He grabbed his backpack and entered the building. Didn't recognize the clerk behind the counter, thank God. She was thin, weathered, maybe five foot two. Her graying, brown hair was stacked on top. She looked used up, old before her time. Couldn't help thinking she knew her product from experience.

Matt picked out a label. Didn't know to look at the bottom of the bottle for its price, only that it was wine and perhaps that was better than a distilled product.

He set the bottle on the counter. Embarrassed. He was sure she could tell he didn't have a clue what he was doing.

"Sixty-four dollars," she said, reaching for a long, narrow sack.

At least he was able to feel chagrin. Something in him still cared how stupid he looked.

"No, please. That's...the wrong..."

He swallowed, screened the shelves.

"Too many choices. Is it for dinner tonight?" the clerk offered.

He nodded, followed her compassionate lead.

"Fish or red meat?" she said.

Think fast, idiot.

"Roast. Pot roast...?" His voice went up, too high.

"Let me recommend something," she said.

Bless her beautiful, discerning heart, he thought. When he left the store he remembered a wise lady who had probably been thrown up against a hard life.

In the morning he felt like he was coming down with the flu, but within an hour his immune system had kicked in and he felt pretty good, and that's when he realized a great release had taken place and he didn't feel pretty good, he felt terrific...damn terrific. Nothing to blame it on, but a bottle of red wine grown in the region of Burgundy, France, by God revelation.

Chapter 32

TWELVE STEP HOUSE
SALT LAKE CITY

"B-12. Start hydration," a man's voice said. "After the first bag put him in the shower. These lacerations are infected. Clean the abrasions also..." He was pointing to Matt's ankles and wrists.

"...after you get the blood work started. Looks like straps or rope held him down. I want to look him over again before you put our scrubs on him. What's this...more needle tracks. I'd like to know where he's been."

"Once dead always dead," Matt said, after the shower. "Shoot me up. Who am I to argue?" he repeated at random, through the night, between dreams.

Chapter 33

SALT LAKE CITY
THE CLUB

"It's good to see you again, President Burgess," the driver said, holding the limousine door.

Ezra Burgess stepped into the limo. It was a clear, sunny Saturday morning. He was driven, from his home overlooking the Great Salt Lake Basin, to The Club downtown.

Burgess had ridden in his share of limos. This one impressed him with its versatility. It could accommodate half a dozen men, two wheelchairs, and a gurney. Made sense, considering who its owners were. A BYU football game was in progress on both drop-down screens, one at the rear facing forward, the other in front facing back. Both were retractable into the roof.

"Driver?"

"Yes?"

"Eliminate the television."

"Would you prefer music, sir?"

"No."

Fifteen minutes later they pulled into the underground parking of a building adjacent to The Club. At the lowest level of that parking area, they pulled to a stop in front of a metal gate, which retracted into a wall, another underground parking area beyond. The driver tapped a button above his head. A pair of freight elevator doors whispered rapidly apart. The limo eased into the elevator like a stiletto into its sheath.

Six stories above in a conference room without a conference table, Brother Smyth picked up a telephone that was not ringing.

"Yes. Good," he said.

He hung up and with his cane tapped the arm of the chair next to him. Brother Angus opened his eyes.

"He's here," Brother Smyth said.

Angus rose and left the room.

At its fourth-floor destination, a pair of elevator doors slid open to reveal a limousine filling its space. Burgess exited the limo directly into the lush interior of The Club, the scent of evergreens greeting him.

"Better than dealing with downtown parking," Angus said, reaching out to shake his hand.

Down a well-illuminated hall Burgess detected a heavy medicinal smell. It reminded him of his wife's last days in the David O. McKay hospital in Ogden. The two men entered the conference room where Brother Smyth, looking all of his eighty years, remained partially reclined.

Six club chairs, upholstered in an aqua green, deep pile fabric, formed a circle in the room. Each chair had a telephone built into one of its arms. There was a football game on a large plasma television screen Smyth had been watching. He pivoted his chair one hundred and eighty degrees to greet President Burgess.

"That University represents Utah well."

He depressed a button in the arm of the chair and the television screen went blank.

"Good to see you, Burgess. How's this alliance thing going?"

Burgess made his report to the two men. It was brief and to the point. He concluded on a lighter note. "I rather doubt said party will stay in Utah."

"You feel he will do the right thing then?" Smyth observed.

"He has a much sweeter disposition and he knows his life depends on it," Burgess said.

Angus glanced at Brother Smyth. "He is not in custody at this time?"

"I saw no reason to hold him once he understood his responsibilities."

"And he had no visible contact with you over this two-week period?"

There was a knock at the door. It opened without hesitation. A man with a crew cut wearing a short white laboratory jacket lowered a medicinal tray in front of Smyth. He upended a tiny plastic cup holding several medications, sipped from a glass that looked like orange juice, and nodded his thanks to the attendant, who then left the room as unceremoniously as he had entered. The three men sat in silence until the door latch made a distinct click.

"Visible contact? None," Burgess answered.

"I've heard the name before. Can't place it," Smyth wondered.

"His father, bishop of the Bountiful Ward," Angus said.

"Oh, yes. I've met Bishop Alcott. An asset to the Church," Smyth said.

"Five years ago his son was working in the archives. He was in the Cottonwood Stake, making me his then spiritual leader. I brought to the attention of a member of the Quorum of the twelve, with whom I lunch on occasion, that he was removing documents from the archives. He directed me to the presiding bishop's office. They saw to his prompt termination."

"What happened in the interim?" Brother Smyth asked.

"Years ago, I was asked by Brother Benson to be a member of the board of the SMC."

"Strengthening the Membership Committee, yes," Brother Angus confirmed.

"That committee can find and monitor anyone. We've had trouble with historians before. I kept tabs on him for about a year, when he abruptly dropped out of sight. I reviewed his file from time to time and put out feelers. It was like he ceased to exist. Didn't file taxes, didn't renew his license tags or his license. Credit cards went unused. Until Brother Tanner called me from Tanner and Welsely law firm, I assumed something had happened to him."

"How did you discover his earlier behavior?"

"That he was removing documents from Cottonwood Canyon?"

Angus and Smyth both nodded. Burgess uncrossed his legs and took a deep breath. "He was married to my daughter."

The tips of Brother Angus' hands came together at his jaw as he digested this information.

"Not a union I encouraged or was proud of. Carol is an only child. I readily acknowledge I have spoiled her."

"I think we can all plead guilty to that one. The children of money often have a difficult time of it," Smyth said.

"Temple divorce?" Angus asked.

"Immediately," Burgess said.

Without excusing himself, Smyth labored his way to a standing position on unsteady legs. Cane in hand, he hobbled out of the room. When he did not immediately return, Burgess fought the impulse to think he had said something amiss.

This was not a typical day for President Burgess. Feeling uneasy was not a familiar experience, but not today. Today he was seated in an exclusive club where an elite gathering of wealth huddled to conduct a unique business common and personal to each to maintain and preserve the welfare of the true Church. Because they all had it, money meant nothing in the usual sense. The membership was made up of fifty of the wealthiest men in the thirteen-million-member Church.

Brother Angus made no move to leave. "Let's see what the score is."

He tapped a small panel on the arm of his chair, which opened. Under were several dials. He touched one and the giant screen lit up.

Burgess attempted to focus on the game when the phone at Brother Angus's elbow vibrated.

"Yes. Very good."

He hung up, nodded, and rose from the chair.

"Brother Smyth left rather suddenly. Was there a problem?" Burgess said.

"No. You had no way of knowing he would refuse the two million. That was beyond your control. When you found out, you acted immediately.

Excellent work. Brother Smyth only thought it prudent to report these new events to the committee. He knew they would want to know what further steps you took to insure the threat of negative publicity was behind us. He had a therapy appointment after in the pool downstairs. We'll be in touch."

Angus reached to shake Burgess' hand when an afterthought prompted a question. "You are keeping track of this man, this Alcott?"

"Absolutely."

"Do you know where his church records are?" Angus asked.

"I've convened a Bishop's Court. His excommunication is forthcoming, if that's what you are referring to."

Brother Angus leaned closer to President Burgess. "I was thinking along the lines of something a little more definitive…something that might guarantee his reunion with his family in the next estate."

Burgess paused for a moment, almost said the phrase out loud, *blood atonement*, but caught himself.

"That would be up to the committee," he said.

"And so it would, and so it would. Excommunication will have to do…for now."

In the limousine, Burgess sat reviewing the last hour. He hadn't talked to Farley for some time. Hadn't seen him in church. No phone number. Was beginning to think he may have erred in hiring him. Rain had been forecast by evening. As they drove, dark clouds were forming west over the Great Salt Lake.

He reflected on the fact that Brother Angus considered Matthew's soul yet salvageable. If publication did manage to take place, one Matthew Alcott would have earned himself a place among the most damned of all men. He would become what Joseph Smith called a son of perdition, a man beyond redemption. Burgess wondered if he had, indeed, been too lenient when Matt moved to Las Vegas. None of this would have occurred if he had taken care of business the first time.

Chapter 34

SALT LAKE CITY
TWELVE STEP HOUSE

Matt blinked. Everything was black. Figured it must be night. When heavy in withdrawals, he saw Star War's people playing in a band, not snakes or spiders like most drunks. They would point and laugh.

Two black eyes looked at him. Matt moved his head, reasoned that he must be looking into the face of an animal, black, purring, and sitting on his chest. The thought crossed his mind; man looks at cat, looking at man, looking at cat. He moved his head to change the view and found himself staring directly into the bearded face of his once friend and cohort in advanced adolescent mischief, Doctor Rodney Overton, add ten years, twenty pounds, and a PhD in shrinkology. Many a skirt had they terrorized that last year of high school.

Rod was sitting in a chair next to his bed. He leaned forward and picked up the black cat.

"Yoyo, take Relapse," Dr. Rod Overton said.

Matt watched him undoing hand restraints that had been placed on his wrists.

"Can you hear me, Matthew?" Rod asked.

"You had me t…t…tied down?"

"It's been, what, ten years?"

"You had me tied down," Matt repeated.

"Do you know me?"

"Son of a bitch. You have any idea h…h…how tired I am of b… being tied down?" Matt asked.

"What's happened to you?" Rod said.

It caused him to stop ranting and consider the question itself. Matt tried to collect himself. He was ice cold and shaking like a dog shitting razor blades. One eye still swollen shut.

"Don't ask me. I came to you," Matt stammered.

He couldn't hold anything. His hand shook too much.

"I'll give you Thorazine for a couple days if you want it," Rod said.

"Thanks, but I've been chemically lobotomized long enough. I feel like...what's the word...amnesia? Something's nagging at me and I can't find it. I prefer to shake."

A few of the patients helped tease food down Matt's throat. The nurse kept a close watch.

"You need to shave," she said after a week on the detoxification wing.

She was a retired nurse Dr. Overton pressed into part-time service at Twelve Step House. He'd worked with her in the past and knew he could rely on her. Stocky and five foot three she commanded respect from patients and staff.

Matt's vision had cleared some; he was focusing better.

"I'll shave if you'll marry me," he said to the nurse.

"I've seen you naked, thanks anyway."

"I can see self-esteem is not going to be problem around here."

She almost smiled. "Welcome back. Something you might want to know...Dr. Overton spared nothing to keep you alive. You worth it?"

"Tough question. I got a better one."

The nurse paused at the door, looked back.

"What the hell happened to me?"

"Sit here, by me." Yoyo said. "I'm the one carried your naked, stinky ass in here."

There were six wooden picnic tables crammed into a room that could comfortably accommodate four. Each was covered with a checkered oil tablecloth, some red and white, some blue and white, all frayed and time worn. Matt had to shuffle sideways to where he was to sit, Yoyo directing traffic.

"I'm your treatment buddy," Yoyo informed him.

"What's a treatment buddy?"

Counselor's assistant, Tiny Tim, shoved a tray of something cheese-smelling in front of Matt. A mound of orange gruel spread as Matt watched. It was the least appetizing food he could remember seeing. There was a small carton of milk, a whole-wheat roll, and a sprig of something green.

Yoyo knew what he was thinking, smiled, and announced its nutritional classification. "Macaroni and cheese. Get past the color, ain't bad."

Theo at the next table was watching and further announced its nutritional classification. "You'll love it. Something a Montana cow did after ingesting too much food coloring." Then added, "Someone don't like you, man. What'd you do, screw the governor's wife?"

"Had us freaked out, man," Yoyo said.

"Taxi driver gave you up cold, man. Dumped you dead in front of Twelve Step House," Tiny said.

"Not even an Oklahoma suitcase." Yoyo grinned.

"Oklahoma what?" Matt asked.

"Plastic bag, man. You were funny as hell. Kept saying, Morphine Matthew to the rescue. No shit. Laughed my ass off."

"Frosted my chips, man. Like to teach that cabby some manners," Tiny said, before adding, "Eat. You have to eat."

Matt reached for the small carton of milk. Trembling too much, he put it down. Pushed the tray away. Mother hen, Yoyo, opened it for him.

"I couldn't open it either when I was in detox. Here's the way it works. I'll hold the milk. You put your hands on mine, and we rotate the milk for a small sip."

Yoyo's grin showed teeth on one side only.

"What's wrong with a straw?" Matt asked.

"The vegetable's afraid we'd use 'em for other things,"Theo explained.

"Can't eat," Matt announced.

"From the blood work, Doc said you're starving to death. Opiate derivatives and ethyl alcohol. Doc says to see you take your vitamins and eat. Don't mess with me on this. Doc's word is law,"Tiny said with an air of righteous certainty.

Timothy O'Malley. Six foot two and had trouble getting shirts to accommodate his shoulders. Once a cop and a drunk, he earned his way to this job the usual way, the hard way, deferred prosecution, two years during which he became absolutely devoted to Dr. Overton.

Tiny was one of those recovering types that learned by fixed method a certain discipline. "Keep it simple," he said with the same absolute certainty.

Matt pictured him, a Hog Hogan counselor telling some poor little hungover, piss-your-pants wino how it works, and started to laugh. Not wishing to offend Tiny at the comic image in his head, Matt switched to sarcasm.

"In other words, do what you're told without question," Matt said.

"Good. You learn fast,"Tiny agreed.

Shaky, but finally out of detox. Matt was in the day room trying to concentrate on cribbage. Theo, for Theotis, older black guy, shaved clean from his T-shirt in front to his T-shirt in back, was challenging Matt.

Tiny Tim had taken on the characteristics of a shadow. Followed Matt everywhere.

"I sure could use a drink. When's that go away?" Matt said.

"Like makin' love to a gorilla, man. Ain't over till the gorilla's done."

"We could call a cab. Be in a liquor store before they know we're gone."

"How'd you plan to get past that?" Theo asked, nodding in the direction of Tiny.

Tiny gave Matt one of those squared-off, Hollywood movie, tough-guy looks with steel in it when Doctor Overton walked into the room.

"Rod, old buddy, I would like to lodge a complaint. Why does this over reactive ex-cop follow me into the pisser? Is he strange?" Matt asked.

"I thought it prudent," Rod said.

"That's an explanation?"

Rod paid no attention to what Matt said. He walked over to see who was winning and put one hand on Matt's shoulder.

"I'm going to do you a favor and save you from yourself. Theotis takes no prisoners at this game." Looking to Tiny he said, "Let's say two o'clock, my office?"

"Hold up." Matt put his cards down. "You talking shrink stuff? The couch? Are you not happy torturing my ass into some state of sobriety? Do you know how bad I need a drink? You honestly think you're going to shrink my ass as well?"

Yoyo grinned. For him this was turning out to be a wonderful day at Twelve Step House.

"Excuse me, but not in your lifetime. Shrinks are for sickos," Matt continued.

Tiny offered a lopsided smile. "Fatally hip and terminally cool. We'll cure him of that, sir."

"It's good to see you're feeling better. Two o clock. My office," Rod said.

"I need a drink, not a shrink."

SALT LAKE CITY
LATER THAT EVENING

Matt pushed the all-glass door open. It was late, seven p.m.-ish. Tall, slim, immaculately dressed, Paul's secretary was putting on her coat.

Matt wondered if little brother had slipped the wood to her. She was too proper for Matt, but still one sharp-looking lady. Matt pointed to Paul's office, said his name, and turned in that direction. Caught her off guard. He guessed her brain had already gone home because she didn't react, and before she could, he was in. Little brother had his briefcase in one hand and was about to leave. The minute Matt saw his face, the anger ignited and welled up. Totally forgot who he was because little brother could kick his ass any day of the week. He walked directly toward Paul and watched his eyes change expression.

"You turncoat son of a bitch," Matt said.

Matt hit him with everything his used-up, shaking body could muster. It was a right cross to Paul's jaw. No idea he had that much left in him after what he had been through. Matt was as surprised as Paul was.

His brother fell back into an overstuffed chair. Matt leaned back on the edge of his desk, holding his hand. Secretary showed up in the doorway. From what he'd told Matt, she was the best secretary in the city, but not now. Not a trace of efficiency in the whole building.

Flustered, she opened her mouth, looked directly at Matt, and said, "911."

Matt looked at little brother. "You tried to get me killed."

Secretary did it again. Just stood there. "911."

Matt's hand was in pain and he was trembling.

"Yeah. Call the cops. Call the *Salt Lake Tribune* too. I want everyone to know this turncoat bum had me tortured for two weeks."

At the word "tortured" she hesitated, put her hand to her breast, and looked at Paul. Paul, somewhat dazed, said nothing. She collected herself, moved toward the phone.

"Never mind that," Matt told her.

He started opening desk drawers, looking for the bottle he knew was stashed somewhere for clients. He shuffled papers to one side. Nothing. Opened another desk drawer. Couple of file folders, a marriage license, and some legal papers. Matt tossed them on top of the desk out of the way. Opened another drawer.

Paul pointed to the desk.

"Help him. He's looking for the bottle," he said.

Mary nudged Matt out of the way and opened the bottom left-hand drawer. A quart of Cutty Sark—she handled it like it was a live snake. Matt circled the desk, looking for a drinking glass as secretary Mary straightened the papers he had thrown on the desk and went into the restroom off Paul's office. Matt looked in a drawer for a glass. A paper cup fell on the desk in front of him. Secretary half threw it at him.

Matt sat in Paul's chair.

"I rename thee, Judas Iscariot's chariot."

He caressed the sensually familiar shape of an old lover. The bottle felt good in his hand.

"Go away, Mary. Go home," Paul said from the chair.

"I will not!"

Matt turned the cap on the Cutty and realized that nothing, not one person on planet earth, at this moment, could stop him from taking a drink. Every cell in his body was at attention.

Secretary put herself between the two brothers.

The smell of the scotch, thick and hearty, invaded. Matt almost drooled, swallowed. *What happened to your dog, Pavlov?*

A spot of red showed at the corner of Paul's mouth.

Secretary, turning into nurse, headed for a box of Kleenex.

"Look what you've done," she accused.

For ten days at Twelve Step House he'd needed a drink so bad he'd hyperventilated. Paul was feeling his jaw. Matt poured two fingers in a cup and placed it on the arm of the chair Paul sat in. Secretary Mary had knelt in front of Paul's chair, dabbing at his face with a tissue. Not hard to figure that one. Her face held no secrets. Reminded him of a young Katharine Hepburn and definitely in love with little brother.

Couldn't marry in this life, but Matt guessed they'd already talked about marrying in the hereafter. That kind of folklore was popular in this valley. She probably took satisfaction in cornering position of wife number two in eternity. Matt resisted going much deeper into the behavioral license that image conjured. Nothing like a Utah romance, Matt said to himself.

No one said word one when he navigated a swallow of scotch and waited for the second coming.

When Paul finally spoke, it sounded like he was at the other end of a long tunnel.

"They threatened disfellowship and excommunication."

Matt wanted to ask why they were excommunicating him, but at that moment a scotch healing took precedence over all else.

"Screw you. Screw your bishop," Matt uttered, almost a whisper.

"Do you know what happens to your family when they excommunicate you?" Paul demanded.

"You ever had a vodka enema?" Matt countered.

Paul blinked. Secretary Mary went pale.

"Had to be you gave me up. Any idea where I've been for two weeks, asshole?"

The shakes were abating. The calm that followed felt so good it was hard to think. Matt poured another shot in the cup.

"You don't look like you were tortured."

Matt put the bottle down, walked to the end of the desk, and dropped his pants and shorts. Secretary let out a shriek that could pierce armor. There on both cheeks of Matt's white buttocks were the partially healed scars of his sadistic captor. It looked like someone had played tic-tac-toe at their leisure.

"I was told they needed to talk to you, that s all."

"Christ, Paul. I don't even like vodka."

"I didn't know. I had no idea. I'm sorry. I am," Paul said.

"You were right though. You were exactly right. They got some zealot psychopath kept me naked, tied up, and when he wasn't pissing on me I was—something like ten days."

Paul seemed more dazed by what Matt was telling him than by Matt's feeble right cross. Mary had turned milk white.

"Who?" Paul asked.

"You tell me."

By now it was all academic. Mood changed with the booze. Matt forced himself to stand at the window behind Paul's desk. A dark Salt Lake City with lights twinkling for endless miles spread out before him. It was a panorama even Brigham Young could not have imagined. His brother's image was reflected in the window in front of Matt. Paul sipped the scotch, rotated his jaw.

"How can you drink this stuff?"

In the reflection, Matt saw his brother for the first time, like an afterthought, the serious poverty of a man who had lost respect for himself.

"You didn't think they were serious?" Matt said.

Mary, the enabler, was on her knees dabbing at the red spot in the corner of his mouth.

"Offered my publisher two million to kill the book."

Little brother came to life. Pushed her hand away.

"What?"

"You heard me."

"They bought the rights? Who? Not the Church," Paul said.

Mary's mouth was open, again. She and Paul were both staring at Matt, like they were headlights with people attached.

"You know the Church can't get involved. A bunch of business types, the wealth of the valley, all those invested business types. My best guess, an association of CEOs. Church money? Not directly. How could there not be church money involved? Under some organized cover. Keep the negative media out of Zion. Big business," Matt said.

Paul spoke slowly. Couldn't believe what he heard. "Two million? Your book?"

"I refused the offer."

Paul sat up straight.

"Oh. Excuse me. When does the idealist get off his high horse? Never learn, do you. You're the one sets the standard for self-righteousness in our family. Worse than Dad ever was. I can see your epitaph. Big head stone. 'Here lies Matt Alcott, the only person in Utah that was right.'"

Mary began dabbing again. Matt grew quiet. He was trying to figure out who his little brother had become.

Paul headed one of the most respected, well-thought-of law firms in the Salt Lake Valley. Probably worth a good deal of money by now. It occurred to Matt that he was looking at half a man, one who had sold out to the system, given up that one inch of independence that allowed the floodgates of conform and comply to take hold and influence every subsequent decision that moved through his firm.

"You sold out."

"You criticize me, the Church, the philosophy, but you know what, collectively we don't have half your arrogance," Paul said.

They sounded like brothers again. Paul was in his own little cellblock of hell. Matt shut up and let him talk, more interested in the scotch. What's more, he couldn't afford to be more self-righteous than he already was. Paul had a point, the idealist is destiny's pawn, inevitably self-destructs.

"It's the family. They get you through your family, Helen and the kids. School kids are merciless to other kids."

"What are you talking about?"

"Why do you think I'm being threatened with excommunication?" Paul said.

"Yeah. Good question, why?"

"Well, it's not because of me. I'm not the black sheep in the family."

Matt set the bottle down. "You can't be serious? You've always been in good standing in the Church."

"I don't attend as regularly as my family. It's you they're after. They're trying to get to you through me, the kids."

Matt went back to the chair at the desk. "They're threatening my nephew and my niece because of me?"

"It was my daughter that called me. Crying. Scared out of her mind. Said her mother was acting funny. I go home. Helen's sitting in the kitchen. Still has her coat on, just sitting. She has been kicked out of Relief Society. Can you believe that?" He pounded on the arm of the chair.

"Always wondered how that worked."

"She'd been in her regular Wednesday meeting with some of the other sisters, discussing a family in the ward on welfare. They were sitting around a table, sewing a quilt. It was a total surprise." Paul ran his hand through his hair.

"The bishop sent the Relief Society president, one of her best friends, in to get her, and tells her she has to leave. Sharon had never seen her mother like that. I'm a pretty decent attorney, and I didn't know how to explain it to my own daughter."

Matt didn't say anything. His sister-in-law was one damn fine lady, his niece a sweetheart. All because of him.

"They did that to Helen?" Matt confirmed. Shaking his head, he said, "How does one reckon something like that? Jesus. That's violence. Mental rape, betrayal at a whole new level."

"I paid the church over forty thousand dollars in tithing last year."

"Peanuts to them, Paul."

"I can only figure they thought I had something to do with that damn book you've written."

"Justin on his mission?" Matt asked, referring to Paul's son.

"Gone a year now."

"What's he gonna do when he finds out how they treated his mother?" Matt asked.

"I'm not going to tell him and I know his mother won't. She's hardly spoken since it happened."

"I know my nephew. When he finds out, there'll be hell to pay. God, Paul, only reason he went, he didn't know how to tell his mother he didn't want to go."

Paul swallowed. "He told you that?"

"He's always had my ear. Of course I talk to him. Only one in the whole family with any sense."

Silence again. Matt watched Secretary Mary stiffen every time Paul talked about his wife. Figured if he hit little brother again, he'd have to fight her. Paul regained his composure.

"Where you staying?" Paul asked.

"I should tell you?"

"I'm sorry. I am."

Matt sensed he meant it.

"You remember Rod Overton?"

"Yeah. Running that recovery place?"

"Got me in detox now. Viva la scotch."

Matt hoisted the bottle, a salute, a swallow.

"You can leave messages with him for me. Although, ten to one your phones are bugged."

Matt put the cap on the bottle, a reverent maneuver. Left the two of them, Secretary Mary still kneeling, dabbing.

As the elevator doors parted, air from the lobby wafted into the elevator. The hair on Matt's neck moved. Cheap aftershave. Couldn't see anyone in the lobby. Sensed someone, a presence he knew. His heart raced; he reached for the close button and hit the open button by mistake. It was his last breath on earth. He knew it. *Think, fool, think.* The doors finally glided closed. He pushed the button for the tenth floor, held it down. Until the elevator doors opened in front of Paul's office, he didn't inhale once.

In a wave of apprehension it came to him. He had been so doped up for two weeks and in withdrawal for another week, he hadn't been curious about the manner in which he had been treated. Not in a real sense. He was starting to feel again, reliving the experience without being drugged out of his mind. There was a metal frame with straps. Contorted, injected with morphine or heroin. Urinated on, carved up, forced to ingest booze in unspeakable ways, and what else he could only imagine.

Why had bad breath asked no questions of him? He said things to Matt—he was a thorn in God's side—things like that, but hold it. Correct that. He read things. There was always the rustling of paper around or touching Matt's ear. What the hell was that all about? Only one answer made sense to Matt. The whole experience had one purpose. *Scare me*. Be a good boy, Matthew. Be quiet. While this explanation made the most sense, it didn't lessen the apprehension. Something was yet out of plumb. Why had bad breath asked no questions?

Why had he not cut my throat while he was carving hate signs on my ass? Why am I still alive?

Matt hurried back into the office. Paul hadn't moved, and Mary was still kneeling at the side of his chair. As he picked up the phone to call Twelve Step House, he noticed in the mirrored effect of the night window Paul move Mary's other hand away from his upper thigh, the obvious lump under it. Nothing more disgusting than another man's erection.

Matt dialed Rod's number.

"Rod. I think I'm in trouble... Paul' s office. Someone's in the lobby. I don't know. Big son of a bitch. I think so. You mind? I don't think I can take another two weeks. What am I saying? He'll cut my freakin' throat next time. Tenth floor. Door straight across from the elevator. Bring Tiny with you. If he can't get through the front door, he can stand out in front and intimidate the building."

Matt turned to look at Paul, who was all ears.

"Yeah, I'll be catching up on old times with little brother."

As he hung up he was overcome with nausea. The full implication of what it would mean if he were kidnapped again hit him. He felt shaky, weak. Paul climbed out of the chair as Matt walked into the outer office. Through the glass doors he could see the elevator light, indicating the elevator had stopped and was about to open.

The doors parted. A man in a brown suit was standing where only half of him was visible. One eye watched Matt bend down and twist the thumb-turn lock on the inside of the glass door. Paul walked up behind Matt. The elevator doors closed.

"Anyone you know?" Paul asked.

"That's him."

Paul was staring at Matt's color.

Matt opened his eyes. Paul and Rod were shaking hands. Tiny Tim was standing next to him.

"Is he hurt?" Rod asked.

"He just turned white and dropped to the rug. What happened to him?" Paul said.

"He was dumped in the street in front of Twelve Step House. He's lucky to be alive, and I have only a dim idea of what happened to him. Would you have lunch with me tomorrow? I'd like to get your input on this association thing."

Matt was coming around. Recognized Rod's voice.

"You hear that? Tried to kill me." He looked at Paul, self-pity working at full rpms.

"By all means. Tomorrow," Paul agreed.

Tiny threw Matt over his shoulder.

"I can walk, goddammit. Lemme down."

Chapter 35

RESURRECTION CORNER, NEW YORK

Late, only one customer in the One Hump Bar. The door eased open. Cate stood wet, cold, and shivering, her jacket unzipped against the cold rain. James J didn't reach, as he normally would, to pour a coffee.

She looked up at the man she thought of as a big brother. "What's happened? Why hasn't Matthew called?"

Cate sat at the bar, leaned forward until her head rested on her hands.

"It makes no sense to me either," he said.

"We have all that money in our checking account, and no Matthew."

He poured Cate a glass of wine. Her shoulders began to shake. Sitting where they'd spent so many happy hours, exhausted, Cate surrendered to her grief. She shook as she sobbed. His large hands rested gently on her shoulders as though to absorb some of the pain. James J stood quietly watching streamlets of rain run down the front windows.

The large man in the corner booth wearing a brown hat and brown suit under a rain coat floated a ten on the table. He walked quietly out exactly as Humphrey Bogart had done in the movies.

Chapter 36

SALT LAKE CITY
TWELVE STEP HOUSE

Tiny stuck his head in Matt's room as he went by. "Doctor Overton wants you."

Matt banged hard on Rod's office door.

"Come. Is there a reason you knock so loud?" Rod said.

"Didn't want to catch you up against your secretary."

"Encouraging. You do sometimes think of others."

"Please don't shrink mine brain and mine balls, Doctor Mengele," Matt said, attempting to mask the strangeness of this new relationship with his old buddy.

Rod returned to the chart he was reading. At the couch Matt slouched into a full horizontal. The TV Rod used for taped demonstrations was facing him.

"Turn on the game. Let's see what the Jazz are doing," Matt said.

"Your blood pressure is looking better. I see you are not sleeping well. How do you feel?"

"Perfectly shitty, thank you."

Cities, the state of Utah, and a number of associations had honored Dr. Overton. He had lectured extensively. For distraction Matt criticized every diploma and award on Rod's wall.

"All these citations. Man, that's a lot of ass-kissing."

"If you don't occasionally run with the herd, you lose mobility. How do you think I keep this place funded?"

"You've changed. Why am I here?" Matt demanded.

"You were mysteriously dumped on my doorstep and you are an addict. Is that the answer you are looking for?"

"No. And I'm not an addict. I'm a drunk."

"Same thing. You are in treatment. And you are fighting demons the size of freight trains. Humor me, Matthew. Why did you leave Salt Lake?"

Rod slipped a yellow pad on the desk as Matt thought back to that painful time.

SALT LAKE CITY
FOUR YEARS BEFORE

The City of Saints to his back. The City of Sin in his sights. Matt followed the hypnotic white line and pondered the ironies of the last few months. The sign read, LEAVING UTAH, ENTERING NEVADA. His headlights picked up a dirt side road. Beyond the lights of other cars, Matt killed the engine, switched off the headlights. Finally he was in another state. Swore he would never enter the state of Utah again as long as he lived. *Cross my heart and hope to die*, if a grown man can say that sort of thing. Almost pitch black, he stepped out into a night eerie with stars.

Matt unzipped his fly and in a symbolic gesture turned to face Utah. He let the tension out of his bladder.

From one dark horizon to another, a zillion points of light blinked down as though trying to tell him something. Your problems are microcosmic, fool...nobody from nowhere urinating on a nameless byway on a dark night under a heaven filled with stars.

From a different angle, earth would appear just another insignificant point of light. Matt couldn't help wondering...was there somewhere a life worth living?

TWELVE STEP HOUSE
DR. RODNEY OVERTON'S OFFICE

"I was looking for a life that was worth putting the effort into," Matt said.

"What did that look like?"

"I felt like the skin diver surfacing in the ocean. As the waves gently lift the diver, he turns in every direction, can't see land or boat. Nothing but water. Nothing to orient to. The goddamn disconnect is paralyzing. I wanted autonomy and anonymity more than I wanted anything in my life, but I had no compass. I had no North or South. It was devastating. Went from Salt Lake City to a bottle and named it Las Vegas."

Rod was jotting something on the yellow pad of paper. He looked up.

"And?"

"Savage, bitter rage. Felt abandoned, betrayed. All my life I was taught to be honest. I only said what I thought. Wasn't their brand of honest. They couldn't accept the fact that I was thinking for myself, never mind if I was right or not. Then there is that other thing..."

Rod leaned forward, waiting...

"Dad loved the church more than me."

The pencil in Rod's hand looked like it was chasing something.

"How did you avoid suicide?"

Matt turned. "You don't fuck around, do you?"

Rod switched pencils, needed a new sharp tip.

"You're right. Grim. There were times I actually tried to drink myself to death. I don't think we are meant to go from one reality to another overnight. Too extreme." Matt sat, watched the yellow pencil dance. "Emotional anemia. Sober, I couldn't figure out who the hell I was. Drunk, it didn't matter. So, of course, stay drunk."

Rod's ears seemed bigger. There was an intensity about him, like he wasn't sitting on the other side of the desk anymore, but had jumped inside Matt s head.

"I learned," Matt went on, "you can lose everyone you love and somehow go on, but not when you lose yourself. That's when things get dicey."

Matt pictured himself sitting on top of one of the file cabinets behind Rod, looking down, and reading over his shoulder.

"Didn't tell anyone good-bye. Just drove out of town. Never felt so unnecessary in my whole life. Tried to find something to hang on to, live for, some reason for using up oxygen. I'd write a list of things needed to get done. It was a pointless attempt to give meaning to the moment. Everyone I knew was preoccupied with their careers, children, graduate school. Their lives looked full. Mine was a staggering emptiness. Envy only made it colder, ya know. I watched people on the street. Their every step was part of something; a way of life, a people, a history, a place, a cause, a curse, something. When a sense of yourself is gone, it's desolate. I thought about it a lot that first year. Realized I had to believe in something. There I was at the bottom of my life and that's when I discovered it."

Matt paused. The yellow pencil stopped moving.

"It." Rod, eyebrows up.

"The ancient elixir. The magic. The drink."

Rod threw the pencil down. Picked it up. Scribbled something. Matt noticed he had Rod's full attention. *Sometimes I do impress myself*, he thought.

"And," yet coaxing.

"Absolute, universal, unequivocal truth, ya know. You drop that from your internal biosphere, especially if you grew up digesting it with your pabulum, you're screwed big time. I was never taught how to live, only how to..." took a second to find the word, "...only how to church."

Rod's head was moving while writing as though trying to move the pencil faster.

"It was hard. From one of God's chosen to just another human.

Man, that's challenging. You know you have to reinvent yourself, but knowing how, that's the mystery," Matt said.

Rod looked up. "I've never heard a patient put it so succinctly. You're lucky you didn't blow your brains out."

"My shotgun was in the basement at the folks'."

The pencil was earning its keep again. That's when Rod swiveled in his chair, faced the file cabinets against the wall.

"Do you remember the smartest guy in our class?"

"We laid that role on Brainy Brian Billings, didn't we?"

"Do you know what he ended up doing?"

"Assumed physicist, brain mechanic, advisor to the Godhead, something like that."

"Other than me, only one man works on my antique cars."

"Really!"

"We will go by one day. Small garage. You can say hi. I like to go in, hang around and talk to him while he's working, which is a misnomer for him. Never seems to be doing anything but puttering or tinkering. Perfect work. Perfect. He knew I was working on my dissertation. One day Brian picked up a shiny new nut and said it had no more value than a rock without the right thread on it. Then he smiled that Ichabod Crane smile of his and said, our beliefs are the nuts and bolts that mount the engine in place while it's running."

"Yeah. God, yeah. All my nuts had come loose."

The pencil was tugging on Rod's hand again.

"Drink mornings to get going, noon to keep my stomach where it belonged, and...well, don't remember that many evenings. Until I stumbled into AA and started writing again, I just existed. No period of bereavement, funeral, flowers, eulogy, nothing. I am, since that time, no longer self-righteously critical of those who attempt suicide. Some days, enduring a single hour was a miracle. The angst. All I could do...act like everything was okay, and I've never been judged a poor actor. I used to criticize the teenagers that stuck rings in their tits and tattoos on their dicks, but at least they were identifying. Sex was okay, but you can't screw twenty-four hours a day. And money? Bores me, when I have it. So where does a Mormon boy go for help? Not a shrink. Not in this valley."

Rod glanced at his wristwatch. "Something's missing, Matthew."

"Give me a break. I'm making this shit up as fast as I can."

"Here's what I want you to do." Rod stood, leaned his hands on his desk, as though stretching, and looked directly at Matt. "Take this evening and think about all this. Something you might have left out. Consider how you might better help me help you. Make a list. Anything you think might be important. Bring it with you when we meet again."

The yellow pencil rolled across the desk, abandoned.

Sitting alone in his room, Matt was forcing memory, which sometimes worked, sometimes not. He hadn't seen his folks in four years and there was an old truck parked in back. He found a set of keys in Rod's desk.

In case he disappeared again he left a note. Knew Rod would not read it until the next morning, but at least someone would know he was missing. As he drove, thoughts of his father stirred warm memories.

NORTH SALT LAKE CITY
CHILDHOOD MEMORY

He and dad. The two of them together. On the first Sunday following his twelfth birthday he was awakened earlier than usual. A gentle shaking, his eyes opened to find his father standing over him.

"Time for church, son."

And it was his father, and not his mother, who handed him a clean white shirt.

"I like a Windsor knot myself," and Dad showed Matt how to tie it.

His mother's eyes were moist as they hustled past her through the kitchen and out to the car.

It was his first meeting, for men only. He remembered looking out from under the hands of four men pressing down on his head at the audience of bowed heads he was sitting in front of. Thought his father's voice, ordaining him into the priesthood, would never end. After, congratulating handshakes all around. From that day he was taught the things he hadn't learned in Sunday school.

NORTH SALT LAKE CITY, UTAH
EVENING

Matt parked the truck in front of the Bountiful Ward meetinghouse. The hinges on the eight-foot high doors made the same squeaking complaint they'd made four years before. The same chest-high, green leafy plant was still in the lobby. Felt like yesterday.

Dad looked older, almost frail. As usual, his office door was open. He would have heard a vehicle drive up, but he would not look up, not until he was finished or was interrupted. Matt watched him for a minute. Felt the heaviness between them and the sweet, good love of the little boy he'd once been for the best dad in the whole world.

"Hi, Dad."

Bishop Alcott sat quietly looking at him as though trying to figure out who he was. Then he smiled and, ever the gentleman, stood and offered Matt his hand.

"Hello. Hello. Paul said he'd seen you. Back east, I believe."

He was obviously happy to see Matt. That changed abruptly as memory caught up with circumstance.

His father grew old and tired in front of his eyes. The bishop sat down again and picked up the pen. Matt was confused.

"President Burgess called me. He explained that he couldn't stop the...the excommun..."

His father couldn't say the word, couldn't complete a sentence with excommunication in it. Then he did something completely unexpected. Bishop Alcott put the pen back down and rose and looked his son in the eye.

"I don't understand what's happened. Your mother and I... Is there something we've done...?" His hands shot forward in a pleading gesture. "Have I let you down in some way? I've prayed and I've fasted. I've searched my heart. I don't understand?"

His father collapsed in the chair, sobbing silently.

"Matthew, you are a complete mystery to me."

Matt had forgotten the letter Hamilton handed him in New York when he got off the bus. Paul had posted it to Hamilton, as he did not have Matt's address. He glanced at it as they walked through the bus terminal. It was short and to the point.

> *There has been a Bishops' Court. You've been excommunicated. Wouldn't be surprised if Dad has a breakdown. I've never seen him so low. Mom doesn't know yet. Tread lightly, Paul.*

Matt had thought of writing the Church and thanking them, but that would have been too arrogant and self-serving. As he looked into his father's eyes, sarcasm didn't seem appropriate. It was a mixed feeling. His father didn't ask him how he was, where he was living, what his life was like, or even what he was doing in Salt Lake.

Matt shifted his weight, felt a heat build up under his shirt. He knew where his father was coming from and he knew his father would never understand, which fueled the inner rage. He took a deep breath, turned away from the picture in front of him.

"I wish I could give you the answers you want, Dad. I'm sorry you feel the way you do." Matt wanted to scream bloody murder. He looked at the ceiling. He looked at the floor. "Anything I'd say further would only cause you more hurt."

"I don't know how to tell your mother," his father's voice a whisper.

He loved his father. Next to the last person on earth he would want to hurt. And he was doing it again. His rage, shackled behind unfair, was helpless. *Burgess, you unmitigated bastard.* Coming had been a mistake. He turned and walked away, the picture of his father sobbing silently burned in his brain.

On the drive back to Twelve Step House, Matt had to force himself not to think about his father. What was Rod's question? How can you help me help you?

TWELVE STEP HOUSE

"Do you own anything other than a T-shirt?" Rod asked the next morning. "See Tiny for a sweatshirt. He knows where we keep the ones that are left by other patients. I would like you to meet Millie. You feel okay staying with us tonight?"

"On a real mattress?"

Chapter 37

ROD AND MILLIE OVERTON'S HOME
EVENING

Matt was introduced to a pleasant woman with large, wide-set blue eyes. Rod informed Matt that his wife had a PhD in linguistics.

"I have a profound respect for symbol junkies. The world would be better off if there were more of them," Matt said.

Millie laughed, looked at Rod. "I see what you mean."

"How do you live with this bum? He's been torturing me for the better part of a week," Matt said.

"A challenge, certainly," she acknowledged, beginning to have fun with the repartee.

"Millie has just been made a full professor at the University of Utah."

"Wow. Clearly you have an affinity for politics."

Her laugh betrayed her. "Spot on," she said and threw her hand up for a high-five.

Matt felt at home. Rod disappeared into his den, returning after a few minutes with his mail.

"She's far too good for your ass, old buddy," Matt said.

Rod opened a letter. "Plebeian humor, however true."

A little tan pug with the characteristic concave black face would have nothing less than Matt's full attention until Millie patted her leg. The pug jumped into her lap.

"Do you have the flu?" she inquired.

"Residual withdrawals from the opiates," Rod offered, not looking up from browsing his mail.

Who am I, Matt wondered, *but some derelict drunk come washed up on her ol' man's beach, and she is treating me like royalty.* He hadn't expected that. When Rod and Millie spoke to each other, Matt could sense no subtle layers of anything ulterior. They were completely candid with each other. Caused Matt to think of Cate. His breath caught in his throat.

Rod discarded the letter he was reading.

"Matthew, would you mind—take Millie through what you can remember since you got off the plane."

"Does he ever relax?" Matt said to Millie.

She smiled and looked warmly at her husband

"Not about you, I'm afraid. He has wondered about you for years, disappearing like you did."

Matt felt like an ass. He hadn't been the ideal patient at Twelve Step House. He took them through what happened. Covering what he could remember while kidnapped and going to his brother's office. After, Millie was thoughtful, began to shake her head.

"It's incredible. No food of any kind? Nothing but toxins. You must have a remarkable constitution."

"I remember being hosed with water. Cold as a glacier. I think I tried to drink it."

"Frankly I don't know why your heart didn't stop," Rod said. "Electrolyte imbalance. You must have been given some nutrition, something."

"One big blur."

"The morphine kept your metabolism low. That may have contributed to your survival," Rod added, almost as if talking to himself.

Mr. Stubbs, the dog, stared at Matt like he might be a kibble or bit.

"Your story puzzles me." Millie glanced at Rob. "What purpose did those twelve days serve?"

"That is my dilemma," Rod said.

That was when Matt realized why he was there. Rod knew his wife and wanted her mix of opinion and intuition.

They were quiet for a few moments, looking at each other.

The silence felt awkward to Matt.

"Hello, Doctors. Are we talking about anyone I know?"

Millie's voice, alto in range and texture, produced a warm laugh that draws you in.

Matt sat up.

"I'm being published. You didn't know."

The pug jumped off Millie's lap and took up a position on Rod's lap, looking at Matt.

"Book?" Rod said like an echo.

"Everything muddled. I'm all cobwebs. The firm of Welsely and Tanner offered my publisher and me two million dollars to squash publication. I turned it down. Took the advance money instead." Matt shrugged.

"Oh!" Millie exclaimed.

Another silence. The pug was shaking. Rod rested his hand on its rump.

"Welsely and Tanner?" Millie posed.

"One of the law firms the Church keeps on retainer," Rod said.

"Mr. Stubbs needs Alanon," Matt said to break the tension.

"Mr. Stubbs is trying to make sense of anyone who would turn down two million dollars," Rod remarked.

"Paul told me the funding came from an alliance of local businessmen."

Rod looked to Millie. "Paul is his brother, the attorney I told you about."

Mr. Stubbs was nudging Rod's hand.

"I remember, you worked in the church archives at one point," Rod said.

"Took me three years to realize I was there to find and catalogue, nothing else. I find it. They hide it."

"What happened?" Rod asked.

"I was told by the powers that be, what I found, a lost revelation of Smith's, was a meaningless forgery, which was horse shit..." he turned to Millie, "excuse me, crap."

"I prefer horse shit. More definitive," Millie said, interrupting.

"The revelation was dictated to Willard Richards on the last day of his life, June 27, 1844. He'd been told a large mob of agitated men were closing in on the jail. I sense that Joseph knew his time was up."

"Lost revelation!" Rod said.

"I discovered it sleeved behind the cover leaf of one of Young's personal journals. Brigham Young stashed it. Devastating if read in the context of an 1844 mindset. It was before Darwin by fifteen years. Keep in mind; women didn't have the right to vote. The reason? What could be more obvious?

If they voted, by sheer numbers, they would change everything. Smith didn't miss things like that. Martin Luther was big. Luther said, girls begin to talk and to stand on their feet sooner than boys because weeds always grow up more quickly than good crops. Aristotle said the same thing, but with an even colder characterization of female-specific behavior. Simply put, Smith was telling Brigham Young it was genetic tissue that carried right thinking and only men had it. The good seed, the ability to understand the truth, was inherited male to male. It was recessive in the female, dominant in man. Woman could receive and express the gene, but she could not pass it on. I was feverish as I tested the paper. It was of a compatible composition and quality. Was it, indeed, the hand of Willard Richards? No question of that."

"Not in the Doctrines & Covenants?" Rod posed.

"Brigham Young knew better. The ramifications! It confirmed like no other document that if you did not practice polygamy, your soul was damned. The meaning was clear. Monogamy allowed the occasion for too much intimacy, too much variation, and, of course, too much experimentation. Birth control was something Joseph had foreseen. Monogamy was the devil at work, promoting the opportunity; sex for sex' sake. Women being what they were, and with one wife only, the devil was able to do his best work."

"Babies without pleasure. I doubt it," Rod said.

"All this drove me deeper into Smith's life and character. His view of women; they were all Eve, of the profane, and were to administer unto man. What does that say? Here is the seed and there is the dirt. Start planting."

"The words themselves symbolize a subspecies of human. One designed for a specific purpose…to be used," Millie said.

The room was silent. Millie, thoughtful, spoke to Rod.

"Do you remember Becky Wood? I introduced her to you in the parking lot at the mall."

"An older lady? A year ago?" Rod acknowledged.

"I've known her forever. She was the only girlfriend that didn't drop me as a friend over the years because my family was non-Mormon. She's not older. We are the same age. At nine births she told her husband, *no more*. She told me that's when her life turned to hell—as if it wasn't already."

"I understood that was not happening anymore," Rod said.

"I've got to say, it's some old boys club you've got going in this valley. Susan was summoned to her bishop's office first. Both he and her stake president reminded her that she was denying her duty to God and her husband."

Rod said nothing. Matt noticed he wouldn't look away until she returned his look.

"It's hard not to get carried away once in a while. You'd think you'd get used to it, but you don't. You never do. That was the funeral I passed on last month. In her tenth pregnancy she'd turned septic. I couldn't go and listen to them praise her for the grand role she played in bringing to so many the gift of salvation in God's kingdom."

"How did Smith justify this?" Rod asked.

"Keep in mind he kept his mother on a pedestal. He piled elaborate praise on women for the grand role they played in the great plan of salvation. It was woman who went through childbirth and gave Joseph sons to carry on his name. The grandiosity? He never gave that up." Matt stopped. Shook his head. "Forgive me. I do get carried away," he said.

"On the contrary," Rod said.

"Women were never to say no to their husbands. It was saying no to God Himself," Matt added.

Rod extended his legs out in front of him, one leg on top of the other.

"We were taught that in priesthood meetings, as I remember," he said.

"I had to know what motivated him. How he thought. What he hinged his choices on. Many books have chronicled his experiences and the major events in his life, but seldom have they fleshed him out with real feelings and personal dreams and fears. All we get are lofty aspirations and celestial motives. I took a different tack. I wanted the human factor."

Mr. Stubbs was breathing fast, looking first to one then the other.

Matt went on.

"He was a complete failure at intimate relationships. Emma, his wife, learned too late, he nourished on his own grandiosity, loved the self-image he carried of himself more than anything, more than any woman. But he did earn the admiration he craved. I saw much of myself in Smith, which put me off at first. He inspired confidence, both at the pulpit and personally as a spiritual Lothario. Over fifty marriages probably. I could only document about thirty. He went way beyond propriety, was marrying children and women whose husbands were still alive."

"You found all this in the Church records?" Millie asked.

"The practice, convincing a woman to believe him, began early with Emma. Her father forbade the marriage. Did you know he talked her into eloping? 1827. It became habit. Every woman he subsequently married was in some respect an elopement, a way of getting around the traditional, a means of answering his own needs."

"I've read something of this already, haven't I?" Rod wondered.

"To some extent, yes, but I had to know what the seduction really looked like. How did he get their dresses off? Had to get them drunk, literally. Words. It was words were his weapons, his instruments. He got them drunk on words shaped and angled to overcome any inhibition. He caressed them with his vision of paradise, eternal life. The secret liaison titillated. Secret letters were meant to be destroyed. One incident comes to mind. Her name eludes me for the moment...anyway..." Matt rotated his index fingers as though rolling out a scroll.

"Joseph would eulogize the sweet fantasy of romantic dream. He spoke of love so pure it was beyond the understanding of common folk. He capitalized and embellished on the ecclesiastical inventory of supplications, devotions, and beliefs of the time.

"Joseph took them in his arms, looked them in the eyes, and said, 'Only the elite of God's children are capable of experiencing so great a love. Until a more enlightened time, our love must remain God's secret. The world is not yet ready for love's perfection.'"

"No ordinary car salesman," Rod offered.

"We are seduced by our own beliefs...the nature and power of what we do with our symbols," Millie added.

Rod was thoughtful, processing.

Matt leaned back, brought his arms up, interlaced his fingers on top of his head, and continued. "Only love Smith knew was of himself and, for lack of a better word, his loyal subjects. When you were around him, he made you feel special even if it was only a handshake. Radiated charisma. Men like Porter Rockwell, who lacked a sense of themselves, found meaning in their lives by devoting themselves to him, his agenda. Through him their importance was extant. Smith could accept frailty and weakness in the masses, but not in himself. I liked that about him. Offered up an interesting image, a narcissist who could not separate reality from his dreams of greatness."

"Not hard to understand why you're not well liked in some circles," Millie said. "You de-sanitized the man. You're like the artist who gets excommunicated for painting the pope at his toilet."

Rob talked like he was thinking out loud again.

"If there is anything the leadership of the church is jealous of, it is its image. Probably the most appearance-conscious institution on earth."

The professor side of Millie stepped up again.

"It's a worship mentality. Members have pictures of the Twelve Apostles and the First Presidency in their homes like Catholics have of Mary, Jesus, and the pope."

"It's why the shift in missionary activity from Europe to Central and South America. Those cultures precondition a worship posture. The conversion ratios are better," Rod said.

"I can't see two million being offered for an inferior work," Millie offered.

"This is really about turning down what two million dollars represents," Rod said.

"What do you mean?"

"You should be frightened."

Millie, Rod, and Mr. Stubbs all were staring at Matt.

"Oh. Yeah, I keep forgetting," Matt said.

Chapter 38

TWELVE STEP HOUSE

The next morning as Rod and Matt drove north along Foothill Drive toward Twelve Step House, they talked about old times and old names.

Exactly at ten a.m. Matt knocked on Rod's office door.

"I have a ten a.m. with you, right? My memory is a train wreck. I need to make a phone call," Matt announced, tossing a piece of paper on his desk.

Rod punched save on his computer and put it aside. He unfolded the paper. One name only; Cate Lynn.

"You are married?" Rod asked.

"More than married. Cate Lynn is the only woman I have ever loved."

"You didn't love Carol, your first wife?"

"Thought I did when I married her. Compared to the way I feel about Cate, it was something else entirely."

"Sit down."

"What's to tell? I've been brain dead for weeks. I'm remembering more and more. Being away from her is agony."

Rod leaned forward in his chair, waited.

"Ordinarily I can't breathe unless she is in the same room," Matt said.

"When did you last speak with her?" Rod asked.

"That's it. Now I'm too dangerous. My book! I have to break it off until it's safe."

The expanding lump in his throat shut him down.

Rod shook his head. "I don't understand."

Matt tried to respond. Couldn't.

"If you're talking about your book, I'm not buying into that and you know it," Rod said.

Matt knew he'd screwed up. One more careless word, and Rod would throw the equivalent of a headlock on him and crank up the pressure.

"Cate and I are lost to each other. Simple as that. Love's labor, lost. There! You happy?" he said, self-pity oozing from him like juice squeezed from a fat lemon.

"I know ten-year-olds more mature than that."

"Don't fuck with me!" This was followed by an involuntary lurching deep inside. "I'm not rational about this."

A box of Kleenex landed next to him. Matt felt like a fool. Grabbed a handful and, knowing it was useless to try to hold it back, took cover behind the flimsy tissue.

After a minute he heard his old friend's voice. It was mellow and smooth,

"You've been holding this in for a long time. In my book those are good tears, Matthew. Nothing to be ashamed of."

"You don't get it. Cate is the best thing that's ever happened to me. I can't put her in harm's way."

As soon as he spoke, Matt knew he had screwed up again.

"Why? Where's the connection? I don't believe what I'm hearing," Rod said, like he was talking to a child.

Rod pushed harder.

"Let's see then, proposition; if wife dies before husband, it means they should never have married in the first place? Right?"

"Don't you get it? She's too important to me to take the chance."

Matt choked back the self-pity.

"You're reacting out of fear. Long-term relationships are founded on something worth working at."

"If you're right, I'm the biggest asshole on the planet."

"You're going through what is called post acute withdrawal. Your memory is improving, but your emotions are still catching up."

If there was one thing Matt hated, it was when his eyes filled with water. He couldn't force a whisper. His old high school comrade leaned back, folded his hands across an ample stomach. Matt stood up, walked out.

Matt walked past the counter that separated the staff from the patients, lovingly called the vegetable pit. He was on his way to place a telephone call to Cate.

"Matt, you have a letter," said a young, pretty attendant Matt knew as Megan.

"Impossible. No one knows where I am."

"You still go by Matt Alcott?" she teased.

It was from a Salt Lake City zip code. He turned to walk away.

"Need to open it here please, Mr. Alcott," she said.

"You are a cruel woman, Megan. You're going to make some poor bastard a wonderful wife," he said as he opened the envelope.

She blushed. Matt enjoyed funning with her.

He opened the letter, the young attendant looking on. For a few uneasy seconds he stared. The words were pasted together from cut-out letters, like in the movies where the FBI is analyzing and tracing a letter that is thought to be untraceable. It read,

stop the boOk.
Give everything OVer.
She w o n e d get hurt.

Matt had never thought much about gravity, but he did now. He became very aware of his legs. Breathing too fast, he headed for his little cubicle of privacy. Slumping down on the bed, he tried to slow his breathing. Just as he found his Cate, he lost her, and whose fault was it? Yours truly again, Mr. Consistent, Matthew A. Alcott.

The vegetable pit alerted Tiny that Matt had received some disturbing mail. Tiny found Matt and scooped the letter out of his hand. Matt didn't remember Tiny leaving the room.

Attempting to focus, Matt realized he was looking at the inside of a brown paper bag. Someone was talking.

"Take slow, deep breaths, Matthew," the nurse instructed. "Square breathing. You know the drill. Take a breath in, hold it for a count of four. Let it out, hold it for four."

"You don't give up easy, do you?" he mumbled, pushing the bag away.

"Oh good. We're back. The same oversexed Mormon boy I remember."

"How can you say that when I only want you for your mind?"

"Pervert."

She wiped perspiration from his forehead, put the moist face cloth in his hand. That's when Matt remembered and went pale again.

To Rod, who had just appeared in the doorway, the nurse said, "He's back, but I don't guarantee anything, Doctor."

Matt sat up, still dizzy.

"I've got to go. I've got to get out of here."

"And where is it that you are going?" Rod answered.

"They've got her."

Matt looked at Tiny.

"Show him. Show him the letter."

"This letter is only a threat. Read it again. Call her."

"It says they'll harm her."

"It does not say that. No return address. What do they want? Actually, this letter doesn't make a lot of sense. You and I know the Church can't be involved in this or anything remotely resembling anything like this."

"This is worse than when they had me. Ten times worse."

Matt's mind was a cauldron of fears. He needed a drink. Needed to tell Hamilton to call off the book.

"Call home. Until you make a phone call, you don't know anything."

"Can I use the phone in your office?"

Rod motioned to Tiny.

The two men headed for Rod's office. The phone at the loft didn't answer. He called Raven's number at the school.

"Matthew, is that you?"

"Where's Cate? Is she with you?" Matt stammered.

"We haven't seen Cate in a week. She's not with you?"

It was like the last straw, his worst fear. In his imagination he pictured her trussed up and treated as he had been. He felt light-headed. "You sitting down?"

The phone went silent. A voice, clear and strong, said, "You know, Matthew, there is every chance I may kill you, if I ever see you again."

"I think she's been kidnapped."

His throat closed, barely got the words out.

"You give new meaning to the term bastard, you know that?" Raven said.

Matt explained it to her.

"Where are you?" Raven asked.

"Salt Lake City. Have the sheriff call the telephone company, and request they check your phone for listening devices. I'll call you back tomorrow."

"Why would you write a book you knew might endanger people's lives?"

"Chalk it up to stupidity."

He could see Cate in his mind writing sad computer on the blackboard, and when he had new pages she would rave over them.

"She always praised my writing. What am I telling you for? You know what she's like."

"Do you need money?" Raven asked. "I can't send the computers back. We've been using them."

"What computers?" Matt asked.

"Oh God!" Raven exclaimed.

The air was dead; Raven regrouped.

"You didn't know? You supplied the school with computers. Twenty-four, all new. I assumed she had talked to you. Every senior in school is online. We have our own website. Microsoft even had a rep from New York City come to the school to train us on their software."

"Cate did that?"

"She did."

"See if her mother knows where she is."

"Her mother takes your name in vain every day."

"So do I."

"She filled out a missing persons report day before yesterday."

"If you hear anything call Twelve Step House in Salt Lake."

"Did you drink again?"

"It's a long story, Raven."

Matt called the offices of Agent Hamilton Gloss and got the person he wanted to talk to.

"Nice to hear your voice. Hamilton thinks you've been kidnapped by the Danites," Louise said.

"Close. How is the world-class worrier anyway?"

"Better when I tell him you called. We've become quite the Mormon scholars, no thanks to you."

"I'm impressed. You even pronounced Danite with the hard 'a' like they do in Utah."

"You met my niece, Samantha, Sam," she said.

"Like her too. Gave me a lot of money."

"The references were fine, but her managing editor wanted verification on some of the basic tenets. 'Baptism for the Dead' had

Hamilton scratching his head for days."

"I know who does the work around that office, Louise. I'm not ungrateful."

"I'm surprised the women in that church have taken it for so long."

"You're not the first to make that comment."

"The book's printed and with the binder now. Paper, five and a quarter by eight," Louise said.

"Paper?" Matt said.

"Sam wants to do a cloth or hardcover in two years as a collector's edition on one of their imprints. I thought it was a pip of an idea, myself."

"Damn."

"Because you put me in the middle of it, Sam thought I should be at the meeting. Hamilton never had to take me with him before. He was annoyed something awful. I don't believe I've enjoyed myself more. As they say, I owe you big-time."

There was a break in the conversation. Matt was framing how he was going to tell her about Cate.

"You see, Matthew, you've certainly had us jumping," Louise said before adding, "Listen: this is one of the advertising blurbs.

Bad boy author
Matthew Alcott
exposes Joseph Smith,
the prophet of love."

"God. No more, please," Matt said.

"Another.

A tale of tender love.
New York son
and founder of the Mormon religion

was the Hugh Hefner of the new world.
The sexual revolution started as a church."

"Uncle."

"Matthew, they sell books."

It made Matt feel weird to hear how they were touting his serious work. He wanted to be respectful to Louise, but all he had on his mind was Cate.

"When do you think it will be on the shelves?"

"Soon. Like waiting for the other shoe to drop, isn't it?"

His voice betrayed him.

"I had no idea."

"The advance copies and press releases went out to the book reviewers a week ago. I haven't been told the specific publication date. Hamilton doesn't share, but very soon. Probably a week, two. Sam definitely wants you for publicity. Two talk shows have been lined up."

"If I don't find Cate, I'll do personal interviews anywhere they want. Siberia, Jersey. Name it."

"Matthew, what's happened?" Louise's voice was serious.

"I was kidnapped. Reason you didn't hear from me. Now Cate's disappeared."

An audible gasp.

"I'm not sure I understand."

"Her mother filed a missing persons."

"But that's terrible. I'll call Hamilton. What can we do?"

"Stop the press," Matt said.

"You know that will never happen. In fact, they will find a way to use your abduction in promotion. You can count on that."

"Oh God. Cate's doomed!"

Matt hung up, started walking. Nervous and fretful, he moved without direction. The halls were empty. All the patients were in the auditorium. He walked nervously, aimlessly until he found himself standing in the auditorium a few feet from Dr. Rod Overton.

Rod stopped talking and stared at Matt. The audience was silent.

"I just spoke to New York. They are going to use my kidnapping in the promotional materials. It's hopeless. Cate's as good as dead."

After a moment's consideration, Rod addressed the class, "Answer the questions at the end of the section. Timothy will take it from here."

Rod took Matt by the arm and guided him out of the room and to his office.

"Matthew, sit down."

"Too late to stop publication," he said, riddled with anxiety. "What in God's name do I do? I don't know what to do."

He collapsed in a chair.

"There were forty-eight patients in that room. I'm the person they rely on to help them learn how to change their lives. What gave you the right to interrupt?" Rod asked.

Matt's mouth was open, surprise written all over him.

Rod continued.

"I am going to tell you what to do, but I have to know if you are listening. Are you listening?"

Matt was rigid, unable to move, mouth a bewildered gap.

"Here's what you do. Wallow. Feel sorry for yourself, stew in your own self-pity. Then when she shows up dead, you can say you were right."

"Cruel motherfucker." Matt's voice was a thin imitation of itself.

"Listen to yourself. You ask me for help, but I wasn't with you, not in New York, not when you were kidnapped. The only knowledge I have about this mess came from your blood work and your physical condition. But I'll tell you what I believe. Do you want to know what I believe?"

Rod paused, then continued without waiting.

"I believe all the parts and pieces to find her exist. And I believe if you take a minute and stop feeling sorry for yourself, you'll begin to be objective about this, and you'll know where to look for the answers."

"Kick me when I'm down," Matt groaned.

Rod moved around his desk and jabbed him in the head with his index finger.

"You're not listening, are you? All you can do is feel sorry for yourself. I don't know anyone better positioned to figure this thing out than you. Take responsibility for that, not her disappearance. Focus on finding her, not on losing her."

Rod lifted a folder from the surface of his desk and left the room.

Matt sat staring at the wall. Rod's words paralyzed him. To think what they might be doing to Cate... Beads of perspiration formed like a mist on his forehead. One drink and the trembling would stop. He knew that. Knew it as well as he knew his own name. What would Cate think? Would she think he had abandoned her? Goddamn it! It was one thing to be betrayed, another to be the betrayer.

That night was the longest night of his life. Except for Relapse, the cat, it was the most alone and helpless he had ever felt. Matt sat on the bed, his back against the wall.

"Why do you hang out with losers, kitty? Ever tell you about my Cate?"

Relapse dug in, found a comfortable warm place.

"She has a black mouse. Hangs on a wall. Makes obnoxious noises. Give anything to hear her talking on that damn phone."

He stroked the black cat.

"Happiness, if you think about it, hangs precariously on the thin edge of happenstance." He put both index fingers to his temples and made a noise like a gun going off. "Focus, fool."

His throat was dry. Intense loss tore at him. One memory floated into consciousness. What might be happening to her made him shudder. He wondered if Cate could feel the rumble of a train going by?

Why am I thinking about trains? God. I'm losing it.

Relapse listened with the blind ear of innocence.

"I came to her broken and she healed me. I've never told her that, but when I hear her on the stairs, my IQ drops fifty points. She owns me."

He could call up the fresh scent of her, the vanilla perfume she liked so much. Feel the echo of her laugh in his bones.

Dawn finally. A patient was snoring in another cubicle. Matt stroked Relapse.

"You know something I don't, don't you, you fuzzy little bastard."

Matt stood up. The cat pealed off his lap, jumped to the floor.

"Trains! I remember trains!"

Rod wouldn't be in for another hour. Matt penned a quick note, put it in his inbox.

It's starting to work. I remember trains. Where I was being held prisoner trains were going by. I could hear them. I could feel them. Back later. Matt

"University of Nevada, Las Vegas. How may I direct your call?"

"Dr. Evelyn Hickman's office," Matt said.

"One moment."

A woman's voice: "Dr. Eve."

The way she enunciated her words, crisp, clear, and alto, Matt could see her. The hiking boots. The broad-rimmed hat. Zero tan lines.

Easy to remember this lady.

Chapter 39

LAS VEGAS
THREE YEARS BEFORE

The intercom buzzed.

"Got one for ya."

Click. It was Jack, his editor.

Jack, typically, was talking before Matt was in range.

"She's the newest addition to the faculty at the university. A herpetologist specializing in desert reptiles."

He pushed a handful of paper at Matt.

"Her phone number."

He tapped the top canary-colored sheet he'd been doodling on.

"Expecting your call. Tone down the snake side of the story. Okay? I'm tired of dealing with the travel agencies and the Better Business bunch. They don't want us scaring off the tourists. Find the human interest angle in this thing."

He threw one hand in the air to reinforce his point.

"She's young, probably youngest PhD over there," Jack said, his arm changing direction. "An expert in desert lizards as well as snakes."

Matt couldn't help thinking that his boss needed a drink.

"Lizards. Right," Matt said, starting back to his desk.

Jack had summoned Matt to do a Sunday feature on the newest addition to the faculty at the University of Nevada, Las Vegas. A PhD in herpetology, she was a snake doctor. Matt pictured a woman with a humpback he could introduce to the gay food editor in the next room.

He set up an appointment with the newest and youngest member of the University of Las Vegas, Nevada faculty. What was going to be eighteen hundred words and a few pictures of specimens under glass became three thousand words and a series of field trips into little-known corners of God's well-kept secrets in southern Nevada. Dr. Evelyn Hickman did not meet expectations. She exceeded them. With a little upper body work she could have featured in any chorus line on the strip.

They left just after two a.m. Timed their arrival for the coolest part of the day, to catch the repulsive little critters when they moved the slowest. He interviewed on the drive, pencil and pad in hand.

"Tell me, how did you get interested in snakes?"

"No idea. I've been fascinated with the desert as long as I can remember. My dissertation was on reptiles of this region. I know of two snake dens and have recorded a third. All between the Silver Reef just above St. George, Utah, and the Mohave mountains in California."

They were on their way to the latest discovery. Matt had a camera for the occasion and would take pictures, but the snake dens actual whereabouts had to remain undisclosed for the obvious reasons.

It was about one hour off road, just this side of the Utah-Nevada border. The story focus was on her, but Matt slugged it All Things Desert, which he explained was still technically correct, considering her love for the desert. Matt wondered if the twinkle in her eye was genetic or mischief. The human interest was easy. He quoted her on the discovery of the third den.

"One of my students came up after class. His grandfather was an old toothless Paiute who'd lived in the area all his life. I was excited and arranged to meet him. He was adamant that they go alone. No photographer. Me only. The old Indian called it a sacred place. He walked me into the hills like he'd visited the place last week. In the whole basin it's the only one you can stand up in."

The basin she was referring to was made up of parts of southeastern California, southwest Utah, southern Nevada, and northeastern Arizona.

"He told me not to go in there if I was with child. He said, if a snake bites me and I live, the child will grow up with snakes in its dreams."

The next part Matt's editor, a coward to the bone, cut out of the piece.

"I told the nice old Indian, 'I'm not pregnant.' He gave me a big toothless grin and, removing his hat, said he would be honored to help me with that."

"Well?"

Matt caught her off guard. Her laugh was explosive, honest.

"Ready with the camera? We're here."

When they had gotten out of her four-by-four, the lean, sexy creature he had driven up there with changed hats. An officious Dr. Hickman emerged.

"Stay right behind me."

She pushed a button on a small voice-activated recorder.

"Tracks visible from yesterday or this a.m. Crotalus cerestes moving from west to east. Short, separated lines, angle about thirty degrees, and the J smaller than usual."

She turned to Matt and said, "First of that species I've seen in this area." Then for Matt's benefit, "No mistaking a sidewinder's tracks."

Matt was taking his own notes. Legs lean and tan, not a decimal less than a ten; shorts loose, revealing.

She would shake the mesquite and sage with her five-foot metal hand probe as they walked.

"Watch for snakes on off-floor shelves. They like to catch the morning sun."

They rounded a massive wall of rock about twenty feet high, and he heard the unmistakable noise that gives the rattlesnake its name. Dr. Hickman half lifted and half threw a small tan-colored snake off to the left where it landed in a bush. Matt wondered if she treated her men like she did her snakes. Behave or get tossed. Dr. Hickman was still talking; recording everything she saw.

"Crotalus viridis, twenty to thirty in clear sight around and inside the entry, various sizes. No births yet that I can see."

About then she looked at Matt. One or two of these evil-looking little critters at a distance was one thing, but now they were everywhere. The urge to quip funny vanished. Matt paled.

"Take a deep breath, for God's sake. I'm not about to carry you out of here." She started spraying repellent all around them. "Journalists! All right. Follow me."

She deposited him on a rock she first checked out for critters. Doctor Hickman took his pulse and watched his color for a few minutes. When she felt he was going to live, she put a hand on one hip.

"All this way, I need to make some further observations. Births seem to be late this year." As she backed away from him, she was talking half to Matt and half to her recorder.

"I think I saw some scutulatus, Mojave rattlers more prevalent in southeastern California."

She was gone. Matt felt a little embarrassed, but what price story? *Journalist faints in snake den.* Pulled his feet in closer and checked his watch. Just past seven a.m. An hour later he was worried she might be snake bit and dead when she came around the massive wall of rock they'd passed going in. She was half dragging a tan-colored bag with her.

"Feel how heavy this mother is," she said.

She offered it for him to heft. Looked like she had just won the lottery.

"She'll give birth to live babies almost anytime. Maybe, hopefully, hold off until class tomorrow."

Matt looked at the bag, shoved his fists deep into his pockets. *Wonderful*. "Is it going to make that noise all the way back?"

They left the area of den number three. All those crawling, coiling critters ready to bite his precious ass produced a condition of near shock.

"If you had to guess, how many people do you think ever see the inside of a snake den?" Matt asked, a new idea dawning.

"You mean besides you and me?"

"Yeah."

"I didn't see any bodies in that one."

"Wouldn't be a bad place to hide something, would it?"

"The den? Would be a perfect place to hide something. Why?" she said.

Chapter 40

LAS VEGAS
THE PRESENT

Easy to remember this lady, he repeated to himself.

"Evelyn. This is Matt, the drunk, ex-feature reporter for the *Las Vegas Sun*."

Dr. Evelyn Hickman swiveled her chair to the left and looked up at a cork bulletin board. The newspaper article, a little yellowed and partly covered with other later bits of information, was easy to see. Evelyn read the title of the piece into the phone.

"All Things Desert. I remember a snake, a crawling, spineless creature who never returned phone calls—poisonous species, I believe?"

"You were always good at defining your reptiles."

"Never thought I'd hear your voice again. Did you call to apologize?"

"Unless you married that microbiologist, I could grovel over dinner."

"He's a snake too. Is that the real reason you called?"

"Are you up for a drive, retrieve a box from a snake den?"

"As long as dinner goes with it. Where are you?"

"Salt Lake. Be there in three days. I'll call."

"You better."

Chapter 41

TWELVE STEP HOUSE

Relapse was playing with it, the cat and the hat. Matt had wandered into the day room. He was alone and doing his best to remember anything that might help find Cate. He sat and watched the cat play. The hat was dark blue, with the yellow braid work removed. Must have been a military school hat of some kind, like an officer would wear.

He picked it up, studied it. Held it by the brim and brought it hard against his leg. Dust clouded up and around him in the morning light, spilling into the room. Still looked pretty good. Yoyo was fond of wearing it.

Matt put it on and pulled the bill down close to eye level. Not a bad fit. Across the room in the window's reflection he could see his nose, mouth, jaw. His eyes were in the shadow of the bill. Perfect disguise. Angle of the light, couldn't tell who was under the hat. Stared at the image for some minutes. Why not? Exactly. What did he have to lose? By mid morning the idea had crystallized.

One thing to do then before he left for Las Vegas. Matt needed answers.

Objective was to go directly to the top, speak with the old man himself. He didn't mean the prophet and president of the Church. Easier to get to the president of the United States. He determined he would talk to old Money Bags. The top dog. The guy with the money, the muscle, the say. He needed to talk to the business type who would know who the sons-o-bitches were who took his Cate hostage.

He'd thought about the violent history both against and by the

Church. Was fighting a Dante-like mentality, desperate men out to protect what man has always fought to have and hold; his family, his God. He couldn't do anything without information.

Matt remembered when he and Carol were married, she would have lunch with her father every week. It was usually at his luxury hotel, The Wasatch. He was at an impasse until he knew more, but he could shake the trees, see what falls. At the very least he would make it clear if Cate got hurt, the consequences would be personal. Hard, when you don't really know who's giving the orders. Could end up in a Salt Lake jail. Without Cate he couldn't imagine going on anyway, and it was the only thing he could think to do at the moment.

Will I end up in a Salt Lake jail? Seventy-thirty odds. At least he had a plan, and he would have one phone call. Jack, his old editor at the *Sun. Give him the story, my kidnapping, Cate's kidnapping, along with the note.*

Only thing in Matt's favor: surprise. *Certainly no one would expect this kind of behavior from yours truly.* He rented a limousine with borrowed fake ID. A great source of illegal information is available from people who have done almost anything for a fix.

It had become overcast, no real threat of rain. Matt drove the limo to ex-daddy-in-law's hotel. The man's net worth had grown. When Matt pulled in front, the parking attendant started walking toward him. Matt pulled the brim of the hat down, dropped the window halfway, and waited.

"You're here for Mr. . . ."

Matt cut him off. "Yes."

"Where is the regular driver?"

"Mr. Burgess doesn't want him to drive if he has a cold."

Parking attendant nodded knowingly and turned back.

Matt's gonads were in his throat. He remembered leaning over the side of a building once and how his nuts literally pulled up inside him. Right now he felt like he was twenty stories up, looking straight down.

A guess and a bluff, but he had to do something. Sure didn't expect what happened. Wealthy people didn't need to spend all day in meetings. That was what underlings were for. Matt assumed Burgess' business meetings were still scheduled at nine a.m. or two p.m. as they had been when he was married to his daughter. Nine-forty in the morning was a good guess.

Couple of motorcycle cops pulled up in the street. Thought he was had, until he figured out that it was impossible. How could the police know what he was doing when he, himself, didn't know? At a quick glance he saw they were just bikers and took a couple of relieved breaths.

Seconds later when Burgess walked out of the hotel, the parking attendant said something to him and waved the limo with Matt driving into the load zone in front of the building.

Someone was with him but had lagged behind, giving last-minute instructions to a secretary in heels trying to keep up. The minute Burgess was in the backseat, Matt buried his foot in the throttle. The back door didn't shut until he hit the brakes to avoid a taxi. Stomach in throat. Panic to the max. Gripped with fear, he didn't stop for traffic or red lights. *Breathe, fool, breathe, you're a dead man anyway.*

Matt noticed several motorcycles had moved in behind and around him. He was overcome with a new panic until he noticed the bikes themselves. All Harley-Davidson. One pulled up alongside, made a motion to roll the window down.

"Where you been, man? We've been looking all over for you."

Matt slowed down. It was the obnoxious biker whom James J had started on the straight and narrow in Resurrection Corner couple years before. The smile on his face must have registered his answer.

"James J sends his best. Says to give you a hand. Where you headed?"

"The Club," Matt hollered over the traffic noise.

"*The* Club?" Bart said.

"Yeah."

"Follow me," and he roared ahead to lead the way.

Matt took off the hat and looked in the rearview mirror. "You know what I want?" It was the first time he looked into ex-father-in-law's face.

Burgess had recognized his voice, refused to speak.

"You or someone you know just offered two million to stop my book from being published. Nothing is going to happen to you as long as you listen to me. I don't care if I get us both killed. If you're half as smart as you think you are, you'll take me seriously!" Matt said.

He was breathing hard and stumbled over his rehearsed words, yet there was a curious energy in his voice.

"If anything happens to Cate, be sure you kill me too. You got it? Not one scratch, got it? One tiny abrasion, a bruise, even a rash and your worst nightmares come true. Eye for fucking eye, I'll come for you Ezra Dickhead Burgess."

Neither spoke while Matt concentrated on what was happening. He knew if they stopped, Burgess would try to get out, which is precisely what happened, but for the Harley biker who kicked the door closed. The caravan came to a dead stop in the middle of the street in front of The Club. Matt turned off the engine, pulled the keys out of the ignition, and got out. He leaned back inside the limo and looked at Burgess.

"I know you know what's going on in this town. Cate has been kidnapped."

Burgess looked older, less fit than when he'd last seen him.

"Is there any doubt in your whole body I won't do what I say?"

There was not fear in Burgess face only revulsion.

"I have to go out of state to get the records. You tell whoever, if Cate is released, I won't go to the newspapers. Can you imagine how much the *Salt Lake Tribune* would like to get their hands on my research? Have a man meet me at the fountain in front of Caesar's Palace, in Las Vegas, this Friday at eleven a.m. I can deliver the research documents at that time."

Burgess said nothing.

"No acknowledgment is taken as an affirmative."

A Harley engine revved.

"Eye for an eye, Burgess."

He tossed the keys hard into the old man's chest, watched them bounce to the floor. Matt pulled the hat back on and climbed on the back of the waiting Harley.

Twelve bikes pulled away and took a right at the next corner, and as they did, Matt watched Burgess exit the limousine. The bikes peeled off and went their individual ways at each intersection until Matt and Bart were alone. At Eighteenth South they pulled into a garage behind a two-story tan brick building.

"Welcome to Residence Twelve. We're almost ready to open," Bart said.

"Your timing couldn't be better. How did you...?"

Matt heard a familiar voice and turned to see Tiny Tim make a standard three-foot-wide door look like it had been built too small.

"Easy. I walked into an AA meeting last night when Bart announced James J had called looking for one Matt Alcott. Shouldn't tell Yoyo anything," Tiny said.

"When Cate disappeared, James J called." It was Bart talking. Not the Bart he remembered. This one had been clean and sober two years.

"We got feelers out, man. See what we could come up with, but we're getting a strange picture. We're not dealing with your average criminal type here. Rich and powerful is difficult to figure. Up against people who are the law, can do any goddamn thing they want."

"The guy in the limo, what was that all about?" Gabe said.

"He's the one you are talking about, one of the most wealthy members of the Church. Owns enough of this valley to know everything that goes on. I doubt a seagull shits he doesn't nod first," Matt said.

"No shortage of balls in your family. You the guy with the book?"

"Guilty. I don't think they know how to deal with 'no.' I get this letter says they have Cate and I have to give them all my research and stop my book from being published."

"Count yourself lucky you didn't call the police. I don't know two dudes on the Salt Lake Police force that aren't Mormon," Gabe said.

Bart dropped his hand on Matt's shoulder. "How can we help?"

"I'm not sure. Cate's mother put in a missing persons report, but that was in New York. I don't have a clue where she is. That's why the limo ride. I told President Burgess I'd go to the media about a kidnapping if I didn't see her by Friday."

"What did he say?"

"I might as well have been talking to Brigham Young's statue."

"What about the FBI? You think she was hauled across a state line?" Gabe asked.

"Yeah, ordinarily. But there's a hitch. Church staffs its security posts with FBI retreads."

"You were hosed before you got out of bed this morning," Bart said.

Matt looked pale. "She had nothing to do with any of this, as innocent as it gets."

"Look, you need anything, James J says you get it."

"I can't tell you how much I appreciate that. If I had a clue how you could help, I wouldn't hesitate, believe me."

"Here's our phone number. Ask for one of the twelve. We call ourselves the Twelve Apostles."

Even if he'd wanted to Matt couldn't hold back the smile.

"Fashionable."

Chapter 42

SALT LAKE CITY
THE BIG BLUFF

Matt bought a car. Cash. Figured after the limo ride, best place for him was out of town. Tiny dropped him off to pick up a Jeep Sahara at a local dealership. A stick shift, do seventy-five easily before it started to float. It was for Cate. God, what? A pinch of the positive. All this time she had been driving a 1976 AMC, flat-fender CJ5 James J had restored. It was about time James J got his jeep back.

Las Vegas was an eight-hour drive. How extensive the surveillance on him was, from parties unknown, he could only guess. The only thing he could think to do was bluff. Had to get Cate back. If they had all the roads staked out, he would make some off-road detours. Matt was not uncomfortable tooling about in the southern Nevada desert.

It was turning evening as he left the highway in North Las Vegas. Felt good to be back. Pulled into the parking lot, a small joint with a big name, North Las Vegas Lounge, A Drinking Establishment. The eye adjustment took a minute. The silhouette behind the bar was familiar.

"Thought you'd have made your fortune by now and sold this place," Matt said.

"Jesus, Matt. That you? Don't tell me you're sober?" the bartender said.

"North Las Vegas Lounge did it to me."

"I guess I should always put a little on the long shots. You just cost me fifty bucks."

"Ouch. Who gets the money?" Matt asked.

"Remember Cap Three?"

Brad Cummings had flown the Air Force F-111s. At retirement the closest thing he had to a home was the North Las Vegas Lounge. It was across the street from Nellis Air Force Base, so he stayed. Matt reached into his pocket, peeled off a fifty.

"I got a deal for you. I need to be incognito for a day or so. Park my wheels out back and I'll cover the fifty you lost to Cummings."

"No way, man. I did three 401Ks on your liver. Leave your rig out back. I'll keep an eye on it." He hesitated. "I'll do better than that. Here." The bartender opened the till, pulled out a set of keys, and put them next to the coffee he put in front of Matt.

"There's a pickup in the shed I use for odd stuff. Put yours in there. You take the pickup. Worth it to see you sober."

Got everything done he needed to the next day. Time to get visible again. He picked up his jeep Sahara. Had given old Money Bags plenty of time to inform whoever might be interested in his whereabouts. He assumed he was being watched. Top down made it easy to see him. He pulled into the back parking lot at Caesar's Palace. Breakfast in the hotel restaurant at ten a.m. He stood out in front by the fountain until eleven-thirty. Figured this was when they would find him and probably place a radio transmitter locator-type thing on the Jeep somewhere. They could follow him to Snake Den Number Three to retrieve the records if they wanted.

Hadn't been able to reach Evelyn. *She's a married woman, Matthew. Leave her alone.* Coward can go in the desert by himself. Matt couldn't wait any longer. Drove through Mesquite, Nevada, and into the low hills thinking, *How do I get myself into these things?*

Had no more idea how he was going to get the box out than he did putting it in. He'd picked up some lighter fluid. That might do the trick. The day they stored the box in Den Number Three, Evelyn went ahead, said, "When I tell you it's okay, you bring the box and just put it down. Then get out."

That was then.

The gun Matt bought had buckshot bullets for a seven-millimeter Smith & Wesson revolver. Evelyn would shoot him with his own gun if she knew. Matt approached cautiously, but didn't see one snake as he cleared the twenty-foot wall of rock just before coming on to the entrance to the den. Something inside wasn't in the right place to be the box he had stored there. Odd something. Moving closer and at a better angle, he slowed his stride. The hair on his neck moved. It was a person. No snakes anywhere. The person was wearing shorts. Matt would know those legs anywhere. Evelyn. Was there any chance on God's earth it was not Evelyn? His skin turned ice cold as he entered the den and stood looking at her. Eve was on her side, her mouth open as though gasping for air. Matt felt faint. Fell to his knees, vomited violently.

"No, not you. Goddamn it."

Surprised at hearing his own echo, he turned away. Couldn't look, her face contorted like that. Nothing was moving around the inside parameter of the cave. No noise of any kind except his shoes on the cave's floor. He touched her legs where the puncture marks were. Rock-hard skin.

"You dirty bastards. You dirty, fucking bastards."

Over and over the sound of the Smith & Wesson barked in his ears. He emptied every round into the dark crevices at the floor of the den.

He drove back to Mesquite for a sheriff. Told them who she was. The box he'd left four years back was gone. No reason to mention it. Too complicated to get into that.

"No mystery here," the sheriff said.

It was typical to this part of the world. When working for *The Sun*, he learned there was a dark under shadow that ran through Nevada's southern parts. In how many cities across the country do you read headlines, averaging maybe twice a year, Body Found in Desert? More often than not the discoveries were made by someone's dog while its owner jogged in the outlying areas. This was just another body in the desert. How was he to explain her as an unwitting player in an ecclesiastical-political power struggle? Exposing the truth can get you killed.

The sheriff wiped the inside brim of his Stetson with a handkerchief. "Should never have worked this den alone, no matter who she was."

The *Las Vegas Sun* gave it a quarter column on page eight. *Prominent herpetologist dies of snakebite.*

Matt called his old editor, Jack.

"The autopsy report said she had enough venom in her to kill a rhinoceros, asphyxiation brought on by rattlesnake venom. Coroner quit counting at something like thirty sets of punctures," Jack said.

"Evelyn Hickman was murdered," Matt growled. "Coward bastards made her go into that den and retrieve the box by herself without her equipment. Then they made her go back in and stay there. One snake bite acted on immediately is one thing. More is guaranteed lethal. She always carried anti-venom and had repellant that smelled like dragon shit."

"Prove that? You show me hard evidence, I'll print it. What was in the box?"

Chapter 43

Matt drove back to Salt Lake City in agony. Only the worst came to mind, but if there was the slimmest chance, he had to explore it. Another pay phone. He didn't try to get to ex-father-in-law. When Burgess's secretary answered, he blurted out his message.

"This is Matt Alcott. You tell your boss if Cate does not show up within twelve hours, I'm going to the *Salt Lake Tribune* with her kidnapping, and Burgess' name will figure prominently in my report."

The line was silent. He wondered if she was still there.

"Do I need to repeat that?"

A pause.

"I have it."

Chapter 44

SALT LAKE CITY

Matt, chin on chest, headed for Twelve Step House.

Tiny Tim gave Matt a humongous hug when he walked through the door. With friends like him he'd never need a chiropractor.

"Doc's in his office. There's a message for you."

Doc walked into the room.

"Paul's waiting for you. Called me himself. Wants you in his office the minute I see you," Rod said.

Matt was motionless. "Come with me, will you? Someone killed Evelyn."

"Who's Evelyn?" Rod asked.

Tiny Tim drove them in the Twelve Step van. On the way over Matt told the two of them where he'd been. Missing church records, rattlesnakes, and a dead herpetologist.

"How many people have to die because they know me, Rod?"

"Illegitimate question," Rod declared.

Little brother was well connected in the City. Could only be a good omen, he hoped. Matt was grateful Paul's office was a short ride. Good news was all he could handle.

"What do you think this is about?" Tiny asked.

"Police are probably waiting to arrest me," Matt said.

Chapter 45

PAUL'S OFFICE
SALT LAKE CITY

Mary, faithful, devoted secretary, didn't smile as they filed in. "He cleared his docket for you. You may go directly in."

Knowing the romantic fix she had on her boss, Matt guessed they would never be friends. Paul frowned when he saw three people enter his office. He offered his hand to Rod. They shook hands.

"Hi Rod, no offense, but what I have is for Matt only," Paul insisted.

"I don't trust myself. They're here for your protection," Matt said.

Tiny stepped forward. "I'm Tim Malloy, Mr. Alcott's bodyguard."

Paul glanced at Matt, then Rod.

"He's a former policeman. Gonna help me find Cate," Matt said.

Rod touched Tiny on the shoulder, motioning him to sit behind them.

Paul seemed annoyed. "I've been asked to talk to you, but...Matt, you have to take this seriously. Did you kidnap your ex-wife's father?"

"Next time I'll feed him vodka for two weeks," Matt said. "Old Money Bags knows where Cate is. Even if he doesn't know, he could find out."

Paul shook his head in disbelief.

"You idiot. He is a prominent businessman. There is no possible way he could be mixed up in anything like this."

"I took you for naïve, not stupid," Matt said.

Paul's forehead became white and pasty. He took a deep breath, restrained himself. "My firm has done some work for one or two of his companies. He's an honorable, straightforward businessman. I know this will be the end of any further business from him," Paul said. It was a clear accusation.

"He's a pragmatic businessman. World of difference."

"You're paranoid. This man has lunch every month with a member of the twelve," Paul said.

"Yeah, well, who had lunch with Cate?" He looked at Rod in desperation. "What do I have to get to these dense bastards on subject?" Matt felt himself beginning to shake. "No skin off your self-righteous ass, is it? Only your rich clients carry any weight around here."

Rod put his hand on Matt's shoulder. "Calm down, Matthew. Paul, it's my understanding that Cate's mother filed a missing persons report in New York."

He was attempting to inject some sanity into the conversation when Matt came out of his chair.

"I'll tell you what to do with your client."

Rod motioned to Tiny Tim. "Hold Matt."

Rod needed only to say it and Tiny Tim had Matt by the shoulders. Paul took his cue and out of fear and revenge, placed a solid right on Matt's jaw. Seeing the error of his ways, Tiny dropped Matt and stepped in front of him. Rod talked them down to a shouting match.

"You hit me, asshole," Matt said from the floor.

"I owed you, you arrogant prick."

Paul's secretary entered the room. "I'm calling 911."

"Just close the door," Paul said without looking at her.

She slammed it. Matt, back on his feet, had to crane his neck to see around Tiny.

"Tell me Cate's okay," Matt said, feeling his face begin to swell and hurt.

"I can't tell you that. The call to me was from Tanner at Tanner and Welsely. I'm to convey to you that Burgess has no idea what you're talking about," Paul said.

"Does Dad know you're associated with kidnappers?"

"Must be out of your mind. The people who offered to buy your manuscript are business people. That's the extent of it."

"Bullshit. They write checks, they make deals, kidnap people. That makes 'em real, and Cate is missing. That's real too. Doesn't anyone get it!"

"They made you a legitimate offer. That's the end of it."

"Yeah and your brain's not connected to your asshole either," Matt said, trying to stand up.

"That's it, the message I am to give you."

Matt, wobbly, attempted to get in a chair.

"Rodney, for God's sake, talk some sense into my fool brother," Paul said.

Paul became aware that Rodney had turned psychologist and was studying his face

"I believe you believe what your clients have told you, but Matthew has a point. There is a woman missing and people don't just vaporize."

"They insist they had no hand in this and I believe them," Paul said.

Tiny helped Matt get into the chair.

Little brother took a deep breath before he spoke. "You know . . . all of this is off the record."

Rod nodded. Tiny looked like he would squeeze little brother like a pimple if Matt wanted.

"There is a suggestion . . ." Paul said hesitantly.

"You been holding back," Matt accused.

"They want this cleared up as badly as you do. I'm told to tell you that they hold no ill will toward you, and they are using all their resources to resolve this thing."

"Ill will toward fuck! What about Cate?" It was clear to all in the room that Matt was not rational. Enraged, he tried to stand. Rod looked at Tiny and pointed at Matt, who then couldn't get out of the chair. Tiny holding him.

"That's it, I'm going to the *Tribune*," Matt said.

Paul's phone buzzed. Annoyed, he picked it up. "I said, no interrupt… Okay. Yes. Okay."

He was looking at Matt when he put the phone down. "Shut up, Matt. There's a man, might have something to do with this."

"Who? What's his name?" Matt said.

"I don't know," Paul said.

"Is that all you have?" Rod asked.

"No. They want you to go see your ex-father-in-law, Brother Burgess. Apparently he knows of this man," Paul said.

"President Burgess," Matt said.

"Not anymore."

Chapter 46

BURGESS HOME
SALT LAKE CITY

Ezra L. Burgess, past president of the Cottonwood Stake, would be in his home office. Matt knew that. He also knew Burgess would be figuring a strategy. Matt had no idea what to expect.

The lady who opened the large oak door spoke his name.

"What is it with you? I divorce you and four years later you're still ruining my life."

"Carol?"

Bewildered. The voice was hers. Hair had never been blond, and the face was at best an imitation of the girl he had once been married to for eternity.

"Don't be smart," Carol said.

Matt was temporarily disoriented. The voice coming out of the face put him off, her body even more so.

"My God, how many times have you had your tits lifted?" Matt said.

All that anger being squeezed out through those beautiful features was as diabolical as it gets. Her eyes, too, bothered him. They were her eyes, but at the same time they were not. Matt couldn't, within the time frame he was standing there, reconcile the image he was looking at with the one carried in memory. He wondered if it showed.

"You've been excommunicated," Carol blurted venomously.

He couldn't mistake the pleasure in her voice.

"Your records are still here, in our ward. The bishopric met and un-churched you, you apostate bastard," she said, pushing the words through her teeth.

She was holding the door from fully opening. Matt attempted to push past her.

"Yeah. I heard."

"I will personally see that you are my servant in eternity," Carol said.

"I'll take the fire and brimstone, thanks."

"I can't imagine what attracted me to you," she said, reaching, trying hard to wound him.

"Truly, one of the great mysteries."

He put his back to it, pushed past her.

"You bastard. You've ruined my father's life too."

Coming from her it sounded like a compliment.

"Father dearest in the throne room?"

She didn't answer as he walked away from her and toward the library.

When Carol and he first started going together, Matt wondered why her father hadn't remarried. As time went by he began to understand. They talked every night, father and daughter. She owned her father, had the strangest power over him. The only personal interaction he had with anyone was with her.

Burgess was behind his desk. As Matt approached, a man stepped out from behind one of the bookcases. He was dressed in blue shirt and pants, was about Matt's height, but more stocky. Matt remembered him as a gardener. Wished he'd brought Tiny Tim in with him. As the man did not move toward Matt, he continued.

Burgess rose from his desk and turned his back on Matt. It was a move he used to establish authority.

"I have one question for you," Burgess said, reaching for his cane.

Matt knew his ex-father-in-law blamed him for everything. Knowing where he was coming from made it easy to read Burgess, who couldn't help himself and turned to see the effect his words were having. Burgess pointed the cane directly at Matt.

"You are a treasonous son."

On the drive over, Matt had made up his mind that he would not call him Brother Burgess. He would call him shithead.

"And you are getting senile, Ezra. That was a statement, not a question."

"Nothing is more contemptible than a self-righteous fanatic with a cause," Burgess said.

"And I was wondering, what is more dangerous than an arrogant, self-righteous old fool who thinks his way is the only way?"

"Are you aware that you've sinned against God, that you've placed your immortal soul in grievous peril?"

Matt's eyes did a roll over.

"I keep forgetting what planet I'm on. You know why I'm here! A woman has been kidnapped and you know where she is."

"That is absolutely not true," Burgess said, jamming the cane into the carpet.

"Then why was I given your name by a prominent law firm as the man who knew about this?"

"I heard of a man that was watching you. I don't know him. I know of him. That is the extent of it," Burgess said, leaning on the cane, his hands trembling.

"Liar!"

Matt knew this humiliated the old man, especially because it was him that he was answering to. If it was anyone else it might go differently, but not the ex-son-in-law.

"You heard me." Burgess' voice was quivering.

Matt's assumption had been correct. The old man wasn't about to implicate himself and was attempting to divert anything that might be construed as suspicious as far away from himself as possible.

"Now get out before I slap a kidnapping charge on you for that limousine stunt," he demanded.

Matt sat down, crossed his legs. Burgess' eyes were cold, hard.

"I had a duty to call your father, inform him of your excommunication. When I did, I spoke to a man with a broken heart. What does it take to turn a missionary for God into the antichrist?"

The conditioning was deep. Matt was almost sucked into the old mindset. Prodigal, wayward son, come home to disgrace and shame. Burgess was cunning, knew exactly how to leverage emotions, coerce with words. Obvious why he was picked to be a stake president, Matt thought. He stood, squared off to the old man, something he had never done when married to his pride and joy.

"Don't bring my father into this. You don't stand that tall. My father is a decent man, and you, you miserable bleep, are nothing but a spiritual shill. You're nothing without the membership. They give your empty, bullying life its substance."

Matt was spitting the words, listening to what he was saying and wondering where they were coming from.

"And another thing, Ezra…" Matt bore down on the name like it was something nasty-tasting. "There is a mother who wants me to call her every night. She wants to know where her daughter is."

"Get out of my home," Burgess snarled.

"You arrogant old bastard, the man you've got working for you played Jazz basketball with my gonads for two weeks, and now he has kidnapped an innocent lady and doing God-knows-what to her. Tell me where she is."

This infuriated Burgess. His hand was shaking as he raised the cane and brought it down hard.

Matt had forgotten about the other man, the gardener, who now had him in a bear hug from behind. Burgess was old and thin, but he managed a good solid blow to Matt's forehead.

It was freaky. A hard hickory cane like that would hurt like hell. Matt felt nothing. He realized he was looking up as these thoughts were spinning through his head. Two men were looking down at him when without warning Matt's head exploded with pain. He didn't remember getting to his feet. Nor did he know why he was flying, but he was doing just that and with the gardener in front of him.

When perception caught up, Matt realized he was outside of the Burgess home and midway between the floor above and the ground below. Glass fragments everywhere caused him to shut his eyes tight.

He slammed into the ground with a grunt. There was another grunt. The gardener was moaning next to him. Matt looked up. The large window at Burgess' office was without glass. Popcorn-sized shards of glass lay all around Matt and the gardener. Every move to get up cut knees, elbows, and hands.

Someone lifted Matt to his feet.

"What happened?"

It was Tiny Tim's voice.

At a noise from above, Tiny and Matt looked up.

"Shoot him," Burgess said.

Carol was standing next to her father, a nickel-plated revolver in her hand. Matt found himself looking directly into the muzzle.

Tiny pushed Matt. The thirty-eight Police Special made an angry report. The gardener jerked.

"Run."

Rod arrived moments before and was watching from a patio off the kitchen a few feet away.

"Run," he shouted again as he hurled a sprinkler head at Burgess' daughter.

Burgess disappeared.

Carol leaned out of the opening and re-aimed at Matt, who was just entering the house though a sliding patio door.

Another shot fired. It pinged off the cement patio and spiraled off into the cottonwoods.

Matt navigated the stairs to the next level. He burst into Burgess' office. Empty. He heard a car start. Burgess and daughter were gone.

At that point Tiny Tim came into the room.

"Address book," Matt said and started looking through Burgess' desk.

"You're bleeding, Matt," Rod declared as he walked in the room.

"I'll start the van,"Tiny Tim shouted.

The knot on the top of Matt's head was swelling. He felt a little fuzzy and handed the leather-bound address book to Rod as he stepped into the vehicle.

In Rod's hands the pages began flipping over, one after another, in rapid succession. At the H's he stopped, turned back a page.

"What does *Odd Jobs* mean to you?" Rod announced out loud.

Matt's eyes met Rod's for a fraction of a second.

"Head for Redwood Road," Rod declared studying the page. "Farley Harper. It's seems to be a trailer park."

"That old man is all gristle," Matt said, holding a towel to the lump on his head. "The old bastard wouldn't tell me shit.

"Where we going?"Tiny Tim said.

"Five hundred South Redwood Road. Space number eight."

Chapter 47

SALT LAKE CITY
AN OLD TRAILER COURT

It looked derelict. A total of nine trailers. Harper's was in a corner at one end. No grass. A few bewildered wild flowers.

Matt was first out when the van stopped. Couldn't get the door of the trailer to open. Tiny Tim pushed him aside and twisted the knob until it made a sharp metallic clink and turned freely. All three of them recoiled as the odor from inside followed the thin metal door out. The smell gave rise to a vocabulary of offense. Matt peered inside into the world of what could only be a pathetic, lonely, human animal.

"Man has the palate of a grizzly," Tiny said.

The first thing to catch the eye was not the layers of garbage and dust balls, but the homemade signs that were Scotch taped to the walls. AVENGE THE BLOOD OF THE PROPHET. ORRIN PORTER ROCKWELL, SON OF THUNDER. Another read, DANITE LEADER, yet another, COMMISSIONED BY THE PROPHET JOSEPH SMITH, AVENGER-IN-CHIEF FOR THE LORD.

"Oh God, oh God." A muffled wail was coming from Matt. He hadn't been inside for thirty seconds when he doubled over, instantly sick to his stomach.

Rod motioned to Tiny Tim. "Put him in the van, Timothy."

Tiny grabbed Matt's arm, slung it around his neck, and deposited Matt outside.

"What is he doing to Cate?" Matt said.

"It's time to think about backup," Tiny said.

He disappeared back inside the trailer. A moment later he exited pressing a cell phone to his ear. Rod stayed in the trailer a long time. When he came out he was looking at the ground. Tiny and Matt stood watching him as he paced, slow and haltingly, back and forth; finally he raised one hand, his index finger like a baton.

"We are obviously dealing with a functionally retarded man."

They both knew not to interrupt.

"Dull, normal IQ with an obsession. Cate is being held exactly where you were. It only makes sense."

"The same shithole, cold basement I was in." Matt instantly felt cold, shivered.

"Was it a basement?"

"I don't know. Felt like it."

"This man didn't kill you, Matthew, and there is no reason to believe he would kill Cate. As a matter of fact, she would be considered a prize, where you were more of a...what?...in the service of the Lord. This man has little control over his life. He likes to hold and play with his victims. He needs them alive. This is as close to intimacy as this level of intelligence gets under the circumstances."

Rod talked as though to himself, figuring it out as he went.

"Not necessarily a basement either. An old abandoned building maybe. Some place where a person can shout all day and not be heard."

"Oh God." More tortured images exploded in Matt's head.

"Cate can't be alone, not in the dark."

Rod turned away from Matt. His brow darkened. In anger he turned back and looked directly at Matt.

"Do you believe we can find her?"

There was a long pause.

"I have to find her."

"Good. Because if we are going to find her, I need you focused."

"I'm good," Matt said as he flashed on Cate occupying the same contorted apparatus he had been bound to, cold and naked. Where he had to go to picture it was madness, too painful for the natural mind.

He thought of a place designed by man to terrorize man, blackmail the human mind, give birth to the sinner. For a moment Matt became light-headed.

Tim shook Matt.

"Pucker up, man. The Twelve Apostles are here."

Blasts of hog exhaust vibrated the air. Two by two and two more loped into the trailer court. The noise overrode the morbid images in his head. Matt opened his eyes as several more bikers peeled off the main road and rolled toward them.

Tiny introduced Rod to Bart. Rod then stood on the top step of the mobile home.

As the bikers turned off their engines and walked past Matt, each one said something.

"Hang in there, man."

Another slapped him on the shoulder, and one bushy red beard stood in front of Matt, a giant smile widened across his face. Slowly he reached behind his back and produced a large bone-handled hunting knife.

"Human bone," he said, pointing to the knife's handle. "Been months since I killed anyone. I'll personally bring you his balls. We'll tape his fuckin' eyes open and feed 'em to my fuckin' dog. Ha ha. Ha ha. Ha ha."

He laughed like happiness was a drug and he had overdosed. Something wild behind his eyes gave Matt hope.

Tiny said something to Bart, who pointed to Rod.

"Lock it down. This here's Dr. Overton. He's gonna walk us through it."

"Thank you for coming, for helping us. I can't help thinking..."

Rod paused, changed his mind, and with his thumb pointing behind him to the mobile home at his back said, "The man we want to find lives in this... Large man, only wears a suit from what I can gather. He's not too swift. I'm confident, if we put our efforts together, we can find the location of the place where the girl is being held. Might be something like the basement of a house, or an old factory...maybe an abandoned warehouse. Might be an unused industrial area. The key is the railroad. When Matthew was being held by this man he could hear and feel trains as they moved. We stay close to the tracks. Check out every building."

"What about Ogden or Provo?" the biker with the bushy red beard asked.

Dr. Overton thought for a moment.

"He is too limited, like a small animal that would be disoriented outside his own territory, his own little world. Say we work from Woods Cross to just south of Riverton at the turn of the mountain and west of I-15. Let's make that our first sweep. Every abandoned edifice where you can feel and/or hear a train."

Bart took over.

"All right, listen up. Let's cut the valley into sections, like six. Two Hogs to a section."

Matt couldn't listen anymore. The task seemed enormous. Gloom like ice filled his gut. His hands trembled. He flickered in and out of an exotic emptiness, a moment when everything felt painless.

Matt was aware of someone shaking him.

"Focus, damn you, focus. Cate. Think about Cate," Rod said.

Tiny driving. Aware that he'd passed out, Matt put his hands over his face. Rod swiveled in the passenger side chair, looked at him again, a psychologist's eye, probing. Rod reached for his arm. Matt watched him hold his wrist before pulling his arm away.

Matt couldn't handle the thought of what was happening to her. He remembered the conversation with Rod. Wallow in your own self-pity. He wanted to scream his lungs out. Rod's voice cut through the fog.

"Tell us exactly what you can remember when you were dumped in front of Twelve Step House. You've never told us how you got in a cab naked. What happened? Anything you can remember. Why we didn't think to do this before is unconscionable."

Matt thought of Cate. This time no dark peace invaded. He thought of the big man and felt his blood rise.

"I was dumped."

"We know that. What happened before you were deposited at Twelve Step House?"

With effort. His mind searching.

"That's what I'm telling you. I was dumped before. Before that. First time, it was an alley, bricks, not asphalt. It was dark, a brick building…a restaurant…it was after that, the cab that took me to Twelve Step House."

"What kind of restaurant?" Tiny seemed to come to life.

"I'm not sure I can…" Matt worried.

"Relax. Take a deep breath and think back. Was there a sign? How about a smell?" Rod asked.

"Shit. Nothing's coming to me."

"Chinese?" Tiny proposed.

"No."

"Mexican?"

"No."

"How about pizza?"

"Pizza. Yes. Yes!"

"Small place? Big place? Signs? Color of the building?" Rod threw out.

"When you came out of the alley, was the pizza joint on the right or left?" This time it was Tiny who asked the question.

"On the right. There was a yellow cab in front."

Tiny swerved to the side of the road. The van rocked violently. He put on the brake, released the lock on the driver's chair, and swiveled to look at Matt.

"How long was the ride from the pizza place to Twelve Step House?"

"Short. I think. I wasn't very with it."

Tiny did a U-turn, wheels squealing, and put them on the freeway.

"Do you remember the name of the pizza joint?"

"The light hurt. Couldn't see. It was night, but everything was too bright."

"You were blindfolded for two weeks. A full moon would have looked like the sun," Rod said.

Minutes later Tiny made a right turn into an off-ramp. A left, another, and they pulled into an alley.

"Was the brick building on your right or on your left?" Rod asked.

"Yes. No. Yes. Like this. Exactly, I think, like this."

"Get out. Walk it," Rod said as he exited the cab.

Matt stood in front of the van, looking around. Rod behind him. Tiny shut the engine down and followed.

"It was dark."

"Close your eyes. Were you standing?"

"I was on my hands and knees before I leaned against the building."

"Then kneel. See if the brick feels the same. Were the bricks worn and splayed at the edges like these or new with more defined edges?"

"Not new. Like these, I think. God, I don't know. The confusion. I remember. I was crawling. Used the building to stand up."

"When you get to the end of the alley…put your hand over your eyes…what was the surface like? Were you standing? What was your impression as you came out of the alley?" Rod was pushing questions like a machine gun.

"Okay, okay. My knees hurt."

Matt knelt; felt the alley surface, crawled to the building, felt its bricks. He attempted to read his own impressions. It seemed right, but nothing jolted him conclusively.

"You were pretty drugged up. Take your time."

Matt walked along the building, holding onto it with both hands. Kept his eyes closed.

"I was making my way along like this, half leaning on the wall. That's funny. I was carrying my clothes under my arm."

The bricks ended. He cleared the building. To his right there was a Laundromat. Next, above the entrance door was a sign, New York Pizza. Beyond that a few other small businesses.

"Here. Right here. This is where I was. I know it."

The three men walked out in front of the pizza restaurant and into the middle of the street. It was as though they knew what they were about to see. Each did a three-sixty and stopped at the same view with the restaurant at their backs. They were in the middle of a two-lane street, the occasional car avoiding and honking. Three miles out was an abandoned set of buildings.

It was Rod's voice, deep, resonant. "Ladies and gentlemen, I give you the old Army Reserve building, shut down for years. Unless I ill remember, it was a foundry before that. Some barracks were added for later military use, Second World War."

As they stood squinting to see what they could, a train traveling north cut between them and the buildings.

"Train!" Matt and Rod almost said it in unison.

A passing sedan hit its brakes, spun out and onto the side of the road, barely missing three men running toward a van in an alley next to a pizza joint.

Tiny was first in the van. He dropped the clutch before the engine had time to build up rpms. The engine died.

"Make a right," Rod said.

The engine was flooded. Wouldn't start. Tiny put the transmission in neutral, jumped out, and pushed the van until it was rolling. He jumped back in, dropped the transmission into second gear, and let the clutch out. The engine rolled over and purred.

"During the second World War, those buildings were used for castings of metal parts for jeeps and B-29s. It would be a perfect place to stash someone." Rod rummaged through memories.

Tiny found a side street he remembered. A chain-link fence ran all the way around the compound. They drove the fence until they came to a gate.

"It's locked," Matt said.

"Gonna ram it," Tiny said, shifting down.

"Get closer," Rod suggested.

The lock had been opened and hooked back through the chain to make it appear locked. Matt leapt out, pulled the chain loose. The gate swung wide.

Hope surged. Matt felt stronger. They drove around a one-story building to a large, six-story, concrete structure. A gray four-door sedan was parked in the shadow of a loading dock. Tiny brought the van to a stop. They sat in silence, looking at it, when something in the shadow moved. Rod leaned forward.

"Did you see...?"

"Yes. I saw it."

Tim headed the van in the direction Rod was pointing.

"That's him," Matt shouted and jumped out of the van running.

They were at the north end of the long structure. Matt was moving fast as he closed in on the brown suit.

Farley bent forward, leaving only a shoulder as a target. Matt ran straight into him and bounced off like a toy person. He hit the ground, winded. Farley saw two other men in the van and disappeared inside the building. As the door shut behind him, Matt heard a steel bolt slam in place. It was a steel door, in a steel frame with a dead-bolt lock.

Tiny put the van in neutral, set the brake, and got out. He sized up the door as he approached it. He couldn't get the door to budge and began looking for something to work with. Not much lying around, couple of old crates, small pile of railroad ties, and other odd junk discarded years ago.

"Bring one of those railroad ties," Tiny said to Matt.

Matt could only get one end off the ground. He made a futile attempt to drag it. Tiny took it from him, held one end against the steel door, the other toward the van's bumper.

"That'll work. Bring me that wood crate."

Rod had moved into the driver's seat. He brought the front bumper up against the railroad tie. Matt slid the crate under it. Both men stepped back as Rod applied some throttle to the van. There was a metallic clink, and the door buckled, allowing them access to the interior of the building.

Tiny disappeared inside. Seconds later he returned.

"It's darker than the inside of Toby's ass in there. We need a flashlight."

The van didn't have one, but the gray sedan did. Matt waved it in victory.

"Excellent," Rod said as he headed for the broken door.

Inside, Matt flipped the switch. Nothing. The batteries were burned out. They stood helpless, waiting for their eyes to adjust. The old foundry had wire-glass skylights in the roof, two rows of them running north and south with the building. Years of baked-on dirt rendered them marginally helpful.

At this end of the building it was open all the way to the roof. After a minute their eyes began to adjust and they could make out forms and shapes. There was a maze of rooms used for product supply, fabrication, quality control, and more. There were furnaces for forging and swaging metals. Spaces for assembly and transport.

A conveyor belt was located to the left of a door that was locked. Matt climbed on the dust-laden belt and worked his way into the room beyond. He found himself standing alone in the dark, stillness wrapping itself around him. Goose bumps the size of hubcaps glazed his skin. The thought of Cate in this place turned his stomach to mush. He found the lock on the door, but, warped out of square, it would open only a couple of inches.

"Get back," Tiny said.

He bent the door enough for them to squeeze through.

"He couldn't have come this way," Rod said.

"There's another door. Looks to be going west," Tiny offered.

Rod tried it. "Locked."

Matt found a small, steel access door, three feet high, two wide.

"Must be for machinery repair," Rod said.

Matt could fit. He stuck his head in. "Pitch black in here."

He dropped to his knees, squeezed in, and began working his way in to see if there was another access door on the other side. Felt his way by inches. He realized he was kneeling in a thin paste-like substance.

"Yuck. What do rat turds feel like?" His words didn't echo. Talking out loud dulled some of the fear. He turned to go back, but couldn't see where he entered. "Where are you guys?" There was no answer. "Hey. We're talking disoriented here," he said, shouting. He heard soft, even, rustling noises. They were all around him. "Rats in here."

Rod's voice surprised him. "I don't see enough bio matter for animal forms. Beetles probably."

He found a wall with his forehead. Of course it was steel, built, no doubt, like everything in this valley, with an eternity mentality, to last through the millennium. His head throbbed something awful. He checked to feel if he was cut. Couldn't tell, so much crap on his hands. Matt worked his way around the inside of the steel room until he found a door. No way of knowing if it was the same door he came in by, but it did have an inside latch-handle. There was just enough room to squeeze his shoulders through.

Shafts of light were coming from the skylights above. He got to his feet to find he was in an open area with latticework, steel floors above and below he could see through. The layout was entirely different.

"Where are you guys?" The air was dead. "Anyone hear me?" he shouted.

There was a muffled voice off to his left behind a cluster of three large galvanized pipes running through to the floors above and below.

A few cautious steps and he was on a walkway with a handrail. He could dimly see through the latticed steel floor to the area below. *Don't look down, Alcott.*

Following the handrail, he tried to make sense of the room. It was open in the middle with a crane above. The floor pulsed under him. He started to turn to see the cause when he was pushed from behind. Flailing, Matt was propelled out into the open blackness below. His hand struck the steel flooring off to his right and he managed to grab hold.

"Help!" Matt shouted.

Hoping to find something else to hang on to or climb, he looked up to see a large shadow lean over him.

"She's mine," the shadow said.

He knew the voice. It was Farley with a handful of Matt's collar. He knew it was the end of his life. Then he realized the big man wasn't pushing, he was pulling. He hoisted Matt up to his level. His expression puzzled Matt. He was staring at arrogance and contempt, Goliath looking at David, laughing at his puny foe.

Matt kicked and twisted and managed to squirm loose. He ran for a dark corner and found it was a hunk of steel machinery. He leaned to one side to keep his balance, but fell. On his back, a foul odor drifted over him. He remembered bad breath and kicked hard with the other foot. Pay dirt. Got him in the face. The big man was stunned for a second.

Matt managed to stand. Which way to run? He had no sense of direction. In the half-light he could see bad breath was ten feet away, wiping blood from his nose.

"Farley Harper. Is that your name?" Matt said.

The place was dust everywhere, so fine he could hardly feel it. Matt swung a handful of the silky dust at the bear-like shadow. Reticulate powder. It didn't carry a foot. Hung in the air like a cloud.

A voice that sounded like it came out of a well said, "You are a sinner."

Farley put his hand in his pocket. Matt heard the unmistakable metallic snap a pocketknife makes when it opens.

"Cate's not a sinner," Matt shouted.

"The Lord has given her to me for a helpmate," Farley said, his voice emphatic.

"You touch her, I'll kill you," Matt shouted.

"I am here to avenge the blood of the prophet," he snarled.

A glint of light from a skylight above gave the blade the look of a machete.

"You gonna cut my throat?You gonna blood atonement my ass, you ass?"

Farley started toward him. Matt could see no way out. Cate flashed through his mind. He hoped she would come to know he hadn't abandoned her. *I love you*. Weird. So many thoughts in the flicker of a second. Knew he was done for.

"Tim," Rod said. "I think there is a door over here."

"I heard something."

The two shuffled through shadows, came to another door.

"Locked."

"Let me try it." Tiny Tim checked the door. "Yes. It opens away. Stand back."

A roof leak had rusted it paper thin. Tiny slammed his shoulder into the door with all his force. The noise echoed and they were able to push through.

A muffled "Help" reached them.

Rod motioned to his left. "Off this wall."

Farley had him again, forcing him down to the steel deck.

"Where's Cate?' Matt shouted.

"Mine," Farley growled.

He put a foot on Matt's chest while wrapping a chain around his ankles. He couldn't breathe from the weight of the big man. Farley hadn't cut his throat. It took seconds to know why. Matt was being shackled to a block and tackle and was being pulled higher and higher. The click, click of a chain pulley registered. The chain bit into his ankles like fire.

He saw himself, like a stuck pig hanging in the blackness, the blood spurting from his neck, taking his worthless life with it. Matt realized he was looking directly into the face of hell, only upside down and spinning. One moment he was looking at Farley, a large knife in his face. The next he was peering out over nothing. Farley was guiding the chain pulley assembly Matt was fettered to beyond the edge of the steel flooring, out into the open shaft used for bringing materials up inside the building. Farley's face, upside down, would come in focus, then disappear as Matt spun. He knew he was about to be sliced open and gutted like a pig.

"Say your prayers," the big man said.

Doomed and knew it. Upside down and doomed. *Get smart* ran through his head. It occurred to him that saying his prayers might, indeed, be exactly the right thing to do.

"Dear God. Please forgive me for my sins."

Farley's sense of respect for all things religious, especially a prayer of redemption, caused him to hesitate with the knife. Matt scurried mentally to call up things to say that would distract him.

"I will repent of all my sins if you spare me. I will be good. I will repent. Dear God, please forgive me and please forgive Farley too, because he doesn't want to go to hell for the mistake he is about to make. Please forgive Farley. And please let Cate go. She has nothing to do with this."

"No." Farley's voice more of a growl.

At the mention of Cate's name, Farley made a fist. It felt like a padded sledgehammer. Black infinity below. Farley had let go of the chain, and Matt began spinning and swaying away, then back to catch another blow. The big man had his own personal punching bag, and all Matt could do was listen to the grunts he was making while he was being turned into hamburger. Matt saw the knife up close.

"Dear Lord, help Farley understand that I have him by the balls," Matt hollered and clamped down as hard as he could. The one he got hold of filled his hand. Farley let out a noise that sounded like a dog's yelp.

"Oh shit. Oh shit, oh shit," Matt sputtered.

He saw Tiny Tim coming at Farley with a pipe in one hand. As the two squared off to each other, Matt found himself hanging directly between the pipe and the knife.

Farley was stronger, but Tiny was faster. The knife and the pipe made a metallic clanking noise as they ricocheted and bounced their way down to lower levels. Farley and Tiny wrestled, heaving from the right of Matt to the left. It was like two concrete slabs slammed into each other.

The combat jostled and bounced Matt first into one machine, then another. All he could see was two titan shadows colliding. He was swinging at what must have been a twenty-degree arch and hit something hard and sharp. He tried to grab Farley and was flung into Tiny. He blinked to see Rod working the chain pulley assembly to bring Matt back to the steel grate decking. His ankles were inflamed with pain. Mountains of flesh insulted each other next to him. Farley, protecting a treasure, fought with great fury, but too many pizzas and cholesterol clogged the pipes.

Winded, Farley was on his stomach with his arms bent behind his back. Something strange happened that caused Matt and Rod to look at each other. This mountain of a man began to cry. It was like stepping in something smelly that couldn't be scraped off. Both realized that this enormous person was little more than a large boy.

Matt turned away embarrassed, for what he wasn't sure. This great hulk of a man crying like an adolescent boy whose pony had to be put down was weird, awkward, and did not digest. Tiny took a white plastic tie out of his pocket and put it around Farley's wrists.

"You carry that stuff around with you?" Matt asked Tiny.

"Old habit. Used to be a cop."

Tiny pushed Farley against a railing and used another plastic tie to secure him to it. They searched his pockets for keys, but found none. The brown suit was ignorant enough to think he wasn't defeated. He strained against the railing. The cuffs of his shirt turned red where the sharp edges of the ties cut into his flesh. Finally he quit moving.

Matt and Tiny followed Rod down a set of steel stairs and through an open overhead door probably for use by forklifts. The shadows were deep in this part of the old building. Matt hollered, "Cate," at the top of his lungs and listened as the words died against thick cement walls.

"Any idea where we are?" Matt asked.

"We were headed south when we entered," Rod answered. "Without seeing the skylights, I'm only guessing."

Tiny grunted against a door. "We need a crowbar or at least a tire iron."

"Where did you find the pipe?" Matt asked.

"That was the only one I've seen."

Tiny managed to break through a door. The next door wouldn't budge. Reinforced hollow metal doors with steel hinges.

Thank God, a break. It had glass in the upper half. Glass with wire in it. They managed to break it and push most of the glass out of the way with a broken two-by-four. Tiny reached through and unlocked it, but the door was blocked at the floor. No alternative. It was up to Matt to crawl through and move whatever was in the way. He started through. At the point of no return, wire and glass were digging into him and he found himself helpless to move either way.

"I'm stuck."

Tiny tried to lift and push at the same time. Matt held on to the doorknob to help break the fall.

"Ouch."

"What's holding the door shut?" Tiny said.

"Gimme a damn minute, will ya."

There was a two-by-four wedged against a wall and the door. Matt kicked and kicked. Trying to help, Tiny pushed, and the door slammed into Matt's head, knocking him down.

"You should get out of the way," Tiny said, lifting him to his feet.

"We must be getting close." Rod handed Matt what was left of one leg of his pants caught in the wire when he fell to the floor.

His ankles were still on fire from the chain, and now one leg stung like salt in an open wound where the wire had etched its signature in him. Blood ran down his leg and into his shoe. He tied the cloth around his leg as tight as he could make it. At least they were making some progress through the old building. Matt leaned over and forced himself to take a few deep breaths.

"Rob. How about the fire department? They have break-in tools," Matt suggested.

"The Twelve Apostles would be faster," Tiny commented.

"Call them both. Call the Marines," Matt said, leaning against a wall.

Rod brought his cell phone to his ear. "Too much steel. We want emergency med techs standing by also. "

Rod started to work his way back out of the building.

Another large room, several levels high with iron stairs and steel walkways, opened up to Tiny and Matt. Visibility from the skylights was a little better.

"Door down there, I think."

Tiny took the lead, disappeared down into the darkness.

"Door. Stand back."

There was a boom. Tiny stood, rotating his shoulder. The door hadn't moved.

"Don't know how many more of those I got left in me."

He froze, looked at Matt funny.

"Did you hear something?"

Matt's ears were ringing from having been hit by the door.

"What?"

Tiny, moving along another descending ramp, disappeared. Matt followed. His equilibrium off, he bumped into Tiny.

"I know this smell. I've been here before," Matt said.

Matt shouted at the top of his lungs, "Cate!"

They came into another room.

"Cate!" Matt shouted again.

Tiny's face lit up. "A woman s voice."

"Cate!"

"Matthew?" It was muffled, but it was Cate.

Some form of relief ran through Matt. He leaned against a wall. Thought he was standing until he realized he was on his hands and knees.

"Jesus, take a deep breath," Tiny said.

"Never mind me."

There was more light in this area.

"What happened?" Rod said, moving up behind them.

"Weird. He heard her voice and he went straight down," Tiny said.

"He belongs in a hospital bed, Timothy. He's still detoxing. Backup is on its way."

Rod put his ear to the door and elevated his voice.

"My name is Rodney Overton. I'm an old friend of Matthew's. Are you all right?"

"I'm okay. Is Matthew there?" Cate asked.

"He's right here," Rod returned.

"What's wrong with him?"

"Nothing, honey. I'm fine. Are you okay? Has he hurt you?" Matt said, now standing.

"Matthew?" Cate asked.

Rod and Tiny stood quietly, looking at Matt.

"I'm here, honey."

"You won't hurt Mr. Rockwell, will you? He's been very kind to me."

Tiny Tim looked at Matt, his face one long question mark.

"You have to know Cate," Matt said.

Rod spoke through the door again. "How long have you been here?"

A small, bewildered voice answered, "I don't know. A month, two? But I read the Book of Mormon," her voice stronger, "the whole book. Mr. Rockwell has been teaching me about the Church. He went on a mission, too, like you did."

Matt got a funny look from Tiny.

"Someone should be outside when they arrive. I found an outside door in the last room," Rod said as he left to meet the EMTs.

An old metal air vent, which looked like it was part of some later modification, went across the ceiling and into the same room Cate's voice was coming from. There was a shelf-like workbench built at the wall, making it accessible. Matt climbed onto the workbench, marking a blood-smudged trail. He tried to shake the pipe loose.

"Maybe I can get to her through this," he said, banging on the pipe.

"Only thin straps holding it...metal though..." Tiny instructed, picking up a two-by-four in a corner. "Watch yourself," he said, swinging the wood against the corrugated pipe.

It worked. Tiny managed to break one section loose and bend it aside.

Standing on the workbench, Matt was nose high to the air vent. Still feeling wobbly and shaky, he lifted a bloody sneaker and said, "Gimme a boost."

Tiny raised Matt to where he could host himself into the opening of the air duct. He crawled forward until he came to a narrowing. It was tight. He forced himself deeper in by pushing with the toes of his sneakers, but found himself stuck in a metal coffin, unable to go forward or back. In the closeness of the duct he was sweating profusely.

He heard a muffled shout. "Farley broke the railing. He's loose in the building."

A sense of desperation overcame Matt. He was trapped, but he still had a voice.

"Die, Farley, you feeble-minded fuck. Die!" Shouting made his ears ring. "Touch her, shit-for-brains, and you're dead, you're fucking dead."

More muffled shouting from below.

Arms pinned to his sides, Matt kicked with all his might, both feet from side to side. A vibration. He thought the building was coming down, and shouted at the top of his lungs when one shoe came off. He thought he heard Farley's voice and laced the air with more obscenities. It felt like the building shook. A cold sensation, he felt air on his legs.

Under his weight the pipe separated. Matt found himself suspended by one of the straps that had held up the two severed ends of the pipe he had crawled into. He was hanging on for dear life when he looked down.

Below—standing transfixed, like people watching a UFO hover—were three firemen, two paramedics, a policeman, Doctor Rodney Overton, Tiny Tim Malloy, and several black leather jackets all staring intently skyward at a strange man hanging precariously out of the broken ends of an air-conditioning duct. Cate, wearing a floor-length white dress with long sleeves and a petite green apron, looked up and said, "Matthew?"

Under his weight, the straps holding the pipe broke.

Matt sat up, dazed, and wobbled his way to his feet. Cate ran into his arms, buried her face in his chest. A moment, less, she pulled back, frustration ballooning, and pounded on his chest.

"You didn't call me. Why didn't you call me?" Pressing her face in his chest she repeated the question. "Why, why?"

Matt looked at Rod, a smile starting to spread across his face when his knees buckled.

Rod turned to the paramedics. A motion of his hand directed them to their work.

Cate looked at the paramedics. There was fear in her eyes.

"Is he dead?"

"St. Joseph's Hospital. Both of them. I'll follow you in my car," Rod said.

Chapter 48

SALT LAKE CITY
ST. JOSEPH'S HOSPITAL

The next day Tiny took a handful of patients in the minivan to visit Matt at the hospital. Cate had been checked out by the doctors and released. She and Millie were at the mall shopping for clothing for her and Matt. When they arrived Doctor Overton was making notes in the chart. A large bandage hiding one eye gave Matt the look of a swami. He had small sets of stitches on every limb and one rather large set on the inside of his left leg.

Yoyo was first in the hospital room, talking as he entered.

"I'm here, Matthew. Mother is here. Oh, my God, you look awful. Tell me all about it. Mother will take care of it." He slid his hand under the sheet and grabbed Matthew's penis. "Oh, thank God. You're all in one piece," the excitable Yoyo said, ecstatic with expectation.

Matt, sedated, could only frown.

"Yoyo?" Dr. Rod Overton said.

Yoyo huffed off to a chair as the others entered the room. All the hellos done, Tiny started laughing. Then, shaking his head, he told what happened.

"I couldn't make sense of it. Matt ran right at the big guy, bounced off him like a Ping-Pong ball. Later, when he heard her voice, he dropped like a lead turd. I'm telling you, nothing he did made sense."

When they stopped laughing, Tiny continued. "I'll bet he never gets laid. Pass out in the middle of a good fart."

Matt could only blink and give a half nod. For Yoyo it was too much excitement for one day. He crossed his legs and smiled nervously.

Rod added his perspective.

"We were looking up at an air vent that was shouting obscenities. Within a nanosecond we were watching a half-dressed human missile hurling toward the earth. Matt was covered with soot, blood, and beetle feces. It happened so fast we couldn't make sense of it, that is, in time to at least break his fall."

Matt tried to smile. Lip was too swollen. Rod looked at him.

"Three weeks isolated in that dark hole, Cate's in better health than you are."

"You made a respectable bounce," Tiny Tim added.

Yoyo doubled over. The smell of urine followed.

"Yoyo. You piss your pants again, you'll walk home, I swear to God," Tiny threatened.

Matt tried not to laugh. It hurt too much.

Chapter 49

RESURRECTION CORNER, NY
THE ONE HUMP BAR

James J hadn't felt good and had gone home to rest. The latest round of chemo and radiation treatments were taking their toll on him. Matt was making coffee and talking to Carl and the sheriff. Crazy Helen had come in and was rolling her eyes at poor old Mr. Wylie over a cabernet sauvignon she was convinced gave her a sexy aura. The phone rang. It was Cate. Matt was again enjoying the lilt of her voice—a music that owned him.

"The Louise lady called."

Matt could tell she was sitting on the bed, bouncing like it was a trampoline.

"Your book's out. I'm coming. We'll drive to Manchester and go to the bookstores."

Matt grew quiet, looked over at the raised platform where James J's Harley sat.

"Are you there?" Cate asked.

"Pack our bags, honey. We can schedule plastic surgery in the next county, change our names."

"Oh stop. I knew you were going to say something stupid. Ask Carl to cover for you. Are you going with me or do I go alone? I want to buy a copy of your book. I want to put it in the One Hump where everyone can see it."

MANCHESTER NEW YORK

Matt hardly muttered a word the entire drive to Manchester. This wasn't like being a newspaper journalist. This was different, more final. Cate drove. Occasionally she would reach over and squeeze his hand.

It was turning dark when they arrived. An older brick building with accessible parking. A different bookstore than when he and Cate had met his brother Paul and his agent, Hamilton Gloss. That was in a new shopping center with scientifically engineered indirect lighting that depressed the hell out of Matt. A bookstore that looked like it might have a history itself lifted his spirits. The ivy-covered brick walls were further encouraging of a now jovial mood.

Over the years, the expanding interior took advantage of every nook, cranny, and closet to display books. Matt couldn't help thinking, *Rich treasures lie within*. His eyes fell to the display at the entry.

The cover was dark blue with a lighter blue imprint in relief of a handsome man with a long face and straight nose. He was wearing a coat with a high collar and was encircled by the busts of four beautiful women. A woman with a dour expression was seen in the background looking on. The handsome man, holding a book pressed tightly to his chest, was staring off into the heavens.

Matt was wearing his lucky baseball cap that James J had given him. Each of his pigeons received one at their first year birthday. It was made with lettering that read: "I had my last drink at the One Hump Bar."

The new book's display was impossible to miss as you entered. A round, heavy man with a beard that looked like it might have birds living in it was holding Matt's book, flash-reading the back cover.

Cate disappeared into the store.

Feeling frisky, Matt tapped the book the guy was holding.

"You don't want this. It was written by a tedious drunk with lousy attitude having a bad day. Would you like me to sign it for you?"

The guy leaned away until he read the words on the hat. He then grinned and handed the book to Matt.

A malnourished clerk with horn-rimmed glasses behind the counter saw what looked like someone playing a trick on an innocent customer and jumped in the middle of the fraud. While it wasn't really his store, pride of employment put him into battle mode.

"Please. Sir," the clerk said as Matt finished signing his name. "Don't do that. You disfigure a book, you buy it."

"I am sorry. I didn't think the guy would say yes. He called my bluff. I didn't know what else to do. I mean, I think he's going to buy it, and I was only having a little fun. God knows they don't let me out that often anymore." Matt said.

"Who are you?" the clerk demanded.

Pointing to the stack of books with his name on them, Matt said, "These books should be burned. They are an insult to God and Mrs. Alcott, and I won't leave until you take them off the shelf."

Heads turned, people were watching. A small crowd began to gather. Matt was glad Cate wasn't around to make short work of the fun he was having.

"You must leave this store immediately," repeated the indignant clerk.

"I will not. Not until you burn these books," Matt said, waving one of the books at the red-faced young man.

"I can call the police, you know," the clerk said in his most threatening tone.

"You are insufferable!" Matt said. "Now you're going to sell this book to the police and corrupt them too. Have you no shame?"

Matt, indignant, turned to huff out of the building and ran smack into two uniformed police officers who immediately took him to the carpet. It seemed one of the other clerks had already called the police, and it also seemed that the police department was just around the corner.

Matt's silent chortle went unnoticed as his face hit the beige carpet. He heard the click, click of the handcuffs. When Cate's sneakers appeared next to his face, he could have sworn they were frowning at him. With all his might he tried not to chuckle aloud. Her expression, as the police lifted him to his feet, was the first thing he saw.

Matt turned directly to one of the officers.

"I did it. I confess."

Ruckus over, the books flew out the door. Matt signed them all and promised to do an author reading a week hence. When he finally worked up the courage to look at her again, Cate was wagging her head.

"I can't take you anywhere anymore."

RESURRECTION CORNER
THE ONE HUMP BAR

"Honey."

Cate's voice was barely a whisper over the phone.

"It's over. James J slipped into a coma and died a few minutes ago."

She was at the hospital in Danville.

The bar was filled, everyone waiting. Matt turned. Nodded. Brought the phone back to his ear.

"Damn. I wanted to be there."

"He knew where you were and that you were looking after things. That's the way he wanted it."

"On my way," Matt said.

Cate's eyes said everything. The two stood with their arms around each other next to James J's hospital bed. She finally let go. Matt held her while she sobbed.

Two orderlies looked in. They had a stretcher with them to transport the body. Upon seeing Matt and Cate, they rolled it to one side. Said they would go for coffee.

"A couple of hours ago he kicked everyone out but me. 'Go home,' he told them, 'find something useful to do, besides annoying my sick ass.'"

Matt faced James J, leaned forward, and put both hands out on the bed to prop himself up.

"You're the one taught me to be honest with my feelings." Matt took a deep breath before continuing. "For always being there, thank you. For leaving me, you really piss me off."

Cate smiled big-time, happy with her Matthew.

"Let's go home," she said.

"Feel like I'm abandoning him."

"He's not here anymore," she said, taking his hand.

They left.

Cate rose early, started calling people.

"Our phone bill will look like the national debt," Matt mentioned.

She smiled and kept dialing.

"James J left the bar to Residence Eight, and guess who the executive custodian in perpetuity is?" she said.

"Really?" Matt said, acting like he didn't know.

"Well, along with Fonzie, you, and an attorney in Danville. No one trusts me with money. I know that much."

"Do I know the attorney?" Matt asked.

"Doubt it. He's not an alcoholic. It's a precaution in case either you or Fonzie fall off the dry wagon."

"James J never said word one to me."

"Did he tell you he wanted to change the name of the One Hump? *Transitions, A Bar and Coffee House.*"

"Like a Starbucks with booze?" Matt ventured.

"No. It's the new wave in getting clean and sober. You're done, but you don't know how to stop. Well, at Transitions you get connected. There is always someone to hang with, talk to, drinking or not."

"He had no family. What about the jeep, and the Fat Boy and Knuckles?" Matt wondered.

"He was hoping you would take an active part in Residence Eight."

"I thought you had to be a Harley type?"

"You do." She beamed.

"Really. The Fat Boy is mine?"

"You'll look good in black," Cate said.

"Only reason I didn't before—it was their deal, their own little piece of the American pie—sober bikers."

Matt was quiet for a minute.

"Damn. Pretty sneaky way to make me a Residence Eight sponsor. I'm his replacement."

Matt swallowed. More of a gulp. He turned away to process what had happened.

Cate didn't need to see his face.

"I better get down there," Matt said, referring to the bar.

Being the unofficial hub of Resurrection Corner, Darwin's Place, and Dansville, someone had to open the bar, especially today.

By noon the bar had filled up with commiserating locals. The next day Resurrection Corner looked like a Harley-Davidson convention. Matt had no idea James J's reputation was so large. He thought he knew most of James J's speaking engagements at AA conventions and the like. Not close. Knuckles, the rebuilt bike, had been featured in two magazines.

Knowledge of the work he'd done setting up Residence Houses for battered women reached from California to New York. People in recovery came from Denver, Dallas, Phoenix, Salt Lake City, Chicago, Windsor, Toronto, Winnipeg, you name it.

It quickly became evident that Resurrection Corner was not equipped for an invasion of this proportion.

Town Council met, decided to sponsor an evening buffet every day for a week. Charge by donation. Ordered ten Johnny cans. Matt called

Sister Angela, explained what was happening, in case any strangers stumbled onto the address and came sightseeing. She called the archdiocese and spoke to her mother superior.

The next day she and another nun, Sister Temperance from Chicago, were standing in front of the One Hump when Matt arrived to open up. A third nun would manage the safe house for the week. Mother Superior didn't hesitate, not for James J. She sent temporary replacements out where necessary. It seemed the archdiocese held James J in high esteem.

Money started pouring in, donation money in honor of James J. Bikers were calling other bikers, telling them about sober bikers and Residence Eight. Fonzie and Cate opened a special escrow account at the bank. That week alone they deposited over $40,000. Harley types turned into an army of previously untapped support for James J's dream.

Sister Angela and Sister Temperance, in their black habits, were everywhere. They knew what needed to be done and they knew how to delegate. Matt took instructions like everyone else. Every now and then Sister Angela, overcome, would stop, sob into her hanky, cross herself and move on.

Curiosity about the shelters for battered women was huge. The nuns and the twenty bikers who were its original sponsors became information brokers, talking to people from all over the country. Six of the Twelve Apostles from SLC came roaring in to pay respects and attend the funeral.

When James J was still capable he asked his biker brothers if they would bury him on Knuckles in some pleasant meadow in the hills. The boys went to work. To keep the Department of Health happy—compliance and all that—as well as to present the proper image for the local authorities, a casket was buried in a grave in the local Danville cemetery.

One of the local biker's family owned the mortuary and managed the cemetery. All was properly certified. Until the day of the burial, you could stumble on James J sitting on a chair in the walk-in fridge in the back room of the One Hump Bar.

Five-gallon coffee percolators were strategically placed everywhere an electric extension cord would reach. There were several AA meetings daily. Even the sheriff quit drinking. The high school let out early every day, and the kids did all kinds of things to help, including making a temporary new sign. Transitions: A Bar & Coffee House. Everyone pitched in, Cate's mother too.

Crazy Helen was in paradise. She let half a dozen motorcycle types sleep in her front yard next to the lilacs and even use her bathroom. She offered the other half of her bed to one old biker who called her his dream girl.

Matt had become famous, not because of a book, but because James J was his sponsor.

Third day Matt was sitting next to the sheriff in the One Hump. Sheriff's face melted into a wry smile as he sipped a coffee.

"Do you realize, I could arrest half the black leather in this town and close out one-tenth of the unsolved crimes in three states?"

Matt hoisted his coffee to the sheriff. "Look at the money you're saving city and state."

Sheriff raised his coffee mug. "James J."

There were Cocaine Anonymous, Marijuana Anonymous, Narcotics Anonymous meetings, as well as Alcoholics Anonymous meetings, all in James J's honor. Some in Danville. Others at the One Hump, standing room only. Many took place in the street at the same time.

Couple bikers borrowed a truck. When they returned they had a welding rig and an empty fifty-gallon metal drum. Every day, late afternoon, they had a barbecue Texas would envy.

The Danville AA Angels planned the funeral with Sister Angela as adviser. By God, they would bury him like he wanted on his Harley.

James J and the unique 1947 knuckle-shaped headers with the extended arm bars that looked like an ape hanging from a tree would ride together forever.

Those wily bastards took a front loader into the hills and enshrined him in a green valley at the edge of a narrow meadow. When James J knew his days were numbered, he'd ridden out there with Fonzie and marked the place. Wanted to be buried wearing full leathers.

Motorcycle magazine, *The Rider*, sent a reporter with a camera, but they couldn't let her attend the funeral. The site had to remain a secret; otherwise, some drunk biker would likely dig James J up to have a drink with him. The reporter persisted.

"Lose the camera. Blindfold both ways?" Fonzie declared.

She agreed.

"Done," Fonzie said.

The afternoon of the funeral Raven rode behind Fonzie, matching helmets. His Hog. His broad. They were an item now. Cate and Matt stood with Raven, Sister Angela, and Fonzie, who was officiating.

James J Flannery's funeral took place in a small valley in the hills in upstate New York, officially on his way to Harley heaven. They stood around the grave, which looked like a crater made by a small bomb.

Started at dusk. Can you imagine sixty-four Harley-Davidson engines winding out and roaring at near redline rpms for fifteen seconds? Leaves fell out of trees. Matt figured he lost two decibels of hearing that evening.

Couple of leather jackets talked. One Bartholomew Young from Salt Lake and another John Crowder from Seattle. When Bart came to the end he said, "I take my bandanna off for no man but one," and removed his bandanna, showing himself to the world, a bald biker.

The moon came up early and the clouds backed off just enough. Black leather shines a certain way by lunar reflection. They could see James J below ready to kick-start that baby into full throttle and scream through hell spreading his own kind of fire—sober fire.

"He rides into hell with sobriety in each hand. Devil will have to relocate to Georgia permanent. Either that or take his turn chairing meetings," Fonzie said at the beginning of the gravesite ceremony.

Then silence. Two full minutes, James J motionless in that hole. People stood with their arms around each other. Couple of black leather jackets bawled like babies. Matt couldn't hold it back either. Said, "I've gotta learn to swear. Only thing that says the way I feel."

Cate was joyous all day. Smiled at everyone.

A few who had been close to him were allowed to share an anecdote. Hearty laughter. Tears of joy. Nothing like an AA wake. Best funerals in the universe.

Sister Angela Maria stepped forward, praised God, thanked God, and blessed all Harley-Davidson bikers all over the world. Even the sheriff said a few words. People were laughing and crying at the same time. Serious laughter too, the kind that washes away emotional rust created by hard living.

When it was little sister's turn, Cate pulled Minnie Mouse out of her bag and stepped forward until she was leaning over the hole.

"Call me, big brother," and chucked that damn phone into the pit. Matt bit his lip.

After the hole was filled in, they replanted. The shrubs and trees removed before the front loader started digging were carefully set back in place by way of a Polaroid taken earlier. Now they served as James J's headstones. He was buried in a ceremony celebrating who he was. One set of seasons, only a tranquil green valley would mark his remains.

The front loader had been trucked into the hills earlier in the day to dig the hole. Matt, Cate, Fonzie, and Raven had followed to watch. They got there in time to see the bikers lower Knuckles in place with a chain attached to the bucket. James J was lowered in place the same way. Looked like a too ripe banana. Strange popping noises came up out of the hole when the bikers shaped his body into the proper posture and duct taped him in place.

"My God, those people are fearless," Raven said to Cate.

Matt couldn't help thinking, after what they put themselves through, hell is a truck stop with bad food.

Chapter 50

RESURRECTION CORNER

Coffee in hand, Matt sat looking at his computer. The screen seemed overwhelmingly large and barren this morning. He rose, poured the fresh pot of coffee in the sink, steam temporarily enveloping him. A new filter dropped into the cone-shaped tray. The plastic ladle made twice the trips from the can of coffee to the tray.

Cate and Matt put a small down on a single-level, three-bedroom, leaving the Resurrection Corner bank account in pitiful shape. Even though he knew taxes were inevitable, they surprised him.

Worse, he felt cheated because he couldn't watch the lumps under the quilt stir and jostle as Cate awoke in the mornings. It was ever the same; she would sit up, look around until with heavy eyelids, she found Matthew. When she located him she would fall back and sleep for another ten minutes, another hour.

It was an important part of his day, a prelude to the never-ending mystery of his quiet joys with Cate. Nothing serious. Little things. The stuff he'd kill for. In the new house it was impossible. He felt cheated, sitting alone in the kitchen.

Fourth morning bare feet whispered down the hall and one of his sweatshirts came around the corner.

"I don't like our new house. I'm always looking for you." It was her sleepy voice, as shivering, she wedged her way between him and the computer to take over his lap.

He carried her back to bed.

Noon, he could hear a pigeon cooing. His eyes opened to find Cate sitting cross-legged on the bed, the phone to her ear, Raven on the other end. Matt lay looking at her through half-open eyes. He realized he was thinking of her instead of himself, a freedom he was happy to know.

Cate noticed he was awake and pivoted the mouthpiece away from her chin.

"Let's rent out the house and move back to the loft."

Matt reached for the phone.

"I'll call you back," she said to Raven.

"Carl's number."

Speed dial. She punched it in. Handed him the phone. The voice of his old partner from the remodeling days answered. "Carl, how fast could you and I pull the walls in this place?"

"Interior or exterior?" Carl said.

"Inside."

"Not that easy. Have to shore up at the barring points first."

"Put up posts."

"Posts."

"Can you start today?"

They put up four eight-inch, round steel posts and ran two eight-inch steel I-beams twelve feet apart that paralleled the full length of the structure, and the walls came tumbling down. Cate and her mother quilted the posts and beams to match. Cheerful, bright colors when entering by the front door, more subdued when coming in at the rear.

The atmosphere in the kitchen was festive, carnival. The bedroom: various purples with something resembling a scarlet rose. Here and there a flash of lightning behind clouds. At the fireplace it was warm and relaxed. Where they put his computer was animated and playful with small stuffed critters standing, lying, and hanging about. When someone came by to visit, they walked straight to Cate's oval-shaped kitchen table, drawn by a warm, cheerful presence Raven called the oxygen of Resurrection Corner.

RESURRECTION CORNER
THE NEW HOME; ONE ROOM

The keys made their muted snapping noise under Matt's fingers, the distinct plastic sound of a computer keyboard. Minnie Mouse was no longer a threat to sanity. Riding a Harley somewhere. Her replacement, a turquoise-colored cordless, began to announce itself. Matt was grateful it was a noise that didn't pull fingernails out.

"If that's Hamilton, I'm in the Andes."

Samantha Perness, his publisher, asked Hamilton to plead, threaten, blackmail, and cajole. Anything to get Matt to do author readings at bookstores. Adamant thus far. He was grateful it wasn't Louise who called him and asked. Lady could shame a shadow out of its corner. Matt sensed she respected his decision.

Cate picked up the phone.

"He says he's not here." She listened, laughed. He knew it wasn't Hamilton.

"Hey, Doctor Rodney. You guys haven't come to see us yet. We have room now and guess what? Our high school principal is writing you a letter."

There was a pause. Matt looked up at Cate.

"I told the whole school about you. Everyone wants you to give the commencement address at this year's graduation ceremony. It's at the high school in Danville. You would be wonderful. And guess what..."

Poor Rod. It was hopeless to try and keep up. For most men, "Yes" or "Uh-huh" was the most, if fleet of tongue, a guy could squeeze in.

"My expiration date has come and gone. Four years and counting... Yeah. I am. I'm a keeper. You have to meet all our friends, and I have an idea. How about why don't you and Millie move out here. The lot next door came with the house and you can have it. All you have to do is build on it..."

"Honey, give me the phone," Matt said.

"How many people have an address that reads, Resurrection Corner?"

"The phone," Matt said, reaching.

"His Majesty wants to cut me off. I must be giving something away again."

It was the second pause where Rod was allowed to talk.

"I never thought of that. He does have to sleep sometime, doesn't he? Give my love to Millie. I wish she lived next door. We miss you guys."

A dull clonk vibrated through Matt's skull. The phone slid down the front of his nose, held by its short antenna from above.

"She struck me with the phone and it's your fault," Matt said.

"You are fortunate it was not what you deserve," Rod returned.

"You seldom call. Who died?"

"I found this website. It was called www.catesinsurancepolicy.net. It referred me to five others with various names…"

Matt couldn't help laughing.

"Websites. My personal favorite is www.Smithscomedy.org."

"You think this up?"

"Not me. According to Raven, it was the kids at the school."

"Raven?"

"Cate's best friend. Teacher at the high school. Students scanned every document I had. In a kind of classroom ceremony, they pumped all of it, everything—every word I walked out of Salt Lake City with—into…how did Raven put it…into the great galactic mind, the Internet."

"When did all this happen?" Rod asked.

Cate was sitting Indian style next to him.

"I was in Salt Lake with you. Cate bought twelve computers for the senior class. In my name, if you will." Matt said it more for Cate than Rod.

"She must come from a well-to-do family," Rod said, probing.

"Not really."

"Don't tell me..." Rod said, still fishing.

"You're getting warmer."

A pout began to spread across Cate's face.

"She's a genius, you know," Rod said.

"Rod said you're a genius," Matt echoed.

"No he didn't," Cate threw back.

"Called me a liar, Rod. You tell her."

He put the phone at an angle against her ear so they could both hear.

"I did not get to know you very well, Cate Lynn, but from what I observed, you belong in the behavioral sciences. Millie is sitting here. She agrees. I think you have a rare talent for reading people. You could make a fortune picking juries," Rod said.

"Tell Millie I miss her," Cate said, turning the phone back to Matt.

"They got a plaque with my name on it at the school," Matt said.

"Memorialized while alive. That makes you someone important then."

This was Rod at his most playful.

"Remember that when you talk to me. Anyway the kids went on-line. Raven said to the senior class, 'If the kidnappers haven't let Cate go by now, she's probably already dead.'"

"Risky."

"I think those kids were the only common sense in this whole mess. Not like they didn't know Cate. She's a teacher's assistant at the school. From what I gather, bunch of students approached the principal. Johnny Baget, senior class president, said, *If Cate's already dead let's make them pay*. A junior, Jennifer Shepard, one of the top debaters in the state, said, *If she's not dead and we put this information on the net, then they have no reason to hold her*."

"Amazing."

Cate was smiling again as she listened.

"Course, none of us knew what we were dealing with," Matt stated.

"What are you saying?"

"Rogue element. Farley Harper."

"Oh, yes. Rockwell reborn."

"That reminds me, I have a question for you, my truant friend."

Matt thought for a minute.

"Depends."

"On what?"

"Who's asking, shrink or friend?"

"How many sets of records did you make?"

Matt started to laugh. More like an evil snicker.

"You don't want to ask that question," Matt said.

"You didn't. Tell me you didn't. I've been afraid of something like this. Where is it? Where is the other set of documents?"

"You sitting down?"

"Alcott. You are a certifiable penis."

"I was thinking cad. Did Mary's tulips seem robust this year? Can't imagine better fertilizer. So what happened to the loose cannon?"

"Farley Harper? His brother's declined to put up bail. Figured the best place for him was where he can't hurt anyone. Reporter for the *Tribune* did the story on him. Refusing to let anyone cut his hair."

"Bastard had her in the trunk of the car from New York to Utah," Matt said.

"He will do no more harm. After the trial his permanent address will be Point of the Mountain."

"Burgess? What about him?"

"Nothing and you will hear nothing. No organization on earth can create a veil of silence like this one," Rod said.

"Which reminds me. There is a question I need to ask you."

"I'm listening."

"When I was in little brother's office I saw something. He keeps a bottle of booze in his desk for clients. I was looking for the bottle when I saw it...a marriage license. Wasn't paying attention to anything except finding the booze. Figuring the marriage certificate belonged to a client, I tossed it on the desk with a bunch of files I was looking under. Paid no attention to it then, but Paul pointed to the desk and said to his secretary, 'Help him. He's looking for the bottle.'"

"I'm listening." Rod said it like *so what*.

"Well, he wasn't pointing at the desk per se, he was pointing at the top of the desk where the certificate was. When he said it there was a different tone to his voice, more urgent.

"She physically brushed me aside, opened one of the large bottom drawers, and fished out a bottle, which she shoved in my face. Turning her back on me, she made a move I can only think was gathering something from the surface of the desk. Paul has a small restroom in his office. She went in there for a moment, came back, and handed me a paper cup. Now here is the funny part. There were paper cups in the bottom desk drawer where the Cutty Sark was. Didn't notice it until I returned the bottle to the drawer. So I know she knew the cups were there. The marriage certificate was no longer on the desk."

"You were distracted," Rod added.

"I think I'm still recovering from the near overdoses of drugs Farley Harper was giving me."

"Post acute withdrawal can last six months," Rod instructed.

"Couple days ago, middle of the night, I sat straight up in bed. I know what the names are on that marriage license."

Cate was leaning forward, listening intently.

"Matthew?" Rod said, attempting to get his full attention.

"What bothers me, and it's really been bugging the hell out of me..."

"Matthew, stop," Rod said.

"It was not a state certificate. Nor a county for that matter."

"I don't think this is something we should discuss over the phone," Rod said.

"It was a church certificate—Mary Lanningham to Paul E. Alcott."

"Matthew. For God's sake. Come to the party. These are things most regular members are not privy to. You cannot talk about this over the phone. Please treat this seriously."

"I'm an investigative reporter. Freelance, but still…I don't think they quit, Rod. In 1906, the Church was thought to have finally honored the federal manifesto of 1890. Bullshit. I think they just went deeper underground."

"All right. That's it. I'm going to hang up."

"These people are secret mongers."

"And secrets breed secrets, I know," Rod said.

"Look at the temple ceremony."

"I thought you knew. I never went through the temple."

"But you knew about the big changes the Church made in 1978."

"Vaguely."

"People were no longer led in the ritual that explicitly demonstrated cutting their own throats if they divulged what they did and saw inside. Secret mongers."

Cate's eyes looked like the shutter of a camera growing wider and wider.

"All those small offshoot churches that broke away from the main church, Brigham Young's church, most were over polygamy. In fact that's why they broke away, to keep the commandment of multiple wives."

"All right, Matthew," Rod said, interrupting, "I'm just going to say this. If this thing runs as deep and far up as you think it does, I don't think there is anything they would not do to stop you."

"Section 132 has never been revoked or renounced."

"Oh for God's sake, Matthew. Not over the phone. Okay. I'm going to hang up."

"They are still practicing polygamy. I intend to prove it."

"Mercy."

Click.

MORNING
RESURRECTION CORNER

She knew his moods. Knew them better than he did. The time felt right. A quilt around her shoulders, Cate pushed between Matt and the computer. He eased back in the chair, making room as she straddled his legs, put her head on his shoulder, and pulled the quilt in tight around them both.

"Never was there a person who wakes up so slow," Matt said, stroking her hair.

In the back of her mind they needed some face time together, and what better time to clean up a few loose ends.

"You put all that money in our bank account. Your money," she said.

"Our money," he corrected.

"I bought computers for the school," Cate reminded him.

He tried not to think about the fact that after taxes they were in pretty bad shape.

"As investments come and go, none better," he said as casually as he could make himself say it.

The tax write-offs from the donated computers were an unexpected advantage, though after the fact. He remembered something about foreign rights and wondered when that money might come to their rescue.

"Are you angry with me?" she ventured.

"Why would I be angry with you?"

"For spending the money. I had to do it. They needed the computers desperately."

"I could care less about the money," he said, making a mental note to have the bank put an expenditure limit on any checks she might write. "You want to know if I'm angry at someone. I'll tell you who I'm angry at, people who kidnap my Cate. At them I'm angry."

"Mr. Farley Rockwell," she acknowledged.

"At least he's in jail."

"But I lived through it. I was sick with fear at first. I woke up in the dark. No one would answer me," she said, her eyes filling with water.

Matt began to burn. Within one beat his heart was marching to a charging drum roll.

She felt him tense. "Please, let me say it. Let me tell it to you. Then maybe I can tell it to Raven and Mom. I need to talk about it. Your AA taught me that."

Firm jaw. He took a deep breath. "Okay. I'll listen, but I reserve the right to murder."

"I was groggy and it was cold. I forced myself to touch the cement I was sitting on. It felt so powdery and smelled dusty. I could tell where paint was peeling on the walls. I made myself explore and feel around. A giant with a flashlight brought me food. McDonald's mostly. I thought I was going to die, but he hadn't hurt me. I asked him, 'Am I going to die?' He didn't say anything. I began to think he wasn't going to hurt me. It dawned on me, if I was going to get away I couldn't wait for someone else to do it. I couldn't unlock the doors. Didn't have one of those jack hammer thingies either. Didn't know what day it was, but I knew—I mean, I really knew—it was up to me. So, I began to try things. When Mr. Rockwell came to see me, I made myself ask for things. Small at first. Soap and water, paper and pencil, a book to read. Things like that. When I thanked him, he was like a puppy. That's when I knew I'd get out. He brought me three books. Two comic books and the Book of Mormon. I told him I couldn't read without light. He started bringing me candles and presents. I wrote down questions about the Book of Mormon he never did answer. In the whole book, I couldn't find one heroine to identify with. All about men this and men that. In the end I think Mr. Rockwell was bringing me things twice a day. I asked for a change of clothes. Do you remember a white dress? Full length?"

"With a short green apron?"

"Yes."

"I thought I dreamed it."

"Those were my temple clothes. Mr. Rockwell was going to take me inside the temple. He said he would baptize me."

Cate spoke in a matter-of-fact tone, yet playfully as though he should be jealous.

"He said he knew a secret way in. Late at night and we would wear white clothes and that he had the Melchizedek—did I say it right—priesthood and would marry us. He said I would be his wife for eternity and we would have lots and lots of kids."

When she finished Cate sat quietly, waiting to see what Matthew would say.

"I should have known. You made him your slave too," Matt said.

"It seemed like the only thing to do if I was going to escape."

"You had a plan," Matt said.

"I was hoping, if he really took me to the big temple building, I could hide from him. He doesn't move very fast, and wouldn't there be people in the morning?"

"Any plan was better than none, I guess."

"Doctor Rodney told me you almost died."

"He exaggerated," Matt insisted.

"Liar. Doctor Rodney doesn't exaggerate." Cate returned to picking the fuzz balls off the inside-out sweatshirt he was wearing. "I forgive Mr. Rockwell. He only lived the way he knew how."

"How does that work anyway?"

"What?" she said.

"Forgiving someone. People throw that word around like a volleyball. Truth be told, I haven't a clue what that means."

"James J said it's when we can honestly wish them well, even pray for them." She cocked her head to look at Matt. "Have you forgiven Joseph Smith?"

"He's dead."

"Well, if he were alive today, could you forgive him?"

"If he were alive and breathing?"

"Alive and breathing."

"Today?"

"Today."

"I'd have to go to Hollywood."

"What does Hollywood have to do with it?"

"If Smith were alive today, he'd be in California making films with Lucas and Spielberg."

"Not Salt Lake?"

"The one place he would not be. Church would excommunicate him in a New York minute," Matt said.

"What about you? Have you forgiven yourself?"

"How would I know? But I know who I haven't forgiven—your ex—and I won't either, so don't ask."

"You wouldn't hurt him, would you?"

"Certainly not."

"Liars don't go to heaven."

"You will be the only one there."

"You would deny him of the opportunity to change?" she demanded.

"I would be more than happy to help him change. It's called water boarding."

"You're hopeless," she said, pulling his chest hair.

"Ouch!"

She grew quiet again. "Do you regret we never married?"

Matt had been thinking about the relationships he'd known.

With Carol, it was all appearances. When she told someone what Matt did for a living, she made it sound like he was the chief and personal historian to the Quorum of The Twelve and the First Presidency. The love was selfish. Their marriage certificate had been license to use each other. She gave to get. Matt figured they both did.

Eve, in Las Vegas? She was a breath of fresh air. Emotionally healthy and free. If things had been different, they may have had a good life together.

Cate Lynn, his butterfly, who was she? Always thinking of others. Matt was hard pressed to define his Cate. The first time they made love, it was as though her pleasure was in him taking his. It was the same with all her relationships. Raven's school needed a teacher's assistant. Cate volunteered. Matt needed a computer to write his book. Cate again. Several kids in The Corner wanted careers in computer science. The school only had a couple of relics.

The stories went on and on. What did she do for herself? Why had this never occurred to him before? Those she touched were better off for having known her. Her reward came by way of the rewards others benefitted. She was a freak of nature, an ethical politician.

"I don't need a piece of paper to know how I feel about you," Matt said, before adding, "And, my book would never have happened without you."

Her hand reached up, felt his forehead.

"You don't seem to have an temperature."

He loved it when she touched him.

"Oh, I would have written a book. It would have been penned with impassioned hand and accurate facts, but I'd never have seen what, after all, drove Smith. You gave me that."

"You do worry me sometimes," she mocked as she lay back against him.

"You know what scares me?" he said.

Cate arched her back, leaning away in order to look him in the eye, "What?"

"I was told you would be good for me."

"Who told you that?"

"The town. The whole damn town. Truth is you are too good for me."

"May be hope for you yet," she said, smoothing the wrinkle from his brow with a finger.

"You and I are like two atoms that collide in space. An accident so unlikely, calculating its opportunity would be an incomprehensible number. I steered left off the freeway, led only by the whimsy of a name."

"So, we were meant for each other."

"Exactly. Mystery's perfection," he said.

"A perfect accident."

"Before, in my other life, every choice was dictated out of loyalty and obedience to another man's dream. While I could respect a great leader, I could find no traction living by his ideology. When I finally turned and faced my past, well, that's when it happened. Joseph Smith shaped the lives of millions of people. Writing about him was writing about me, and writing about me saved my life."

Cate leaned back again. Locked into his gaze.

"You have forgiven Smith," she said.

"Don't know. Your department. But there is one thing I still don't understand. Collecting wives. I can't wrap my head around that. I have no more desire to collect women as wives than I have to collect bruises for fun and sport. I'm missing something. How can I understand his need to collect wives like that?"

"I hope you never do."

"I'm serious. If I hadn't met you and I was horny, I imagine I could go to a bordello, but is that the same thing?"

"Different. The idea wasn't to share wives. So different."

"The last year of his life, Joseph married one woman after another. Why?"

"You wrote your book about him and you honestly don't know?"

"Oh, and you do?"

"Duh. He hated that he needed us the way he did."

Cate gave Matt one of her looks. It was the silly look that said, *How could you not know?*

"Sex? Availability?" he posed.

"Women, even the most passive, are too independent. He needed slaves. Men want to be pleasured. Controlling us was a huge pain in the butt, but it was better than the standard cultural alternative. His drive was normal. The need to procreate is normal, innate. Your Joseph person did not understand himself."

"But why did he love women by the numbers so much? Was it as simple as notches on a belt?"

"Love. You think it was love?"

"Well, it wasn't hate!" Matt said.

"Why not?"

It caught Matt off guard. An answer he hadn't expected.

"God, men are dumb," she exclaimed, rolling her eyes across the ceiling.

Matt felt vulnerable, exposed, and downright dumb. Kate looked surprised.

"Apparently I'm the one that is shortsighted for thinking you understood. It was his vulnerability he hated, the constant need to control what he couldn't control. He didn't know it was his need."

"The unexamined life?"

"He transferred it directly to us. Blamed us. If his wife hadn't been so cold to him, Mormonism would be a whole different religion."

Slow motion. There were moments in Matt's life when time stretched, long and compelling, into an elastic suspense. It held almost to the breaking point before snapping back into shape and jarring its host into a new perspective. Matt felt like he had been hit upside the head by an invisible baseball bat.

"He blamed us. Subconsciously he hated us," Cate said.

"Why couldn't I see it?"

"You are comfortable with yourself. You don't need to control anyone."

"It's all about control."

"It's not a secret," she said, making the silly face again.

"God, you exasperate me."

"Not my fault you're so dumb."

The twinkle in Cate's eye.

"I guess I had that one coming. I will get even."

"I'm counting on it."

Chapter 51

RESURRECTION CORNER

That evening in their newly renovated one-room house, Cate Lynn took her pleasure in Matt's pleasure. After, depleted, sleep descended rapidly.

"I don't believe you," she said.

Cate wanted to talk. She always wanted to talk after. The words were fuzzy, almost echoes. Like most men, he could hardly keep his eyes open after. She knew he enjoyed talking about his father, the early years. When he did, she grew quiet and listened as though something reverent were taking place. Her head rested on his arm. He knew she was wide awake, listening, watching.

"Well, it's true," his voice, husky with sleep. "You just made love to a saint!"

"I don't think so."

"Dad told me I was born a saint."

"I think I'd know it if I made love to a saint."

"The last days. Dad said, because I was a good boy in the life before this one, I was born a saint in the last days."

"So?"

"When I was a boy I believed everything Dad told me, didn't you?"

"My daddy taught me not to believe everything boys tell me."

"Smart ass."

Her laughter, his reward.

"I assumed when I was young that, at least I was a good boy in the pre-existence."

"Did anyone ever call you a saint?"

"Mmmm. Good point," he said.

"Last days?"

"Uh huh."

"Then we should to do it again," she said, tugging at him.

"Again?"

His voice broke.

"This time in the missionary position."

A Postlude

RESURRECTION CORNER
4 A.M.

A saint rolled out of bed, made coffee, and opened a laptop computer. Shoulders slumped, he brought up a blank page in the software and sat looking at it. He pushed back, away from the keyboard, staring. Minutes went by. His back straightened. Matt slid forward on the chair. Fingers slowly mounted the keyboard. There was a gentle tap, tap, tapping sound of the plastic keys. The screen mimicking its rhythmic cadence scrolled out...

Theme: THE GOSPEL OF LOVE'S SALVATION
Working Title: COMES AN END TO SECRETS

He designed a new culture out of the ashes of the burnt over district in upstate NY where the New Baptists, Methodists, and the Congregationalists brought tent preaching to a whole new level of hell, fire, and brimstone.

His name was Joseph Smith, Jr. and he bucked the local Christian fair and made of religion a new world and a new doctrine, multiple wives at its core. Few times in the annals of history has a single individual changed the direction of human progress so radically. Rational people don't do things like that. Joseph Smith was not a rational man. The man most think of as a prophet, seer, and revelator was little more than a misogynist who couldn't have what he wanted, but had figured out early on that the magic was not in the gold itself, but in its lore.

end

CPSIA information can be obtained
at www.ICGtesting.com
Printed in the USA
FFOW03n1041051213
2591FF

9 781432 788933